ON STORMY SEAS

Siobhan Dunmoore Book 8

3RD FLEET

NUNQUAM RETRORSUM

Eric Thomson

Published in Canada
By Sanddiver Books Inc.
ISBN: 978-1-989314-82-1

Sanddiver
Books Inc

— One —

"It seems Dunmoore almost started another war with the Shrehari a few days ago, sir." Leila Gherson, the Special Security Bureau's Chief of Staff, said after Blayne Hersom accepted her call. "I'd say the disinformation and deception plan is going perhaps a little too well."

Hersom, the SSB's director general — tall, lean, in his early seventies with an aging aristocrat's tight features and thick gray hair — allowed himself a smile as cold as the South Pole in a blizzard.

"Where Dunmoore is concerned, anything we do can never go too well, Leila. She has the devil's own luck. By all rights, she should have retired from the Navy as a captain after being passed over for promotion one final time and be working on tramp freighters. Instead, she's riding roughshod through the Zone at the head of her own battle group, unconstrained by the rules that govern every other naval formation." Hersom tapped the polished desktop with his fingertips, eyes narrowed as they speared Gherson. "What happened?"

"If you'll recall, our sources fed false information to Naval Intelligence concerning a putative human trafficking operation in the Erlach system, just outside the Shrehari Empire's sphere of control. Another bit to keep Dunmoore's battle group hopping around the Zone chasing mirages so our assets could work undisturbed. It worked twice before, so a third time wasn't out of the question."

"Yes." Hersom nodded irritably. Like all good chiefs of staff, Gherson was detail oriented and couldn't help restating things. "I do recall."

Even though the Special Security Bureau had wide-ranging responsibilities, of which covert operations in the Protectorate Zone were only a small part, Rear Admiral Siobhan Dunmoore had been a thorn in Hersom's side since before the end of the last war. As a result, he tracked anything that might involve her.

"Either it was bad luck, or someone told Shrehari intelligence of illegal goings-on in Erlach, and they decided it worthy of investigation. When Dunmoore arrived, she came across five *Tai Zohl* ships masquerading as corsairs and running silent at one of the planet's Lagrangians. In her after-action report to SOCOM — which landed on the desk of our source, by the way — Dunmoore states the Shrehari went up systems and attempted to arraign the three ships she took with her on the raid, calling them pirates. They lit her with targeting sensors when she tried talking her way through it."

Hersom let out a derisive chuckle. "Let me guess. She unmasked, proving her ships to be naval units in disguise, and identified herself as Rear Admiral Dunmoore, the flame-haired she-wolf admired by their *Kho'sahra*."

Gherson nodded. "Got it in one, sir. That made the Shrehari stand down just as they were powering weapons."

"And ended the Q ships' usefulness until they're modified by a yard to no longer resemble the ones now in the Shrehari Deep Space Fleet database." Hersom shook his head. "Ah, the joys of two great powers operating undercover in a part of space where neither should deploy naval units as per the binding peace treaty that demilitarized it. At least it means three of Dunmoore's ships, *Iolanthe* included, lost some effectiveness since someone now has visuals of them unmasking. Not that the *Tai Zohl* would share with our assets. But the Shrehari now have undeniable proof of the Navy's activities in the Protectorate Zone and will act in some fashion, if only to increase their presence rather than lodge a diplomatic protest. I'm sure the Fleet's top leadership aren't overly pleased with Dunmoore at the moment."

"I couldn't say, sir. Our source doesn't have that sort of access. Besides, I'm sure Grand Admiral Sampaio and Admirals Lowell and Doxiadis will excoriate Dunmoore behind closed doors if they do so. She's been remarkably successful until we found a way of tripping up her last three missions. And they can't make a big stir without admitting they've given orders that deliberately violate the Treaty of Ulufan. No one will accept the excuse Dunmoore entered the Zone under the hot pursuit provisions allowing naval units to chase fleeing pirates who've just committed a crime in Commonwealth space."

Hersom tapped his fingertips on the desktop one last time.

"Well, let's not miss our chance to recover some of the ground our assets lost because of Dunmoore's depredations if Lowell shortens her leash. I'd still prefer her battle group under 3rd Fleet command instead of Armed Forces HQ. She'd be a lot more constrained and controllable."

"I'll send you the copy of Dunmoore's after-action report, sir. That was all I had."

"Thank you, Leila."

***

"You saw Siobhan's latest?" Rear Admiral Ezekiel Holt, who headed the counterintelligence branch, dropped into the chair facing Vice Admiral Kathryn Kowalski, one of the newly appointed deputy chiefs of operations, and placed his coffee cup on the table.

They were in the Fleet HQ cafeteria in one of the isolated booths reserved for flag officers on temporary release from their offices and overburdened schedules. Kowalski, a tall, slender blond in her mid-forties with intense blue eyes and shoulder-length hair, nodded.

"Yes. And if you plan on telling me we still have traitors in our midst, I figured that out myself. Once is happenstance, twice is coincidence…"

"And three times is enemy action. Since she's pulling out of the Zone with the ships she had at Erlach, I'm sure that thought also occurred to her. I'm going ahead under the assumption our SSB friends across town have a copy of her after-action report by now. They'll use the reprieve to regroup, perhaps even resume their attempts to get the 101st under 3rd Fleet control and treated like any other naval formation. But the damage she's done to SSB assets, allies, and operations, let alone organized groups like the

Confederacy of the Howling Stars, won't be repaired soon, if ever. So, in that respect, Siobhan has done what we needed to pacify the Rim Sector and a good chunk of the Protectorate Zone without our government getting notes of protest from the Shrehari ambassador."

"True." Holt, who now sported more silver in his hair than Kowalski, took a sip of coffee. "And she's had her three years in command. Are the seniors miffed at her blowing the 101st's cover? I tried sounding out my boss, but he's not commented yet."

"They're aware she had no alternative under the circumstances. Besides, it was bound to happen one day, and we're lucky she was the one who dealt with the Shrehari commander. That defused the situation more quickly and easily than if it had been any other rear admiral." Kowalski raised her coffee cup and took a gulp. "As you said, she's done three years, so her tour is up whether or not the CNO is mad at her."

"What job did you finagle for her?"

A sly smile lit up Kowalski's face.

"Oh, you'll love this, Zeke. Remember telling me you suspect there are people in 3rd Fleet HQ who might be bent? Senior folks?"

He nodded.

"It would explain several operational failures, along with suspected peculation and other forms of corruption." Another sip. "We really need to start planning for a dedicated internal affairs organization completely outside the chain of command that can swoop in and investigate senior officers who might otherwise escape justice."

"No arguments here. Creating a federal police force with a professional standards branch whose mandate covers all parts of the Commonwealth government, Armed Forces included, is well overdue. But back to your question. I had planned on bringing her here where she could learn the ins and outs of surviving the demented bureaucracy while paving the way for her third star. But that's no longer the best option."

Holt cocked an amused eyebrow at Kowalski.

"I'm sure Siobhan would agree wholeheartedly. She's the only flag officer who made it a mission in life to never set foot in the puzzle palace. So, where will she go?"

"To 3rd Fleet HQ. The chief of staff for operations billet will be vacant shortly when the current incumbent steps down. Were your lot involved in him putting in for early retirement? I didn't think he was the sort who'd do questionable things."

Holt searched his memory for a name to go with the position, then shook his head.

"Not that I know. But, I understand working for Admiral Keo, the 3rd Fleet's deputy commander, can make or break an officer's career. Maybe he drove Berg into considering a less demanding and stressful career subsidized by a healthy military pension."

Kowalski's smile widened. "Maybe Siobhan can drive Hogue into retirement. She's not one of Lowell's favorite people."

"Meaning she's politically connected since Lowell would have signed off on her appointment."

"Let's call it one of those compromises our seniors must often make. Hogue didn't distinguish herself during the war, nor since, but she can whisper good words for the Fleet in certain senatorial ears and has done so at Lowell's request. Strictly back-channel stuff, you understand."

Holt shook his head. "A throwback to the prewar way of doing things? Siobhan's going to love that."

"3rd Fleet has been less than impressive in the last few years, Zeke. Considering it's responsible for the Rim Sector, our most turbulent frontier? Subtract the successes of Siobhan's 101st Battle Group and 3rd Fleet's ability to keep its area of operations safe for civilian shipping becomes the worst of all border formations in the entire Navy. The only reason Sampaio hasn't relieved Hogue yet is because Siobhan's been covering for her lack of aggressiveness. Even politically connected admirals can face consequences when they can't fulfill their responsibilities."

"I see." Holt drained his coffee cup. "You're sending Siobhan as chief of staff for operations to shake up 3rd Fleet."

"And dispose of anything that needs flushing down the vacuum ejection tubes. 3rd Fleet isn't what it was in Admiral Nagira's day, Zeke. Not even close. There's rot at the top, and I just can't figure out where. Knowing Siobhan, she'll throw the place into turmoil within forty-eight hours of arriving and harpoon the guilty parties."

"Then the next and equally important question is who gets the 101st, presuming it stays on the order of battle. I can name at least half a dozen admirals who have their own views on the subject, none of which agree with yours, let alone our aims. Worse yet, most of them want it out from under SOCOM and answering to one of the fleet commanders."

— TWO —

"Did the message packet include a missive from HQ concerning our latest misfire?" Gregor Pushkin, the 101st Battle Group's flag captain, asked as he helped himself to a cup of coffee from Rear Admiral Dunmoore's day cabin urn. "Since it was your eyes only, I figured it might have included a dressing-down from someone with four stars on the collar."

"Oh, ye of little faith," Dunmoore replied in a sardonic tone.

As was her routine once *Iolanthe* had picked up messages from the nearest subspace array after returning from a raid in the Zone, she'd closeted herself in her private office adjoining the flag combat information center. And as was Pushkin's regular routine, he'd joined her a few minutes later to read those messages before the relevant ones were disseminated to the captains. In this case, Devall of *Iolanthe*, Leung of *Gondolier*, and Navarra of *Mikado*. One of the battle group's other ships, *Thespis* under Commander Thorin Sirico, had been on a solitary cruise and would be heading home as well while the remainder were in port for crew rest and ship repairs.

Once *Iolanthe* and her companions docked at Starbase 30, Dunmoore's entire command would be in port for the first time in over six months, and after the latest operational failure, she figured the 101st needed to regroup and reassess tactics. But without her.

"Why would HQ be cross with me when what the history books will surely call the Incident at Erlach stemmed from an intelligence failure? That Shrehari spy ships were there in great number when we showed up was bad luck — the explanation I favor — or because of the aforementioned intelligence failure. I did the only thing I could to avoid fresh hostilities."

"True." Pushkin dropped into the chair across from her. "So what was flag officer commanding eyes only in the message packet?"

Dunmoore sighed softly as a sad smile lit up her narrow face. "Orders proclaiming the end of an era."

Pushkin's hooded eyes narrowed. "They're relieving you of command again?"

She raised a restraining hand. "Peace, Gregor. I had my three-year run as commander of the 101st. That's pretty much what any flag officer gets nowadays. Too many ambitious admirals and not enough command billets. But this time, I'll walk off *Iolanthe* with my stars on my collar. Have no fear. Unless a court martial relieves me of them, they're mine until I retire, unlike the temporary wartime commodore star I gave up after the armistice."

His air of suspicion hardened.

"And what's your next assignment? Some obscure job where they'll let you rot for ten years?"

Dunmoore chuckled.

"Not even close. I'm the 3rd Fleet's next chief of staff for operations, a clear step up and certainly not obscure. I'll be moving the naval pieces around in the entire Rim Sector, and as a bonus, I don't have to pack up and move. My little house in Marseilles is only a quick hop from HQ."

"You seem rather unfazed by the orders if you don't mind my saying so."

She shrugged.

"I knew my time was ending, Gregor. It's the way of things. As staff assignments for a rear admiral go, this one is decent. I feared I'd find myself riding a desk on Earth, constantly fending off the Good Idea Fairy. And we can share a cup of coffee whenever you're in port."

"Meaning?"

Dunmoore's radiant smile lit up her features. "Congratulations, Commodore Pushkin. You get the 101st."

"What?" The word came out in a strangled voice as he sat back with an air of astonishment. "I didn't even know I'd made the cut-off line."

"Well, you did. But I see the hidden hand of friends on Earth behind our respective appointments. You and I know things aren't well at 3rd Fleet HQ. I wouldn't be surprised if the dysfunction we've noted in the last year is at least in part responsible for our operational failures. Admiral Hogue certainly is unhappy she doesn't have the 101st under her command, and Oliver Harmel's replacement on Starbase 30 hasn't been particularly friendly with us."

"Yes." Pushkin scowled. "He does make it seem like we're a nuisance, not a friendly lodger formation sharing the base's support and facilities with his battle group."

"That'll change once I take up my new appointment. Count on it. And I won't even have to put a flea in Quintin Anand's ear. He'll change his tune without prompting once I'm the one riding herd on him at Hogue's behest."

A broad grin split Pushkin's face. "Oh, glorious day. I'll finally have a friend in high places."

"Don't get too excited. I'd be shocked if I was Admiral Hogue's pick to replace Hanno Berg. He's retiring. Early from what I understand, so there might have been issues between him and either Hogue or Keo."

Pushkin made a face.

"Or both. The esteemed Deputy Flag Officer Commanding 3rd Fleet has a reputation as a harsher taskmaster than Hogue, with only a fraction of the charm. And he's looking for his fourth star, like all vice admirals. But," Pushkin's smile returned, this time with a hard edge, "Horace Keo might regret pushing you around."

A snort. "Well, I'm certainly not his pick."

She'd had several run-ins with Keo over the eighteen months since he'd taken over as deputy commander. He was another like Hogue who resented having a SOCOM battle group operating in what they considered their area of responsibility, with no say in the 101st's employment or about the logistical support Earth demanded they give Dunmoore. But even though she'd been unfailingly polite, Keo, unlike Hogue, never tried hiding his dislike of her.

"With either of them, I'm betting on you, Admiral. Just remember your friends from SOCOM."

Dunmoore smirked at him. "With you as flag officer commanding the 101st, no danger of my forgetting."

"When are the new appointments effective?"

"Your promotion is already posted, so I just need to present your star in front of *Iolanthe*'s company on the hangar deck to make it official. I kept a set from my time running Luckner. If you'd like, I could pin one of them on you."

Pushkin's smile more than made up for his earlier frown. "That would be one hell of an honor, Admiral."

"Then they're yours, with my best wishes and my gratitude. When we're done here, I'll brief the captains. We can link *Gondolier* and *Mikado* and make you a commodore before going FTL on our final leg to the Dordogne system."

"And the change of command?"

"Impatient?" Dunmoore gave him a mischievous grin. "My orders are handing over the 101st and reporting to Admiral Hogue as soon as we reach port. Therefore, we'll do it on Starbase 30, with every ship's company represented on parade. Chief Guthren will take care of everything, so don't get involved with the planning other than rehearsing your part, okay?"

He inclined his head. "Understood. Do we get a reviewing officer?"

"If someone from SOCOM or Fleet HQ was coming, they'd have said so. This leaves Hogue as the most senior Navy flag officer on Dordogne, and it would be bad politics to give her the idea she might have authority over the 101st. So, no. We'll do it without a reviewing officer, though we'll invite all commanders and up from 3rd Fleet, 30th Battle Group, and Starbase 30, along with the senior chief petty officers."

"Why do I think your new boss won't be pleased?"

"She'll be sitting in the front row of spectators if she accepts my invitation. Other than that, she can be as miffed as she wants. If I invite her as the reviewing officer, I know people on Earth who won't be pleased, and their opinion matters more in the long term."

Pushkin burst into laughter. "That's the Siobhan Dunmoore we all love — ready to give the brass heartburn in the name of a good cause."

"My current boss reports to Grand Admiral Sampaio. So does hers," she replied in a prim tone. "I'll report to Admiral Hogue after the change of command ceremony. I'll pay for it, but as they say back home, them's the breaks."

"After this momentous news, I hesitate to ask about anything else in the message packet."

"There's nothing else. Let me get the chief in here, and then we'll link up with the captains."

When Guthren heard the news, he pumped Pushkin's hand with such enthusiasm that Dunmoore thought his entire arm would come off.

"We'll see that you two get a change of command ceremony fit for the finest flag officers in the known galaxy," he said, a satisfied smile on his square face as he looked at each of them in turn. "I trust I'll stay with Commodore Pushkin as command chief?"

"That's the idea."

"Suits me just fine, Admiral." Guthren turned to Pushkin. "The commodore and I had our differences during the early days, but if I can't work for you, then I'm glad to work for him."

Pushkin grinned at Guthren. "Likewise, Chief."

"Okay. Now, to get things organized. While you speak with the captains, I'll rouse the cox'n and get all crew that isn't in their racks or at critical posts on the hangar deck in thirty minutes. We can discuss change of command during the rest of our trip home, and I'll round up the battle group's cox'ns as soon as we dock. Leave it to me. The Starbase 30 chief owes me a few favors I'll collect in a worthy cause." Guthren stomped to attention, saluted, and marched out of Dunmoore's office.

"Now, there's a man who saw more of our trials and tribulations than anyone else, Admiral. I'm glad he's staying on with me. But I'll let him go if you ever usurp Hogue and need a command cox'n."

***

"Dunmoore? They're appointing her as our new chief of operations? Unbelievable." Vice Admiral Horace Keo, Deputy Commander, 3rd Fleet, turned an exasperated gaze at the ceiling as if summoning the Almighty's help. Sixty, with silver-shot black hair, an angular, craggy face, and watchful dark eyes, Keo came across as a consummate, professional flag officer whose appearance and deportment was always beyond reproach. "Were you even consulted?"

"No." Admiral Eva Hogue, a few years older than Keo, thin, with a sallow complexion, shoulder-length brown hair parted slightly to the left, and a gaze that rarely, if ever, held a hint of warmth, shook her head. "The CNO's office told me of her assignment, which will be effective once she hands the 101st Battle Group to her successor. Apparently, she's inbound with her remaining ships."

"Why would the CNO not even consult you?" Keo asked in his resonant baritone. "What about the custom of allowing fleet commanders to choose their own senior staff officers?"

Hogue let out a humorless laugh. "That custom has been honored more in the breach than not since the war, Horace. I think they're afraid nepotism might return. No. We're stuck with Dunmoore."

"I don't like it, sir. Dunmoore is a loose cannon who could cause untold harm to the efficient functioning of your command."

"Then it's your job to make sure that loose cannon is tied down," she replied with a hint of petulance. "We can't refuse her appointment, nor can we simply place her on a shelf and let one of the senior staff officers run operations. From what I hear, she's considered a superb battle group commander by the CNO, someone who still has career potential at the highest levels."

Keo scoffed.

"If she doesn't buckle down and adapt, that potential will evaporate quickly. I didn't tolerate her predecessor's attempts to undermine me, and I won't tolerate hers." He rubbed his chin, eyes narrowed. "Who gets the 101st now? Please tell me it's not another SOCOM hotshot who'll ignore us and run amok, breaking the treaty provisions on every patrol. Better yet, tell me we're taking the 101st under command, so all nonsense stops

once and forever. Eventually, someone will trigger a crisis with
the Shrehari, and then where will we be?"

Hogue grimaced. "Sorry. Dunmoore's flag captain is promoted
to commodore and will take over from her directly."

"Gregor Pushkin? Why? He's about as stubborn, disrespectful,
and rules-be-damned as Dunmoore, but with a fraction of the
personality."

"HQ doesn't want a newcomer upsetting SOCOM's neat little
undercover operation specialized in evading the Treaty of
Ulufan's provisions concerning the Protectorate Zone. That, and
other things which best qualify as blacker than black and
therefore questionable under the Code of Service Discipline."

Keo shook his head. "Lord, grant me strength. These wartime
yahoos should have been put out to pasture years ago."

"I won't argue the point. It would have been better for the
Navy if Dunmoore and her coterie of unconventional warfare
officers weren't promoted out of sequence and had been forced
into retirement. But she'll be your responsibility by the end of
the month, and I have no doubt someone in the CNO's office
will watch us. Her last-minute reprieve and two-step promotion
three years ago prove she's finally found a new protector, which
is one reason I haven't protested her appointment. Please keep
that in mind, Horace."

— Three —

"Looks like Admiral Hogue and the entire 3rd Fleet top brass showed up," Commodore Pushkin said in a low tone as he glanced through the starbase hangar deck control room's one-way transparent aluminum window. "And in full fig with swords. She doesn't even look miffed from a distance."

He and Dunmoore, also wearing the dress uniform prescribed for flag officers, with medals, accouterments, and naval swords were waiting for the parade commander, Captain Trevane Devall, to call the assembly to order at precisely eleven-hundred hours. A company stood for each ship of the 101st under its captain, the companies lined up by order of the ship's seniority.

"All the better to chew me out tomorrow morning when I report for duty," she replied in an amused tone. "Not that Hogue would do so. She didn't become flag officer commanding 3rd Fleet without understanding naval politics."

"Our ship's companies look sharp, though."

She smiled at him. "That they do, for a bunch of scruffy unconventional warfare spacers. I'm sure many in the audience are wondering how they managed to look like regular Navy personnel."

Pushkin let out a snort of amusement. "Blame Chief Guthren for shattering rumors we're only untrained mutts who like breaking every rule in the book and pissing on everyone else's carpets."

"They are doing us proud, aren't they?" Dunmoore said in a wistful tone.

"I wish the original bunch who piped you off *Iolanthe* thirteen years ago were there to see that it all worked out in the end. A lot of us took it hard, you know."

"There are a few, Gregor. You, Guthren, and if I'm not mistaken, I spotted a chief petty officer third class who once gave me my broad pennant among the spectators."

"Vincenzo?"

"Older, leaner, and looking every millimeter like Guthren's darker-haired clone."

He grinned at her. "Old home week, here we come."

Before she could reply, a disembodied voice, that of the narrator, one of *Iolanthe*'s more mellifluous lieutenants, echoed across the vast starbase hangar.

"Good morning, and welcome to the 101st Battle Group's change of command ceremony between Rear Admiral Siobhan Dunmoore and Commodore Gregor Pushkin. At this time, the parade commander, Captain Trevane Devall, will call the formation to attention to prepare for Admiral Dunmoore and Commodore Pushkin's arrival. I would ask that all spectators please stand."

Devall's voice rang out, their cue, and they gave each other one last glance.

"Ready?" She asked.

"As ready as I'll ever be." Pushkin breathed in deeply, then released it and smiled. "After you, Admiral."

They marched through the open airlock in step, left hands grasping sheathed swords, stiff right arms swinging, the sound of their heels loud in the silence. The eyes of every spectator followed their progress across the compartment as they headed for the dais where a rear admiral's flag hung on a white flagpole. Once there, Dunmoore stepped on it and faced the parade while Pushkin took position to one side.

Devall gave the order to present arms, and the band from the 13th Marine Regiment broke into the traditional general salute ruffles and flourishes. Carbines snapped up, swords swept down, and Dunmoore raised her hand to her brow.

When the music died away, Devall gave the order to shoulder arms, Dunmoore's hand dropped, and the narrator asked the audience to sit. Devall marched up to the dais and saluted again.

"Would the admiral like to inspect the battle group?"

"With pleasure, Captain." Dunmoore stepped down and looked at Pushkin. "Please join us, Commodore."

Dunmoore, Pushkin, and Devall marched down the ranks to the strains of traditional airs, Dunmoore stopping now and then to exchange a few smiling words with a crew member. Contrary to the last time she'd relinquished a battle group, this felt like a more joyous occasion — the sense of her job well done and the next step in her career about to unfold.

As they returned to the dais, the narrator announced, "Rear Admiral Dunmoore and Commodore Pushkin will now sign the instruments to transfer command of the 101st Battle Group."

At that signal, two spacers carrying a table and another two carrying a chair each appeared from behind the dais and carefully set up in front of it while Devall ordered the formation to stand easy. Once the spacers had left, a lieutenant from *Iolanthe* appeared with a folder and two old-fashioned writing implements. He pulled three identical parchments from the folder and placed them on the table — one copy for Dunmoore, one for Pushkin, and one for the official files. They sat side by side and signed each document, then stood and shook hands while the audience applauded. The lieutenant retrieved the parchments, and the spacers took the table and chairs.

"Admiral Dunmoore will address the 101st Battle Group for the last time."

Turning her back on the spectators, she took a few steps toward the waiting companies.

"As you well know by now, I'm not much for saying more than needs to be said, let alone making long speeches. So, I'll keep it short. It was the greatest honor of my career to serve as your commanding officer over the last three years. The record of wins you racked up will stand against any comer for a long time. Every last reiver, pirate, smuggler, or Shrehari corsair—" She paused as a spontaneous chuckle erupted from the ranks. "Yes, even they will remember the day they tried to stare down the 101st and lost. I know you'll keep this part of the Commonwealth frontier safe under Commodore Pushkin, who's been part of our victories since the start. I wish you good hunting. Long live the 101st Battle Group. *Audaces Fortuna Juvat.*"

A roar of approval rose from the assembled spacers as they thumped their carbine butts on the deck while officers tapped their swords on their sheaths.

Dunmoore, with the sort of dignity seldom seen, raised her hand slowly in salute, held it for a few heartbeats, then dropped her arm, made a precise one-hundred-and-eighty-degree pivot, and marched off toward the side of the dais where Pushkin waited.

"Your turn," she whispered as she came within earshot.

Pushkin marched out to where Dunmoore had stood as the cheering died off.

"Members of the 101st Battle Group, I can think of no greater honor than becoming your commanding officer and Admiral Dunmoore's successor. I know you will continue as you've started under her by being the best hunters in the known galaxy." He paused, then repeated the battle group motto. "*Audaces Fortuna Juvat.*"

But instead of rejoining Dunmoore by the dais, Pushkin nodded at Devall, who marched off to take position in front of *Iolanthe*'s company and drew his sword. He turned around to face the audience.

"Admiral Dunmoore, if you would take the dais one last time."

She climbed onto the small, low stage and drew herself to attention as the narrator's voice came through the hidden speakers.

"Please stand."

Once the audience had complied, Pushkin ordered the formation to remove headdress.

"Three cheers for Admiral Dunmoore. Hip, hip, hip."

"Hurrah."

The first strains of Auld Lang Syne wafted across the hangar.

"Hip, hip, hip."

"Hurrah."

The Marine band played another few bars of the traditional farewell song.

"Hip, hip, hip."

"Hurrah."

The band played the entire piece this time as a pair of spacers lowered Dunmoore's flag. But contrary to her expectations, Dunmoore didn't feel any tears welling in the corners of her eyes. For everything, there was a season, and her season of battle group command had ended as it should.

When the music died away, Pushkin ordered the formation to replace headdress while the spacers folded the flag. Then, surprising even Dunmoore, as the band burst into Will Ye No Come Back Again, over a thousand voices joined it. The spacers with her flag marched up to the dais, saluted, and handed her the folded triangle of fabric, her two stars showing. Once they'd stepped aside, Pushkin ordered the general salute, ending the ceremony.

But this time, Dunmoore didn't walk off to board a shuttle and face an uncertain future. Instead, she headed toward the nearest airlock leading to a neighboring compartment for the post-ceremony reception. She would rather have taken the next shuttle to the surface and headed home, where she could have enjoyed a dram of single malt alone in her garden and reflected on the future. But protocol demanded she not leave before Admiral Hogue and Vice Admiral Keo. Dunmoore had already made her private farewells with her captains, officers, and crews in the days leading up to the ceremony and felt no need to swap war stories while sipping indifferent Dordogne wine and nibbling on mass-produced hors d'oeuvres.

She found herself alone in the reception space with the serving staff for several minutes while Pushkin dismissed the parade, and the narrator dismissed the audience. Then, with Hogue in the lead, the crowd appeared and headed for the tables to help themselves. Dunmoore stood on one side, out of the way, intending to let people approach her if they wished. This was Pushkin's day now that his broad pennant flew over the 101st, and he should rightly be the center of attention.

And as she expected, Hogue and Keo made a beeline for her while their aides fetched wine glasses.

"Welcome to 3rd Fleet, Admiral," the former said with a smile that didn't reach her eyes. "A nice ceremony. Pity you didn't have a reviewing officer to give it that crowning touch. I would have gladly accepted, you know."

Dunmoore inclined her head. "Thank you, sir."

"I suppose you'd like a week or two of leave to settle on the surface?" Keo asked. "I understand you own a house in the suburbs of Marseilles."

"Yes, sir. I do. But I'll only need until next week. Would my reporting for duty on Monday morning suit you?"

Dunmoore's eyes caught people shying away at seeing her engaged with Hogue and Keo, who weren't known for suffering protocol breaches lightly. A shame because she would have enjoyed chatting with many and thanking them for their support over the years.

Pushkin wasn't as shy when he finally entered the room and made a beeline for her.

"Admiral Hogue, Admiral Keo, thank you for attending the ceremony."

Hogue inclined her head in greeting.

"Commodore. Congratulations on your promotion and appointment. I hope you have a successful tour of command."

"Thank you, sir."

"You can rest assured 3rd Fleet will keep supporting the 101st Battle Group to the best of our abilities."

"I would never doubt it. Please enjoy the reception. Now, if you'll excuse me." Pushkin smiled at Hogue and Keo, then gave Dunmoore a quick nod that said, talk to you later, before turning to meet the throng of well-wishers waiting for him.

"And that's our duty done," Hogue said, draining her wine glass and handing it to her aide. "We shall see you Monday morning, Siobhan."

"Yes, sir. Enjoy the rest of your day."

"Thank you." Hogue turned to her aide. "Make sure my pinnace is ready."

"Already done, sir."

Keo held Dunmoore's eyes for a few silent seconds.

"I look forward to profiting from your extensive experience patrolling our area of operation's outer edges, Dunmoore. Until Monday."

"Until then, Admiral."

With them gone, Dunmoore waded into the noisy crowd, chatting with people here and there, accepting congratulations for her appointment and giving old comrades one last handshake.

But she couldn't find Chief Petty Officer Vincenzo, who seemed to have shunned the reception, and after another forty-five minutes, Dunmoore found Guthren, who'd arranged for *Iolanthe*'s pinnace to take her down.

"Time, Chief. If I spend another five minutes in this white noise chamber, my eardrums will explode."

"Your shuttle is waiting on the Furious Faerie's hangar deck, sir. Shall I walk with you? I could use a break from this din myself."

"With pleasure." She looked for Pushkin, and when he met her gaze across the room, Dunmoore nodded at the exit, then headed for it, Guthren in tow. Pushkin at once disengaged from the people surrounding him and made his way in her direction.

"Time?" He asked when he joined her at the door.

"Yes. This is your party, not mine, and I'm getting a slight headache. I'll be glad for a quiet afternoon at home watching the clouds scud past."

"When are you reporting to 3rd Fleet?"

"Monday. That gives me five days to unpack, restock the house and relax. Thanks for letting *Iolanthe* loan me the pinnace."

"There will be a staff car waiting at the spaceport," Guthren said. "We'll have you home within the hour."

Dunmoore stuck out her hand. "Thanks for everything, Gregor. You're the best friend anyone could have."

"It's me who should thank you, Skipper. No matter who signed the orders, I owe you my star and the chance at a long and fulfilling career."

She smiled at him. "We owe each other, Gregor. As good friends do. Now go enjoy every second of that command. Three years go by all too quickly."

—Four—

The driver of the staff car from Joint Base Dordogne's motor pool, a quiet young spacer, helped Dunmoore carry her luggage, including a small container with her personal effects, to the bungalow's front door. Her house, built in what was known locally as the Mediterranean style, with white stucco walls, a red tile roof, and a broad veranda, sat in a quiet hilly suburb northeast of Marseilles, the star system capital. Up here, the air was fresher than in the waterfront city bordering a long, narrow bay with countless inlets on all sides. Equally convenient, Joint Base Dordogne, home to 3rd Fleet HQ among other Navy, Marine, and Army units, was a mere ten kilometers further inland, which meant easy travel to and from work without entering the city.

"Thank you." She gave him a smile.

"My pleasure, Admiral." The young man came to attention and saluted. "With your permission?"

Dunmoore returned the salute. "Granted."

The front door unlocked at her touch, and the indoor lights came on. As she stepped over the threshold, a disembodied female voice — the AI butler — said, "Welcome home, Admiral. The property is secure and in good order. All is working within the expected parameters, and I turned the environmental systems on an hour ago. The air should be clean and the indoor temperature at your preferred setting."

"Thank you, Jeeves."

"Shall I transmit the grocery list you sent earlier, now that you're here?"

"If you would."

"Done."

She headed for her bedroom, unbuttoning her dress uniform tunic along the way, and changed into shorts, a light shirt, and sandals — her preferred getup when she was at home alone, something she hadn't enjoyed in several months. Meanwhile, her sole service droid pulled the luggage and container into the hallway and shut the front door.

Unpacking didn't take long. Dunmoore had spent most of her life traveling light and quickly stowed her clothes in the closet. The items she kept in her shipboard quarters — books, souvenirs, and the clock with the silhouette of a knight on horseback on its face, found new homes in her living room, along with her sword and the departure gifts from each of her ships.

However, she didn't expect the presents hidden at the very bottom and smiled to herself, knowing Pushkin and Guthren were responsible. A bottle of twenty-five-year-old Glen Arcturus, another of cognac which usually bore an eye-watering price tag, and half a dozen bottles of fine red wine bearing a commemorative label with the 101st's crest and the dates of her command.

A note covered in Pushkin's handwriting was stuck to one bottle. It said, Skipper, don't drink it all in a single session. Save some for when we come to visit.

"Oh, I will," she murmured.

Shortly after storing the wine in the cellar and the rest in her bar cabinet, the store droid delivered her groceries, and she made herself a late lunch which she took on the shaded terrace, alone and without immediate responsibilities for the first time in a long time. It felt peaceful and strange, but after the meal, she stretched out in her hammock and fell asleep at once, waking as the sun kissed the horizon over the Western Ocean, turning the fluffy clouds marching across the sky a brilliant orange.

Above her, on Starbase 30, Gregor Pushkin would rest before his first formal function as battle group commander — a mess dinner in the base's wardroom for his officers and selected guests. He'd asked if she wanted to attend, but Dunmoore had declined because she believed an outgoing commander should clear off as soon as possible and stay away for a bit.

Instead, she went for a leisurely stroll around the neighborhood, anonymous under a floppy hat and sunglasses. How many of her neighbors knew she was one of the more infamous admirals in the Commonwealth Navy remained debatable. Beyond the occasional friendly hello, she'd not spoken with any of them at length.

Of course, Dunmoore had been away most of the time. Why she even bought the house remained somewhat of a mystery to herself and her closest friends when she could have taken flag officers' quarters in the Joint Base Dordogne's residential area.

But she'd spent so little over the years that her bank account simply cried for a few large purchases. The house had been one.

Her car, tucked away in the attached garage, was another. Indulgences, yes, but since her appointment was to 3rd Fleet HQ and not elsewhere, they became less questionable now that she would get at least another three years out of them before selling and moving on.

Pushkin and Guthren, comedians that they were, had nicknamed her house Dunmoore's Lair and her car Dunmoore One. She would miss seeing them daily after so many years together in the same ships. But such was life. Battlegroup command was the highest aboard starships in peacetime, and even if she made it to four stars and fleet command, she wouldn't do so in space. Her time riding the hyperspace bands, looking for action, had ended permanently, without a chance of reprieve.

Night had fallen by the time she took a solitary supper on the terrace with a bottle of the commemorative red wine gifted to her by Pushkin and Guthren. She glanced up at the starlit sky, hoping to catch Starbase 30 as it orbited around Dordogne, and raised her glass.

"Fair winds and following seas, my friends."

By the time Sunday evening rolled around, she'd exhausted her patience at the leisurely pace of inactivity and looked forward to her new responsibilities playing chess with starships and battle groups as Admiral Hogue's chief of staff for operations. Considering her knowledge of the Rim Sector and the vast swaths of space beyond, where the Navy shouldn't go, it could get interesting.

***

"Well, well, well. Admirals Kowalski and Holt, Fleet HQ's most notorious fixers, enjoying a Friday afternoon drink here of all places. And in civilian clothes, at that. Who'd have thought it?"

Lothar Waterston, Undersecretary of Defense for Political Affairs, took an empty chair and joined them without so much as a by your leave. The terrace of the Geneva Weinkeller, overlooking a Lake Geneva that shimmered prettily under a cerulean sky, was empty, the lunch patrons having left and the supper patrons still hours away.

"How about you piss off, Lothar?" Ezekiel Holt said in a conversational tone. "We're waiting for friends, and you're not one of them."

The balding, narrow-faced, sallow-skinned undersecretary gave him a toothsome grin.

"Come now, Admiral. Is that any way to treat a Defense Department colleague?"

Kowalski turned her basilisk stare on the man.

"Speak your piece and leave, Lothar. Before Zeke forgets his manners and sics his investigators on your bent ass."

"See, Zeke. That's how you do it. Be more like Kathryn and less like a smart ass who never outgrew his days as a lieutenant trash-talking his betters behind their back."

Instead of rising to the bait, Holt took a sip of his white wine and waited.

"I hear you two have been playing creative nepotism games again. Dunmoore as chief of staff for operations at 3rd Fleet and her minion Pushkin taking the 101st Battle Group?" He shook his head in mock disapproval. "That's crass, even for you. She's no more qualified for the job than he is, and neither should still be in the Navy. Many people in this city are unhappy with that situation, some of whom you should take care to avoid offending more than necessary. Now, what's done is done, but no more giving your friends preferential treatment, and to hell with the Navy's needs."

"Who says we're engaging in nepotism, Lothar? The CNO approves all flag officer appointments and promotions. If he doesn't like a recommendation or doesn't think an officer is right for the job, he says so and doesn't sign off on the orders. As you know, even if you're a civilian drone with delusions of adequacy."

"Ooh." Waterston made a face. "Zeke's questionable sense of humor is rubbing off on you, Kathryn. You should hang out with a better class of people, preferably not those wearing a uniform."

"Hard to do in Geneva. All you find around here outside Fleet HQ is low class and no class. And that's just those working in government."

"Does Grand Admiral Sampaio know about your propensity for disparaging your betters?"

"I'll have to ask him, though I suspect he and I share the same opinion about many subjects. Anything else you wish to say?"

"Don't mess with the senior appointment plot again, Kathryn. After this, Dunmoore and her coterie get shelved before they create the sort of havoc we can't afford."

Holt's right eyebrow crept up. "Who's this we that can't afford nice things?"

Waterston climbed to his feet. "Shall I tell the boss message delivered and understood?"

"If you want. Goodbye, Lothar. Don't bother us again when we're off duty and enjoying a glass of wine."

"And say hi to Blayne Hersom for me," Holt added.

"Why should I do that?"

"Because your ass belongs to him, not the SecDef. Regularly losing to Blayne at golf makes it worth his while keeping you around." Holt raised his glass. "Now be a good little boy, and don't let the doorknob hit you in the ass on the way out."

Waterston wiggled his fingers at them. "Cheerio." Then he turned on his heels and left.

Kowalski turned to Holt. "Hersom's man in the SecDef's office, eh? Figures."

"We've suspected for a long time but finally got proof this week. Please don't ask me what or how."

"It explains many things, such as operational leaks that caused Siobhan's last few missions to fail. I hope Admiral Doxiadis is making sure the SecDef no longer gets briefed on anything that matters."

Holt grimaced. "My boss doesn't know yet, but once he does, he'll try. Whether it'll work is another matter. The SecDef likes to be in the know."

Movement by the entrance caught his attention. "Speaking of the devil. Make that plural."

He raised his hand, and moments later, Admiral Zebulon Lowell, the CNO, and Admiral Jado Doxiadis, the Chief of Intelligence, both in elegant civilian suits, took the other two chairs at their table.

"Was that Lothar Waterston I just saw climbing into an official car outside?" Doxiadis asked.

"He is rather unmistakable. Yes. And he'll have seen you, which makes this even better."

"Why?"

Holt took a sip of wine before summarizing the conversation.

"If Lothar's masters are worried about how we're moving pieces around, then we're on the right track," Lowell said once Holt finished.

The latter pulled a small, oblong object from his jacket and placed it on the table. "My jammer is active." He turned to Doxiadis. "If you'd like to check, sir."

Doxiadis produced an identical jammer, consulted its built-in display, and nodded. "I confirm. We're clear to talk. So, what was Waterston really about, Zeke? This is hardly the first time we've moved our people where they're needed and ignored suggestions or pressure from the outside."

Holt smiled. "Funnily enough, Lothar the Loathsome is one of the items I wanted to discuss, sir. We established beyond all doubt he's Blayne Hersom's man inside the SecDef's office."

A thunderous expression creased Lowell's forehead.

"Sonofabitch. He's why missions in the Zone have failed recently, isn't he?"

"Likely. Waterston has access to almost everything we send the SecDef. And that means Hersom is reading the stuff as well, probably at the same time."

"Options?" Doxiadis asked.

"We can terminate Lothar, although Hersom will realize why and find another source we might not uncover for a long time. Or we can restrict what the SecDef sees, which will raise questions in due course. Or we can feed the SecDef disinformation, stuff that's true except for a few vital details only we'll know about. Any of the options will only give us a temporary reprieve. Only eliminating the SSB as an entity will bring a definitive solution."

"Disinformation it is," Doxiadis said. "And please add your conversation with Lothar to the file."

"I recorded it, sir. It'll be in the file verbatim."

Kowalski guffawed at Holt's statement. "Oh, marvelous."

"Why?" Lowell asked.

"Zeke used some salty language with Lothar. And so did I. The man was asking for it. Besides, insults just slide off him without leaving a mark."

"One thing concerns me, though," Holt said, serious once more. "Why did Lothar show up right after we linked him with Hersom to deliver a warning that might have been more appropriate when we announced Dunmoore and Pushkin's appointments?"

Doxiadis frowned. "You're worried he heard we found out and is firing a warning shot across our bow, either on his own or at Hersom's behest?"

"Yes, sir. And if Hersom is pulling Lothar's strings in this instance rather than the SecDef, we might have problems cropping up soon enough."

"You think I should speak with Hersom? It's been three years since I last warned him the wages of deceit were death."

Holt shook his head.

"Since it might tip our hand, not just yet. But I'll put more eyes on Lothar for now."

"Your call, Zeke. If he needs to be taken out, then so be it. Anything else concerning him and Hersom?"

"No, sir."

Lowell nodded once. "Alright. Let's order and move to the next item on the agenda."

"That would be 3rd Fleet and its remarkable lack of success in stopping traffickers."

— Five —

On Monday morning, a few minutes before oh-eight-hundred, Siobhan Dunmoore settled her car into the spot marked COS Ops, between those labeled DComd and COS Admin, in front of the flat-roofed three-story 3rd Fleet HQ building. Like most at Joint Base Dordogne, it was built on a standard pattern typical throughout human space — banks of polarized windows, stone cladding, pinkish red, in this case, flag posts in front of the door and a large sign announcing its occupants. The installation, a throwback to the ancient Roman castra concept, was also based on a universal design, with two main avenues intersecting at right angles in the center, quartering it.

Dunmoore climbed out of her car, a gray, sleek, but not particularly flashy model produced on Dordogne, and glanced up at the gray clouds, wondering what Gregor Pushkin was doing at that moment in the day cabin that had been hers for three years. Her former command wasn't due to return on patrol for another two weeks while its ships resupplied, carried out minor maintenance tasks, and made adjustments to their camouflage so they wouldn't be easily recognized after the encounter with the Shrehari.

It meant crew members would enjoy shore leave, some with their families, others sampling Dordogne's recreational delights.

But she knew Gregor had no planetside home. He would divide his time between visits to the surface, enjoying Dordogne, and the quiet of his suite aboard *Iolanthe*. By common accord, they wouldn't speak again until after his first patrol as flag officer commanding the 101st. It was only fair to both as they settled into new and unexpected roles.

Besides, the new 3rd Fleet Chief of Staff - Operations being too friendly and chatty with the commodore commanding a battle group answerable to SOCOM against the 3rd Fleet commander's wishes wouldn't be considered politically correct.

She tugged on her tunic hem — the dress of the day at 3rd Fleet HQ was the same as aboard a starship in port — adjusted her beret, and fetched her briefcase from the back seat. The car door closed silently as she walked toward the transparent aluminum outer doors, which parted at her approach.

An invisible security arch in the lobby scanned her credentials. It matched her biometric data with what was on file, and the inner doors opened to an airy, three stories tall central atrium with a polished granite floor. Twin winding staircases at the back framed a large silver naval crest while display cases overflowing with mementos lined the walls. Wide, carpeted corridors led off the atrium on each side. The sign above the one on the left said *Executive Suite*, the holy of holies where mere mortal officers feared to tread.

The two ordinary spacers sitting behind a gray, granite reception counter just inside sprang to their feet at her arrival, seeing as how she ranked immediately behind Admiral Hogue and Vice Admiral Keo by dint of her appointment.

"Good morning, Admiral," the senior of the two said.

She smiled at them. "Good morning. And how are you?"

"We're doing okay, sir. You know your way around?"

"Yes. Thanks." She'd visited enough times in the last three years to find her new office and that of the other principal staff officers without a guide.

The executive suite corridor was paneled in wood the color of liquid honey. Ornate brass plates hung above each door, announcing the job title of the occupant. Admiral Hogue's suite — office, conference room, and antechamber — occupied the width of the building wing at the far end. Vice Admiral Keo's suite sat to the left, while the 3rd Fleet's command coxswain's office was on the right.

Dunmoore knew both connected with Hogue's suite through private doors. Her office and that of her colleague, Rear Admiral Alvin Maffina, the Chief of Staff - Administration, were the next ones on either side, both suites smaller than Keo's but larger than that occupied by the coxswain.

When she entered her office suite, a lean, freckle-faced, middle-aged lieutenant with gold cords dangling from her left shoulder stood with alacrity from behind a neat desk by the open inner door and came to attention. She wore two and a half rows of ribbons above her tunic's left breast pocket, some of which dated back to the Shrehari War, meaning she was a mustang, someone commissioned from the ranks, and not an Academy product. She had the look and could clearly claim more Navy time than the average two striper.

"Welcome, Admiral," she said in the raspy voice of someone who'd inhaled fumes from shipboard fires caused by enemy action. "I'm Anna Ramius. It's an honor to serve you."

Dunmoore was momentarily taken aback. She'd never considered her position came with a flag lieutenant, someone who'd handle her agenda, schedule, correspondence, and other administrative matters so she could focus on her primary responsibilities.

Then she held out her hand.

"A pleasure to meet you, Anna. After three years as a two-star in *Iolanthe*, I wasn't expecting a flag lieutenant, but I'm glad you're here. I see you're a veteran of the war. We'll have to compare notes and see if we fought in the same places."

A faint smile of pleasure softened Ramius' hard features.

"Aye, sir. And our paths did cross, but you'll not remember me. I was a petty officer when the war ended. Made chief third before the Navy decided I should become an officer."

"I figured as much."

Ramius pointed at the inner door.

"Your office is ready for you, sir. Can I get you a cup of coffee or tea?"

"Coffee would be great."

"Sure thing. Admiral Hogue would like to see you at eight-thirty."

Once Ramius had vanished into the corridor, Dunmoore entered her office and studied her surroundings. As she remembered, the walls were half-paneled in the same pale wood as the hallway. Standard issue naval art hung from the walls —

wet navy battle scenes, plaques from various units and formations, starship schematics, and the like.

Her large wooden desk occupied the center of the room. A stand of flags framed by tall windows on either side stood behind it. The windows looked out over the parade square and let in plenty of natural light. An oval conference table surrounded by a dozen chairs occupied the corner to the left of the door, while a settee group with sideboards and table lamps occupied the corner to the right. Her quarters in *Iolanthe* would have fit inside the office with room to spare.

She hung her beret on the coat rack behind the door, placed her briefcase on the desk, then dropped into the high-backed leather chair and surveyed her new domain. Or rather, her inner sanctum. Her domain was the 3rd Fleet operations center one level down, inside a blast-proof casing that could withstand a kinetic strike from orbit. If her memory wasn't playing false, a private lift was hidden away either in this office or the outer office, so she could reach the ops center quickly and without fuss. And bypass most of the security checkpoints.

At that moment, Ramius entered her office with a mug bearing the 3rd Fleet's crest. "Black, without sweetener, right, sir?"

Dunmoore gave her a smile of thanks as she placed the mug on the desk.

"Got it in one. By the way, I recall there's a private lift to the ops center around here."

Did she see a brief look of disapproval on Ramius' face?

"Yes, sir. It's behind the paneling next to the closet in the outer office. The security lock has been coded to your biometrics. Of course, it's also coded to admit Admiral Hogue, Admiral Keo, and Admiral Maffina."

"And you?"

"No, sir."

"Can the other aides use it?"

"Admiral Hogue's and Admiral Keo's aides. Not Admiral Maffina's."

"Then please tell security I want you added to the list. There's no sense in making you take the long way if you need to find me urgently and can't get in touch via the secure network. In fact, have Admiral Maffina's aide added as well."

"Yes, sir." She nodded at the virtual display hovering over one corner of the desk. "You'll find your messages and the briefing notes awaiting your approval in the queue. I'll fetch you two minutes before your meeting with Admiral Hogue."

"Thank you, Anna." Dunmoore picked up the coffee cup and took a tentative sip. Not quite Navy standard like what they served in *Iolanthe*, but it packed a flavor punch, nonetheless. "Nice."

"I'll leave you to it then, sir." With that, Ramius vanished, closing the door behind her.

The first thing Dunmoore pulled up was an organization chart of the 3rd Fleet operations branch, parsing the names and job titles, looking for people she knew either personally or by reputation. She'd be meeting with them individually or in small groups over the coming days as she settled in.

Largest of her divisions, the operations center itself numbered plenty of commanders, lieutenant commanders, and chief petty officers under captains in charge of the duty watches, along with lieutenants, petty officers, and ratings to take care of the administrative needs. Over a hundred in all, divided into three watches which continuously relayed each other every eight hours. And that was only one part of her remit.

She also oversaw the intelligence, current operations, and planning divisions, which totaled another hundred officers, chief petty officers, and ratings. And, of course, she'd be the one issuing orders to the fleet's battle groups in Admiral Hogue's name.

A knock on the door broke through her focus on the organizational details, and she glanced at the time readout. Oh-eight-twenty-eight precisely. The door opened, and Ramius poked her head in.

"Your meeting with Admiral Hogue."

"On my way."

When she entered Hogue's suite, her senior aide, a lieutenant commander, looked up from his desk but didn't stand.

"Please go right in, sir. The admiral is waiting for you."

The office door slid open silently, and she entered. Hogue sat in splendor behind a desk that made Dunmoore's look dowdy and her office a cramped closet. Windows on all three sides made the already ample space seem even bigger.

The configuration, however, was like her office's — a stand of flags behind the desk, a conference table to one side, and a settee group to the other. Five chairs stood in front of the desk, the center one occupied by Horace Keo.

"Good morning, sirs," Dunmoore said in a bright tone, smiling as she walked across a polished wood floor inlaid with the crest of the 3rd Fleet, a circle enclosing crossed tridents above a watchtower. It bore the motto *Nunquam Retrorsum*, meaning Never Backward in Latin. "I hope you had a good weekend."

"Tolerable," Hogue replied. "Welcome to 3rd Fleet, Siobhan. Please sit."

As she did so, Keo nodded at her wordlessly.

"Thank you, sir."

"Since we're all busy people, I'll come straight to the point. Your predecessor had the operations branch running smoothly, and in the way I like. So, please take some time to acquaint yourself with the functioning of the headquarters before proposing changes. And please don't modify any procedure or protocol before discussing it with Horace and me."

"Of course, sir. I'm not in the habit of changing things for the sake of change."

"Good. Well, that's all I wanted this morning — to welcome you to our family. I hold weekly executive meetings with Horace and both chiefs of staff every Wednesday at thirteen hundred hours. That's where you'll keep me, Horace, and Alvin, up to date on routine matters pertaining to your branch. You may carry on."

Keo climbed to his feet, imitated by Dunmoore, and said, "Yes, sir."

He glanced at Dunmoore. "Let's go to my office. I'd like to discuss a few things."

— Six —

"Let me make a few things clear, Dunmoore," Keo said once he'd settled behind his desk and she in one of the facing chairs. "First, you work for me, and I work for Admiral Hogue. You never go to her directly on any matter. Always go through me."

"Understood, sir."

"Second, you heard what the admiral said about procedures. I'm happy with how things work now and don't want changes. If you have ideas, run them through me first."

"Third, I expect you and Alvin to sort out disagreements between yourselves. I don't enjoy refereeing between two rear admirals."

"Yes, sir."

"Four, you always run proposed changes to battle group orders, patrol routes, and anything else touching on their deployment through me first."

"Understood."

Keo stared at Dunmoore for what seemed like an eternity.

"You know, I can't fathom how you made rear admiral without spending a single day as a higher formation headquarters staff officer since you were a lieutenant before the war. To my eyes, that makes you singularly unsuitable as the 3rd Fleet's number three in the chain of command. You simply have no experience in how things work. Besides, I've read your essays on the conduct of the war and did not find them particularly cogent either. No wonder you spent ten years as a post captain after the armistice before someone rescued your career with an out-of-sequence promotion to rear admiral. It must be nice to have patrons in high places."

Since Keo obviously didn't expect a reply, Dunmoore simply held his gaze and remained silent.

"It's only fair you know you were neither Admiral Hogue's nor my choice as COS Ops. But here we are, so I suggest you make the best of it by learning the job quickly and becoming an integral part of the senior command team. You have a reputation as a loose cannon, which might be handy in SOCOM, but not here. Tie yourself down and work within the parameters Admiral Hogue and I have set, and we'll get along splendidly. Otherwise, your tenure might not be lengthy, and I don't need to tell you senior rear admirals relieved from such a high-profile appointment no longer have career prospects, highly placed friends notwithstanding."

Dunmoore inclined her head by way of acknowledgment. "Yes, sir."

Keo's eyes narrowed as if he'd sensed something, but Dunmoore had maintained an impassive and respectful appearance all along, knowing he didn't like her and never had.

"Oh, and you'll run everything through me before mentioning it at the admiral's weekly executive meetings. I don't enjoy getting blindsided by an issue you and I haven't discussed beforehand."

Another nod. "Absolutely, sir."

"That was it. Get yourself familiar with all the active files and deployments."

***

When Dunmoore re-entered her office suite, Lieutenant Ramius gave her a strange look but said nothing beyond asking whether she should schedule meetings with the division heads and the operations center's watchkeeping directors.

"Please do. If any are free this morning, I can see them as early as possible. I'll meet with the directors during their shifts, so none should come in while off duty."

"Yes, sir. I'm on it." A pause. "Perhaps you can see Captain Horvat now. She's the Alpha Watch director."

"Good idea. Don't summon her up here. Check to see if she's free; if so, let her know I'm on my way. She can take me on a tour of the ops center." Dunmoore smiled at Ramius. "By the way, I'm acquainted with all my direct reports in some fashion. Most of them were young lieutenant commanders when they took my class at the War College, and I ran across the others here and there over the years."

All, of course, were veterans of the Shrehari War but were still relatively junior officers when it ended. Yet they were now senior captains who'd done their time as commanding officers of starships and shore units. Thinking about the passage of time,

Dunmoore felt just a little old for a moment. It must have shown on her face because Ramius chuckled.

"None of us are getting any younger, Admiral. Let me call Captain Horvat and tell her you're on your way. Since there's no emergency on right now, otherwise, we'd have heard, she'll be glad to show you around."

Dunmoore remembered Freya Horvat as a stocky, energetic officer with a shock of platinum blond hair, enigmatic green eyes, and a voice that could rouse the dead. And when she finally made her way through the security gates guarding the ops center, taking the long way like everyone else, the woman who met her at the door hadn't changed much. A few more wrinkles and laugh lines at best.

"Admiral Dunmoore." Horvat's smile was just as infectious as before. "I gather I'm the first of the directors to welcome you. Please enter your domain."

"How have you been doing?"

"Since I barely survived your classes at the College?" A laugh. "Grand, sir. Just grand. Luckily my ship didn't have the pleasure of being evaluated by RED One during your time as its director."

"A good tour of command, then?"

"Outstanding."

She ushered Dunmoore into the ops center, a vast room with a high ceiling dominated by a three-dimensional holographic representation of the 3rd Fleet's area of operations at its center. Small icons of assorted colors floated in what was commonly known as the tank, representing the last known position of Commonwealth naval and ground units, civilian ships who'd filed a sailing plan, and suspected or potential hostiles as per intelligence reports.

Workstations with large displays surrounded the tank in two concentric rows, each housing an officer or chief petty officer responsible for a particular segment of the AO or a specific deployment. Offices opened onto a mezzanine overlooking the bullpen, one for the watchkeeping director, the others unassigned and available for visitors if, for example, Dunmoore wanted to spend a few hours working here while overseeing a specific operation.

As befit the beating heart of 3rd Fleet HQ, silence was paramount. Watchkeepers held barely audible conversations among themselves, even in the break room under the mezzanine. Fascinated by the holographic projection as always when in an operations center, Dunmoore spent a few minutes studying it close up while exchanging nods and smiles with the watchkeepers who'd meet her gaze. One, in particular, caught her eye, a chief petty officer third class who saved her life long ago on a ship decommissioned and scrapped a few years before the armistice. She gave him a quick sign that meant I'll speak with you later, then followed Horvat up a flight of stairs to the director's glass-walled office.

"Someone you know, Admiral?"

"An old shipmate, Chief Petty Officer Guido Vincenzo, Vince to his friends. He was with me in *Stingray* and *Iolanthe* during the war."

"Ah, yes. Chief Vincenzo has been with us for six months. Solid, smart as a whip, and rather quiet. He's easily the equal of any lieutenant commander on my team."

"Glad to hear you say so. He and I went through a few hairy situations together. I'd like to speak with him for a few minutes after we're done if you don't mind. It can wait if he's working on something that requires his full attention. Neither of us is going anywhere."

"No problems, Admiral. Should you want some privacy, the office next door is yours whenever you need it."

"Thank you." Dunmoore settled back. "Tell me about your normal shift, Freya, and the things you figure are going well or need improvement."

As Horvat spoke, Dunmoore, sensitive to the undercurrents in the HQ, especially after her one-sided conversation with Keo, thought she detected hesitation in her tone. Almost imperceptible pauses while she searched for words. And that wasn't the outspoken, daring officer she remembered from spirited debates at the College.

Equally strange, Horvat should have remembered Dunmoore preferred outright candor to equivocation, yet her turn of phrase sometimes seemed overly ambiguous rather than clear and direct. But perhaps it was no more than a captain with a commodore's star in her eyes trying to give the new boss as rosy a picture as she could.

Dunmoore asked a few probing questions about the standard operating procedures, then thanked Horvat for her time.

"And now I'll have a few words with Chief Vincenzo on the way out."

"Be my guest, sir. After all, he and I work for you."

She left Horvat in her office and took the stairs down into the bullpen, Vincenzo watching her approach with his dark, intelligent eyes.

"How are you doing, Chief?" She asked in a soft tone once she reached his workstation.

"Great, sir. And you seem to be prospering."

"What winds of fortune bring you here?"

He shrugged.

"A career mangler with a sense of humor, I suppose. It's been mostly shore assignments for me since leaving *Iolanthe* back in the day. Once I made chief," a grin appeared, "it became nothing but staff jobs keeping officers from stepping in it."

"I thought you enjoyed serving aboard starships."

"So did I, but here I am. This is a rather good billet. I get to see a lot of stuff happening, and during the slow times, I'm working on a degree in war studies."

Dunmoore's eyebrows shot up. "Looking for a commission?"

"Maybe. But the subject is interesting in itself."

"You can count on your former captain's recommendation if it comes to that."

"Thank you, sir." A pause. "And you can count on me for anything, like always."

***

"I have Captain Tsang ready to come over," Lieutenant Ramius announced when Dunmoore returned to her office. Tsang, the N2(Intelligence), Captain Rodriguez, the N5(Plans), and their respective divisions were in the neighboring building, which closed off one end of the parade square at the center of the 3rd Fleet's quadrant. It connected with the main HQ building via an underground passage which was much beloved by all during severe weather, especially when one of equatorial Dordogne's tropical storms roared in from the open ocean.

"Then give him the word."

Dimitri Tsang, wiry, black-haired with a square face and deep-set dark eyes, appeared at her office door only five minutes later. Another of her War College students. She remembered him as industrious, inquisitive, and occasionally argumentative but always armed with cogent facts.

Dunmoore gave him a welcoming smile and waved him in. "Glad to see you again, Dimitri. Grab a chair."

"Likewise, Admiral," he said in his usual flat tone as he complied, studying her all the while. "Welcome to 3rd Fleet HQ."

"Thank you. And how are things? You've been here now what? Eight months?"

"Yes, sir. Eight. Going as well as can be. I enjoy the job. It's probably the most fun I'll have until retirement."

"You plan on leaving early?"

"No." He shook his head. "But I'm likely terminal as a post captain and won't get another assignment this close to the action. Most of the senior Intelligence Branch people are on Earth these days."

"And how's business in the N2 world?"

Tsang grimaced. "A mixed bag, if truth be told, Admiral. You may have noticed the quality of what comes in hasn't been great in recent months. I understand the 101st scored three goose eggs in a row because of faulty intelligence."

"You understand correctly."

"Well, 3rd Fleet patrols along the Rim frontier haven't been doing much better. It's been even longer since one of our battle groups scored so much as a simple seizure for unpaid registration fees."

"Any idea why?"

Tsang shook his head. "Not a clue. My division doesn't actually develop intelligence. We collate it from many sources — our ships, those of neighboring formations, Fleet Intelligence, etcetera. And those sources have struggled to generate precise estimates. Honestly, I'm at a bit of a loss."

***

"Is Dunmoore going to be a problem?"

Vice Admiral Horace Keo, standing by his palatial apartment's panoramic windows overlooking the Marseilles harbor, shrugged, even though the call was audio only.

"Probably. She has a reputation for sticking her nose into things that don't concern her, acting without permission, and overriding her superiors' wishes. That's why she's only a rear admiral when she could be sitting in Eva Hogue's chair right now."

"How is that?"

"Dunmoore finished the war as a commodore thirteen years ago. She reverted to captain but, by all rights, should have regained that first star within a year or two. A few years after that, rear admiral — she has influential friends in the CNO's office — then making it to vice admiral could have been another three or four. Someone with her war record and successful command of a special operations battle group would easily be considered for a fleet command."

"Unlike you."

Keo's face tightened with anger at the jibe.

"My friends are no longer around to help my career. Some of them because of Dunmoore's actions in the latter part of the war. I know I won't make four stars. It took me too long to reach three."

"You have my sympathies. Just keep in mind your job is to make sure she doesn't cause us grief. It shouldn't be too hard. Dunmoore doesn't only have friends on Earth. She has implacable enemies as well."

Keo turned away from waters shimmering under a full moon.

"How about you help yourself by helping me keep her under control? She's just a human with normal appetites, needs, and desires. And since she probably knows she should be commanding 3rd Fleet instead of a lazy, inefficient political appointee, Dunmoore will carry a grudge."

"Just like you."

— Seven —

After speaking with Ewan Loziro, N3 (Current Operations) and Raina Rodriguez, N5 (Plans), and when he reported for duty at sixteen hundred hours, Haru Mifune, the Beta Watch director, Dunmoore felt little wiser about the inner doings of the 3rd Fleet's operations branch. All painted a rosy picture, except Tsang, and he placed the burden of blame on outside agencies.

Yet she knew they had glossed over the negatives and emphasized the positives for her benefit. It was almost certainly a manifestation of the common idea that staff couldn't give the new chief reasons to search dark corners for the organization's faults. She'd seen it before the war when 3rd Fleet Headquarters lived aboard the orbiting starbase, and she was a watchkeeper in the current operations center's precursor as a mere lieutenant. And again, throughout her career, when dealing with higher headquarters. None of her direct reports would voice concerns until they thought they could trust her, and even then, in most cases, only when they saw an opportunity to advance their careers — the curse of a peacetime Navy.

She still hadn't spoken with Brianna Kim, the Gamma Watch director, who'd come on duty at midnight, but she would catch her before oh-eight hundred the following day before Kim signed off. And though she hadn't been one of her students or a passing acquaintance, let alone an old shipmate, Dunmoore somehow knew Kim would sound very much like her colleagues Horvat and Mifune — all was good. No changes or improvements could make the functioning of the operations center noticeably better. And perhaps all three were correct.

Dunmoore glanced at her briefcase, then decided she didn't need to carry work home, at least not that night, and shoved it into a desk drawer, which she locked with a biometric signature. Then she headed for the door, grabbing her beret along the way.

"Time to quit, Anna. It's been a full first day, and the rest of the week looks just as action-packed."

"I won't argue with you, sir. Enjoy your evening."

"You too."

Dunmoore's AI butler had made sure the house was ready for her return from work when she pulled her car into the garage. Though the late afternoon air was sweltering under a cloudless sky, the indoors were at a pleasant temperature. Her evening meal was simmering as per the program she'd set that morning, and a chilled bottle of Dordogne Riesling was waiting in the refrigeration unit.

The only thing missing was companions with whom to share her meal, either in her quarters or in the wardroom. Living alone after all this time would take getting used to, especially since she'd spent the last three years never taking a solitary evening meal after a long day's work.

She slipped out onto the terrace after sunset, with a dram of the Glen Arcturus, and spent a long time staring up at the stars, looking for the orbital station where her former command would still be docked. But in vain once again.

That night, she had strange dreams for the first time in ages and woke at sunrise feeling fuzzy and unsettled. With nothing else to do until she dared show her face at HQ, lest she gave her staff the wrong impression, Dunmoore slipped on gym clothes and, for the first time in a long time, went for a ten-kilometer run around the neighborhood in the cool morning air.

She was at work by seven-thirty and immediately headed down to the operations center for her interview with Captain Kim, the Gamma Watch director, who'd be relieved at oh-eight-hundred and head home. But, as expected, Dunmoore heard nothing that Horvat and Mifune hadn't already mentioned.

By the time she returned to her office, Lieutenant Ramius was waiting with a fresh cup of coffee and the morning summary which was, not unexpectedly, short and held no surprises. As Captain Kim had mentioned, the overnight shift was quiet.

Dunmoore barely had time to finish the report when knuckles rapped on her office door jamb. She looked up to see the smiling face of her colleague, Alvin Maffina, the chief of staff for administration. A few years older than her, with thick silver hair, ruggedly handsome features, and warm brown eyes, he wouldn't have seemed out of place as a candidate for the Commonwealth Senate. His branch provided logistical support to the 101st, and they'd gotten along reasonably well over the previous three years. He was not one to seek conflict. On the contrary.

"Good morning, Siobhan. Sorry I wasn't there yesterday to welcome you. But I am here now, so welcome."

"Thanks, Alvin. Grab a pew."

"Don't mind if I do." Maffina closed the door behind him and dropped into a chair.

"Got data overload yet?"

"It's manageable."

"But not as simple as running a battle group from the flag CIC, I bet."

She couldn't help but smile at his good humor. "No, but I'm not exactly surrounded by unknown senior staff or learning new procedures."

"Anything I can help you with?"

"Are there any issues involving both of our branches I should know about?"

He shook his head. "Nothing that needs our attention. Folks work well with each other around here and do their best to resolve matters at the lowest level possible. Hanno Berg and I rarely had to reach down and make folks smarten up."

"Good to hear. Any idea why Hanno pulled the plug so unexpectedly? I would have liked to speak with him and get pointers, but he dropped off the sensor grid right after turning in his uniform."

Maffina shrugged. "I couldn't say. It took all of us by surprise. Not that Hanno had any illusions he'd ever get a third star, but there are plenty of interesting rear admiral billets he could have filled until reaching his normal retirement date."

"An attractive civilian job offer, maybe?"

"Perhaps. Though he discussed nothing of the sort with me or anyone else, and he wasn't the type to keep secrets."

"Do you know if he was staying on Dordogne?"

Maffina shook his head. "No. But he wasn't from here. If I recall, he's from Scandia, so maybe he went home. Did he leave you handover files?"

"None that I've found or that Lieutenant Ramius mentioned."

"Ah, well, she's new to the COS Ops flag lieutenant job. You knew that, right? Hanno's aide asked for a transfer to a starship and is now patrolling the frontier somewhere."

Dunmoore, who'd been focusing on her senior staff, hadn't scanned Ramius' file, something she regretted.

"No, I wasn't aware, but that's my fault for not asking. She seems at ease in the job, as if she's done it for a while."

A chuckle. "That's because Anna Ramius was Admiral Hogue's junior aide until last week. The admiral figured it would be easier if she gave you someone who was already experienced at the job and picked herself a replacement, seeing as how she has Lieutenant Commander Dewint as her senior aide."

"That's very generous of her."

Maffina's smile widened.

"I think she's worried you might find adapting to a higher formation headquarters as a flag officer more challenging than usual, seeing as how you've not served in one since you were a lieutenant before the war."

"The price of clean living, I suppose."

Maffina let out a bark of laughter. "You do not enjoy staff jobs, do you?"

"It's not so much a matter of enjoyment as one of happenstance. I spent the war aboard starships, then taught at the War College before leading Readiness Evaluation Division Team

One, and from there, back to starships. No complaints, mind you."

"I'd think not. Well." He climbed to his feet. "I'll let you keep gulping down information by the metric ton. As I said, if you need anything, just ask."

"Thanks, Alvin."

Once more alone in her office, Dunmoore turned to stare out the window at the parade square, currently doing duty as overflow parking, like most days of the year. Officers unexpectedly taking early retirement and falling off the galaxy's edge weren't unusual. Many turned in the uniform because they simply couldn't deal with things anymore and wanted to get as far away as possible. Though she hadn't known Hanno Berg more than in passing, he'd left the impression of a calm, thoughtful officer.

And why had no one mentioned Ramius was Hogue's former junior aide? That, along with the rosy picture painted by her direct reports, made Dunmoore wonder whether she was being 'managed' as often happened in the military when a less than desired commanding officer took over. After all, she'd done it to Admiral Petras. But that begged the question of why she wasn't wanted as COS Ops. The billet was for a rear admiral who'd done a full tour in command of a battle group, meaning she qualified. It couldn't be her lack of previous staff experience. By the time flag officers successfully commanded a formation in space, they knew how the staff system worked.

After a few minutes, she turned back to her desk and called up the files Ramius had helpfully queued in order of urgency and importance. Inevitably, the first of them was the quarterly budget review covering not only the expenditures of the operations branch but also those of every formation and unit under 3rd Fleet's control, along with the forecast for the next quarter. Someone in Alvin's N8 (Finance) division had helpfully highlighted areas of concern, including the increase in operating costs for several battle groups. She took notes because it might come up at Admiral Hogue's weekly executive meeting, then went on to the next file.

By the time Ramius poked her head through the door to remind her it was noon and ask if she should fetch a meal pack, Dunmoore felt more than a twinge of despair at all the non-operational work her responsibilities entailed. It made her wonder whether relinquishing her rank to get a billet aboard a starship was still an option. But considering someone back on Earth had arranged for her appointment without consulting Hogue, she was sure her request would get lost in the ether.

Sixteen hundred hours had come and gone by the time Dunmoore called it quits and sent Ramius home, wherever that was. She felt more exhausted than at any other time in the recent past but had plenty of notes on the more pressing issues for the next day's meetings — one with Keo at eleven-hundred and the other with Hogue at thirteen hundred.

After an early night and another morning run, Dunmoore spent most of the morning digesting more files until it was time for the meeting with Keo. When she entered his office, Alvin Maffina already sat with Keo at the conference table, and she joined them at the latter's gesture.

As they went through the current issues, Dunmoore quickly understood Keo was managing Hogue by deciding what she would see and rule on and what would remain within the staff. Or, more precisely, what Keo himself would decide. But considering the scope of Hogue's command responsibilities — hundreds of starships, orbitals, and ground installations, well over a hundred thousand people, and the most contentious frontier in human space — was that not normal? After all, a staff's responsibility was relieving a commander of the minutia so he or she could concentrate on the mission.

Yet the way he managed the information flow from the chiefs of staff to the commander took it one, if not two or three steps beyond what the Staff Officer's Handbook prescribed, and she was intimately acquainted with its provisions after her years at the War College. Usually, a deputy commander wouldn't act as an information filter between his superior and the fleet's principal staff officers, who were expected to know what should and shouldn't be brought forward.

Equally interesting was Keo not kicking any of the decisions back to the two chiefs of staff. Perhaps he assumed that if they raised an issue, Maffina and Dunmoore wanted him to adjudicate. The few times Dunmoore suggested a course of action, he either confirmed in a manner that suggested it was his sole prerogative or told her to try again and come back later.

When she and Maffina shared a quick lunch in the flag officers' dining room, which was little used unless visitors wearing stars were in town, she mentioned Keo's ways struck her as unusual. Maffina gave her a grin and swallowed his latest mouthful.

"Trust me on this, Siobhan. Humoring Horace Keo is much easier and less anxiety-inducing than quoting the relevant Staff Officers' Handbook paragraphs. For what it's worth, Admiral

Hogue would rather have Keo deal with most matters that don't absolutely require the fleet commander's attention. And Keo, in turn, would rather we rear admirals defer to him on most issues."

Dunmoore let out a soft grunt. "That'll work when it's quiet, but if things go to hell, having a bottleneck between the staff and the commander will make sure things break."

"Perhaps. But don't let Keo know you think he's a bottleneck. It didn't work out well for Hanno. And besides, we're at peace, which means the flow of information and decisions can be less than instantaneous. After all, by the time we receive an incident report from a forward battle group, it'll likely already be resolved or on a path that can't be changed without creating additional difficulties. Which leaves the non-operational stuff, and I've yet to see a situation demanding urgency." Maffina finished his sandwich and washed it down with the rest of his water. "Just let him do the talking this afternoon. If Admiral Hogue asks you a direct question, make sure your answer is one that was vetted by Admiral Keo this morning."

They finished their meal in silence. Then, pads in hand, they reported to Hogue's reception area.

The executive meeting struck Dunmoore as more than a bit strange. It turned out to be a dialog between the Commander, 3rd Fleet, and her deputy, with the two chiefs of staff playing the role of a Greek chorus. Dunmoore and Maffina didn't so much brief Hogue on the current issues as speak in Keo's support when he raised those he believed were of interest. Never mind that Dunmoore figured one or two of her own merited at least a passing mention but never made it past Keo's list of permitted subjects.

Dunmoore wore her best bland expression throughout and noted Maffina doing the same. Yet even though she had no experience working in a higher headquarters at this level, she knew keeping the chiefs of staff as mere adornment, the sort who'd nod on command, wasn't right. And she wondered whether it merited a coded message to Kathryn Kowalski, who obviously engineered her appointment, and Ezekiel Holt. He was the closest thing to a Grand Inquisitor the Armed Forces had.

She spent that evening on her terrace, slowly sipping her one allotted glass of Riesling while reviewing the day's events. Perhaps it was too soon to contact her friends, yet the more she thought about it, the more Hanno Berg's sudden resignation and disappearance struck her as odd. But how would she search for his whereabouts with no one at 3rd Fleet HQ noticing?

— Eight —

"You'll never believe who I heard from," Ezekiel Holt said as he placed his tray on the table and sat down across from Kathryn Kowalski in the flag officer's section of the HQ cafeteria.

"Your family, complaining about the time you spend at work?" She gave him an amused look as she speared a spring roll section with her fork.

Holt made a face at her. "Hardy, har, har. No. Siobhan sent me a private message, encrypted with the key I gave her, wondering if I could determine the whereabouts of her predecessor, Hanno Berg. She hasn't been able to find any traces of him using overt means and doesn't want to risk being caught snooping."

"Did she say why?"

He shook his head. "No. But it wouldn't have been necessary. I know how she thinks. Siobhan figures something's wrong with Berg's unexpected retirement and, from what I can tell, disappearance."

"A case for counterintelligence or a little side job?"

"Side job for now. But if our Siobhan is getting antsy about things two weeks into the appointment, I was right about 3rd

Fleet HQ giving off a faint aroma of decay." Holt picked up his chicken and bacon sandwich and took a healthy bite.

"Oh, I never doubted your instincts, Zeke. She's there because of them. But please make sure Siobhan has backup embedded in the staff in case she stumbles across something that might make her push a detonator just to see what happens. You know how she acts when she's out of viable options."

"Already taken care of. Remember, I'm the one who suggested we find a way of placing friends in 3rd Fleet's high places a while back. How's the plan to keep Lothar in the dark?"

"So far, no one's noticed the briefings are a little sparser on details than usual. Or at least not that the CNO can tell. The 101st should head on its next mission soon if they haven't already left, and we'll see whether our intelligence is faulty or we still have a leak."

***

"I thought you might like to know your former command broke out of orbit just now," Captain Horvat said when Dunmoore accepted her call from the operations center. "They didn't file a navigation plan, however."

"Not surprising. I never filed one in three years, either. Thanks for letting me know, Freya."

"My pleasure, sir."

And there it was. The first actual demarcation between her previous life and her current one — *Iolanthe* heading out on patrol while she remained on Dordogne. She'd experienced it before when leaving her beloved Q ship right after the armistice, but this time it was different. Instead of being shunted aside, she'd taken a step up to a more senior position, but she still couldn't quite find her balance.

Keo was a micro-manager, which had become clear quickly and probably explained some of the unease among the senior officers. Yet there were ways of dealing with his type by subtly controlling the information flow and managing him, though she needed to ensure he remained unaware. A tricky proposition.

But by her third week, Dunmoore realized Maffina was doing it. That gave her greater confidence, especially since she now had a firm grasp of the issues and files and had spoken with each member of the operations branch as she visited the offices and various ops center shifts.

However, there was no getting around the fact her job was administrative. No playing chess with starships and battle groups. In fact, her chess set languished at home, unloved and collecting dust. Beyond the lack of worthy opponents, she simply didn't have time during a typical working day and lived a solitary life outside work. And that solitude was sitting heavily on her shoulders.

She was the third highest ranking Navy officer in the star system and the entire sector, making friendships with other officers impossible. And after a lifetime in the Service, she wasn't sure she could relate to civilians. Of course, there was always Alvin Maffina. Yet he had a family, and, although their working relationship was decent, his manner toward Dunmoore made it clear he wasn't interested in adding her to his circle of friends.

So she spent her weekends sightseeing and hiking along mountain trails in the cooler, sparsely inhabited interior of Dordogne's primary, equator-spanning continent.

"Admiral?"

Ramius' voice over the intercom broke Dunmoore out of her reverie.

"Yes."

"An encrypted message for your eyes only has arrived. No sender tags. I'm forwarding it to your queue."

Dunmoore was nonplussed for a few seconds, then remembered — it could only be Zeke or Kathryn.

"A personal missive from a friend, no doubt. Must have tacked it onto a regular subspace packet. A tad irregular unless it came from a starship in deep space, but we've all done it often enough, right?"

Ramius chuckled. "And how."

Dunmoore glanced at the time readout as she called up the message. "It's almost sixteen hundred, Anna. Why don't you sign off and head home for the weekend?"

"Thank you, Admiral. I believe I will."

"Any big plans?"

Ramius chuckled. "If I make plans, then it won't be relaxing. I'll see what my partner wants to do. We'll probably go sailing or scuba diving. Something on or under the water. It's supposed to be a scorcher tomorrow and Sunday, even for Marseilles. You?"

"I'll drive inland and hike one of the wine roads along the Saône River. I haven't visited the area yet."

"In that case, enjoy. The wine tasting is excellent, but too much of it, and it could be a short hike."

"Noted."

"Have a great weekend, Admiral."

Once Ramius was gone, Dunmoore decrypted the message using the algorithm provided by Ezekiel Holt three years ago, and it was indeed from him. As she read, a frown creased her forehead. Hanno Berg had clearly vanished, and without close family or friends who might miss him, no one knew he was gone.

Holt's people had established that he cleared his quarters on Joint Base Dordogne and moved his personal effects out. Where he put them was unknown, just like his whereabouts. He'd neither rented nor bought new accommodations nor owned property on Dordogne as far as the investigators could tell. The local customs and immigration enforcement agency had no record of him leaving the system. Nor could the investigators find evidence he'd tapped his bank account since the day he moved out of the senior officers' quarters. Although it seemed low on funds for someone drawing a rear admiral's pay.

But there were many ways to drop off the sensor grid on a world like Dordogne, which had extensive organized crime and official corruption problems like most older worlds. Buying a new identity that would pass muster with law enforcement wasn't difficult if you had plenty of money and knew who to ask. Then there was simply settling in the backcountry under an assumed name and paying with untraceable cred chips.

But without a friend or relative filing a missing person report or evidence pointing at foul play, the Dordogne Gendarmerie wouldn't investigate. And since Berg was a civilian, he no longer fell under Armed Forces jurisdiction, meaning Fleet Security couldn't look for him either. Officially.

However, Zeke would issue a be on the lookout notice to both his branch and the military police, naming Rear Admiral (retired) Hanno Berg as a person of interest.

Dunmoore entered the self-destruct code and watched the message dissolve into its constituent electrons, then turned to stare out the window at a parade square rapidly emptying of cars as the daytime staff headed home for the weekend. Was her predecessor a victim of foul play, or did he simply decide to disconnect from society for a bit? He wouldn't be the first who needed time and space to re-evaluate his life, and without the help of close family or friends, a situation Dunmoore knew only too well.

She took one last look at her work queue, then decided she wouldn't open a single file until Monday, unlike Admiral Keo, who, it was rumored, worked steadily throughout weekends. A single touch shut down her workstation, and she left the building empty-handed and fancy-free.

***

"What do you think happened to Hanno Berg?" Kowalski asked when Holt confirmed his jammer was active, and both had ordered their customary glass of white wine. The terrace of the Geneva Weinkeller was unoccupied, as always, when they met away from HQ to discuss sensitive matters before the supper rush started.

Holt grimaced. "Berg didn't have a history of mental or emotional issues, nor did he have known enemies. A freshly retired rear admiral doesn't just vanish without a trace on a world like Dordogne."

"Has Admiral Doxiadis declared it a security matter yet?"

"No. Besides, Berg isn't carrying much top secret information in his head. As Siobhan no doubt found out by now, the COS Ops job is administrative. The big operational decisions concerning 3rd Fleet's deployments are made here."

"How long before the matter becomes official?"

"Perhaps it never will. Berg is a grownup, retired from the Armed Forces, and not contravening any laws, be they federal or Dordogne's. He can do as he sees fit with his life, and that includes vanishing. But don't worry, I have people looking, and they've also asked people they know to look.

"Speaking of disappearances, is it true—"

Holt raised a restraining hand. "Hold on to that thought. I just spied our chiefs emerging from the unmarked staff car."

Moments later, Lowell and Doxiadis, also in civilian attire, entered the terrace and headed for their table.

"All is clear?" The latter asked as he sat.

Holt produced his jammer. "That's what mine says."

Doxiadis consulted his and nodded. "Confirmed."

A waiter appeared with two wine glasses moments later, having been warned by Holt, and left menus.

"Item one concerns Hanno Berg." Holt relayed what he'd told Dunmoore in his message. "Unless you want direct action now, I'd rather let matters develop. If misfortune befell Hanno, then there's nothing we can do, anyway. And if not, then he'll reappear at some point."

Lowell took a sip of wine, then said, "Just in case it wasn't voluntarily, I hope Dunmoore is watching her six."

"Ever since the assassination attempt three years ago, sir. I'm not worried for the moment. Item two, which Kathryn was about to raise when you arrived, concerns Lothar the Loathsome. He, too, has disappeared. Officially, he's on sabbatical from the SecDef's office since a few days ago. Apparently, it was sudden, but all the required authorizations are in his personal file, including the SecDef's sign-off. He was last seen leaving the Defense Department's main building. Since then, nothing. No records of him using public transportation, no pings from his private vehicle, and no attempts to access his private funds. His apartment has been empty since that day, but we haven't entered to see whether he packed a bag. I don't consider the matter sufficiently urgent to risk annoying the police if my agents get caught. Lothar lives in a high-security building, so I'd rather get a warrant when and if required."

"What do you think happened?" Doxiadis asked.

"No idea, sir. But he and Hanno Berg vanishing within a few weeks of each other could be more than just coincidence. We're still developing the situation. But my first thought is that the SSB realized we're no longer feeding the SecDef all the information, meaning Lothar's usefulness in that role was over. Whether they're redeploying him after a reasonable waiting period or ending his employment remains in pure speculation."

"All right," Doxiadis nodded. "Keep a watching brief on the matter. Since Waterston is civil service, we don't have official jurisdiction. Next?"

"You've heard rumors Judy Chu was perhaps not a fully autonomous, self-propelled Secretary General of the Commonwealth as everyone assumes, but a front for a Centralist cabal?"

Both Lowell and Doxiadis nodded, and the former said, "Considering the efforts deployed in some quarters to squelch said rumor, it has to be at least partially true."

"We've looked at who might be in that cabal, and one name came up repeatedly — Sara Lauzier, our honorable junior senator for Pacifica. After two terms as her father's close adviser, she knows the ins and outs of the SecGen job and would be the perfect puppet master pulling Chu's strings. And since she wants to be dear Judy's successor once the latter finishes her second term, the more influence and control Sara can exercise in the Palace of the Stars while waiting for her turn, the better."

Lowell nodded sagely. "It makes sense. I can't have been the only one surprised Chu got the top job. She may have been a sharp and often deadly political operator in her decades as a senator, but she cannot grasp the big issues in a non-partisan way. And her former Senate colleagues know it. I always figured she took over from Charles Lauzier for reasons unrelated to her suitability, let alone her qualifications."

"Got it in one, sir. That's what we think. Of course, it's another watching brief for us, but we must remain aware that Sara Lauzier will push Centralist policies through Chu without waiting until she's SecGen."

Kowalski frowned. "And we're nowhere near ready to confront the Centralists if they try a constitutional coup d'état to realign the political firmament away from the OutWorlds."

"Can we speed up the move of SOCOM HQ to Caledonia?" Lowell asked.

"It'll be at least six months before Joint Base Sanctum is ready to receive the advance party, and we can begin trickling in the rest. Completing personnel transfer without the political side noticing will take eighteen months, minimum. But we could move up the timetable to create the new Logistics Command HQ as soon as the current batch of buildings is ready. Unlike SOCOM, we'll pull the new staff from outlying units instead of wholesale transfers from Earth, which SSB won't notice. They'll probably have to double up with SOCOM for a while, but the sooner we put our people out of reach, the better."

Lowell grimaced. "It's still a lengthy job, but there's no avoiding that, not if we want to keep it sub rosa."

— Nine —

Dunmoore aimed her car eastward at the Saône River valley shortly after oh-eight-hundred Saturday morning, ready for a day-long hike through forests and vineyards, far away from Marseille's hustle and bustle. Even after three years of home port leave every few months and now living here full time, she had yet to figure out why the locals preferred spending their weekends on the sweltering shores of the Western Ocean. But choose it they did, rather than relax in the cool and clean air of the interior where native vegetation commingled with that imported from Earth by the first settlers.

Dordogne was a place of contrasts. Its globe-spanning northern polar region, from about sixty degrees latitude to the pole itself, was nothing more than taiga and tundra, with a small ice cap in the middle. The only habitable continent, a vast swath of land connected to the taiga in the north and spilling over the equator until the southern polar latitudes, was home to almost all humans on the planet, their agriculture, and their industries. A broad, tumultuous oceanic passage separated the southern tip of the continent from the tiny Antarctic cap, which was nothing more than a precarious sheet of ice sitting atop a rocky remnant.

But the passage itself was more perilous than any in human-settled space, and no surface ships had ever attempted it, not in the entire history of Dordogne since the first settlers. As the locals liked to say, there was no law, no humanity, and no God south of sixty. The widely spaced island groups populating the ocean that wrapped around two-thirds of the planet were equally uninhabited because they had nothing to attract colonists.

But the mass of land running from north to south, bulging widely at the middle, was as fertile and welcoming as any beyond Earth and easily supported the three hundred million humans who called it home. And since most of them were concentrated on the east and west coasts, the interior remained, even now, an oasis of calm and natural beauty, productive without human activity seeming intrusive.

Dunmoore had discovered what the locals forgot during her first home port vacations. She was no stranger to hiking expeditions in the hinterland, some of which covered many days and hundreds of kilometers. But the sheer size of the landmass meant a lifetime of exploring on foot without ever covering the same bit of land twice.

Whether overdeveloped and thoroughly tamed Earth would have offered her as much, though her habitable landmasses were more significant, was questionable. Micromanaging Keo notwithstanding, being 3rd Fleet's chief of staff for operations had to be better than any rear admiral job in Geneva.

When she reached the northern end of the Saône wine country, Dunmoore hoisted her day pack and sent the car ahead to her planned endpoint automatically after making sure it was linked with her personal communicator in case of changes. The air was clean, the morning sun cheerful, the sky blue, and the valley a beautiful green on either bank of the slow-moving river.

Dunmoore spent the first hour and a half alone on the trail, serenaded by birds, amphibians, and a light breeze ruffling the leaves. She could scarcely have found a more peaceful spot this close to her home. But she still missed the stars, the camaraderie of a crew, and crossing countless light years chasing enemies of all that was good, true, and beautiful.

Eventually, other hikers, in singles or pairs, appeared from various feeder trails connecting the main path to parking areas, hotels, and villages. Dunmoore dutifully nodded and smiled at those who would meet her eyes, though she remained silent. And she soon found herself irritated by those who insisted on holding loud conversations or, worse yet, speaking on their communicators — voices that shattered the harmony of nature.

Shortly before noon, she turned into the lane leading to the Vignoble des Fleurs d'Azur, a boutique vineyard with an attached restaurant that offered wine tasting with a meal. Dunmoore had visited a little over a year earlier and found the rustic atmosphere relaxing, the simple country dishes superb, and the white wine much to her taste.

She was relieved to find the dining room less than half full and the people speaking in quiet tones while enjoying their food. The seating arrangements were simplicity itself — a long table lined with chairs that encouraged communal dining and conversation between strangers visiting the vineyard.

As politeness and tradition demanded, Dunmoore took the next empty chair and dropped her daypack on the floor against the wall behind her, where it wouldn't hinder serving staff. Not that it held anything valuable, merely water, trail food, rain clothes, a first aid kit, and spare socks. She carried her personal communicator in a vest pocket, along with her funds, identification, and work communicator — senior officers in 3rd Fleet had to be reachable through official, secure means at all times.

Dunmoore smiled politely at the people seated next to her and murmured a gentle *bonjour*, then turned her eyes on the old-fashioned slate board with its list of daily options. A few moments later, a smiling, plump woman in her fifties appeared from behind the long bar and made her way across the room.

"Welcome, Madame. Is this your first time with us?"

"No." Dunmoore shook her head. "I was here last year and thoroughly enjoyed my meal."

"Have you made a selection?"

"I'll take the three-course prix fixe with the wine tasting option."

The woman bobbed her head. "Certainly. I'm sure you'll find our kitchen is still one of the best around."

She vanished for less than a minute and returned with the first glass of wine, a crisp white with just a hint of natural carbonation. Dunmoore took a little sip and smiled. Still a lovely vintage.

As she placed the glass carefully on the smooth wooden tabletop, the door opened, admitting a tall, fit-looking man carrying a daypack. He walked over to the table and, with a smile, dropped into the chair across from Dunmoore and placed his pack at his feet.

The man, whom Dunmoore pegged as being in his fifties, had a thick head of luxurious silver hair swept back from a high forehead and a neatly trimmed silver beard framing a rugged, handsome face. Deep-set gray eyes on either side of an aquiline nose met hers as he said *bonjour* in a deep melodious voice. Dunmoore replied with a nod and a smile, then took another sip, wondering whether she should engage him in conversation.

One could never quite tell how well overtures would be received, even though making a bit of small talk was considered polite when sitting across or beside another unaccompanied diner at these communal tables. And she'd been complaining to herself about a lack of interaction with other human beings outside work.

"You're walking the Saône Trail?"

He nodded. "Yes. A day out in nature, away from the city, is the best way of bleeding off stress that I know."

"Likewise."

"I'm Victor Herault."

"Siobhan Dunmoore."

"You've been at this vineyard before?"

"Once, last year. The food was superb then. I hope it's still so."

Herault smiled, revealing even white teeth.

"No worries. I come here every few months, and it's always top-notch. Ah, here we go." He looked up at the landlady, who placed a wineglass in front of him without waiting for an order. "Thank you, Camille. And I'll have the three-course prix fixe, please."

"Certainly, Monsieur Herault."

"*Merci.*"

"They seem to know you well here," Dunmoore said once Camille walked away.

"Oh, Camille and I have been acquainted for years. You see, I buy Fleur d'Azur wine directly by the case."

"You're a merchant?"

He smiled, revealing those teeth again.

"Yes. I'm in the import-export business, and Dordogne wines fetch a reasonable price throughout the Commonwealth. Mind you, this vineyard isn't the only one I buy from, so I'm known across the continent. And what do you do, Siobhan?"

"I'm in the Navy."

"Sailing starships across the galaxy, eh?"

She shrugged. "Not now. I'm filling a shore billet, but I spent many years in space throughout my adult life."

"A veteran of the Shrehari War?"

Dunmoore nodded. "Yes."

Camille reappeared at that moment with two bowls of soup and placed one in front of each. "*Bon appétit.*"

"Thank you."

Herault studied Dunmoore with a pensive gaze as he dipped his spoon in the rich, meat-filled broth.

"You wouldn't by chance be the famous Admiral Dunmoore whose daring raid brought the Shrehari to the armistice table?" He whispered in a tone pitched for her ears only.

She gave him a wry smile. "Guilty, but I'm enjoying a day away from my responsibilities, so please forget you heard me say so."

"Done." He winked at her with a complicit smile. "Where are you headed after lunch?"

"Downriver on the Saône Trail. I started further east this morning, near Neuve Chapelle. You?"

"The same." He pushed his empty soup bowl away and sighed. "Wonderful stuff. You're not a Dordogne native, are you?"

"No. I was born on New Tasman. A hardscrabble place that'll never amount to much, I'm afraid. I no longer have close living relatives there, so I don't lay claim to a home world. It's an old Navy tradition. May I assume with a name like Herault, you're from this star system?"

"Indeed. I'm a Marseillais down to the marrow of my bones, as we say here."

Camille reappeared with a tray, took the empty bowls, and laid out plates of succulent pork roast slices swimming in a white wine and mustard sauce over homemade egg noodles surrounded by a variety of local greens. She then produced two glasses of the wine paired with the main dish.

Dunmoore beamed at her. "That smells heavenly."

"Just wait until you taste it, Madame." A proud smile lit up Camille's face before she bustled off.

Both she and Herault fell silent as they enjoyed their meal. When their plates were empty, Dunmoore sat back in her chair, glass in hand, and sighed.

"I could get used to thinking of Dordogne as my new home world. At least until my employer moves me to a new billet in another star system. The food and the wine alone make it among my favorites."

A pleased smile lit up Herault's face.

"We are proud of both, just as I am proud to bring our vintages and delicacies to the wider galaxy."

"Do you have Shrehari customers?"

"Not yet, but I think that too shall come. In the meantime, my company imports Shrehari ale, which has gained many aficionados here. Mind you, it is an acquired taste, one I haven't quite developed."

Dunmoore chuckled. "Somehow, I get the impression you don't plan on it."

"No."

"It has become something of a favorite among our Marines, though. At least the ones on my last ship. And now I know where the logistics department bought the stuff — from you. I tried a sip once. Can't say it's my thing."

Herault grinned. "You're obviously a person of impeccable taste. By the way, the 13th Marine Regiment is my best customer. They can't get enough of the stuff for their messes."

Dessert, accompanied by a tiny glass of ice wine, capped off the meal, and soon enough, Dunmoore and Herault stepped out into the early afternoon sunshine.

"That was nice. Just enough to satisfy and not so much you feel weighed down for the rest of the hike," he said. "Would you like company for the rest of the trail? I don't walk too fast, and if you're tired of chatting, just tell me to shut up."

Dunmoore glanced at him with an amused look.

"You're assuming I'm the slow, silent type, Victor. But yes, I wouldn't mind if we continued together. I have spent little time with civilians in recent years."

They shouldered their packs and headed up the vineyard's pathway toward the trail, Dunmoore feeling contented for the first time since leaving *Iolanthe*. Victor Herault was a pleasant conversationalist.

"So, now that we can't be overheard, I should mention that your name has come up in some of my circles, the sort that tracks senior Commonwealth officers because they have their place in the Marseilles social hierarchy, whether they know it or not. Being the third highest ranking flag officer in the entire star system and a war hero to boot gives you quite a cachet. If you haven't received invitations to soirees and other events yet, it's simply because they're letting you settle in first."

"Do my fellow flag officers attend?"

"Oh, yes. Admirals Hogue, Keo, and Maffina often cut dashing figures in mess uniforms dripping with medals at charity and other events. The Dordognais have a thing for splendid uniforms. Wait until you're introduced the first time." He gave her a knowing grin.

"Now, I'm worried."

"Don't be. Our elite social sets may live rarefied existences above the noise of downtown Marseilles, but they don't bite. Often. Or hard. And certainly, your reputation being what it is, you'll be feted." He paused for effect. "At least until your first faux pas."

Dunmoore let out a groan. "You realize that my lack of familiarity with civilian life definitely includes a dearth of knowledge about behaving in polite society, where the rules differ from those covering military conduct."

"What is it you uniformed folks say? Adapt and overcome?"

"That's the one. We also have a long list of aphorisms about, to put it in terms my spacers would understand, screwing up the antimatter containment."

"For some reason, I think they use a word more pungent than screwing. Am I right?"

She gave him a sideways grimace. "You are. But such language, when spoken by a rear admiral, is frowned upon."

"I bet you have a long list of war stories where pungent expressions figure prominently."

"Perhaps. You have some amusing tales of deals gone wrong on the bad side of the Rim Sector, right?"

Herault chuckled with genuine warmth.

"Oh, do I ever. Let's trade while we walk. It'll make the kilometers pass faster. Tell me about a wartime caper you pulled off."

"That might be difficult. Most of my operations are still classified."

"This long after the war?"

"You and I will be ancient before they're declassified if it ever happens."

He smirked at her. "If you told me, you'd have to kill me, right?"

"No. We're no longer allowed to shoot people on sight. It takes special permission."

Herault seemed momentarily taken aback by her casual tone, then said, "You're kidding, right?"

Dunmoore gave him her sweetest, most innocent smile, the one her crew knew presaged trouble, and said, "Sorry, that's classified."

— Ten —

"That's me." Dunmoore indicated the sign pointing toward one of the parking areas. Dordogne's sun was already touching the western horizon, which was a lot closer this far inland.

"Me as well. Synchronicity?"

"If you believe in such things. We Navy people have a much less romantic view of the universe."

He let out a snort. "So I gather, based on your stories. I'm not sure I'd have made it through the Academy, let alone the junior officer assignments you barely escaped with your career prospects intact."

"You asked for amusing stories, and those of my awkward years as an ensign and a lieutenant fit the bill. After that, it's either stop tripping over your toes or find another line of work because the Navy doesn't forgive once you've had time to learn better."

"No doubt. Like I said, I'd have washed out early and often. But blowing off the whole carrier pilot bit as fit for AI-assisted monkeys? Priceless."

"That's not what my wing commander thought at the time, but I got the last laugh. The Navy no longer fields dedicated carriers; Marine Corps noncoms and warrant officers fly most ground attack craft, and we use Navy fighter task groups for close-in orbital defense. However, it's still officers only at the controls. Not that my being right earned me many friends, especially after I published my War College papers, but that's another set of tall tales."

"For another day, maybe?"

She gave him an amused look. "Perhaps. I'm sure our paths will cross again if my fate is being inundated with invitations to social events."

At their approach, two cars, parked near each other, came to life — Dunmoore's and Herault's. Where hers was an ordinary, mass-produced vehicle, his clearly came from a manufacturer specializing in luxury custom builds.

"I was more thinking of sharing a path, perhaps on another weekend. There must be lesser-known marvels in the region I can show you. Or if you're willing to go further afield, the continent's temperate areas are also full of stunning sights. You haven't fully experienced Dordogne until you stand on the very southern tip of Cap Némo and watch the mighty ocean currents rip by with no land until the Antarctic. Nothing should survive in those waters, but they're teeming with native life. Or the Great Sandy Isle, on the far side of the Western Ocean, only a short suborbital hop away. Sunsets over towering sand dunes create a magical ambiance you can't find anywhere else in human space."

Dunmoore burst out laughing at his infectious enthusiasm.

"All right. I'll think about it. Thank you for a lovely afternoon."

He placed his hand over his heart and bowed. "The pleasure is entirely mine, Madame Siobhan. Or should I stand at attention and salute?"

"Heavens, no. I get enough of that during the week. How about we get in touch in two or three weeks and plan a nature hike? Your choice of locale."

"It's a deal."

Dunmoore's car door slid open.

"Have a safe trip back to Marseilles."

"Oh, I guess I didn't mention it, but I'm spending the weekend at my country retreat, about thirty kilometers north of the Saône, in the alpine foothills. Perhaps you could visit some day. It's about as lovely a little château as you will find anywhere."

"Maybe." She dumped her day pack on the rear seat. "Thanks again for the conversation. Shall I give you my private address?"

"No need. I'll find it easily enough, just as I'm sure you'll dig up mine. Until next time." He climbed into his car and vanished behind the closing doors.

Dunmoore watched him pull out of the lot and turn right on the country road running parallel to the Saône River before hopping into her car. But instead of telling the AI to get going, she sat for a few minutes, digesting her afternoon. Victor was indeed a pleasant companion, and a very fortuitous one, just as she was wondering about ever meeting new people to make up for friends now roaming the stars without her.

"Let's go home."

"Acknowledged," the AI replied in its androgynous voice.

Moments later, the car moved off so smoothly that she might never have noticed if she hadn't been staring out the window.

Once on the country road, headed in the opposite direction, she called up the Dordogne net on the primary display and searched for him.

Her new friend was indeed a big name in the import-export business and in Marseilles' elite social circles as a star entrepreneur, philanthropist, and potential candidate for the Dordogne Senate. He had two adult children, but his partner, their mother, was no longer in the picture or even in the star system. Belatedly, Dunmoore realized she could have asked if her predecessor had been active on the Marseilles social scene and how, so she could not only get a feel of what was expected but of the man who'd vanished so unexpectedly after taking early retirement.

The almost vanished sun had turned distant clouds into fiery orange columns rising from the Western Ocean by the time Dunmoore's car pulled into her garage, but she was no wiser about what had happened that afternoon. Only one other person knew of her plans — Lieutenant Ramius — yet a man such as Victor Herault walking into that restaurant tucked away behind a small vineyard, where diners sat at a long, communal table, seemed all too fortuitous.

Once in her home office, she fired up her secure workstation and composed a message for Ezekiel Holt, encrypted it, and routed it to the Joint Base Dordogne's communications division for the next regular subspace packet to Earth. After a hearty, albeit solitary supper, she spent a few hours on the terrace, looking at the stars and reviewing her day. Spending a few hours conversing with another human being, one who didn't wear a uniform to work had been more welcome than she could have imagined. And Victor Herault was oh so charming but in an understated way. His tales of deals gone wrong and high society missteps kept her chuckling for most of the afternoon hike.

But a lifetime of dealing with betrayal had left Dunmoore leery of coincidences that were too good to be true.

***

"Siobhan made a new friend," Ezekiel Holt announced when Kathryn Kowalski waved him into her office. "But she reached out to her old friend, yours truly, for a background check."

"Glad to hear it. Paranoia saves lives, especially since she's been targeted for assassination before. Now give."

"He's a Dordogne entrepreneur, aged fifty-eight, by the name of Victor Herault. Two grown kids, no spouse. She left him and the children years ago, moved off-world, and disappeared. So far, we can't find a trace of her anywhere, but the Commonwealth is big and filled with folks who changed their identity so they could start a new life."

"What sort of entrepreneur?"

A wry smile tugged at Holt's lips. "Import-export."

Kowalski let out a bark of laughter. "Really?"

"In his case, it's not a euphemism for unsavory or secretive business. His company specializes in exporting Dordogne wines, cognacs, and food delicacies and importing those of other worlds, including Shrehari ale. In fact, he's the purveyor of the latter to the 13th Marine Regiment and the Marines in *Iolanthe*. Business must be good because he's a wealthy man and hobnobs with the

Marseilles elite. There's even talk of launching a political career at some point."

Holt took a sip of coffee while letting Kowalski absorb his words.

"Why do I think that's not all?" She asked after a moment of reflection.

"Because you're smarter than the next ten flag officers combined. And yes, I know flattery will get me nowhere. Marseilles isn't just the star system capital. It's also home to a large and powerful criminal underground known as La Pègre, a collective of organized crime groups who've divided Dordogne among them and mostly cooperate. However, there have been takeovers, hostile or otherwise, in the past."

"And you think this new friend of Siobhan's is one of them."

He shook his head. "Not directly. But the OCGs have their fingers in every legitimate enterprise on the planet, especially those who primarily deal with imports and exports."

"Trafficking."

"Exactly. Counterfeit products, including food and wine, drug transshipments, human trafficking, anything that attracts duties and excise fees, and a massive amount of money laundering. I'd say the various police forces on Dordogne have been fighting a losing battle since well before the war, but that implies they're doing more than just nibbling at the fringes for the sake of appearances."

"Corruption?"

"Big time, although it's concentrated in Marseilles where the police service is a byword for graft, payoffs, and other forms of professional misconduct. The city government has tried many times to bring in Dordogne Gendarmerie officers, but since the corruption extends deeply into the bureaucracy, the outside investigators never make headway. And when one of them gets too close, they suffer a convenient, although rarely fatal, accident. At least not the first time."

"Nice. And we have a major Fleet installation just outside that charming city."

Holt shrugged. "The Pègre stays away from our folks. We taught them a few harsh lessons during the war, which ended with several of their senior people having those convenient accidents, all of them fatal. Mind you, we still have our own corrupt trash who seek out the OCGs to earn a bit on the side or get revenge for many imagined slights, and the criminals rarely turn them away if they pass the smell test. So, it's no worse than on any other world with OCG problems, meaning almost every single one in the Commonwealth."

"You'll be telling all this to Siobhan, I hope. She's well up on interstellar organized crime but a bit naïve about the domestic sort."

"No worries. But back to Victor Herault. As far as we can tell, he's as clean as any other successful entrepreneur based in Marseilles, so I'm not overly worried he might be a covert attack vector. I doubt the SSB or its minions can turn a man of his stature and wealth into an operative. But now that she's mentioned his name, we'll be watching him because some crime bosses can keep their illicit activities so low profile that they'd fool their own mothers."

"Is the SSB in any way involved with the Dordogne OCGs?"

"Possibly, maybe even probably, but we've not seen any indications so far. By all appearances, the Dordogne SSB detachment conducts its business solely with the Gendarmerie and otherwise keeps out of sight."

"You have people on Dordogne watching them?"

"Every SSB detachment across the Commonwealth has its own counterintelligence minders — part-time, of course, but we still know what they're doing."

A thoughtful look crossed Kowalski's face.

"Can those minders neutralize the entire detachment on order, if necessary?"

Holt gave her an inquisitive frown.

"Do I want to know what prompted that question? Probably not. But the answer is yes, although if we get enough warning, we can reinforce them to guarantee a first strike will succeed."

"Some day, we'll have to deal with the SSB, Zeke. We can't let a psychopath of Sara Lauzier's sort employ a corrupt, politicized law enforcement agency to advance the Centralists' aims once she becomes SecGen, and she will. That'll spell the end of the Commonwealth and the start of the Third Migration War, which we won't survive."

"No arguments here." He drained his coffee and stood. "Let's keep Siobhan's off-duty adventures to ourselves, okay? I'd rather the CNO doesn't think she's finally going off the deep end."

"No worries. Now that she's developing a personal life, I'm all in favor of giving her space. Besides, she knew well enough to have you check up on this Victor."

— Eleven —

Dunmoore took one last look at herself in the mirror and made a face. The silk, short-sleeved apricot-colored blouse over smooth gray linen trousers was apparently the height of fashion for afternoon charity receptions at the Marseilles Yacht Club, as were the flat-heeled dress sandals. When the invitation to the Saturday event arrived the previous Tuesday — she suspected Herault of being involved — Dunmoore had researched the proper attire and discovered she owned nothing suitable. And so, after work on Wednesday, she headed straight for a clothing store and a stylist recommended by Lieutenant Ramius. The latter appeared pleased her admiral would make her Marseilles society debut in a chic venue where non-members only entered by invitation. And those invitations were rare.

Of course, her fellow flag officers had also received invitations and would attend. Being seen in such company was good publicity for the Navy and stroked the ego nicely.

She adjusted the drape of her blouse one last time, although it didn't matter, tucked her communicator in one pocket and her credentials in another, then headed for the garage where her car waited. It would drop her off at the club, return home under AI control, and come fetch her when she called.

The weather, as always at this time of year, was spectacular, with nary a cloud in a sky so blue it almost seemed artificial. A quick fifteen-minute drive took her to the waterfront just north of downtown, where she climbed out by an open gate set in a quaint fence of artistically forged metal bars. There, a security guard scanned her credentials, matching them with the invitation issued by the Greater Dordogne Food Bank Network — today's organizer and beneficiary of the gala — and ushered her in with much scraping and bowing.

An elegant older woman, also in silk blouse and trousers, though vastly more expensive looking than Dunmoore's, greeted her at the clubhouse door with a radiant smile. Her shoulder-length silver hair framed a narrow, aristocratic face dominated by twinkling blue eyes.

"Hello. I'm Genevieve Bloch, the event's hostess, and you must be Admiral Siobhan Dunmoore. Welcome. I understand this is your first time here, even though you have lived on Dordogne for a few years."

"Please to meet you, Madame. Yes, this is my former battle group's home port, and I own a house just outside the city, but I spent most of that time in space. I only recently joined Admiral Hogue's staff at Joint Base Dordogne."

"Well, I'm sure this will be the first of many occasions we'll meet. I understand you know Victor Herault. He's already arrived. You'll find him on the terrace, through there, along with your fellow admirals."

"Thank you." Dunmoore returned her smile, then walked through the open door into a marble and granite foyer that wouldn't have been out of place in one of the chateaus so lovingly reproduced on Dordogne using old Earth examples. Images of serious men and women adorned one wall — the club's current executive — while the massive painting of a racing sailboat cutting through stormy waters filled the other.

Signs pointed her to the main reception room, which gave onto a granite-floored terrace covered by a network of artistically draped awnings to keep away the afternoon sun and funnel the gentle, cooling offshore breeze. Tables with the items up for auction lined three sides, while a bar tended by four white-jacketed men occupied most of the fourth. At first glance, Dunmoore figured there were well over a hundred and fifty people in attendance.

She stepped to one side of the door, searching the crowd for known faces and quickly spotted her superiors and Alvin Maffina clustered around Senator Pierre LeRoy, Dordogne's senior representative on Earth. Handsome, square-faced, clean-shaved, with an amiable smile and thick black hair, he had a reputation as a charismatic speaker and consummate politician.

Unfortunately, in Dunmoore's view, his support of the Centralist cause espoused by Sara Lauzier made him the sort of politician she didn't much like. But before she found Victor, Admiral Hogue spotted her and made a come here sign with her left hand since her right held a champagne glass.

Dunmoore snagged one of her own from a passing waiter with a tray and cut across the terrace.

"Good afternoon," she said in a cheery tone as they widened the circle to admit her. She gave LeRoy a formal nod. "I'm Siobhan Dunmoore, Senator, Admiral Hogue's new chief of staff for operations."

"So I hear. Pleased to meet you, Siobhan. I hope you'll find your stay on our beautiful world pleasant and fulfilling."

"I already am, sir."

"You know, I remember your heroic rescue of my friend and colleague Sara Lauzier and her travel companions. A terrific job you did there. Admiral Hogue is lucky Earth assigned you to her staff."

"Thank you, sir." Dunmoore pointedly glanced neither at Hogue, Keo, or Maffina to gauge their reactions. "All in a day's work, though. Nothing out of the ordinary for the Commonwealth Navy."

LeRoy took a sip of his champagne and nodded.

"True. Yet, many of us in the Senate are worried the criminal depredations on the Rim frontier aren't abating. Since you have recent and extensive experience in those parts, what are your thoughts? And can you offer potential solutions?"

Dunmoore doubted it was a deliberate trap to make her speak out of turn in front of her superiors, but if she spoke her mind, the effect would be the same.

"The why isn't particularly mysterious, Senator," she replied, carefully choosing her words. "Space is immense, starships are tiny, and the mechanics of interstellar travel being what they are, some civilian vessels will always be vulnerable to determined pirates. But 3rd Fleet is doing everything possible under Admiral Hogue's leadership. You can rest assured of that. Our patrols stop a lot of criminal activity before it happens, and most of it is never reported."

"I see. But still, one ship falling victim is one too many." Another sip of champagne. "Can I deduce we need more Navy units patrolling the frontier? Should I form a Senate delegation and speak with Grand Admiral Sampaio?"

Dunmoore was searching for an answer when she heard a familiar voice behind them.

"Pierre, my old friend. I see you're monopolizing the Navy's senior leadership."

LeRoy turned his amiable smile on Victor Herault.

"Professional deformation, *mon ami*. We were discussing security along the Rim frontier. You all know Victor, I assume."

"We've met before," Herault answered, "including Siobhan, who I will now kidnap from you. There is something I want to show our newcomer, if you don't mind, Pierre."

"First, satisfy my curiosity, Victor. How did you meet Siobhan? She's not been assigned to 3rd Fleet for long."

"In the best possible way, while sharing a meal at the Fleur d'Azur vineyard's restaurant, one of the finest in the entire wine country."

"Lucky you. Please introduce her around. I'm sure Admiral Hogue won't mind, will you, Eva?"

"Not at all. We can talk later, Siobhan."

Dunmoore nodded at her. "Thank you, sir."

As Herault led her away from the group through a growing throng of guests, nodding here and there as he smiled at acquaintances, he murmured, "I figured you needed rescuing, if not from Pierre, then from your superiors. Pierre LeRoy is a typical politician, a blowhard with questionable morals who never held an actual job. But he has influence in all corners of society. Eva Hogue and Horace Keo form his most loyal audience whenever we have these parties."

Something about his tone rather than his words made Dunmoore wonder whether there was more than just a smidgen of disdain for senior admirals making nice with the star system's leading Commonwealth Senator when Armed Forces members had to be visibly apolitical.

"I probably shouldn't ask this, but why do I think you're not overly fond of my superiors?"

He gave her a sideways grin as they headed for the furthest display table.

"Birds of a feather and all that. You'll find we smile a lot at each other while looking for a place to slip in a dagger. Especially where politics are concerned — it's a bit of a blood sport here since there's an even split between those favoring greater autonomy and those wanting more governance from Earth."

"And where are you in that spectrum?"

Victor let out an amused chuckle. "I'm where I can make the most money, my dear. And that means not pissing off either faction. You?"

She gave him a wry smile as he snatched two champagne glasses from a passing tray before leading her into a quiet corner.

"No comment."

"A wise position to take in these surroundings."

"So, what did you want me to see?"

"Me." He gave her a self-deprecating smile.

"Well, you are more amusing."

"Oh, I was hoping for more than that, but I shall take what I can. We should intently study the items on offer for auction. That way, no one will disturb us."

"Should I bid on anything?"

"Heaven forbid, Siobhan. Nothing here is worth your consideration. It's all heavily marked up to give it cachet, but once the charity deducts its share, the rest is nothing more than money laundering."

Dunmoore gave him a surprised look. "Why would you admit such things to me? Surely you know my reputation."

Herault let out a delighted burst of laughter.

"Charity events in Marseilles — on all of Dordogne, for that matter — are multi-purpose. Those who use the occasion to launder funds will give more generously, the charity profits, and everyone will be happy. If you wish to remain unsullied, so your reputation as the Navy's avenging angel doesn't suffer, I suggest you don't bid at any auction."

Dunmoore let out the sort of snort that would have attracted a veteran chief petty officer's notice, and not in a good way.

"Unsullied? I spent a good chunk of my career in special operations. If you're a man of the galaxy, you'll know that means I carry the Almighty's flaming sword and to hell with mere angels."

Herault bowed at the waist. "Admiral. I bow before your righteousness. What would you say if I told you I knew of a way out of here unseen now that we've made our mark and will always be remembered as stellar supporters of the Dordogne Food Bank Network?"

"Only if I can make a private donation and assuage my conscience."

"Look them up on the net. They take about every form of payment." He drained his glass. "Must not let the good stuff go to waste, especially since my company provides it free of charge. But I won't be annoyed if you don't. Best we make tracks now. I see the lovely Genevieve making her way to the winner's circle, meaning wealthy patrons are about to feel the pinch of charity."

She placed her half-full glass on the nearest flat surface. "Ready.

"Shame. Not our best cuvée, but it still shouldn't be wasted." Herault snapped up her glass and downed its contents. "There."

He led her around the terrace's perimeter and back to the main clubhouse, where a door opened onto a broad, spiral staircase leading down toward the jetties.

"I moored my boat below us. I thought we might head out into the bay for a bit and watch the auction from a distance. Less noise, better booze, infinitely more congenial company." His eyes twinkled with merriment. "And no admirals who outrank you or senators who rival the most powerful soporific in the galaxy. Best of all, we won't be missed now that they've seen us. Trust me, there's nothing you want to bid on. Leave it for the pretentious nitwits."

"You make playing hooky sound incredibly irresistible."

"Glad my charm still works."

Horace Keo, who'd seen them leave, smiled to himself, though it was a bitter smile.

— Twelve —

Dunmoore still felt relaxed when she settled into her office the Monday after the charity auction. Victor had taken her on a harbor cruise aboard his yacht, a rakish, white, thirty-meter-long craft with five decks crewed entirely by artificial intelligences and service droids. It boasted a large saloon that gave onto a shady open space occupying the main deck's entire aft end, along with several bedrooms, a gourmet galley, scuba diving equipment, small hydrofoil speeders, and a full wine cellar.

They'd even watched the auction on the saloon's wall-sized display via a private feed whose provenance Victor declined to explain. Hogue, Keo, and Maffina had bid on several items, and each walked away with something, though Victor remarked Keo had vastly overpaid, even for charity. She ended up staying aboard for the evening meal but left after enjoying a magnificent sunset, much to Victor's chagrin, well hidden, though it was.

Her good mood had lasted throughout a quiet Sunday at home and even survived the summons to Admiral Keo's office a few hours later.

"Good morning, sir. I hope you enjoyed the rest of your weekend." She gave him a bright smile as she took her by now usual chair at his office's small conference table.

"It was tolerable. But speaking of the weekend, we didn't see you after the auction." For a moment, Keo struck Dunmoore as tenser than usual. "Did you slip out ahead of time?"

"I watched every bit with Victor Herault, sir. Nice sculpture you won. It should look good in your office."

"Things of that sort stay at home." He produced a data chip. "I just finished discussing our current deployment scheme with Admiral Hogue. We're making a few changes to better balance our ship strength in the more active zones. You read last week's intelligence digest, correct?"

"Yes, sir. But if you pardon me, I saw nothing that needs shifting deployments already in progress."

"That's because you're still looking at it as a battle group commander rather than a fleet chief of operations. The new patrol schema is on the wafer. See that messages go out to the affected units by the close of business. One separate transmission for each, not an all-concerned. I don't want to risk opsec by detailing all changes to everyone."

"Yes, sir."

"Dismissed." Keo picked up his reader and ignored her as she left.

The sense of wellbeing that had suffused her until now was gone, and she settled behind her desk, data wafer in hand, more puzzled than ever. Why didn't Hogue and Keo include her in the discussion before deciding the patrol plan needed adjustments?

Dunmoore knew the Rim frontier on all three sides, Commonwealth, Shrehari Empire, and Protectorate Zone, better than any flag officer in the entire Navy. She'd spent the last three years collecting and analyzing data about civilian, Shrehari, and illegal shipping in that area so the 101st could better hunt the latter, not to mention spending a good part of the war patrolling it.

And why on a Monday morning if last week's intelligence digest prompted the changes? It would have been better done before the weekend. Losing two days might not be much in the grand scheme of things, but it was still two whole days.

Dunmoore retrieved the digest in question to refresh her memory, then studied the amended patrol plot. But try as she might, she could not find any justification for it. Worse yet, based on her experience, it would leave several frontier star systems known as conduits for trafficking, more easily accessible by groups like the Confederacy of the Howling Stars and other interstellar organized criminals.

In this case, it would be Mission Colony, Andoth, and Garonne. You didn't chase reivers in deep space. You intercepted them as they dropped out of FTL before crossing a system's heliopause, at a planet's hyperlimit, or on the ground. Once the orders Keo wanted her to issue reached the ships in question, there would be fewer of them watching where it counted. And they wouldn't know the others in their battle group had also shifted, creating gaps in the long-range surveillance net.

After a few moments of reflection, she encrypted the new patrol plan along with her comments and slipped the message into the daily subspace packet for Earth. Maybe Zeke could make something of this strange development. Then, as directed, she prepared individual orders for each affected unit and fired them off using the 3rd Fleet encryption protocols.

The more she thought about it, the more it rankled, and she wondered whether stunts like this had put Hanno Berg — whose whereabouts were still unknown — in conflict with Hogue and Keo, leading to his early retirement.

Then, an idea occurred to her. A dangerous one. She'd set up a shore office for the 101st Battle Group's staff on Starbase 30, so there would always be someone watching their rear, ensuring supplies and repairs were teed up, and passing on orders from Earth for ships out of direct subspace contact. Last she checked, Commander Eduardo Yun, the battle group N4, was still in charge of what she'd termed HQ Rear, and he'd come over with her from RED One, meaning he belonged to her original team.

Dunmoore opened a secure link with the starbase and routed it to Yun's office. When the latter answered and saw who was calling, a big grin spread across his face.

"Admiral. Long time no see. What's up? And what's with the secure link?"

"A notion, Eduardo. Tell me I'm off my rocker."

"Okay, sir. You're off your rocker. But I'm sure you didn't call for free insults from your former N4."

"No. Are any 101st ships still within subspace radio range?"

A guarded look entered his eyes. "Yes."

"And can you still send them intelligence, the sort that might see their captains change plans and proceed to what could be critical areas?"

"Nothing's changed under Commodore Pushkin, sir. The ships that don't go out on a specific mission into the Zone are patrolling likely intercept points or trailing their skirts across starlanes frequented by reivers." A pause. "Why do I feel you're not asking out of sheer idleness, Admiral?"

"I'm going to pass on some intelligence, stuff I just sent to folks on Earth who'll find it interesting. Do as you think fit with the information."

"Go ahead, sir. I'm listening."

"The following systems might see an increase of illegal starship traffic starting in approximately ninety-six hours and lasting up to four weeks." She listed those where ships were withdrawn and sent on new patrol routes.

"Got it, sir. You said you passed this on to Earth?"

"Yes. You'll probably receive similar instructions within the next few days. Which among the systems I listed is more likely, I couldn't offhand say. Maybe you have access to intelligence we don't down here."

A knowing look crossed Yun's face. "Message received and understood, Admiral. Is there anything else I can do for you?"

"No, but you may consider that I now owe you one. Call anytime you want to collect, Eduardo."

"In that case, sir, I'll collect now. I don't know that you can do anything about it, but I would appreciate knowing what is going on."

"Ask, and you shall receive."

"It's a logistics puzzle, sir. Usually, 3rd Fleet is fairly good at getting us what we need when we need it and in the requested amount. But occasionally, since your departure, they shorted us.

Nothing mission critical, mind you, but some deficiencies meant more time in port for one or two of our ships until we sorted it out. I'm talking spare parts, consumables, the sort of thing routinely pushed through the chain at battle groups."

Dunmoore nodded. "Okay. Keep going."

"So, here's the funny part. I have backdoor access to the Joint Base Dordogne logistics system, including inventory changes. This comes under ask me no questions, and I will tell you no lies, by the way, and stuff that comes into the supply chain earmarked for us is being diverted. Not that I see anything nefarious, but if someone is playing silly buggers with our spare parts and consumables, especially if it's for shits and giggles because we're hotshot special ops, I'd like to know who and how I can make it stop. I don't need the extra headaches of arguing with the depot people and chasing down what I need to get our ships back on patrol."

"I'll see what I can find out."

"Thanks, Admiral."

She gave him a friendly smile. "We old RED One relics need to stick together."

"Ain't it the truth? Nice talking to you again."

"Likewise. Dunmoore, out."

***

Rear Admiral Ezekiel Holt spotted movement at his office door from the corner of his eyes and looked up.

"Admiral, please come in. That was quick."

Kathryn Kowalski dropped into a chair across from Holt's desk. "It sounded urgent, and considering how seldom you want to discuss things in the maximum-security zone, I figured time could be of the essence."

"Siobhan sent me a most unusual message. Based on an intelligence digest from last week, Hogue and Keo changed the 3rd Fleet patrol plot in certain Rim frontier areas on Monday morning."

Kowalski's right eyebrow shot up. "They let the entire weekend elapse before acting on an intelligence digest? That seems a tad lackadaisical."

"Oh, it gets better. She sent me the entire new plot, along with her observations. My analysts have prepared a visual projection of the old and new patrol schema. I wonder if you'll see what Siobhan saw." Holt touched his desk's control pad, and a three-dimensional hologram of the Rim Sector, or at least a part of it, materialized in midair beside his desk.

Kowalski studied the old plot represented by purple icons, the new one in blue, the inhabited star systems in yellow, and the uninhabited ones in orange.

"Let me ask this before I pronounce myself. Did the intelligence digest contain enough information to warrant such a redeployment?"

Holt shook his head. "No. And I checked with my colleagues across the floor. They have nothing of the sort. I'm still waiting to hear from the Colonials, but I doubt they'll be more enlightening."

"Then it means someone is moving ships away from our wilder frontier systems, creating openings for traffickers to slip through, deliver or pick up their wares and vanish."

"That's precisely what Siobhan figures. You were right in sending her there instead of bringing her here. Something's rotten in 3rd Fleet, as we suspected. I just didn't think Hogue and Keo were involved."

Kowalski's frown deepened as she let out an exasperated snort. "And since the orders have gone out, it's too late. Damn."

"We could always countermand 3rd Fleet, except they've not yet submitted their weekly status report. But that would make Siobhan's position untenable. Fortunately, she's taken her own action. As you might remember, SOCOM keeps me informed of anything coming from the 101st, and they've been diligent about it. The 101st's HQ Rear commanding officer, Eduardo Yun, sent a message informing SOCOM that based on intelligence he received through a highly reliable channel whose identity he cannot divulge, the very systems named by Siobhan might be at risk of reiver incursions. As a result, he sent all available ships, meaning those not off in the Zone with Gregor, to cover the most likely approaches from the Rim."

Kowalski broke out into a smile and pumped her fist in the air. "Yes, Siobhan!"

"Of course, we — you, me, and Siobhan — could be completely mistaken."

"Doubt it," Kowalski growled. "Things haven't been right in 3rd Fleet for at least eighteen months."

"And if we're right, there could still be repercussions for Siobhan if Q ships assigned to the 101st make intercepts in the target star systems. She knew about the reassignments and can still reach out to her former command."

"True. But let's go ahead with the idea either Keo, Hogue, and maybe even Maffina are bent, or all three, shall we?"

Holt made a dubious face. "I'd only venture on one of the three and leave Maffina out of it from the get-go. And considering Hogue, with family wealth, already wearing four stars, and, because of her nature, disinclined to become CNO or Grand Admiral, she's not a prime candidate for corruption. Which leaves Keo, who's not on the four-star track and not from a family with easy money."

"Okay, Keo then, doing this on his own or convincing Hogue to sign off on his suggestions. Why the sudden change in patrol routes? The latest intelligence digest came out on Dordogne when? The previous Thursday? Did something happen over the weekend that forced the issue?"

"Good question. Siobhan didn't mention any unusual incidents."

"Maybe she hadn't connected the data points when she sent her message. Ask her what happened between the time 3rd Fleet issued the digest and Monday morning. Anything and everything. She may have the answer at hand and not know it yet. The right question will trigger her memory."

A grin split Holt's face. "There's a reason you, me, and Siobhan make an effective team. I already asked. We should have an answer in the next thirty-six hours."

— Thirteen —

What, if anything, happened between last week's intelligence digest and Monday's redeployment orders? Dunmoore stared at the decrypted version of Holt's message, racking her brain. The only thing she could think of that involved Keo and Hogue was the charity auction. But how would it be related to moving patrols away from sketchy star systems known as trafficker way stations?

Then her memory dug up two things Victor Herault had mentioned in passing. First, the various charity galas in Marseilles, including the Greater Dordogne Food Bank Network's last Saturday, invariably served a secondary function as money laundering and other less savory events. She'd thought his statement overwrought or a way of poking fun at the self-proclaimed elites. And second, that Keo had grossly overbid on the items they'd won.

Yet how did those two relate? Overpaying for statues, paintings, and other *objets d'art* to feed Dordogne's disadvantaged wouldn't enrich the buyer or launder funds, would it? But what did she know about sketchy deals? And more importantly, who could she ask, other than Victor, who might wonder why she's curious?

A quick message to Ezekiel Holt listing all events during the relevant period and her comments barely made the daily subspace packet to Earth, leaving her edgy and wondering whether she should investigate on her own. Perhaps it was best to wait until Commander Yun either reported intercepts in the relevant star systems or a matched set of big, shiny zeros, meaning she got it all wrong. In the interim, her responsibilities beckoned, not least of which was the promise she'd look into why the 101st was getting shorted. Not that she'd yet figured out a way of doing so without antagonizing the entire logistics chain of command right up to Alvin Maffina.

Dunmoore turned her chair to face the windows and put her feet on a low credenza. What she needed was an investigator. Someone she could trust implicitly and who knew 3rd Fleet HQ and Dordogne. Someone with smarts and a well-honed sense of initiative. And she had the perfect candidate many meters below her feet in the operations center. But pulling him out of there would leave a hole in the Alpha Watch and attract undue attention. Unless... She swiveled back to her desk and called up the operations branch organization chart.

After the war, the Navy had faced a rather intractable personnel issue — that of too many career petty officers and chief petty officers. Excess officers, recruited for the duration from the merchant service and straight out of civilian life, mostly left on their own after the armistice. But the Navy's wartime expansion among the enlisted had occurred mainly at the ordinary, able, and leading spacer ranks. The additional petty officers and chief petty officers needed by an enlarged Fleet were promoted from those who'd signed on before the war, intending to serve twenty or thirty years, if not more. They thus couldn't simply be released like the short service officers and junior ratings.

And so, the Navy had to find billets for all those professional non-commissioned officers who were suddenly surplus to requirements when a third of its ships were mothballed or sold off. Hence chief petty officers like Vincenzo working as a watchkeeper in the 3rd Fleet's operations center, the sort of job that was reserved for officers before the war.

Replacing a lieutenant or even a lieutenant commander with an experienced, long-service chief often proved beneficial. It also more closely aligned the Navy to the Marine Corps and the Army in the officer-to-senior non-commissioned officer ratio.

But that wasn't quite enough. The Navy then developed the command team concept to employ chief petty officers in jobs that hadn't existed before the war, freeing up traditional chief billets for the senior petty officers coming up through the ranks.

Dunmoore understood the problem like few others and was glad to see more senior noncoms employed in positions once filled by much less experienced lieutenants only a few years out of the Academy. But she'd never liked the command team concept. A ship needed a coxswain, yes. A fleet, a battle group, a starbase, or a ground installation did so as well, along with schools and academies. But senior officers filling staff positions, where the need for a non-commissioned adviser and disciplinarian was minimal? Not so much.

Yet there it was, on the operations branch's organization chart, as she remembered noticing her first day — a vacant branch chief petty officer's billet, the other half of the command team. Dunmoore remembered thinking at the time that the position being unoccupied was a good thing. She didn't need someone sitting around her office looking for a purpose. But now, it represented an opportunity. If she could find a replacement for Vincenzo in the operations center.

After all, Alvin Maffina had a chief second class, though he seemed pretty busy on any day. Dunmoore had never asked what the man did. However, the administration branch was much heavier on enlisted and non-commissioned personnel than operations and dealt with issues where a long-service chief's experience would come in handy, especially one who'd come up through one of the logistics trades.

Obeying her impulse, Dunmoore called Freya Horvat's office. The latter answered after a moment, smiling.

"Good morning, Admiral. And what can I do for you on this fine day?"

"Answer a personnel question. And I'll say right up front I won't override you."

"Fair enough. Fire away."

"I've concluded that I should fill the branch chief petty officer's position—"

Horvat raised her hand. "And naturally, you're thinking about your old shipmate, Chief Vincenzo."

"Precisely. But if my taking him will create a hole in your establishment and mean more work shouldered by the rest of the watch, I'll look elsewhere."

To Dunmoore's surprise, Horvat chuckled. "I gather you didn't look closely at Chief Vincenzo's position, sir."

"No."

"He arrived on the operations branch's doorstep earlier this year with a note from the chief petty officers' career manager asking that we find him a loving home. Admiral Berg, who hadn't asked for more staff — we were full up at the time — shopped him around the divisions. Since there are always more projects in the operations center than people to work on them, I put in my bid. And on the strength of how I proposed to use Vincenzo, he ended up as a member of the Alpha Watch. But in one of my vacant wartime billets. All that to say, if you want him, it simply means returning to my normal establishment. Yes, we'll miss Vince — he's a great guy, a professional in all respects, and smarter than most. However, if you figure you need him, he'll be better employed by you than covering for people on leave and running my special projects. Like I said, he just showed up one day with orders from HQ."

"Thanks for being so good about it, Freya. I really appreciate that."

Another chuckle.

"I remember a War College instructor telling us that the most important lesson is choosing your battles. You can only win so many, and you must make those victories count."

Dunmoore gave her an ironic grin.

"Glad my words are echoing down the years."

"You want to see Chief Vincenzo now, sir?"

"Sure. So long as he's not in the middle of something. Today is fine."

"It's a quiet morning, and everyone is present, so expect him in five, sir."

"Thank you, Freya."

"For you, anything."

"Dunmoore, out."

She turned to look out the window again, lost in thought. Career managers rarely sent people to units that had a full complement. Yes, he was a chief petty officer caught up in the oversupply of senior noncoms, but surely there were places with empty peacetime billets suitable for a bosun's mate, the Navy's jack of all trades. And exactly what had he been up to since the armistice, anyway?

Suddenly, Dunmoore got a sneaking suspicion he was here at Kathryn Kowalski and Ezekiel Holt's behest to find out what was transforming the once glorious 3rd Fleet, scourge of the Shrehari Empire, into a marginally effective formation. And this just as the Protectorate Zone was becoming a major headache because of proliferating mercenaries, reivers, pirates, and traffickers of all sorts, slavers included.

Could Vincenzo be here for a specific reason as well? Perhaps on a similar mission? After all, her appointment had been a last-minute thing because of Hanno Berg's unexpected resignation.

With a sigh, she returned to the files waiting for approval, but her mind wouldn't focus. When Anna Ramius stuck her head in and announced Chief Vincenzo was reporting to the admiral as ordered, Dunmoore felt nothing but relief.

"Send him in, please."

Moments later, Vincenzo entered, came to a halt three paces from her desk and saluted while Ramius closed the door behind him.

"Good morning, Admiral."

"Good morning, Chief."

"At ease, and please sit."

"Yes, sir." As he took the indicated chair, he pulled out a flat, rectangular object smaller than the palm of his hand from a tunic pocket and stared at it for a few moments, then nodded with satisfaction. "We're clear."

"Jammer?"

"Yes, sir. They sweep the entire HQ once a week for surveillance devices, but those who sweep can also install spy sensors on order."

"I guess you're not just an ordinary chief third class assigned as operations watchkeeper. Did Admiral Holt recruit you when he returned to counterintelligence after he left *Iolanthe*?"

A smile lit up Vincenzo's tanned features.

"Never could hide anything from you, Admiral. Yes, I've been one of his investigators for the last ten years. That stuff I told you the first day, those were all cover stories. I'm here because things at 3rd Fleet HQ aren't right. And I know you're the new chief of operations for the same reason."

"Then, at least we're clear on that. How would you like to be the branch chief?"

"If I'm not mistaken, I'm one level down from what the billet calls for."

"Perhaps, but I need an investigator who can go where an admiral would be noticed, ask questions that might be alarming if they came from an admiral, that sort of thing, and the best way to do so is to make you my branch chief."

The smile returned. "I was hoping you'd figure out a way of getting me deeper into the action, Admiral. My instructions were to wait for you, but if an occasion presented, then approach you."

"In that case, welcome. I'll have Anna set up a workstation for you in the outer office. How about I tell you what I've uncovered since arriving, and you can do the same?"

"I'm all ears, sir."

Vincenzo grimaced when she finished relating everything, including her relationship with Victor Herault and his sibylline pronouncements.

"That Monday morning patrol route switch is the third time it's happened since I've been here. If you're right, and I'm betting you are, a thorough review of the incident logs might show evidence the bad guys slipped through star systems left with minimal surveillance. But I doubt it. The whole point is making sure no one finds out."

"I think you're right on that point. We might have more luck checking if anyone from this HQ attended civilian events over the weekend, like last Saturday's charity gala at the Yacht Club. We can let Admiral Holt know if there's a positive correlation."

"That I can do for you without leaving traces, sir. It'll be open source all the way. Consider it on my list. I'll do some checking on Mister Herault's money laundering comment as well. There's no doubt it's happening in a place like Marseilles. The criminal underworld, known as La Pègre, has its tentacles everywhere, including high society. Perhaps especially there. If I can find images of the items Admirals Hogue, Keo, and Maffina won, I'll see about tracking down their provenance."

"And maybe you can help with another issue." She described Commander Yun's missing supplies mystery.

"That should be easy. I live in the chief's accommodations block on base and hang out in the chiefs' and petty officers' mess, so I'm well known as a stand-up guy among my peers, including those working in logistics. Give me some time to work on a few during happy hour. Most can't help boasting when they pull one over on those they or their bosses dislike." The grin returned. "And do some people ever dislike the 101st around here. They accuse it of stealing 3rd Fleet's prey and kudos. Hotshot special forces assholes is one of the many uncomplimentary terms used. Most are worse than that. Much worse."

"Let me guess, the senior leadership is setting the tone."

"Not directly, no, but everyone is aware the admirals, except for you, are annoyed the 101st isn't under 3rd Fleet control, so the loudmouths figure they can dump on your former command with the blessing of those wearing stars. But, based on my survey, they're not even a plurality when all is said and done."

"Good. We should discuss things every weekday morning, say around oh-eight-thirty right here."

Vincenzo nodded once. "Aye, aye, sir."

Dunmoore tapped the intercom. "Anna, could you please come to my office?"

"Right away."

Seconds later, the door opened.

"Lieutenant Ramius, Chief Vincenzo has accepted to become the operations branch cox'n. Please arrange for a workstation in the outer office. Then put him on the same distribution lists as you, and prepare a message to every member of the ops branch, with copies to Admiral Hogue, Admiral Keo, the command chief, Admiral Maffina, and his chief announcing the appointment."

"Right away, Admiral." She smiled at Vincenzo. "Welcome to the holy of holies, Chief. It should make quite a change from pulling shifts day in, day out down in the bunker."

"Thank you, Lieutenant. I'm glad to be working directly for my old skipper again. We had some interesting times together in *Stingray* and *Iolanthe*."

"Then I'm looking forward to hearing your war stories, Chief. The admiral isn't one to tell tales."

— Fourteen —

When Dunmoore arrived at work a week later, having spent an agreeable Sunday at Victor Herault's château, she found a message from Commander Yun in her private queue — the one Anna Ramius couldn't access — asking if she had a moment to contact him.

After setting up a secure link, she called his office on the starbase and found him smiling as he answered.

"Good morning, Admiral. Your intelligence was on the dot. Since I doubt SOCOM will release news that three of our ships captured a pair of traffickers each, so the bad guys don't figure out we caught them, I thought I'd let you know. Five of them were carrying illegal substances worth hundreds of millions of creds. The sixth was crammed with over two hundred youngsters, some prepubescent, kidnapped from rogue colonies in the Zone and destined for short, brutish lives as sex slaves inside the Commonwealth."

Dunmoore gave him a relieved smile.

"That is the best news I've heard in a long time. Please pass my compliments to the captains. They and their crews did the Almighty's work."

"As did you, sir, for telling us where to look. If you get more insights, please pass them along. SOCOM has given us blanket authority to act on reliable intelligence without seeking permission beforehand. Especially now that we've caught human traffickers bringing victims into the Commonwealth, a recent development."

"I shall do so with pleasure, Eduardo. While I have you on a link, I've appointed a branch chief, CPO3 Guido Vincenzo, an old shipmate from the war. He saved my life in those days and had my back for years. I trust him implicitly, as do Commodore Pushkin and Chief Guthren. He's looking into your supply question for me, among many other things, and may contact you on my behalf now and then. Please consider anything coming from him as coming from me."

"Will do, Admiral."

"And once you're in contact with *Iolanthe*, please let Commodore Pushkin know about Chief Vincenzo's appointment."

"No problems. And thanks again for the intel. You saved a lot of young lives — again."

She waved away his compliment. "All in a day's work, Eduardo. Was there anything else?"

"No, sir."

"In that case, until next time. Dunmoore, out."

Once the display faded to black, she sat back, wondering what fallout her superiors would face after the 101st captured six traffickers in star systems their orders left inadequately patrolled less than a week after issuing redeployment orders. And if they did so at the behest of others interested in those valuable cargoes, how would the latter react to losing them?

Of course, only SOCOM and Naval Intelligence, outside the 101st itself, would know what happened. The traffickers would merely realize, at some point, their ships vanished, but not how or where. Here, at 3rd Fleet HQ, no one besides her and Chief Vincenzo, once she told him, would know anything had happened. Wheels within wheels.

Funnily enough, not a single person had commented on Vincenzo's appointment, and he was now a regular in the command chief's office and at his meetings. Lieutenant Ramius reported hearing the latter muttering that it was about time or words to that effect. But as a former chief herself, she found it amusing. At least she and Vincenzo seemed to settle in amicably in the outer office, and she showed no annoyance at him spending a few minutes in private every day with Dunmoore.

When Vincenzo heard about the 101st's intercepts, he pumped a fist in the air.

"Awesome, Admiral. That's what it's all about. And keeping all those innocent souls from depravity makes what we do worthwhile."

"Always. Now, I'd like to find those who got 3rd Fleet out of the way so they could ply their filthy trade."

"Got something for you there, sir. Not much, but a bit. I traced the provenance of the items put up for auction at the gala you attended. That won by Admiral Keo came from the *Maison des Antiquités de l'Occitan*. It's the biggest antique dealer on Dordogne, headquartered in Marseilles, and one with plenty of links with La Pègre. And your friend Victor Herault is right. It's not worth what the admiral paid. The other items, won by Admirals Hogue and Maffina, were minor and worth what they bid."

"So, what is your investigator's nose telling you?"

Vincenzo shrugged in the languid way common to the Marseillais.

"That the scent isn't strong enough for conclusions. But here's the thing. The item bought by Admiral Keo either isn't unique, or he sold it back to the *Maison des Antiquités* shortly after the auction."

"Why would he do that?"

Vincenzo tapped the side of his nose with an extended index finger.

"That would be the trick, right? How does one launder funds? Using dirty money in legitimate transactions that can't or won't be closely tracked by the authorities. The products of those transactions are then cycled through one or more processes until all parties hold clean funds that can't be traced back to the original dirty money."

Dunmoore shook her head. "Sorry. I'm not seeing how this profits corrupt officers."

"They bid on items at auction, perhaps above market value, but who would know other than your friend Victor Herault? It establishes a baseline value, and the charity and its bankers record the transactions. The winning bidders then resell the items to seemingly clean antique dealers for a sum closer to real value, meaning below charity bid. No one investigates financial losses because of bids made to support charity. Except the only substantial funds that changed hands were what the antique dealer gave the sellers. The charity might have received something for its troubles, but only as a blind. The item itself was what they called a McGuffin in pre-diaspora intelligence operations."

"In other words, that black bird statue bought by Admiral Keo represented a bribe he collected once he supposedly sold it back to the *Maison*. He never actually paid for it. No wonder he wouldn't add it to his office decoration. He no longer owns the damn thing."

Vincenzo nodded. "As far as I could find out, he sold it the Wednesday following the auction."

"Still seems damn simple and easy to figure out."

"If you're looking for it, Admiral. But maybe you and I are the only ones scanning those dark alleys where organized crime does its thing. Flag officers acting like the local elites won't attract attention from the local police, and as for the Fleet investigating its own, there aren't enough of us to cover every angle. Admiral Holt might have seeded other agents in the area with orders to keep quiet until regrouping became necessary. But I doubt it. Those hunting corrupt officers are just a small slice of counterintelligence. And the Almighty knows there are more of them than us."

"What about Hogue and Maffina?"

"Sorry, sir. Couldn't trace any sales of antiques, let alone the provenance of what they bought. Doesn't mean a thing. My sources aren't all-encompassing, and even crooks can be patient from time to time."

She gave him a half-shrug.

"Still, we're way ahead of where we were last week. Care to venture any thoughts?"

"I figure Keo, perhaps with Hogue's help, is taking payoffs in return for keeping 3rd Fleet patrols away from places traffickers would use to transship illegal cargoes."

"That's what I figure. And since you've seen the pattern before, minus the 101st intercepting, this last attempt wasn't a one-off."

"I'm sure if we go through the operational logs, we'll find more such incidents. Perhaps even dating back to their predecessors." Vincenzo let out an exasperated sigh. "Like Admiral Holt told me once, we need a dedicated internal affairs investigation unit. There's too much money floating around the various frontiers, and too many careers bogged down since the armistice."

He hesitated long enough for Dunmoore to notice, then said, "Don't take this the wrong way, Admiral, but I also checked out your friend Victor Herault. Like many successful businesspeople in this city, he's up to his ears in links with La Pègre. There's no evidence he is involved in criminal activities either directly or indirectly. As far as I could tell, the man is honest in his business and personal dealings. But two degrees of separation from organized crime can become uncomfortable if the latter decide there's an advantage in making it a single degree of separation by tapping you directly."

A hungry smile lit up Dunmoore's face.

"If the local gangsters try me on, you'll be the first to know, Chief. After I deal with them."

"No doubt, sir. But if they do, please let me know before going weapons-free. It might save us trouble down the road. The local law enforcement agencies aren't much different from the entrepreneurs in some respects, and tolerating the less vicious OCGs so they can control the worst of the worst is part of their philosophy."

"Are they working with off-world, specifically Protectorate Zone-based organizations?"

Vincenzo nodded. "Without a doubt. It's a matter of profits, and interstellar trafficking from the Zone is the most profitable thing in the entire Rim Sector nowadays."

Dunmoore shook her head at his deadpan tone. "What happened to us, Chief? We were honest starship crew members once upon a time, fighting the Shrehari and not worrying about criminals lining their pockets."

"We still are who we were, Admiral. The war we've been fighting merely morphed into something other than missile volleys against Deep Space Fleet assault groups. Senior officers playing fast and loose with patrol routes to let traffickers operate with impunity so they can pad their retirement accounts are a worse enemy than the entire Shrehari navy. And without a shred of honor."

Dunmoore couldn't help but marvel at what the years had wrought on Vincenzo. He'd matured more than most of his wartime shipmates and had surpassed even her wildest expectations, not just by becoming a chief petty officer but a counterintelligence investigator with a clear view of reality as it was, not as most people wished it to be.

"The question is," he continued, "what do we do next? I'll report the latest developments up my chain. I assume you'll be sending your own report to Admiral Holt. If HQ wants us to act, I'm sure we'll get word."

"Ever heard of the adage that once is happenstance, twice is coincidence, and three times is enemy action?"

Vincenzo chuckled. "More than once, from you and from Admiral Holt."

"Let's consider this latest incident — the change in patrol deployment followed by intercepts in the affected areas courtesy of my former command as our happenstance. We can't act on that alone, especially if SOCOM won't acknowledge anything happened, which is the right thing to do — keeping the bastards guessing is our game. But if it occurs again?"

He nodded. "Agreed. And I think that's how HQ will see things. Our normal way of doing things is building an unimpeachable dossier against the bad guys and then ambushing them. Most crumble and confess quickly, leading to more arrests as they implicate others. Rolling up an entire chain of bent Fleet personnel is damn satisfying. And we've done it based on evidence so highly classified, even the judge advocate general of the Armed Forces didn't have clearance. It just meant we gave them a choice between a quiet retirement after surrendering their ill-gotten gains and life in a penal unit on Parth under a new identity. Every single one took retirement."

***

"What the hell happened, Blayne?" Senator Sara Lauzier, a tall, athletic woman in her fifties with long black hair, cold dark eyes, and haughty features, flounced into Blayne Hersom's office and dropped into a chair without so much as a by your leave.

"And good morning to you, Sara." Hersom stared at her with expressionless eyes. "How am I? I'm fine, and you?"

She glared at him for a few seconds.

"Everything works for almost a year and a half, and suddenly, not long after Dunmoore joins 3rd Fleet HQ, a major funding conduit is compromised. I just heard from my friends on Dordogne, and they're livid at the losses but can't explain them since they had arranged everything as before. So, I ask again, what the hell happened?"

He shrugged.

"I don't know, Sara. We're not getting the same intelligence from the top levels at the Defense Department and Armed Forces HQ as we used to. Counterintelligence is becoming wiser to our sources faster than we can replace them. But I can speculate if you like."

"Then speculate."

"Someone in SOCOM or the 101st Battle Group, which has been a thorn in our side since its formation, got wind of 3rd Fleet's patrol plot modifications and came to the correct conclusions. Making targets vanish in such numbers simultaneously is precisely what Dunmoore trained the 101st to do, and her replacement is, by all accounts, just as wily as she was."

"Or Dunmoore is pulling the strings. In fact, I'm sure she's involved. Neutralize her, Blayne. Before she causes more damage."

"That will not happen," Hersom replied in a soft tone. "I won't risk a war with Naval Intelligence by touching her. Tell your friends to be more careful or find other ways of doing business while avoiding patrols."

Lauzier gave him a contemptuous look. "Are you scared of the Fleet?"

"I fear what they might do to the SSB, and so should you, my dear Senator. There's a more radical group of flag officers at the helm these days — Dunmoore and her friends among them — and they have no tolerance for Centralist shenanigans. They will neutralize us tit for tat, should I try, under the heading of what's known as *lex talionis*, the Fleet's newest albeit unofficial doctrine. If you don't know what that means, look it up. And should what I just said not give you pause, perhaps your ambitions are outrunning your common sense. At the very least, find other funding conduits and cut yourself off from your Rim Sector friends before things get out of hand."

Lauzier stood.

"And in the meantime, you could figure out a way of reining-in the Fleet's covert shenanigans. You know how I feel about failure. And you're not my only ally deep inside the government. If you can't handle it…"

Her words still hanging between them, she turned on her heels and left without a backward glance.

"You mean tool, not ally, Sara, darling," Hersom muttered when she was gone. "But tools can turn against you if you misuse them."

— Fifteen —

Dunmoore pulled up behind Herault's car by his château's side door just as the late afternoon sun's golden rays lit up the hilltops to the west. They'd spent Saturday on a leisurely hike nearby, taking their midday meal in a rustic inn Herault swore was a replica of the type found in the region of Earth that gave Dordogne its name.

He was holding a party that evening for friends who owned country residences nearby and wanted to introduce them to Dunmoore, so she'd agreed to stay for the night in one of the château's guest suites rather than drive back to Marseilles at a late hour. Herault had suggested he pick her up at home that morning, so they only needed one car, but she preferred being free to leave anytime she wanted. Vincenzo's warning the previous week still lingered uneasily in her thoughts.

The château, a large, u-shaped, stone-clad, three-story building with steep red tile rooflines, sported a turret at each corner. A massive staircase led up to double oak doors that wouldn't have seemed out of place on a starship hangar deck while mullioned windows pierced the façade in orderly rows. The main house was surrounded by half a dozen outbuildings, with the most significant housing Herault's car collection on the ground floor and a private amusement arcade on the second story. The others hid a small fusion power plant, a gym with an indoor swimming pool, and extra guest quarters, should the ones in the main house not suffice.

All buildings were connected via underground passageways, though stone paths bordered by planters, bushes, and trees wound their way around the park-like estate encompassing a few square kilometers of woodland, hills, and streams.

And based on Herault's offhand description of his neighbors, the Château de Blois wasn't even the most extensive property in the area. Of course, this far from Marseilles or any other major city on a planet whose population hadn't yet filled more than a fraction of the inhabitable surface meant land remained inexpensive. Construction and maintenance, on the other hand?

Where did they get the money to pay for all that? A rear admiral's salary was quite generous compared to the average, yet all she could afford after years of saving was her bungalow on the outskirts of town. Of course, she did not know if and how badly Herault and his peers were in hock to financial institutions. Or underworld financiers, if they weren't among the latter, to begin with.

She climbed out of her car and onto the flagstone courtyard, pulled her overnight bag from the rear compartment, and looked around. This wasn't her first time at the château, but it would be her first overnighter, and she felt a hint of trepidation. Herault had not pressured her into moving their relationship beyond the friend stage, though he'd made it clear, if not in so many words, that he would like to. Spending the night after meeting his wealthy friends and neighbors seemed like a big step. But she wanted to broaden her social circle on the civilian side and had found no better offers.

Dunmoore was still in awe of the château and its carefully manicured grounds. There was nothing of the sort where she came from. Even the wealthiest people on her home world preferred the utilitarian over the aesthetic. Of course, the climate had something to do with it. The sunshine and year-round warmth of Dordogne's equatorial region had no equivalent on New Tasman, where rain dominated the weather patterns.

"Dordogne to Admiral Dunmoore."

Herault's playful tone snapped her back to the present, and she smiled.

"Sorry. I'm not done absorbing my surroundings. This place is utterly enchanting."

"Then let's get you settled in a suite, grab an apéritif, and take a slow stroll around the grounds. The guests aren't arriving for another two hours, so there's plenty of time."

"I'd like a half hour to shower and change first if you don't mind."

"Not at all. I shall do the same."

Dunmoore had brought the outfit she wore at the charity auction, as suggested by Victor when she asked him whether it would be formal. Since her civilian wardrobe still leaned entirely toward the casual, it meant no frantic clothes shopping before the weekend. And that had suited her.

The suite, one of several on the château's second floor, boasted as much floor space as her home. Its bathroom was bigger than her living room. And the bedroom? Given bunk bed stacks, it might comfortably accommodate an entire platoon of Commonwealth Marines.

Dunmoore luxuriated in the vast shower enclosure for much longer than she considered decent, then stood in the warm jets of air that dried her hair and skin more quickly and efficiently than any towel. Once dressed and wearing what little jewelry she owned, Dunmoore found her way down into the main hall, where Adrien, the middle-aged butler, resplendent in a silky white jacket over black trousers, was giving the front of house droids one last check.

He, and his partner Heloise, were the sole human employees caring for Château de Blois. Still, they had a veritable army of specialized synthetics at their command — gardeners, cleaners, servers, cooks, even security droids. Those built for guest-facing tasks seemed almost human, but the majority were unmistakably artificial, though they could understand and execute complex tasks flawlessly and tirelessly. At least until their power packs needed switching.

"Good afternoon, Admiral," he said, bowing his head when he spotted her coming down the stairs. "I trust you, and Monsieur Herault had a pleasant day?"

She smiled at him. "Marvelous, as always. Dordogne is such a beautiful world."

"That it is. Monsieur is waiting for you on the terrace with the apéritif. Gin and tonic, two ice cubes, one slice of lemon, isn't it?"

"It is, Adrien. Thank you for remembering."

An amused smile tugged at his lips. "Monsieur pays us well to take care of his personal guests, Madame. Just follow the main corridor to the reception room and enjoy the sunset."

As she did so, Dunmoore noticed bustling service droids setting up tables in the main dining room. Supper would be buffet style, and the seating informal at round tables for eight. She quickly spotted the host's table, where she would sit with Victor and six of his closest allies.

The reception room next door, big enough to serve as a corvette's shuttle hangar, offered settee groups for dozens of guests spread around a large, polished wood floor, along with two bars where androids in white jackets would serve drinks. Dunmoore couldn't even imagine how much the purchase and ongoing maintenance of this sizeable artificial staff cost Herault.

She passed through the open French doors leading to an expansive stone terrace framed on three sides by the château, with the formal garden bordering the fourth. Benches, vases overflowing with greenery, tables, and statues dotted the space, creating smaller, more intimate spots where guests could relax, enjoy quiet conversations, and breathe in the heady scent of native flowers.

"Siobhan!" Herault, standing by a table overlooking the garden, waved at her. "I have our aperitifs. Let's enjoy this moment of peace before the party."

When she reached him, he held out her drink and raised his. "Shall we toast another wonderful Saturday in a countryside so lovely only the Almighty could have designed it?"

"Sure." They tapped glasses and took a healthy sip. "Nice. I'm really appreciating Dordogne gin. How about you give me a thumbnail sketch of tonight's guests while we amble among the flowerbeds?"

He chuckled.

"Why spoil the surprise? You'll form your opinion of them quickly enough, I daresay, shrewd judge of character that you are. Let's just say they're discreetly wealthy, with all the flaws of their kind."

Dunmoore let out an amused snort as they took the main path.

"What does discreetly wealthy mean, and what flaws, considering that you're part of their kind?"

He gave her a mischievous look.

"It means they're stinking rich but don't throw their wealth around to impress the hoi polloi. Those who should know it already do. As to the flaws, well, I'm not strictly their sort, which they'll tell you if asked. I'm what they call a parvenu. It's not a matter of how many creds or assets one owns, but their source. And how venerable that source is."

"And what am I in this hierarchy?"

"Ah, my dear, you're not part of it. If it weren't for me, you wouldn't be mingling with them at house parties. Not even Hogue is suitable for our little elite society within a society. You'll be a bit of a curiosity tonight, I think. An exotic visitor who is a hero of the Shrehari War. None of them know people in the Armed Forces nor have family members who ever served, so they can't understand what would drive someone to join up and spend a chunk of their lives in deep space or on alien worlds."

"Sounds like a rather aristocratic mindset."

Herault scoffed.

"It would please most of them if the *République Dordognaise* issued patents of nobility, though they'd worry those patents might end up in unsuitable hands."

"Might I be right in guessing they lean toward the Centralists?"

A grimace.

"Probably, but I couldn't say for sure. Politics, religion, and other potentially acrimonious subjects are off-limits in those circles, and it's just as well. Anyone could decide to be outraged by something another might say and use their power and wealth to publicly ruin the perceived offender, so people are careful. It doesn't mean they don't throw poisoned barbs at each other, but always with a smile so that anything said is openly ambiguous and deniable."

"And will they aim those barbs at lesser life forms like me?"

"Heavens forbid. One neither trades pointed witticisms with the hired help in their rarefied world, nor does one insult them."

She stopped and turned toward him.

"Why did you invite me to this party if I'm a lower life form to your friends?"

"Because it's my party and you're my friend. Perhaps also because I'd like to make at least the more perceptive among them realize that there are extraordinary people who don't have hundreds of millions in assets and funds but who spend their working lives protecting those who do and are just as worthwhile."

"Then why not invite Hogue or Keo, who are more senior than I am?"

"Because I can't stand either of them. They're dull, predictable, and arrogant. The people coming tonight know them, and while they would be polite, they'd find your superiors a blot on the soirée. You, on the other hand, are amusing, dangerously perceptive, smarter than the lot of them put together, and self-aware to a degree that would shame my friends. If they knew what self-awareness was in the first place. And, like I said, it's my party, and you are my friend. A better one than many of those who'll attend tonight."

Dunmoore instinctively knew there was more to the story but also realized she shouldn't pry. When and if he felt ready, Victor Herault would tell her. For now, let it remain hidden in the murky depths of a personality that gave little away, not even to her. Though she'd never seen his business side, Dunmoore had glimpsed a character as strong and willful as any she'd known.

— Sixteen —

They spent the rest of their stroll talking about inconsequential matters, and shortly before eighteen-thirty, Herault steered them back to the terrace. As it did so many evenings, the setting sun turned the clouds lining the western sky into a storm of orange and pink that never failed to awe Dunmoore. Holographic torches appeared along the garden walkways and the driveway leading to the gates, lighting up the oncoming dusk and flickering as if they were real.

Adrian materialized seemingly out of thin air when they entered the reception room.

"All is ready for your guests, Monsieur, and a car belonging to the first arrivals, Yohan and Arlette Destroies, has just entered the grounds."

"Then the admiral and I will await them here. Thank you, Adrien."

The butler bowed his head.

"Monsieur."

Then he turned on his heels and headed for the front door, and Dunmoore understood servants, human or synthetic, admitted guests in these circles. Hosts waited in the reception room.

Hopefully, the fact she was with Herault didn't mean anyone would consider her a host as well.

Soon, they heard heels clicking on the marble floor, and a pair — man and woman — came through the inside doors. Both exuded health, youth, and beauty. However, subtle signs in their movements and a vaguely artificial cast to their features gave Dunmoore the impression they were older than they appeared, by as much as several decades.

Though humans lived well past a hundred on settled worlds nowadays, they could only keep the appearance of age at bay through the miracles of medical sculpting. And the Destroies were likely well into late middle age before the onset of the Shrehari War.

Herault spread out his arms, smiling.

"Arlette, Yohan, welcome, welcome. Thank you for accepting my modest invitation."

"You set a splendid table and know your wines like no one else." Yohan, tall, lean, with thick silver hair, piercing brown eyes, and symmetric features, smiled back.

"Oh, you so do, darling Victor," Arlette added. She was an almost identical, albeit female, version of her partner. Who had inspired the other, Dunmoore couldn't tell, but the general effect was slightly creepy. Both wore casual clothes — he shimmering blue shirt and gray trousers, she a pink knee-length dress — that would have cost her at least a month's pay.

"I don't think you've met Admiral Siobhan Dunmoore, the Navy's new number three in the Rim Sector."

Both turned to her with a soulless gaze that could have come from one of the synthetics behind the bar.

"No, we haven't," Yohan said, bowing slightly at the waist. "A pleasure to meet you, Admiral. Welcome to Dordogne."

Arlette simpered briefly in what seemed like a parody of her partner's false courtliness.

"Likewise," Dunmoore responded. "And thank you."

"May I assume you're Hanno Berg's replacement?" Yohan asked in a rich voice curiously devoid of emotion.

"I am. You knew him?"

"Our circles overlapped ever so slightly from time to time."

For a fraction of a second, Dunmoore pictured a Venn diagram and struggled to repress an amused smile. Several new voices came from the corridor at that moment, and Victor Herault gestured toward the nearest bar.

"Please get an apéritif and enjoy the terrace. It is absolutely stunning at this time of day."

The Destroies nodded gracefully and moved off just as the next arrivals entered. During the next fifteen minutes, Dunmoore experienced a whirlwind of introductions. All the guests exuded that natural self-confidence born from wealth and power, and all were unfailingly courteous to her.

When Herault finished greeting the last arrivals, one of the synthetic waiters brought each a gin and tonic and they wandered out to the terrace where most guests were admiring the torch-lit gardens while conversing in typically Dordognais animated tones with plenty of gesturing.

As they circulated among the guests, Dunmoore couldn't help but feel precisely like an exotic specimen being politely studied by humans from a parallel universe. But whether it was because of Herault's comments or not, she couldn't tell. Her imagination would work itself into overdrive under the right conditions. And that evening, surrounded by Dordogne's upper crust with nary a fellow officer in sight, the conditions were right indeed.

Dunmoore felt relieved when the peals of a hidden carillon called everyone to the dining room and buffet tables groaning under the weight of delicacies for every taste, including dishes she'd never heard of.

Only Herault's table had assigned seating, but the crowd quickly sorted itself into groups of eight via some mysterious, perhaps even telepathic means Dunmoore couldn't understand after filling their plates. Wine bottles, red and white, open and held at precisely the right temperature, sat in the center of each table. Herault did the honors for his personal guests, noting these were among the finest his business handled for the export market.

Once all were served, he tapped on his glass with a silver knife until he had the attention of all attendees.

He raised the glass. "To your health, my friends."

The unanimous response came without hesitation, proving this was a familiar ritual. "To your health."

Then, the feast began, with many visiting the buffet tables repeatedly. Dunmoore ate with gusto, savoring each bite and answering questions about her wartime adventures. Herault's tablemates were pleasant, quiet people who made her feel more welcome than others in the crowd, which was no doubt why he chose them from among the seventy or eighty guests.

Eventually, empty plates, drained bottles, and discarded napkins covered the tables, and Victor Herault stood, signaling it was time for coffee, dessert, and cognac or liqueurs in the reception room and on the terrace. Dunmoore took advantage of the break for a quick bathroom visit in her suite, then rejoined the throng.

Still full from supper, she grabbed a small praline and a cognac snifter and, after surveying the room without spotting Victor, Dunmoore headed for the French doors and the fragrant night air. As she stepped out onto the terrace, a woman she remembered as Sylvie Lassieux, trailed by her partner Uta, intercepted her.

Both were olive-skinned, raven-haired, and had youthful features that belied the lack of innocence in their cold, brown eyes. Dunmoore figured they were at least a decade older than she was. Although both were elegantly dressed and coiffed and unfailingly polite, something about them had made her feel uneasy during the introductions earlier.

"Admiral. Or may I call you Siobhan? After all, a friend of Victor's must be a friend of mine." Her smile, which didn't reach her eyes, revealed brilliantly white, even teeth.

"Please do, Sylvie. Are you enjoying the soirée? And you, Uta?"

"Victor always throws the best parties with the best wine and food. And his château is so delightful."

"Without a doubt." Dunmoore did her best to smile back with as much intensity as she pushed back a fresh sense of unease.

"Fascinating that Victor met with a genuine war hero and Sara Lauzier's savior. He's not the type, but you're really enchanting him. We can tell. By the way, Sara is our good friend, so we're doubly grateful for your actions."

"All in a day's work, I can assure you. But I'm enjoying Victor's company. It's refreshing to be with someone who never wore a uniform and can talk of anything but naval matters."

"That must be lovely for both of you. How is your predecessor as 3rd Fleet's chief of operations enjoying his retirement?"

"I couldn't say. Hanno left before my arrival and has been incommunicado since. Did you know him well?"

Sylvie nodded.

"Reasonably. Not from this sort of intimate gathering, of course, but social events in Marseilles with senior Armed Forces officers on the guest list. I do hope Hanno is alright."

Something in her tone caught Dunmoore's attention. "Do you think there could be a reason he isn't?"

Lassieux gave her a languid shrug. "You would know better than us. But I should think the officer in charge of patrolling humanity's wild frontier might attract many enemies among the organized criminal classes who lose illegal cargoes to our ever-efficient Navy."

"They don't make it that personal."

"Oh?" Her smooth brow wrinkled ever so slightly. "Didn't I hear about an assassination attempt on you three years ago, thwarted by one of your officers at the last second? And all because your 101st Battle Group stymied criminals?"

Something about Lassieux's manner grated, but Dunmoore forced herself to keep smiling.

"The reason was never clearly proven. However, I made many enemies throughout my career, not all of them human. Had I died in that attempt, my successor would have hunted down those responsible all the much harder. Had my flag captain, a friend I value beyond all others, died because he stepped between me and the assassin's shot, I would have extirpated every single OCG in the Rim Sector with my bare hands, legal niceties be damned. And when you command a battle group of Q ships, you can do things ordinary naval units only dream about."

"You know, I'm sure some people out there are convinced you still influence the missions of that Q ship battle group, which no doubt continues to cost traffickers a lot of money and hulls. That's enough to keep making oneself a target."

Dunmoore, senses on high alert, wondered whether Lassieux was engaging in more than idle speculation. By now, the sponsors of the traffickers her former command captured would know of their loss, if not who was responsible.

"Even if organized criminal groups are gunning for Navy flag officers, it wouldn't do them much good. We're infinitely replaceable. Hanno Berg retired, and I replaced him. Once I leave this post, the next chief of staff for operations will carry out the same patrol schema and implement the same intercept and seizure policy Hanno and I upheld." Her smile turned predatory. "So should criminals wish to make it personal, let them. It can only end with their loss."

Sylvie and Uta seemed taken aback by her words for a fraction of a second, but their basilisk stares never wavered.

"I admire your confidence, Siobhan. But take it from someone who knows how perilous Dordogne can be if you cross the wrong people. Those who finance the criminals you and your ships are pursuing won't hesitate to strike back if only so they can avenge themselves. Do take care."

Before Dunmoore could reply, they wandered away, leaving her to stare out at the torch-lit garden as she replayed the conversation in her mind. Could someone have traced the 101st's intercepts in systems left lightly patrolled by the new schema back to her?

It wasn't much of a stretch, given the circumstances. Especially if her conversation over a secure channel with Commander Yun shortly after the patrol plan changes went out had been noticed, even though no one could have deciphered it. Then there was her reputation for ruthlessness and scoring unlikely victories, which had enraged the feared Special Security Bureau. Dunmoore was also convinced Sara Lauzier still held a grudge for her premature rescue and the collapse of her scheme.

Which begged the question. Did Sylvie Lassieux just deliver a warning that any further sleight of hand on her part to stymie traffickers might result in a new assassination attempt?

"Cred for your thought, my dear? Or did Sylvie abscond with your tongue?"

Victor Herault's voice startled Dunmoore.

"No. I'm a hundred percent complete and unharmed. It was just something she said."

"Oh? And what was that?"

Dunmoore kept her eyes on the garden, cognac glass in her hand forgotten.

"Tell me this before I answer. Are Sylvie and Uta connected to the Marseilles Pègre?"

Herault's throaty chuckle surprised her.

"Connected? Not that anyone can prove, including the best Gendarmerie organized crime detectives. But ask the right people, and they might tell you our lovely ladies own a chunk of Dordogne's murky underworld. What did Sylvie say that has you staring out into the night?"

"She intimated, not in so many words, that those flag officers who incur the ire of traffickers might want to reconsider their life choices."

Dunmoore glanced at Herault as she spoke and saw him wince.

"Oh. That's not good. Are you sure you didn't misunderstand her?"

Dunmoore shook her head. "No. And now I'm wondering whether Hanno Berg incurred the ire of those traffickers and no longer has life choices to reconsider."

"A bit dramatic, no?"

"You tell me." Dunmoore drained her cognac snifter. "She brought up the assassination attempt that almost killed Gregor Pushkin three years ago after I put some nasty people in the Protectorate Zone out of business — with extreme prejudice, as we say."

He sighed. "Sylvie and Uta can be overbearing."

"A bit?" Dunmoore let out a bark of laughter. "Fortunately, I'm used to dealing with overbearing people."

"A cup of coffee or another cognac?"

"Sure. Pour the cognac in the coffee, and let's find some less dramatic people."

— Seventeen —

The rest of the evening went by in a blur, though Dunmoore didn't see Sylvie and Uta again. Sunday morning, after a late breakfast, she excused herself on the grounds of fatigue and a headache. She drove back to Marseilles for a quiet day at home, reflecting on Saturday night's strange conversation and Victor Herault not being upset in the slightest by it. Or so she thought, though he was solicitous and hovered protectively around her. Equally strange was his absently agreeing to her premature departure as if other matters distracted him. It made her wonder about the entire purpose of the soirée.

She kept a more vigilant eye on her surroundings during the drive and stayed within her property's invisible security perimeter for the rest of the day, pondering her next moves. The more she thought about it, the more she was convinced Sylvie had given her a warning after someone correctly connected her with the six trafficker ships vanishing when they should have had clear sailing through lightly patrolled systems. Were the orders to the Q ships shortly beforehand noticed by an informant in the starbase communications section after she spoke with Commander Yun, despite them being encrypted?

Monday morning saw her back in the office, sipping on a cup of bitter coffee, wondering what to do with the weekend's events and her suspicions. Especially the question of where Admirals Hogue and Keo fit in all that. But was she overreacting? Letting her imagination go wild and seeing things? A knock on the office door jamb pulled her back to the present and her duties.

"Come in, Chief."

Vincenzo, coffee cup in hand, closed the door behind him and took his accustomed seat.

"Good weekend, sir?"

"Strange is probably a better word. How about you?"

He shrugged.

"Did some sleuthing in town. Made a few new contacts. Same old, same old. Want to discuss your strange weekend, or is that too personal, sir?"

"I think I'd better."

Dunmoore recounted her disturbing conversation with Sylvie Lassieux and Victor Herault's reaction after she told him about it. When she finished, a grim-faced Vincenzo shook his head.

"Not good, Admiral. Your friend Herault is right. Lassieux and her partner are big figures in the Dordogne underground. They own almost half of Marseilles through several layers of cut-outs if we can believe my contacts. At their level of play, off-world business contacts in the Zone are assumed. Do you think Admiral Berg crossed them in some fashion?"

She nodded.

"It seems a reasonable hypothesis. He vanished without a trace after something made him resign. Could he have objected to shifting patrol routes for the traffickers' benefit once too often?

From what little I knew of him, Berg struck me as honest. A man who'd seen war like we have and didn't want more of the same."

"Then I suggest we behave as if we're in enemy territory until further notice, sir. I'll warn Admiral Holt. Are you armed?"

"As of this morning." She raised her tunic on the left side to show a compact nine-millimeter blaster in a pancake holster. "Lethal rounds. It's a personal weapon, so there's no trace I've signed something out from the armory. And since I'm a flag officer, the security personnel didn't ask questions when I passed through the sensor arch. You?"

"Always." Vincenzo lifted his tunic as well. "Old chiefs with wartime pedigree also get through security, except mine is service issue, so it passes more easily. Tell you what, though, sir. The fact you armed yourself this morning tells me your gut instinct is howling. And I can't remember it being wrong in all the years you were my skipper. Sylvie Lassieux gave you a warning. Which means she and her organization know we intercepted the traffickers when they should have enjoyed clear sailing, and they think you sent ships from the 101st to plug the holes in the patrol network left by Admiral Keo's changes."

Dunmoore grimaced in turn.

"I was hoping you'd talk me down, Chief. But if we take all of this as a given, it means there are OCG infiltrators in 3rd Fleet HQ and aboard Starbase 30, particularly in the communications division."

"The bad guys got an assassin aboard Starbase 30 three years ago, sir. And that assassin vanished without a trace. My gut instinct tells me he had help from infiltrators or compromised Fleet personnel. They or people working for the same organization are still there since we never found them." He gave her a humorless smile. "I figure your arrival as 3rd Fleet chief of staff for operations sent a shock wave through the Dordogne underworld and their allies in the Zone. The last thing they wanted was the Rim Sector's most preeminent hunter in charge of deploying ships. Especially if she kept links with her former command, something they probably took as a given, considering Commodore Pushkin is one of your oldest friends."

"And they caught me speaking with Commander Yun, even if they didn't know the subject. Shortly after that, he sends out orders, and those systems with holes in the patrol schema are suddenly death traps for traffickers. What can we do to shut down that part of the bad guys' network while I figure out what's happening at the senior levels? They'll try again."

"Of course, they will, sir. Hence the warning Saturday night. The market is still thirsty, and they'll be keen on pushing through another run. Though I suspect they'll look at other systems as transshipment points."

"But I'll know which ones if the patrol scheme changes again."

"Precisely. And once those orders come out?"

"I'll become target number one." She exhaled slowly. "But then, if they figured I did it once, do you think they'll take the chance of me ignoring the warning and secretly deploying the 101st as stopgaps again?"

"That's the problem, Admiral. We can't tell. Your disappearance or demise shortly after Admiral Berg's, when HQ knows what happened to the earlier trafficker run thanks to your intervention, paints a big target marker on the Dordogne Pègre. And they'd be aware of it. Their leaders are neither foolhardy nor stupid, which is why the police can't make any inroads. Either they hope their warning will work, in which case they don't know you, or they'll reconsider and make sure you have an accident before new orders come from Hogue or Keo. Nothing fatal, just something to get you out of the way for a week or two."

Dunmoore made a face. "Sylvie Lassieux struck me as someone who prefers terminal solutions."

"I'll see what I can find out about Lassieux and her friend Uta." He hesitated for a moment. "And do some more checking on Victor Herault. Lassieux catching you alone at his place the other night to deliver a warning might not have been a coincidence. After all, it's clear your friend socializes with underworld figures, although it seems difficult not to do so in Marseilles. I'd also venture his legitimate business interests aren't quite up to financing the lifestyle you've described. If you give me all the guest names you remember, I can see if they're also connected."

"Sure." Dunmoore rattled off those she recalled while Vincenzo made notes. "And you'll inform Admiral Holt?"

"As soon as I can. This is the sort of development he's likely expecting."

She gave him a sardonic smile. "There's no likely about it, Chief. You and I are here for a reason, and we've established what that is."

"Battle stations, then?"

"Heightened vigilance. For now. Part of me still hopes I'm taking the words of a not particularly pleasant individual too seriously."

"Then it's best to make that part smarten up, sir. When someone powerful threatens me, even if it's in not so many words, I take them seriously. How's the security at your residence?"

"Top-of-the-line civilian stuff. I wasn't home a lot while I commanded the 101st. If someone wants to break in, they'll find it almost impossible without heavy equipment, such as industrial lasers. Between the butler AI triggering the alarm and the security company showing up, they won't have time to get through. And yes, I set it to full fortress mode last night. No one was getting in."

Vincenzo nodded while giving her a knowing look.

"You use a security company. That means anyone who wants to harm you won't try while you're inside Fort Dunmoore, Admiral because they'll be aware of your dispositions. It means an attempt to take you off the board won't happen there."

"If at all."

"Let me keep investigating while you swallow a double dose of paranoia every morning. The next time Admirals Hogue or Keo order changes to the patrol schema that leaves star systems open to traffickers, we can take extra precautions with your safety whenever you're here or at home."

***

"How likely is all that?" Vice Admiral Kathryn Kowalski sat back with a frown once Holt relayed Chief Petty Officer Vincenzo's report.

"Both of them have excellent instincts, and Vincenzo's been doing this sort of job for over ten years, so he's seen enough to know. It's highly likely, I'd say." Holt took a sip of his wine, eyes on Lake Geneva's flat surface shimmering in the late afternoon sun. "And before you ask, we can't order *Iolanthe*'s embarked Marine Pathfinders to guard her night and day until we can fumigate 3rd Fleet HQ and roll up the Dordogne end of the trafficking cooperative."

"Then how will we keep Siobhan safe? We need her here at some point."

"Vincenzo is making sure she stays paranoid, and he's quietly rummaging through the Marseilles underground, looking for the most likely threats."

"And when he finds those threats?"

Holt gave her a wintry smile.

"I guess you haven't heard of Admiral Doxiadis' latest brainchild. He decided intelligence needs its own special operations section. It's so hush-hush I shouldn't have told you, and you know everything that's happening behind closed doors."

"And what will this special operations section do?"

His smile widened.

"Everything and anything too black for Marine Pathfinders or special forces operators. Or at least things they can't do without added help. Lone agents or agents working in pairs who can infiltrate the opposition, collect intelligence, engage in acts of sabotage, and assassinate whoever we name as a threat to the Commonwealth's security and stability. It's been up and running for a while, though still thin on personnel."

"A Fleet counterpart to the SSB?"

A nod. "Yes, except they're on the side of good, not evil."

"Who are those agents?"

"Marine, Army, and Navy personnel, officers, warrant officers, and command noncoms handpicked from the various special forces communities and within the Intelligence Branch. People we know are loyal to the core and who've been conditioned against interrogation. I'll see about sending a few to Dordogne as soon as possible, so they can keep an eye on Siobhan and intervene if ever things go pear-shaped."

"And take care of any threats Vincenzo finds, so they need not imitate poor Gregor and become human shields once the opposition triggers an attempt."

Holt tapped the side of his nose with an extended index finger.

"Just so. We're dealing with soulless beings whose demise can only improve the human condition."

"A pretty cold way of looking at it."

"Once you know what evil lurks inside sociopaths, you never want to give them the slightest chance of acting on their desires. Especially the sort who finances the abduction of children and their sale into sexual slavery and premature death so powerful deviants can slake their thirsts. And Dordogne has more than its fair share of those who need terminating."

— Eighteen —

"Any plans for the weekend, Admiral?" Chief Vincenzo asked as he walked out of the HQ building with Dunmoore shortly after sixteen hundred on a sunny Friday, joining a trickle of officers and enlisted personnel heading home.

She'd been stuck in meetings all day beginning at oh-eight-hundred, and they'd not had their usual morning chat. Instead, Vincenzo had fallen into step beside Dunmoore after she dismissed him and Ramius, declaring she was done for the week.

"No. I haven't heard from Victor, and the idea of hiking alone with my sidearm isn't particularly appealing."

"Just as well. Has anything happened to Monsieur Herault?"

"He's on a last-minute business trip and coming back only sometime late next week. When I couldn't reach him on his private communicator, I called his office, and that's what the executive assistant said."

"Off-world?"

"The assistant wouldn't say. Are you doing anything?"

"Weekends are the best times to make new friends in low places." They stopped by Dunmoore's car, and Vincenzo briefly glanced around. "My jammer is on, Admiral. I heard from home this afternoon. They're taking the situation seriously enough that backup is on its way. They may or may not identify themselves, but they'll act on any intelligence you or I uncover related to your conversation with Madame Lassieux. I'm the conduit, and I'll receive communications instructions. The idea is giving you as much plausible deniability as possible."

"Black ops people, then."

He nodded.

"Not from my bunch, but an outfit answering to the same admiral as my boss. If you need anything over the weekend, don't hesitate to call. Even if it's just a gut feeling. And please don't leave your fortress unarmed under any circumstances."

She smiled at him.

"I promise."

Vincenzo drew himself to attention and raised his hand to his brow.

"With your permission, sir."

Dunmoore returned the salute.

"Enjoy your weekend, Chief."

"Thank you, sir."

Vincenzo marched off steadily toward the base's cantonment quarter, back straight, chin up, like a recruitment poster chief petty officer. The sort who could spot slouching spacers from five hundred meters and put the fear of the Almighty into them.

Dunmoore unlocked her car, tossed her briefcase on the passenger seat, and climbed in. The door closed behind her, and she retrieved a hand-held Tempest-C Mark Four battlefield sensor from the briefcase. Vincenzo had given it to her earlier in the week with the admonition she shouldn't question its provenance. She then ran an in-depth scan of her vehicle before waking up the power plant, just in case. When the sensor found nothing of note, Dunmoore switched everything on and headed for the eastern side gate.

As per Vincenzo's recommendations, she now took a different gate at random every time she entered or left the base, and a different route to her home, also at random. Of course, there were only so many ways of getting there, but so long as she didn't take the same one as that morning or the previous afternoon, it would keep possible watchers guessing. Yet the options narrowed as she neared her neighborhood, and Vincenzo had made it clear her greatest point of danger was within the last kilometer before her residence since there were only two ways in and out of her quiet back street.

But this afternoon, just like the others since Monday, she spotted no one who might show even a bit of interest in her unremarkable car. As always, she didn't link in with the centralized traffic system's remote-control service, preferring to drive herself rather than be driven, which pleased Vincenzo. However, her car would still appear in the system as required by law. No one on Dordogne, or on most of the Commonwealth's developed world, could use a ground car, let alone an aircar, without allowing the system access to its location when in movement.

She reached her house without incident and pulled through the front gate, which opened at her approach, along with the garage door. After parking inside, but before leaving the car, Dunmoore interrogated her AI butler about the state of the security system and whether there had been any incidents.

"Nothing to report on the security front, Admiral," it replied in its mellifluous voice. "All systems are active, and the perimeter is now locked down. You received one delivery via drone, which I accepted on your behalf. It is inside the security compartment waiting for your instructions — a bottle of champagne labeled Contessa DuClos, and a bouquet of golden roses in a crystal vase. The sender is Madame Sylvie Lassieux, and a card is attached to the delivery. Scans showed nothing more than what should be there."

Dunmoore's eyes widened momentarily at hearing Lassieux's name. A peace offering? If so, it was a mighty generous one. The Contessa DuClos was Dordogne's premier champagne, renowned throughout the Commonwealth, and cost over a thousand creds a bottle, making it too expensive for ordinary mortals.

She knew nothing about roses but suspected they were equally pricey. Did the gift represent another phase in an ongoing campaign to keep her from interfering with the lucrative illegal trade from the Zone? Her butler wouldn't be able to detect the sort of well-hidden attack vectors used by assassins — poison in the champagne or toxic substances on the flower petals, for example. Something that would kill her and vanish from her bloodstream before rescuers could find her, leaving the authorities with no other explanation than sudden cardiac arrest, which described every death for which there was no apparent cause.

The security compartment, an airlock with an unobtrusive outer and inner door between the main entrance and the garage, served primarily to receive deliveries when she wasn't home, which was most of the time. Her AI butler would open the outside door, allow the drone or human making the delivery to deposit the items, then lock it again once they were gone. The size of a closet or a small dwelling's foyer, the security compartment was armored. It could hold hostile humans, droids, and modest to moderate explosions, though in the latter case, not without damaging the house itself. It came standard on dwellings in her neighborhood, and a version of it could be found in most homes in and around Marseilles. The locals had long ago learned the principle of trust but verify.

Dunmoore climbed out of the car with her briefcase and, on entering the house, put it on a sideboard in the hallway and retrieved the battlefield sensor again. Then she unlocked the security compartment's inner door and scanned the gifts, both in a wicker basket adorned with silky bows sitting on the delivery table. She suspected the bows were made of genuine imported silk, another luxury — but detected nothing untoward.

A cream-colored envelope, twenty centimeters a side, was tucked among the magnificent golden roses and bore her name in what seemed to be actual handwriting, an affectation of the wealthy on this world. Her name only, though. Not her rank. Dunmoore gingerly took the envelope from the basket and opened the back flap, revealing a thick parchment card with ragged edges. She pulled out the card and found the same handwriting on one side.

Dear Siobhan, please accept my most abject apologies for my behavior at Victor's soirée. I sometimes go overboard with my notions, and Victor informed me that I made you acutely uncomfortable, for which I cannot forgive myself. I hope my inadequate gifts make up for it, at least in a tiny part, and I shall show you that I'm not as strange as you might perceive, so you may expect an invitation to another exclusive party within the next few days.

Sincerely, Sylvie Lassieux

If the note's aim was putting Dunmoore at ease, it failed. Something about its wording and the repeated use of the first-person singular seemed both overwrought and slightly menacing. Yet it and the gifts were clues. She slid the card back into its envelope and placed the latter back in the basket. Since neither champagne, no matter how expensive, nor flowers interested her, she left the basket in the security compartment and sealed its inner door. Then, she transmitted a brief report along with the scans to Vincenzo's private address, using the standard counterintelligence encryption Holt had given her and headed for the bedroom to change out of her uniform.

By the time she sat in her favorite shaded spot on the backyard terrace where no one could see her save from above, a glass of ice-cold Riesling in hand, Dunmoore had decided she would play along with Lassieux. Not by opening the champagne bottle or bringing the roses into her house, but by accepting the invitation she would shortly issue.

Either Dunmoore was right about Lassieux, in which case, learning more about her could only help, or she was merely a little strange and beyond local underworld activities, largely harmless. Vincenzo wouldn't like it, but if his friends from intelligence's new black ops organization arrived before Lassieux's invitation, she could have covert bodyguards who shot to kill.

Shortly after she polished off another autochef-prepared meal, her personal communicator chimed for attention — Vincenzo.

"What's up, Chief?"

"I got your message and the scans, sir. You're doing right to leave the gifts in the security compartment. I can be by in the morning, say around oh-nine hundred, to pick them up and have my good buddies in the military police battalion run them through their forensics section's sensor suite. Just keep the card — in your security compartment, of course. No need for the MPs to know it's yours."

An ironic smile lit up her face.

"Won't they suspect you might be dealing with this matter on behalf of the admiral for whom you're working?"

"There might be a fine line between suspecting and knowing, but it's one we try to avoid crossing."

"Plausible deniability."

He nodded.

"Especially in this case."

"When do you think you'll hear about backup?"

"Any day, sir." He gave her a searching look. "Does that mean you plan on accepting whatever invitation may come and would like someone watching your six?"

"That's what I had in mind, yes."

"Then it's best I do it, sir. My colleagues from another parent — let's call them the cousins — will want to remain hidden in the background, and that makes close protection impossible." He shrugged. "There's nothing strange about a cox'n covering his admiral. I remember Chief Guthren doing it often. I'm sure Madame Lassieux has her own muscle — you just didn't notice it at Victor Herault's château, or she felt on friendly territory and didn't bring it."

"Okay. Consider yourself hired."

"One more thing, sir. Another friend let me know that *Iolanthe* and the task group Commodore Pushkin took on a cruise are back in town. If you'd like additional top cover from friends you can count on."

"Noted, and thank you."

"See you tomorrow, Admiral."

— Nineteen —

The following day, Dunmoore settled into one of the front veranda's wicker chairs, coffee cup in hand, to wait for Vincenzo. She hoped he wouldn't be scandalized by seeing his admiral in green cargo shorts, an oversized yellow tee shirt, and flip-flops. It would be another sweltering day, and she had no intention of spending a single uncomfortable moment because she was overdressed.

A few minutes after nine, Dunmoore spotted Vincenzo's personal car, a dark red, boxy, utilitarian thing that had seen better days come slowly around the curve from the next larger street. All the passenger compartment windows were open, and she spotted not only a smug-looking Vincenzo at the controls but two grinning characters who seemed inordinately pleased with themselves.

She told the butler to open the gate and allow the car in. When it came to a gentle stop, Gregor Pushkin, and Kurt Guthren, dressed more or less like she was except for proper walking shoes, jumped out.

"Vince offered us a lift, and we couldn't say no," Guthren boomed.

"To be honest, he called us last night and mentioned that you'd be glad for the company," Pushkin said. "The chief and I have some downtime after our last patrol, and you mentioned taking care of our rations and libations the next time we were in town."

"The guest bedrooms await," Dunmoore replied, aware she was smiling broadly enough to seem a little foolish. When Pushkin walked up to her, she gave him a hug. "It's good to see you, Gregor. I've missed our little family in the last few months."

She then gave Guthren the same bear hug, causing him to blush just enough, so Vincenzo would notice.

When she released him, Pushkin nodded at the younger man.

"Vince mentioned something about you stirring up trouble and needing wingers to watch your back."

Dunmoore nodded.

"Eduardo filled you in on our conversation a while back?"

"In detail. That's why we showed up on the spaceport tarmac this morning without waiting for an invitation. We came fully loaded, and Vince briefed us on the way here." Pushkin quickly lifted the hem of his tee shirt to reveal a blaster, like Dunmoore's, in the same type of holster. "Chief Guthren brought his, and we have spares. I hope you're following Vince's advice?"

Dunmoore imitated Pushkin's gesture.

"I'm slowly getting used to it on my hip, if not the idea of a Commonwealth Navy rear admiral carrying when she's at home. In peacetime."

"You of all people understand there's no real peacetime. We're all still fighting the dark and dirty little war — us aboard ship and you in the cesspools of corruption we call shore establishments."

"It isn't that bad around here." Dunmoore nodded at the open front door. "How about I buy you spacers a cup of coffee and a plate of sticky buns? It's a beautiful Saturday morning, and we have all the time in the world."

"Except me, sir," Vincenzo said, pulling a box from the back of his car. "I'll have a quick gulp of joe, pack up your gifts and meet my buddy in the MP battalion lab. She's supposed to show up around eleven, and I don't want to keep her waiting."

Guthren turned to Vincenzo and gave him a broad wink and a leer.

"A she, is it, young lad? And a meathead at that. I may have taught you too well back in the day."

"Which, in retrospect, was perfect, considering where I've been working for the last ten years. They finished the job you started so well, Chief."

"What did I tell you in the car, Vince? When we're not on the parade square, it's first names among us grizzled chief petty officers. But be a good friend and toss our dunnage out. It looks like the admiral will let us stay."

Once Vincenzo had done so, Dunmoore waved them into the house, chuckling.

"I guess I should set ground rules for old friends staying in my guest bedrooms — first names only under my roof."

Guthren glanced over his shoulder as he entered the living room.

"Aye, aye, Admiral. But please don't embarrass the young chief here by making him call you Siobhan. There are limits."

Vincenzo grinned at his old mentor.

"Thank you, Kurt."

"Understood." Dunmoore pointed at the terrace beyond the French doors. "Sit while I get the coffee and bun tray. This reminds me of another house rule — I'm the host, you're the guests. You will let me do as I wish, even if it means I'm serving you."

"No worries," Pushkin replied as he led the chiefs into the backyard.

When all four had a coffee cup in hand and a small pastry in front of them, Pushkin asked, "How secure is your property in terms of what we can and can't say aloud?"

Dunmoore nodded at Vincenzo.

"He's swept it regularly for surveillance devices since we started suspecting all wasn't right at 3rd Fleet HQ. The house is one big jammer when I'm at home, making it impossible for anyone to overhear us even from next door."

Vincenzo pulled his device from a hidden pocket and stared at it.

"We are protected. Though I suggest truly sensitive stuff be discussed indoors only. Nothing in this universe is perfect, not even spook-grade gear built to Naval Intelligence's exacting standards. We do not know who we're dealing with here. Is it just your average Dordogne OCG with interests limited to this star system? Is it the sort of OCG who plays with the interstellar set roaming the Zone and other nasty parts? Or is it something connected with our friends from the SSB? We can't fine-tune our dispositions until we know the answer, so we must always expect the worst-case scenario for everything."

Guthren stared at him, shaking his head.

"You used to be an honest bosun's mate, Vince. Now you sound like an agent from spook central. What happened?"

Dunmoore burst out laughing at Guthren's plaintive tone.

"A pied piper named Ezekiel Holt happened after he left *Iolanthe* and returned to counterintelligence. From what I've seen, Vince becoming one of Zeke's operatives was a shrewd move. He's a natural at the business."

"And it's a lot more challenging than being a divisional chief aboard a frigate, let alone branch chief in a formation HQ, that's for sure." Vincenzo grinned at Guthren. "As you well know, having done your bit in Special Operations when I was just a wee little ordinary spacer pup."

"I won't argue the point. I'm just glad you have the admiral's back again. There's no better one than you for the job."

"She can tell you about how we slipped back into old habits." Vincenzo shoved the last bit of sticky bun in his mouth and chased it down with the rest of his coffee. "I have a task to accomplish."

"You can always join us later," Dunmoore offered.

A sly grin.

"Thank you, Admiral. But my MP friend booked me for the rest of the weekend. I'll call when and if I have anything."

Guthren guffawed as he slapped his thighs.

"That's the Vince we all know and love. You go, tiger."

Vincenzo stood and re-entered Dunmoore's house to box Lassieux's offerings. And after a loud goodbye, he let himself out.

"Did Zeke know you were coming here when he planted Vince?" Pushkin asked.

"No. He arrived well before Hanno Berg announced his early retirement. But Hanno's departure gave our friends on Earth an opportunity. Knowing Zeke, he hoped I'd pull Vince into my orbit and use his skills to help me discover what was happening. His appearance at the change of command parade was to make me aware he was in 3rd Fleet HQ."

Guthren shook his head.

"Vince, the super spy. Well, the lad is certainly sharp enough for that sort of job. If I would ask for anyone at your back, he's it. And as branch chief, no one will question him being always within three paces of you when you're out and about."

Pushkin drained his coffee cup and put it on the table.

"Do you think there will be another sudden change in the patrol scheme that might call for my ships to fill gaps with no one noticing?"

"Certainly. Your people cost them hundreds of millions in profits and recovered witnesses they'd rather see dead. They'll try again because the demand hasn't gone away. On the contrary. The next shipment will be worth even more."

"And you think they figured out you sent my ships via Eduardo as soon as you realized what the new patrol plot meant?"

Dunmoore nodded.

"They have informants in many places — 3rd Fleet, Starbase 30, Joint Base Dordogne, Earth. Consider the sequence of events. First, I implemented Keo's orders concerning the new schema. Then, I spoke to Eduardo for the first time since I stepped ashore, and shortly after that, he sent encrypted messages to the 101st's ships not with you in the Zone. A week or two later, six traffickers failed to reach their rendezvous. It's not much of a stretch to pin the loss on me. Especially if they have people in the right places, such as Fleet HQ, who can read the after-action reports and track what happened to your prizes, their crews, victims, and cargoes, even if they headed straight for Parth where everything vanished from the sensor grid."

"My prize crews just got back from Parth, if you're wondering," Pushkin said. "The victims are being cared for. The villains will find hard labor a terminal disease, and their ships will be taken into service as minor undercover vessels."

Dunmoore gave him an appreciative look.

"Efficient."

"There's more business than we can handle, as you know. Can't sit on our duffs waiting for the Navy to move at its speed. Anything you pick up and can feed us, please do so. Running raids into the Zone based on outdated intelligence isn't doing it. The buggers are getting smarter just as we're getting faster, even if Zeke's bunch are choking off intelligence conduits to the SSB and its minions." He allowed himself a slight grin. "Consider the 101st under your unofficial orders for missions that can't be mentioned to anyone, let alone acknowledged after the fact. If SOCOM doesn't like it, they can have a chat with Zeke and Kathryn."

"Taking a risk with your career, Gregor."

He let out a bark of laughter.

"Career? I was supposed to retire as a commander. Here I am, a commodore and flag officer commanding the elusive and deadly 101st Battle Group, successor to the legendary Admiral Siobhan Dunmoore. I'm so far past the point of risking my career that I can't even imagine the concept. I didn't think I'd make it past lieutenant commander when I first reported to you in *Stingray*."

"Funnily enough, I can relate to that sentiment. I'd raise a toast, but since it's not even ten, I'll just offer another cup of coffee. Then we can discuss how you space dogs would like to spend your first day ashore after a combat cruise."

"I'll gladly take another helping of the good stuff. A question, though, since coffee fetching just made it pop into my mind," Guthren said. "What about your aide?"

"Anna Ramius? Why?"

"You never had a flag lieutenant before, and Vince told us she used to be Hogue's junior dog robber. Is she trustworthy?"

"So far, yes. She's a former chief who took her commission, so she and Vince get along fine. But now that you ask, Anna is one of those people who mastered the art of being efficient, always there when you need her, and invisible to the eye when you don't."

"You think she might be Hogue's eyes and ears in your office?" Pushkin asked.

"Maybe. If so, it doesn't really matter. We're all answerable to the commander-in-chief, 3rd Fleet. So what if she relates doings in my office to Hogue's senior aide, who passes them on to the admiral? Vince is the only one who knows what's going on, and he makes sure Anna can't listen in on our discussions behind my closed office door. But I think she's okay. Does her job quietly and efficiently, unlike a freshly promoted lieutenant still impressed with his Academy class ring."

Guthren grinned at Dunmoore.

"And she's probably elated that her admiral is so low maintenance."

"Being able to quit at the same time as the rest of the day staff keeps her smiling." Dunmoore finished her coffee. "And now on to more important things. What would you two space rats enjoy doing today?"

— Twenty —

Dunmoore, Pushkin, and Guthren looked like anything but flag officers and a command chief petty officer as they strolled along Marseilles' chic waterfront promenade. Brightly colored shorts, tee shirts, hats, and wraparound sunglasses, made them indistinguishable from locals enjoying a Saturday afternoon. Munching on rich, chocolaty ice cream cones while trading jokes completed a picture of total insouciance in the best Dordogne tradition.

Even spacers on shore leave from the 101st didn't recognize their former and current leaders, or at least pretended not to, though Guthren, with his keen eyes hidden behind stylish shades, spotted many of them. But as befit an old chief enjoying a bout of liberty, he professed to ignore them as well. No one wanted to make nice with the command chief while off duty planetside. Getting away from the chain of command was the whole point.

Of course, one thing differentiated them from most idlers enjoying the sparkling sunshine on the inner bay waters — all three were armed. Although Dunmoore suspected that more than a few locals were carrying as well, those employed by various security firms and their underworld counterparts. After all, the three- and four-story granite, steel, and glass luxury apartment buildings fronting the promenade belonged to some of the wealthiest people in Marseilles.

They found an empty bench and watched sailboats skimming across the harbor, dodging slow-moving yachts and each other as they finished their cones.

"This is nice. Why didn't we come here to slum around before now?" Guthren asked.

Pushkin gave him a sideways glance.

"Because we always try to get away from people when we go ashore after weeks of living in confined quarters? Or travel around Dordogne to take in the sights and explore the untamed wilderness, or laze on a beach far from the madding crowd? When's the last time you simply slummed around on liberty rather than cram a lot of civilian life into a quick vacation?"

"Point taken." The chief nodded. "Makes me wonder whether I should buy a house around here and put in for a job at the local head shed when my time out there is done. I've lived on less hospitable worlds. Not as corrupt and with such a pervasive mob problem, but pleasant weather makes up for bad people who let ordinary citizens live in peace."

"I plan on enjoying my time here, but once my turn as COS Ops is over, I'll sell the house, the car, and pretty much everything else."

"Earth?" Pushkin asked.

"That's what Kathryn threatened. I've avoided staff duty at Fleet HQ until now, but my reprieve has an end date."

"And once you retire?"

Dunmoore shrugged.

"Certainly not New Tasman. I was thinking of going back to Caledonia. I enjoyed living there while teaching at the War College and it was a good homebase during our time in RED One. Plenty of Fleet personnel are retiring there these days, taking civilian jobs supporting the Armed Forces now that its footprint is expanding. The way I understand it, a lot of new headquarters are being stood up in Sanctum to get them away from Earth and constant political interference."

"Good," Pushkin said with heartfelt emphasis.

"Caledonia, eh? Now there's a thought." Guthren shoved the rest of his cone into his mouth, chewed, then swallowed. "Something more immediate just occurred to me. Since you'll be dragging Vince to many fancy places, especially this event Sylvie Lassieux mentioned, you should review our good old hand signals."

Dunmoore nodded. "Excellent idea. Why don't we all do that? If invitations show up while you're still on leave, you're coming with me."

Guthren made a sign with his right hand.

"Threat," Dunmoore said.

He nodded, then placed two fingers of his left hand on his right.

"Unlawful above threat." Guthren nodded again and waited. "Ah. I see. OCG member."

"Should come in handy, sir. Vince must have memorized more faces and studied more dossiers than the rest of us. We're bound to come across people whose connections aren't general knowledge or thought as benign."

"Noted. I'll memorize the most important ones." Dunmoore's eyes swept the immediate area behind her sunglasses. "Anyone worthy of the combo signal around us?"

"Yep. Several. Mostly muscle." Guthren kept still, though his eyes too were quartering the promenade. "I think at least two of them are interested in us. They're standing under a store awning twenty meters to our starboard. Both are wearing white jackets with rolled-up sleeves over dark shirts. One with a mustache, the other with a full beard."

"Seen." Both Pushkin and Dunmoore replied.

The latter finished her cone and stood. "Let's head in that direction and see what those gentlemen of low persuasion do."

"What a life you lead," Pushkin said, chuckling. "The excitement never stops."

Fifteen minutes later, they stopped at a waterfront cafe with outdoor tables under a striped awning and sat. The men Guthren had spotted were still within sight, though they'd taken a bench beneath a towering palm tree this time.

The command chief shook his head as he scanned an imitation chalkboard with the lunch menu.

"What a way to spend a Sunday."

"You mean us wandering the waterfront aimlessly?"

He looked up at Pushkin. "No. Those two bozos over there. I almost pity them. Tailing us on our day off must be the most excruciatingly boring thing ever."

Pushkin scoffed. "Tough. They could have chosen a job that didn't involve working for mobsters. Mind you, they're well paid, so I don't feel the slightest bit of sympathy."

Guthren patted him on the shoulder. "You're all heart, sir."

They ordered a leisurely lunch and spent two hours eating, drinking, and laughing. Dunmoore picked up the tab, and as they ambled back the way they'd come, she peeled off from her friends and made a beeline for the watchers, alarming her companions. But when Pushkin made to follow, Guthren put a restraining hand on his arm.

"Watch."

Dunmoore walked up to the astonished men who now openly stared at her through their sunglasses and said, "We're on our way back to my place, so you can knock off early. Say hi to the boss for me."

Then she turned on her heels and rejoined the others.

Pushkin glanced over his shoulder when they resumed walking and let out a snort of laughter. "I don't know what you said, but they seemed rooted to the spot, staring at us. Maybe they're just two guys enjoying the day, not mobsters."

Guthren glanced at Pushkin.

"They're from the Pègre, Commodore. Trust me on this. I got images of their mugs." He tapped his sunglasses. "And during lunch, I linked with the local Fleet Security database — Vince gave me back door access."

"So that's why you were fidgeting with your little black box?"

A nod. "Security has them down as known muscle for organized crime. They belong to a group that may or may not be headed by Sylvie Lassieux."

"May or may not?" Pushkin cocked an eyebrow at his friend.

"As Vince told us, they're extremely good at hiding connections around here, thanks to corrupt cops. And since Fleet Security gets most of its civilian criminal information from the local police and the Dordogne Gendarmerie, our data is just as incomplete and compromised."

"Charming."

"Dordogne isn't even the worst star system for this sort of crap, and there's damn little Vince's bunch can do about it except where criminal activity touches the Fleet directly or affects national security."

***

When a uniform-clad Dunmoore emerged from her bedroom the next morning, she found Pushkin and Guthren similarly dressed. Both sported row upon row of ribbons on the left breast, most of them earned during the war, and where Dunmoore wore pilot wings above the fruit salad, Guthren had a naval special forces operator badge.

She smiled at their neat appearance. "My, don't you two wharf rats clean up well when you want to?"

"Only the best when making our manners with Admiral Hogue and reminding her she remains responsible for ensuring the 101st gets all the logistical support it needs."

"About that, Vincenzo is trying to find out why some of the supplies Eduardo orders get diverted to other units. He's not finding much beyond the excuse distribution is based on current needs, not future estimates. But so far, no sign of peculation, and none of the people in the 3rd Fleet logistics control chain seem to live beyond their means."

Pushkin shrugged. "They just don't like us, that's all."

"I shouldn't ask this, but do you have an appointment with Hogue?"

He grinned.

"Of course. And while I'm with her, Kurt will make nice with the command chief. And after Hogue, I'll pop into Keo's office for a quick howdy and then buy Alvin Maffina a cup of coffee before I bend his ear — standard flag officer politics. I'd visit you as well, but since we spent the weekend bemoaning the state of the universe, there's no point. Vince is supposed to have a car waiting for us, so we'll be independent after you drive us in."

She frowned at Pushkin.

"Are you using my branch chief as your dogsbody?"

He affected a look of pure innocence.

"Us? Never. He offers help, and we gratefully accept. I don't know where the car is from, but it'll be clear of listening and tracking devices and won't be traced back to any of us."

"Fine. Breakfast, anyone?"

"It's ready and waiting," Guthren announced. "If you'll step into your dining room."

***

Shortly before seven-thirty, Guthren pulled Dunmoore's car into her reserved spot and shut down the power plant. "End of the line, everyone out."

As they disembarked, she wondered what anyone watching would make of the 3rd Fleet chief of staff for operations arriving with the flag officer commanding SOCOM's 101st Battle Group and the formation's command chief. Not that it mattered.

Dunmoore already knew many around the headquarters, her superiors included, thought of her as a misplaced SOCOM officer whose allegiance to what they termed the regular navy was suspect.

And for anyone involved with organized crime who suspected she'd set Pushkin's Q ships on the traffickers, it would be more confirmation Dunmoore was pulling hidden strings behind Hogue and Keo's backs.

As usual, Ramius was already at her desk when she entered the outer office. Vincenzo was also somewhere in the building since his beret hung from the coat rack he shared with her aide.

"Good morning, Admiral." Ramius had her usual smile.

"Good morning, Anna."

"The overnight log is in your queue. No unusual entries. Nothing urgent in the correspondence folder and no messages. Evidently, it was a quiet weekend. Would you like a cup of coffee?"

"If there's a fresh urn, then yes, please." Dunmoore headed for her desk.

"As fresh as can be." Ramius climbed to her feet and vanished across the hall. She returned moments later, holding a mug emblazoned with the 3rd Fleet's crest.

"Thank you."

After taking a sip, Dunmoore went through the Beta and Gamma Watch logs, and, as Ramius had said, nothing unusual happened. Besides, they would call her at home if anything significant cropped up. She signed off electronically, prepared the one-paragraph summary for Hogue and Keo, and fired that off to their message queues. Then she opened the correspondence file.

Again, nothing much, not even a missive from Zeke or Kathryn, but there was a private message from Sylvie Lassieux. An invitation, in fact. Dunmoore frowned. Why to her work address and not at home? Unless she wanted word of the invitation to reach her superiors' ears.

Rear Admiral Siobhan Dunmoore and a guest are cordially invited to celebrate Sylvie Lassieux's birthday at the Grand Casino this coming Saturday at nineteen-hundred hours. Please RSVP via return of message.

Her eyebrows rose in surprise. And a guest? Were those Lassieux's men on the promenade? She saw a small postscript at the bottom of the invitation — formal wear was de rigueur, and personal security attendants would be admitted, one per guest.

Formal wear. Dunmoore knew she had none and doubted Gregor did either. What did bodyguards wear for such an occasion, and did either of the chiefs have it? Because all four of them would go to what would surely be one of Dordogne's social highlights and count many interesting people among its guests. And that meant clothes shopping in the next day or so.

When she arrived home, Dunmoore found another car parked in the driveway but off to one side so she could access the garage. Ordinary, though well-cared for, she knew it had to be the loaner Vincenzo had rustled up. Only those with the proper access codes, such as her house guests, could have opened the front gate.

Dunmoore found Pushkin and Guthren on the back terrace, enjoying a cold beer in the shade, clad once more like vacationing spacers on a warm planet.

"The admiral returneth." Pushkin raised his dew-covered bottle. "Get changed. I'll have a fresh peg for you when you're back."

Once in shorts and a tee shirt, Dunmoore gratefully accepted the beer and took a healthy swig after dropping into her favorite chair.

"So, how did your visits with the brass go?"

Pushkin made a face. "Hogue was polite and infuriatingly vague."

"As she was with me when I had the 101st."

"Keo was abrupt, even brusque, and almost passive-aggressive."

Dunmoore snorted. "Yep. He's like that with me still."

"And Maffina was all oily smiles and fake bonhomie, making promises he doesn't for a moment intend to keep. But I reminded them who I was, what I did, and what their responsibilities vis-à-vis the 101st were, by orders from Fleet HQ."

She turned to Guthren. "And how was the command chief?"

"As usual. Concerned with minutiae. Please never offer me a job like that. Every time I see him, he seems a little closer to chucking it all away out of sheer boredom."

"No promises."

He gave her a disconsolate grunt. "That's what I figured."

"And in other news, we're all going to a big birthday bash at the Grand Casino on Saturday, Vince included."

— Twenty-One —

Marseilles' Grand Casino, sitting at the heart of a splendid park on the bay's north shore, a mere ten-minute walk from the promenade, shimmered softly under projectors hidden among bushes and trees, looking for all the world like a fairy-tale castle. Dunmoore had read somewhere that its architecture was based on an old Earth casino from the nineteenth century in a place called Monaco.

Her car, under Chief Vincenzo's deft guidance, whispered up the flagstone driveway and around the fountain to the grand entrance, where valets and security staff, resplendent in black trousers and short-sleeved white jackets, waited to greet the guests. When they came to a precise halt at the foot of the stairs, under a canopy made to look like wrought iron and glass, Vincenzo and Guthren climbed out of the front seats and opened the back doors to let Dunmoore and Pushkin out.

When a valet stepped forward to take the car, Vincenzo shook his head, tapped the controls in his pocket, and watched the doors close automatically before the vehicle, now under AI control, drove off to wait at home. The valet bowed at the neck and returned to his place by the stairs.

Dunmoore and Pushkin wore sober evening clothes — high-collared silk jackets over black trousers, his severe and just as black, hers a soft shade of lavender and flared at the hips. The chiefs wore tailored black jackets over open-collared black silk shirts and black trousers, what Vincenzo had called the formal bodyguard uniform for muscle owned by the rich. Their loose and unbuttoned jackets provided easy access to blasters carried in shoulder holsters. Both flag officers carried their smaller sidearms at the hip, beneath their jackets, where they weren't quite as readily accessible for a quick draw.

Since this was, at least in Dunmoore's mind, work rather than play, she'd footed the bill for Vincenzo's suit, but even though she'd insisted, Pushkin and Guthren had paid for their own.

They took the stairs, Dunmoore and Pushkin side by side, each chief behind his flag officer, and entered the ornate, high-ceilinged foyer where security personnel in evening clothes checked invitations and discreetly glanced at the readout from the sensor arch surrounding the door.

"Rear Admiral Siobhan Dunmoore and Commodore Gregor Pushkin," she announced when the lead security man gave her a questioning look, eyebrows minutely raised.

He briefly dipped his head.

"Welcome, Admiral, Commodore. The Casino is honored to have officers of your renown among the guest this evening. I would, however, ask that you and your party turn over your weapons. We will keep them safe and return them when you leave."

Dunmoore's smile held little warmth. She said, in her honeyed tone, the one her companions knew signaled danger, "I'm afraid that won't be possible. Our sidearms are Fleet issue and cannot leave our persons, let alone be handled by civilians. We're well versed in their handling, better than your people or the bodyguards of the other guests. Now shall I contact Madame Lassieux?"

At that moment, an older, better-dressed version of the man materialized from a hidden control room behind a nearby wall panel. He put a hand on the lead security officer's shoulder and spoke in a soothing voice as other guests entered the foyer.

"The admiral is within her rights, Jean-Pierre."

"Of course, Monsieur." Jean-Pierre bowed at the waist and indicated the inner doors. "Welcome, Admiral and party. We hope you'll enjoy your evening."

As they walked away, Pushkin muttered, "That's the first time I've been called a party."

She gave him a sideways grin. "I guess someone finally figured out you were a fun guy."

"Hilarious. Don't give up your day job."

A pair of attendants in dark suits just inside the main reception room bowed as a disembodied voice announced, "Admiral Siobhan Dunmoore and Commodore Gregor Pushkin, Commonwealth Navy."

"How very medieval," Pushkin muttered sotto voce, though he kept a pleasant smile as the nearest guests applauded politely.

Sylvie Lassieux, resplendent in a shimmering red and gold, high-collared cheongsam dress, broke away from the nearest group and made a beeline for them, beaming. At the same time, Guthren and Vincenzo, in their bodyguard roles, cased the broad, high-ceilinged space with polished marble columns surrounding an open central area, dividing it from chair groupings, bars, and tables groaning under plates of finger food.

"My dear Siobhan. You honor me by coming."

Lassieux took Dunmoore's outstretched hand in both of hers and held it for a moment.

"I wouldn't have missed it for the world. Thank you so much for the invitation."

Lassieux turned to Pushkin, taking his hand.

"And you, Commodore. May I call you Gregor? A good friend of Siobhan's is also a good friend of mine."

"Please do, Sylvie."

She glanced over their shoulders at the two chiefs and dismissed them as unimportant.

"Come, let us find you a glass of champagne."

Lassieux turned on her heels and, after exchanging a quick glance, Dunmoore and Pushkin followed while their putative bodyguards moved off to one side where a dozen or more stoic-looking men in dark clothes stood along the wall, eyes constantly sweeping the room.

When the chiefs took up their positions, the nearest minder, a swarthy, bearded man with bulging muscles and the eyes of a dead fish, asked in a low voice, without turning his head, "You guys Navy?"

"Yep."

"Figured. Never seen your faces around the circuit before."

"Circuit?"

"Parties. Events. Meet-ups. The sort of thing our principals do to stay rich."

Guthren let out a soft chuckle.

"Staying rich ain't a preoccupation in the Navy. Staying alive? That's another story. Lots of call for our sort to get active on the circuit?"

"Nah. No one wants a war. Them that don't have protection, though, they find out about new friends pretty fast, if you know what I mean." A pause. "You guys carrying military hardware?"

Guthren nodded. "Yep."

"No need for a personal security license, then?"

"Nope. We just need orders, and when an admiral issues those, things get done."

"She the war hero who raided the bonehead capital?"

"That she is. Me, my buddy here, and the commodore with her, we were all on the mission."

This time, the muscle turned to glance at him.

"No shit?"

"None whatsoever. Hell of a thing, too. Later, we were all in the honor guard on Aquilonia when the SecGen and the Shrehari dictator signed the armistice. First time I ever looked a bonehead in the eyes at that close a range."

"Shit." The man shook his head.

"Who's your boss?"

"Antoine Calvert." When Guthren didn't react, he added, "Runs the biggest waste management company in the star system. In fact, he's talking to your admiral right now."

Guthren felt a faint nudge from Vincenzo and saw him flex his fingers at waist height. However, instead of stretching, the younger man was using the hand signals they'd adopted from SOCOM years earlier. And those signals told Guthren what he already suspected. Calvert was a huge organized crime figure.

The chief couldn't help but wonder how many more members of the Dordogne Pègre were among the elegantly dressed guests. Vincenzo had mentioned that most of the planet's wealthiest people hobnobbed with top OCG leadership members when they weren't one and the same. Apparently, money could buy entry into the best clubs and circuits, to use the bodyguard's term, provided you kept its provenance discreet.

The evening might be interesting after all. How often did a command chief petty officer get to see the crème de la crème partying in places that barely admitted flag officers, especially when a bunch of them employed people who were legitimate targets for the 101st Battle Group out on the frontier?

***

Dunmoore, aware of Guthren and Vincenzo standing in the shadows, had caught the latter's hand signal. She knew immediately who he meant, though seeing Antoine Calvert as one of the biggest mob bosses on Dordogne gave her a touch of cognitive dissonance.

Distinguished, elegantly dressed in a suit that must have cost the equivalent of a year's pay for a rear admiral, his old-fashioned manners befit those of a courtier at one of the pre-diaspora royal courts on Earth. He appeared in his late sixties or early seventies, with thick, silver hair brushed back from a high forehead. Intelligent brown eyes framed a patrician nose above full lips. His square, seamed features gave him that gravitas so beloved by politicians everywhere, and as soon as that thought arose, Dunmoore wondered if Senator LeRoy was on the guest list.

Judging by the people she'd met so far, he wouldn't have been invited on the strength of his personality or fortune alone. And since he was friendly with Hogue and Keo, who also weren't in attendance, Dunmoore figured she might displease all three once they found out. And they would.

Which, of course, raised the question of why Sylvie Lassieux had invited her and a friend. Somehow, it seemed excessive to atone for her words at Victor's soirée. A Victor who still hadn't returned from his business trip.

"You must have marvelous stories to tell, my dear," Calvert said, eyes twinkling.

"I do. But they're all classified, so, unfortunately, they'll have to remain untold." Dunmoore exchanged a quick glance with Pushkin, who was chatting with Melanie Calvert, Antoine's spouse, and every bit his equal in elegance, courtliness, and apparent age.

"But of course. How does the old expression go? Your missions are so secret that if you tell me about them, you'd have to make me vanish?"

For a moment, Dunmoore saw his eyes harden and lose their sheen of humanity.

"We don't do that. At least not nowadays," she replied with a smile meant to be mischievous. "Or so I'm told by Fleet Security."

"Hah! I do so enjoy your sense of humor. It pushes the unwritten bounds of our boring, polite little world, which is refreshing." Calvert's smile, warm though it seemed, didn't quite reach his watchful eyes. "You're such a delightful addition to Marseilles society. Victor is taken with you, as are Sylvie, Uta, and many others. A genuine war hero named in battle by the Shrehari *Kho'sahra*, with a reputation for ruthlessness and efficiency. The savior of my good friend Sara Lauzier and her companions, many of whom I am also honored to count as friends."

"Please, Antoine. I was merely doing my duty as a Navy officer."

"Pshaw." He waved her objection away. "You're a cut above everyone else and bring a certain panache to this soirée no other naval officer of my acquaintance can manage. I daresay you'll be climbing even higher in the coming years, perhaps become the flag officer commanding 3rd Fleet, for instance." His smile became positively radiant. "What a good fit that would be. Your experience of the frontier is unmatched. I'm pretty sure you can make whatever you want happen, given sufficient resources. And with friends in the right places, anything is possible."

She shrugged off his compliments. "Perhaps."

"We shall surely see, my dear Admiral. Sara and so many others still owe you a debt of gratitude. But I'm keeping you from mingling. It's been an absolute joy meeting you and Commodore Pushkin. I'm sure we'll see each other regularly now that you've entered Marseilles society."

With that, he gave a courtly bow of the head, touched his spouse on the arm, and they wandered off.

"You know," Dunmoore murmured as she and Pushkin headed toward the nearest buffet table, "I think I was just offered a bribe to keep my nose out of unusual happenings in frontier systems and strictly do my job as Hogue's COS Ops. Meaning, obey orders and don't interfere, and the local magnates use their political pull on Earth to get me more stars."

"You think they figured out what we did?"

She nodded.

"They undoubtedly have informants at 3rd Fleet HQ, aboard the starbase, and at SOCOM on Earth, perhaps via the SSB's good offices. We're not dealing with stupid people. On the contrary."

"Considering they're giving you a chance to back away instead of attempting to take you out doesn't speak well for their grasp of your character."

"These are people who believe everyone has a price, and they're right. You and I do, just as much as Hogue, Keo, Victor, or Sylvie. Ours is simply something they can't imagine, and no one alive can pay. The lure of a four-star admiral's billet doesn't even come close."

"What's your plan?"

She gave him a predatory smile he knew only too well.

"Play along until we're ready. I'll let Zeke know what's going on."

— Twenty-Two —

"Caught any likely fish?" Guthren asked once Dunmoore's car whisked them away from the Grand Casino well after midnight. The city was still as bright as ever, with plenty of evidence the Marseillais enjoyed partying until the wee hours of the morning.

Dunmoore and Pushkin looked at each other and chuckled.

"Funny you should mention fish. Tonight struck me as almost biblical. I'm reasonably sure they offered me a bright future among the wealthiest in the star system and the lure of four stars on my collar if I did my job as chief of staff for operations with due diligence. Apparently, Sara Lauzier and her clique have plenty of close friends on Dordogne."

"Especially Antoine Calvert, sir?" Vincenzo asked. "The reputed boss of bosses. Owns the biggest waste management company within half a dozen light years."

"A very gracious man, who made much of my status as a war hero." Dunmoore snorted. "I haven't been feted as a war hero anywhere until here. Tonight."

"They buttered you up good and hard, did they?" Guthren asked.

"Everyone I spoke with after Calvert made a point of welcoming me into their circle and assuring me that I had a bright future, but the subtext always intimated I had to fit in and keep fitting in. If they consider me a threat because they suspect I somehow placed ships from my former command across a trafficking run, why not just arrange for an accident?"

"I think I may have an answer for that," Vincenzo said. "It goes back to the somewhat strange sense of honor among the Pègre."

Guthren scoffed. "Honor?"

"Among other things, during my investigation, I found out the local OCGs have this thing where they consider themselves honor-bound to try co-opting someone into working with them rather than use threats or violence as a first resort."

"So that was a co-opting attempt I experienced? It makes me wonder if and what they tried on my predecessor."

Pushkin grimaced.

"Maybe he wouldn't cooperate and didn't want to say no because he understood a refusal would mean things could get kinetic. That leaves taking early retirement and vanishing."

"Except they might have taken him out anyway, to serve as an object lesson. I wonder whether Keo or Hogue know more than they'll ever admit."

"Or whether someone from Calvert's crew will corner you and hint at Berg's fate if you hesitate. An intermediate step, so to speak."

Guthren shook his head.

"I don't know. Are those people really dumb enough to figure someone like the admiral can be bought? Or are they just messing with us?"

"It's more likely they can't understand the concept of integrity," Pushkin said. "In their world, people are bought and sold all the time. Everyone has a price, and most hold themselves cheaply. What would a rear admiral whose career languished for ten years want? To make up for it with quick promotions, of course. Throw in hobnobbing with the elite and gifts to follow, so she can afford the best there is, and for someone like Calvert, the idea of refusal is alien. The Almighty knows he bought plenty of politicians that way, Senator LeRoy included. Not that he was in attendance tonight, but still."

Another scoff. "Then they don't know her."

"No, they don't," Dunmoore said. "And we'll use that blind spot to find the traitors working for them."

Pushkin glanced at her.

"Until the next time you get orders to change patrol routes. There's no way you'll risk letting traffickers through if you can get my ships into place, not when it means saving hundreds, perhaps thousands, of innocent lives. If they've decided you were responsible for the most recent intercepts, they won't forgive a replay, not after they offered you all you might desire tonight. At least according to their lights."

"I'll just have to make sure I stay a step ahead of them when it happens."

***

"Siobhan really is a marvel of adaptation, isn't she?" Kathryn Kowalski shook her head in admiration once Holt relayed Dunmoore's latest report. "But I'd be happier if she wasn't swimming among organized crime sharks who have no reason to trust her. Do you think her chief is right about the OCGs giving her a chance to come on board with them merely by doing her job as COS Ops? That it's a matter of honor among thieves, so to speak?"

Holt nodded. "I'm sure of it. Just as I'm becoming convinced her predecessor is no longer among the living because he walked away from the Pègre and opened the way for Siobhan, who quickly cost them a fortune. Berg may have been hiding before, but if he never left Dordogne, Calvert's people would have found him."

"So, how do we minimize the danger for Siobhan and her friends? They have a role to play in the coming years, and we don't have time to recruit others of their caliber — if we can even find the like nowadays."

"She wouldn't be in this position if we had a properly constituted internal affairs division, but I repeat myself ad nauseam on that subject."

Kowalski smirked. "You do. And we'll get there. Patience, Zeke."

"The officers from the special operations section should arrive on Dordogne imminently and contact Chief Vincenzo to discuss the next steps. That's the best we can do other than pray Siobhan's instincts don't fail her. The sooner she can pin 3rd Fleet's problems on either Keo or Hogue, the better. Then we can force an early retirement or two and unleash Siobhan to clean up HQ and Starbase 30, for starters."

"While we leave the SSB with a warning they should stay out of it."

"Of course. But Blayne Hersom likely won't listen. Not when Sara Lauzier is quietly continuing her drive for the top job. She needs funds, and those come from many friends, including Siobhan's new pal, Antoine Calvert, provided their own revenues keep increasing. Cutting off said revenues will, naturally, trigger an adverse reaction."

"Does Blayne have ambitions under the next Lauzier administration?"

Holt let out a bark of laughter.

"When did you ever meet a senior SSB executive who didn't have any? He doesn't want a cabinet job or another lucrative appointment. No, like all his predecessors, Blayne dreams of expanding the SSB into a powerful federal police force capable of dictating terms to the Fleet on all matters within the Commonwealth sphere. Not that Lauzier is crazy enough to give any SSB director general that much power. Nor will her backers accept an interstellar law enforcement agency that can plug the gaps between the Fleet and star system police forces. There's too much money flowing through those gaps. But Sara will use Blayne by dangling possibilities before his nose and perhaps even giving him more scope."

Kowalski made a face. "I won't ask how you know all this."

"Good. Because I wouldn't answer."

"Oh, I can guess, and I bet Blayne and Sara do not know how deeply an unnamed unit has penetrated their organizations."

"And vice versa, never forget that. Hunting down SSB moles is a full-time job for many of my people."

***

A middle-aged man with a forgettable face, wearing nondescript casual clothes, leaned against the bar beside Vincenzo and dropped three untraceable cred chips on the polished wood.

Without looking at Vincenzo, he said in a low voice, "Hey, Vince. It's been a while. Uncle Josiah says hi."

The chief replied in the same tone, without turning his head, "Hey, Lou. Fancy meeting you here. How is our uncle?"

"Still nostalgic about the days of furious faeries."

"Same as our Aunt Si."

The two men finally glanced at each other, satisfied each was who he purported to be, and neither had spoken words that would have signified danger — abort the meeting. Lou, or at least it was the name in the message from counterintelligence on Earth laying out the recognition pattern, picked up the cred chips — they'd been another recognition signal. Obviously, Lou had seen pictures of Vincenzo so he could identify him, but the man's face was totally unknown to the chief.

"Gus is waiting outside. How about we take a walk? You got your hardware?"

Gus was the name given to the other agent in the message. "Always."

Vincenzo and Lou left the bistro, a small, quiet place in one of the suburbs near Joint Base Dordogne, and crossed the street to where another unremarkable man sat on a park bench, watching the last of the sun vanish behind the rooftops.

"Found cousin Vince," Lou said.

"Hey, Gus."

The second man was unknown to Vincenzo as well.

"Vince. How are they hanging, my friend?"

"The way nature intended." Vincenzo reached into his pocket and pulled out his jammer. "I'm active if either of you wants to confirm."

"Already done," Gus said. "I caught you on the way out the door."

"Then we're good." Vincenzo nodded at the park. "Let's take a stroll and talk. You can start by telling me about the last report from either myself or Aunt Si you read before leaving home. Then I can fill you in on what happened since."

Lou gave a concise and accurate summary of Dunmoore's latest report, the last bit of proof he and Gus were the Naval Intelligence Special Operations Section agents he'd expected.

"Okay. Plenty of things happened since you lifted off, my friends." As they ambled along, eyes looking for anyone suspicious, Vincenzo recounted the intervening events, especially the gala at the Grand Casino and Calvert's covert attempt to bribe Dunmoore.

"The corollary to that offer," he continued, "is what they'll do when she uses the 101st against the traffickers again — and she will if she sees a risk — instead of just shuffling 3rd Fleet around and leaving things at that."

"What's your assessment?" Gus asked, one undercover professional to another.

"They'll take her out," Vincenzo replied flatly. "Just as I suspect they did with Hanno Berg, her predecessor."

"Okay. That's one thing you need to keep us informed about. In the meantime, we'll look for potential targets among the opposition, people whose removal will seriously mess with their chain of command and their ability to operate. We can retaliate in ways they'll always remember if they try anything."

"Big bang or little bang?"

Lou smiled.

"Both, my cousin from another uncle. What we end up doing to the bad guys might give local law enforcement the sort of heartburn to make them wish they were dead. Gus and me, we're a two-man wrecking crew. No limits, no rules of engagement, just one imperative. Keep Aunt Si alive, and if ever they try anything against her, terminate the lot of them with extreme prejudice. Even those who wear the same uniform as we do if they've gone over to the other side. And if we run across SSB operatives involved in this matter, they also go down."

— Twenty-Three —

"Victor! You've returned." Dunmoore beamed at Herault when he appeared on her living room primary display a week after the Grand Casino party. Pushkin and Guthren had left several days earlier, their leave over, and were back aboard *Iolanthe*, preparing for the next patrol.

He gave her a rueful smile. "The trip took a little longer than expected."

"Long light years?"

"A bit. But sometimes, new clients insist on meeting face-to-face, and considering the money involved, it's worth the aggravation of interstellar travel. How did you keep yourself amused without me?"

Dunmoore couldn't help but smirk at his cheeky question.

"Well, let's see. I entertained old wartime comrades for two weeks. We traipsed down memory lane often enough to make it seem like we did the north-to-south trail ten times. Then, we attended Sylvie Lassieux's birthday party at the Grand Casino, where I met many prominent Marseillais, like Antoine Calvert, who made me feel incredibly welcome."

"Wonderful. Antoine is a gentleman of the old school."

"I noticed. He certainly thought I might still go far in the Navy. Bless him. He's more optimistic about my career than I am. And then there was…" Dunmoore named every notable person she'd met, many of whom Vincenzo fingered as having underworld connections.

"Then I suppose you made quite a splash. I must thank Sylvie for inviting you and seeing that you met the right people while I was gone. All is well besides your growing social status?"

"As can be. Shall we wander wine country next Saturday? I've been sticking around Marseilles during your absence."

A faint, though noticeably pained, expression crossed his face.

"I'm not sure I can free myself this coming weekend. The consortium I'm part of recently experienced a severe setback, which means redoubling my efforts to recoup our losses. Sorry."

As he spoke, a faint sense of unease tugged at Dunmoore, though she kept her composure, hoping her eyes kept her thoughts well hidden. Did Victor just admit he was one of the financiers behind the traffickers captured by Gregor's Q ships or worked for them? If so, did he realize they suspected her of engineering the intercepts? Or was her imagination spinning tales without substance by seeing the enemy everywhere?

"Was that the reason for your trip?"

He nodded.

"Yes. The interstellar import-export business can be brutal. It's a big, nasty universe out there, as you know. Losing expensive cargo to pirates, malfunctions, or natural causes can devastate a bottom line."

"Is that what happened?"

"We know several shipments didn't reach their intended destination, leaving the customers and us to face big losses."

Was he using the oldest trick of all — telling the truth without revealing anything? Or was this really a case of similar circumstances?

"I'm sorry to hear that. And yes, the universe is unfeeling and unforgiving."

A wry smile tugged at his lips.

"Almost as much so as your Navy, right?"

"When the commission of certain capital crimes is involved, yes."

"Such as?"

"Human traffickers would be at the top of the list. Many of them met their maker under the guns of my battle group."

He winced.

"Is it me, or has a chill wind just passed over the comlink?"

"Sorry. I shouldn't be talking shop when you've experienced a nasty loss, Victor. If you find yourself unexpectedly free next weekend, just call. I'd like to see you again and discuss more pleasant subjects, such as a wine variety you've not yet had me taste. And you can bend my ear about your troubles without me making tasteless remarks, such as my terminating traffickers with extreme prejudice."

Herault's smile returned, although it didn't reach his eyes this time.

"Deal. Have a pleasant week, and we'll talk again in a few days. Goodbye, Siobhan."

"Until later."

The screen went dark, and she sat back with a thoughtful expression. Then she switched on her secure tablet and composed a message for Zeke detailing her conversation with Herault. After encrypting it, she routed a copy to the communications center for the next Earth-bound subspace packet and one to Chief Vincenzo.

***

"Good morning, Admiral."

Dunmoore, who'd been staring out the office window while sipping her morning coffee the following Wednesday, swiveled around.

"Good morning, Chief. Close the door and grab a pew."

When Vincenzo, mug in hand, had done so, he watched her for a few seconds. "You seem preoccupied. More than normal, I mean. Has Mister Herault called again?"

"No." Dunmoore put her cup on the desk and leaned back. "Admiral Keo just passed down another change to the patrol schema. He claims it's based on yesterday's intelligence digest."

"So soon after the last one?" Vincenzo's forehead creased into a frown. "Perhaps Herault arranged a fresh series of shipments to compensate for the ones his consortium lost."

"Perhaps. Like last time, the digest doesn't provide enough data to warrant a patrol schema change in the frontier star systems." She tapped her fingers on the arms of her chair. "But if the changes are to help a fresh wave of traffickers, they make little sense. At least not as much as the previous adjustments."

"How so?"

Dunmoore tilted her head slightly to one side, eyes narrowed. "How about you read Admiral Keo's notes and tell me what you think?"

"Sure."

She pushed her reader across the desk, then called up a three-dimensional holographic projection of the Rim Sector. For the next five minutes, Vincenzo read and re-read Keo's directive while studying the projection. Finally, he put the reader on the desk again.

"We've always assumed traffickers from and into the Zone prefer sparsely populated habitable worlds a few light years from the edge of the Commonwealth sphere for their transshipment and distribution hubs, sir. Law enforcement is sparse on the ground, and the Navy is the only authority watching the orbital approaches. Since sketchy traders are common in places where the major shipping lines don't go because it's not profitable, traffickers often slip through. We found several of their hubs hidden away, far from settlements on those worlds over the last few years. But they're easy to abandon, dismantle or destroy and rebuild elsewhere when no one is looking. All they really need is a landing strip, buildings to store merchandise, barracks for humans being trafficked, and planetary officials who are lazy or prone to close their eyes in return for bribes."

Dunmoore nodded.

"That's the theory, yes. It makes places like Mission Colony, Andoth, and Garonne, to name the places where the 101st intercepted the latest wave, ideal. Go on."

"This patrol plan change weakens surveillance in the Marengo and Nabhka systems, which aren't as convenient to Zone traffickers, especially Nabhka, where we've never found evidence of anything more than customs evasion. But the real puzzler is Jock's Hole — there's nothing but a mining colony on a formerly habitable world."

"Okay. You've found the bits that puzzled me. What are your deductions, Chief?"

"There are two possibilities, sir. Either they decided to move the next run far away from their usual hubs, or this is a test to see what you'll do with the information. I doubt traffickers of sound mind will use Jock's Hole as a transshipment point — any unexpected ship will light up the mining complex's threat board like a Founder's Day festival — and Nabhka has no history of being used by Zone-based outfits. Which leaves Marengo as plausible, but only for a few ships. Their greatest asset is slipping through surveillance nets unnoticed or ignored by local authorities. Too many so-called traders arriving at once or in a brief period will raise questions."

"Meaning you think this is my chance to prove I've accepted their offer without them risking a single ship?"

Vincenzo dipped his head once.

"Almost certainly, sir. The only question I have is why they think you couldn't figure it out."

A feral smile lit up Dunmoore's face.

"Because, as usual, my enemies underestimate me. They're used to dealing with senior officers who didn't spend the last three years chasing traffickers deep inside the Zone, taking the sort of risks that make normal flag officers blanch."

"Then what are your intentions?"

"First, you'll write a report for Admiral Holt on the matter and send it off as soon as possible."

"It'll go out on the daily subspace packet, sir. No problems."

"Then I will send out the orders to the affected units, and we'll see what happens."

"No contacting Commodore Pushkin?"

"Not even to pass the time exchanging old war stories. Neither you nor I will speak with anyone in the 101st or on Starbase 30. If I'm wrong and traffickers go through, then so be it. But I'm right. I can feel it in my bones. This is to see what I'll do after being wooed by the better part of Dordogne's high society crooks. The run after? It will be real, and we will figure out a way of alerting Gregor with no one on the OCG payroll noticing."

"Roger that, Admiral. Should I let my cousins from another uncle know? Their orders are to close in when the threat level goes above basic."

Dunmoore thought about it for a moment, then shook her head.

"Best not, just in case they're watching me closely if this is a test. No changes to our routines. Nothing that might show we're on high alert."

Nonetheless, Vincenzo met Lou at the bistro that evening and updated him on the latest developments. What he and Gus would do with the information was up to them. But he made it clear someone was keeping track of messages and comlinks between folks on the surface and the 101st Battle Group routed through 3rd Fleet's communications center. At their next meeting, Lou gave Vincenzo a miniature surface-to-orbit radio capable of operating on encrypted naval channels. It had no serial number and no sign of provenance. Later that night, Vincenzo tested it by calling *Iolanthe* directly and asking for Kurt Guthren, who he also updated. The radio performed flawlessly.

Unexpectedly, Victor Herault called Dunmoore that Saturday to invite her on a pleasant, leisurely stroll through wine country the following morning. Perhaps she'd passed the test if it had been one and not an actual trafficker run.

All patrol routes returned to normal a week after Admiral Keo concluded that intelligence was chasing shadows.

***

"Did she figure out it was a fake, a test? Or has she decided discretion is the better part of a successful future?"

Keo walked over to the windows and stared at the fog rolling in from the Western Ocean, blotting out the seaward end of the extensive harbor. The weather matched his mood, clear one moment, damp and gray the next.

As before, the link was audio only, so Keo allowed himself an irritated grimace.

"I don't know. But basing decisions about the future on this one event would be foolhardy. In fact, trusting her at this point would be even worse. For someone like Dunmoore, you need leverage."

A chuckle.

"Yes, leverage does work, doesn't it, Horace? We'll give it a go and see. Just keep your units dispersed, so our smaller runs get through. There won't be a larger convoy for a bit, so we have time to work on her."

— Twenty-Four —

"Looks like Siobhan passed the test. Or at least this test." Holt dropped into his accustomed chair across from Kowalski and took a sip from his mug. "And according to reports, no ships worthy of interest entered the systems affected by the latest patrol plan change, which confirms her gut instinct."

Kowalski nodded thoughtfully.

"That means there's a high probability the next time will be for real. They have big losses to recoup."

He nodded.

"Siobhan needs to be extremely careful and ready for blowback, even if the opposition can't detect her passing secret orders to the 101st."

"In the meantime, I'm convinced there will be attempts to compromise her, so she has no choice but to dance to their tune or walk into the Dordogne counterintelligence office and make a statement which could end her career."

"Or walk away like Hanno Berg."

Holt grimaced. "He tried, but it's a given Berg's dead by now. My people, helped by the special ops agents sent to Dordogne, are uncovering signs the Pègre, perhaps aided by the SSB, likely compromised him with a honey pot operation. He tried to escape without asking for our help, hoping retirement would cut the bonds that tie, but those people don't forgive."

"What do you figure they'll try on our Siobhan? She can't be bought with offers of wealth or power. She doesn't engage in illicit activities, has no known addictions or propensities considered deviant by the Fleet, and no skeletons in her closet, at least not ones that would raise eyebrows here."

"We know that, but the mob bosses on Dordogne don't. I'm not even sure the SSB understands who she is beneath the ruthlessness they've encountered at many turns. Both consider everyone corruptible or susceptible to blackmail because that's the slice of humanity they deal with, and they're right more often than not. Meaning they'll try the usual forms of discreet and insidious corruption to build a dossier that might paint her in a bad light if it ever surfaces. We call it making someone take the golden ticket. It'll mostly be as gifts, the sort a rear admiral shouldn't accept, and Siobhan will refuse.

"Except the dossier will show her taking whatever they offer and convincingly, too. If turning her into their creature through bribes doesn't work, they'll slowly increase the pressure. Perhaps with veiled threats against her career, her reputation, her friends — thankfully, what family she has is on New Tasman, and she hasn't spoken with them since before the war — and perhaps her colleagues. The only positive in this is that they need to move fast, which means they can't take their sweet time working on her. Another wave of traffickers intercepted before reaching distribution hubs inside the Commonwealth may spell doom for many people on Dordogne and elsewhere, including Earth. As you might recall, Sara Lauzier isn't a forgiving soul and needs substantial political donations as fast as possible to finance her drive for the top job. Buying the votes of her fellow senators is one of the most expensive activities in the known galaxy."

"Do you think Blayne Hersom might be involved in trying to corrupt or control Siobhan?" Kowalski asked.

"Probably. He still holds a grudge for what she's done to his various operations in the past."

***

"This is magnificent."

Dunmoore leaned against the lookout point's railing and let the gentle offshore breeze caress her face while the mingled aromas of ten thousand flowers in bloom filled her nostrils. Beneath them, a string of beachfront villas stretched out along a sheltered part of the coast for dozens of kilometers in either direction.

The water, from the turquoise of the shallows to the deep blue of the depths, sparkled beneath the late morning sun while white wave crests danced in the distance, beyond the broad barrier reef system running along the western coast like a living breakwater against tropical storms.

"Why do I think you've never visited the Topaz Coast in the three and a half years you've called this planet your home port?" Victor Herault, standing beside her, asked.

"Because this is the exclusive playground for the wealthy and powerful. Grubby flag officers aren't invited."

"You're right about the first part, but not the second. Flag officers friendly with those who own properties along the Topaz are most welcome."

Dunmoore glanced at him.

"What do you mean?"

"Let's get back in my car, and I can show you."

He'd picked her up at home that morning, for the first time, with promises of a surprising Saturday, asking only she pack an overnight bag, including swimming gear. After reading Zeke's latest missive two days earlier, detailing how she would now be offered a golden ticket to bind her, she'd decided to humor her new friends, just so she could see how far they'd go. Unfortunately, she didn't have time to warn Vincenzo about her latest trip and hoped the Navy issue communicator in her pocket would give him or his so-called cousins a beacon they could follow.

"Show me what?"

"Ah." He held an index finger to his lips. "That's the surprise."

"Do you have a little place here?"

He gave her a languid shrug and raised his hands, palms upward, in the typical Dordogne fashion.

"Of course. Everyone who matters does. But I rarely visit. My heart beats faster in wine country, so I let friends use the beach house. They, in turn, help me with my business. Everyone profits, and everyone is happy. Tell me, do you enjoy scuba diving?"

"Why?" She climbed into the passenger seat of the racy sports car while he took the driver's side.

"The Topaz Coast boasts the best inshore diving within a thousand kilometers. And you'll find every villa has the equipment and personal propulsion craft."

"Noted. Not that I'm able to enjoy such amenities."

He turned his head and gave her a mysterious grin as he gunned the car back toward the main road running along a ridge overlooking the most desirable tract of land on Dordogne. They turned west after less than a kilometer and approached a security arch blocking the way. It slid aside at their approach, and Dunmoore realized the Topaz Coast was probably the biggest gated community in human space.

They wound their way through two switchbacks down the escarpment and finally reached a private road running along its base in both directions. Herault turned north and drove for a few more kilometers past high walls, towering trees, and discreet lanes that ended in tall gates until he turned left, toward the beach, down one of them.

When they were within a few meters of the solid wood gate, it split apart, and both halves slid to the side, revealing a stone driveway bordered by thick bushes dripping with a rainbow of flowers. At the end of it stood a two-story mansion of gray granite topped by a red metal roof.

"Stormproof," Herault said, nodding at the structure. "With metal shutters that can secure windows and doors to shrug off anything coming ashore from the ocean. Not that it happens often. We get a bad typhoon once or twice every few years."

"Is this yours?" Dunmoore's head was on a swivel, trying to take in the expansive grounds where gazebos and other small structures hid among the vegetation. "It's gorgeous."

"No. Mine is next door. Not that I use it much since I prefer my château. This is one of Antoine Calvert's many properties. He has a principal beach residence five kilometers north of here."

They pulled into a circular drive and stopped in front of stone stairs leading to a broad, covered porch where double doors of transparent aluminum were slowly swinging inward.

Dunmoore gave him a curious look after he urged her to climb out.

"What are we doing here, Victor?"

"A few more moments, please." Herault led her through the doors, which closed soundlessly behind them. The temperature indoors was pleasantly cool, even after the few moments they'd spent outside in the tropical sun, and the delicate scent of fresh flowers tickled their nostrils.

He took her on a tour of the house, pointing out the amenities, of which there were many. Dunmoore could not help but marvel at the indoor swimming pool, hot tub, and gym. Or be impressed by the service droids silently waiting in their alcoves for orders. Of course, the finer things in life were also taken care of — a wine cellar, a fully equipped wet bar, and a gourmet kitchen. And for guests, a half dozen suites along with a master suite almost as spacious as her entire bungalow.

When they returned to the living room, which gave onto a covered terrace overlooking the water, she turned a crooked smile on Herault.

"Thanks for showing me how Antoine lives, but I would have preferred seeing your property. This one, though beautifully furnished, doesn't feel lived in."

"As I said, Antoine doesn't live here." He beamed at her. "But he's offering you the use of the property for as long as you want. Consider it yours — a home away from home where you can relax and forget the travails of running 3rd Fleet. Where you can invite your old friends when they're on shore leave or host parties for your new friends. As you saw, it's a straight run down the national road from Marseilles, not even an hour. Less if you take an aircar — incidentally, there's a landing pad on the side of the house. Your Navy friends can visit you directly from their ship with a shuttle. And," his smile widened, "there's a path to my property. A few minutes' walk, and we can visit each other."

Dunmoore raised her eyebrows.

"Why? Why is Antoine lending me this place?"

After Holt's latest message, she knew what was going on but needed to hear it from Herault.

"Because he admires you. To him, you're a war hero who got a raw deal after the armistice, and he's trying, in his own way, to make up for the government's unjust treatment."

"Really? Letting me use this place, which I couldn't afford to rent for a night, seems a little over the top."

Herault gave her a typically languid Dordognais shrug.

"What can I say? You made quite an impression on him at Sylvie's party. Antoine is a generous man to his friends and considers you among them."

Dunmoore narrowed her eyes as she shook her head in dismay.

"Do you and Antoine realize I can't accept this? It might be construed as a bribe."

Herault immediately waved her objection away.

"A bribe? Perish the thought. Antoine isn't gifting you the place; he's merely offering it for your use since no one currently lives here."

"What about the food in the stasis pantry, the wine in the cellar, the expensive booze in the bar?"

"It all comes with the property." A pained expression replaced his earlier smile. "Don't be like that, Siobhan. Let people do nice things for you after your sterling service to humanity. Try it out and see if spending weekends and days off here suits your soul. Antoine would be crushed if you refused his hospitality out of hand."

Dunmoore knew she had no choice but to accept, lest Calvert and company conclude the game was over. She still hadn't accumulated enough evidence to expose the corruption in 3rd Fleet headquarters and couldn't stop now. Not that anyone would accuse her of taking bribes on the strength of accepting Calvert's offer, considering Ezekiel Holt had expected a move of the sort, and she'd be updating him the moment she was back home.

"Fine," she said with an air of reluctance. "I wouldn't want to disappoint a gentleman like Antoine, so I'll try it."

Herault's broad smile returned.

"Excellent. Shall we fetch our overnight bags from the car and settle in?"

"Only if you show me your property next door this afternoon."

"Deal."

— Twenty-Five —

"You reported it to Admiral Holt, so that covers you with the beach house, sir," Vincenzo said when she finished updating him, complete with the location of the place and images she took over the weekend. "Can't be accused of taking bribes if counterintelligence is aware of it. But you can bet the place is lousy with surveillance devices, audio, and video, the latter capable of seeing in the nonvisible spectrum. Our issue jammers can take care of them, but I still wouldn't discuss sensitive matters, just in case, and running jammers nonstop will drain their batteries pretty quickly. Not to mention give the opposition enough time to develop a baseline for countermeasures."

"That, I'd already figured out. Getting you or someone from signals to come down and sweep the place would give the game away."

"Not necessarily." Vincenzo narrowed one eye in thought, lips pursed as he tapped his fingers on his knee. "The opposition would expect you to check on privacy. The trick is not finding and disabling all the sensors, just the most inconvenient ones, then using the rest to practice the art of dezinformatsiya and maskirovka."

Dunmoore nodded. "Disinformation and deception. That's a brilliant idea."

A lazy grin spread across Vincenzo's face.

"And Calvert's gift becomes a proper counterintelligence operation — you using the property is now part of the mission profile. You want me to sweep the place? I can go down in a civilian getup. They'll quickly figure out who I am, but it could just throw them off a little more. After all, the Calverts of the galaxy have their security folks do this sort of thing all the time."

She pulled a small, unmarked metallic card from her tunic pocket and pushed it across the desk.

"This opens everything. Have fun."

***

Vincenzo reappeared the following afternoon and returned the key card.

"That place is lousy with surveillance, including sophisticated video pickup constellations in every bedroom and bathroom, perfect for recording blackmail material. I'm fairly sure more than a few people found themselves working for Calvert after committing indiscretions while enjoying their time at his beach house. It need not even have been questionable activities. A talented artist can do wonders with video. Clearly, they're hoping for something that gives them a hold on you."

"What did you disable?"

"Nothing."

She cocked her head to one side and frowned. "Why?"

"The house is one big three-dee performance box. I could spend a week evaluating what could stay up and what should go down to preserve your privacy and still miss something, so I'll use mobster methods and go back once I can get my hands on a piece of kit that shouldn't be used in civilian places."

"Should I ask?"

"A portable EMP generator. The stuff I found isn't shielded against military-grade destructive countermeasures. Short-range bursts near each sensor set, and it all goes down hard without damaging innocent electronics in the same room. I'll get the droids out of the way first since they're the most expensive bit that could get damaged." He shrugged. "What's Calvert going to do? Complain? That means revealing he gave you Voyeur Manor without disclosing the no-corner-left-private setup, which is a crime on Dordogne. Not that he'll ever be prosecuted for it. But frying the network will send a nice little message."

"But it will remove our ability to play the disinformation and deception game."

He shook his head, smiling.

"No. Once his people realize the network is gone, they'll install backup sensors, but nothing as pervasive as now. Rebuilding everything from scratch would take too much time and leave too many traces. Once the backup is in, I'll carefully adjust it for our own ends."

"I see. If you're looking for my permission, go ahead. And I won't ask from whom you'll borrow an EMP generator."

"Just as well, because what I intend is not only illegal on the civilian side, but on our side too, and Calvert's people will catch me doing it in real-time. I don't know if or how fast they can respond to stop me."

A sly smile lit up Dunmoore's face.

"Then how about the last thing those sensors see is my face? We can head out there on Friday afternoon and cleanse the house. I'll stay for the weekend since Victor hasn't discussed any plans, and you're welcome to use one of the guest suites. After all, the mobsters think you're my muscle, as well as a distinguished chief petty officer of the Commonwealth Navy."

"And it'll let me check if I've missed anything. Sometimes, they build redundancies in such systems, stuff I can't detect because it isn't powered. Sweeping the house a few times over the weekend should reveal those once they go live. But we'll travel in two cars, Admiral. In case I must leave." He tapped a tunic pocket, indicating the surface-to-orbit radio.

"As they say in the N5 branch, it's a plan."

***

"It looks like I'll be spending Saturday evening at Antoine Calvert's place just up the coast for a little gathering," Dunmoore said when she and Vincenzo, both in civilian and carrying overnight bags, entered the borrowed beach house.

"Will you be needing me to accompany you, Admiral?" He asked, playing his role as her shadow for the benefit of the sensors.

"I think it's customary for folks to bring their own security in these parts, so yes."

"Very well, Admiral." He placed his bag on a marble bench in the foyer and rummaged through it, withdrawing a metal box that fit in the palm of his hand. He produced a second, thinner one and mated it to the first. "If you'll settle in, I'll check the house per standard protocol."

"Actually, since I've never watched you do so, I'll accompany you and learn."

"As you wish, Admiral. If I may, I'd like to begin with your private quarters."

"Certainly."

They took the winding marble stairs to the second story and walked down a bright hallway with a toffee-colored tile floor, white walls, and wrought iron light fixtures to the house's southern end. There, Vincenzo opened a polished door of blond native wood, stepped through, and headed for Dunmoore's luxurious ensuite bathroom.

Over the following hour, he led her from room to room, methodically pinpointing the surveillance sensors he'd noted during his earlier visit. He gave them a burst from his EMP generator, nodding every time he took a subsequent reading.

When they returned to the foyer after finishing in the wine cellar, Vincenzo said, "That takes care of what I could find. We should assume there are more and behave accordingly. I'll run a fresh sweep in the morning."

"Understood." Dunmoore's stomach rumbled, and she glanced through the windows at the heights to the east, now bathed in a Topaz Coast sunset's golden rays. "How about a bite to eat?"

"Absolutely. Why don't you enjoy a drink on the terrace? I'll put the service droids to work. Any preferences? When I checked earlier this week, the menu choices were almost endless."

"Surprise me."

Vincenzo snapped to attention and bowed his head.

"One flag officer's surprise coming up."

"You will join me at the table."

"Of course."

***

The driveway to Antoine Calvert's sprawling beach mansion was lit by countless flickering torches, making it seem as if the swaying palm trees and flowering bushes were engaged in a languid, sultry dance under the impulse of the warm offshore breeze. Dordogne's sun had set an hour earlier, and the planet's moons were still below the horizon, giving the Milky Way a place of honor in the cloudless evening sky. The faint thump of tropical music wafted through the car's open windows as Dunmoore examined her surroundings while Vincenzo drove up to the main house.

She climbed out when he came to a stop, and a valet stepped forward. But as before, Vincenzo joined her after shutting the driver's side door and sending the car back down the beach to Dunmoore's villa. He gave the valet a quick nod, then followed her through the open doors.

For the occasion, Dunmoore wore simple but elegant sandals, khaki shorts that ended just above her knees, and a white silk short-sleeved, open-collared blouse. Vincenzo was all in black, the same suit he'd worn at the Casino, minus the jacket. Neither carried weapons on this occasion, though Vincenzo had the surface-to-orbit radio.

Human staff in white shirts and shorts ushered Dunmoore through the house to a crowded terrace overlooking the beach. She snagged a glass of champagne along the way while Vincenzo followed like a black shadow. Though the other bodyguards were inconspicuous, and to the locals invisible, Dunmoore noticed a fair number hovering on the edges, watching their employers.

She let her eyes roam over the guests, looking for their host, Antoine, so she could make her manners, and the first face that jumped out from the crowd was Horace Keo's. Was he merely down from Marseilles for the occasion, or did he also enjoy a rent-free beach house with all the amenities and surveillance sensors a man such as Calvert could buy? If so, no one, not even counterintelligence, knew — otherwise, Vincenzo or Zeke would have said so — which meant he'd at the very least broken several tenets of the ethics code.

Their eyes briefly met, and she nodded pleasantly. At that moment, Dunmoore thought she could see surprise, annoyance, perhaps even a hint of fear cross Keo's tight features. No one had told him she was now part of the Topaz Coast set. But her last glimpse of the man's face before another guest led him away showed the beginnings of a bitter smile and a look of, if not triumph, then satisfaction.

One of the couples she'd met at the Grand Casino noticed her. After exchanging Dordogne-style kisses, one on each cheek, they took her around to make new acquaintances and say hello to those she'd already met, Calvert included.

Eventually, as the evening wore on and many guests became increasingly raucous, Dunmoore found herself face-to-face with

Keo, who seemed as sober as she was, unlike the people around them.

"I heard you'd been adopted into Marseilles society, Dunmoore," he said in a conversational tone. "Well done. It takes most senior officers much longer before they're invited to a party on the Topaz Coast, if at all. Are you down from Marseilles for the evening or staying with your friend, Victor Herault?"

Dunmoore supposed it was inevitable that Keo would hear of her friendship with the import-export magnate.

She shook her head.

"No. Victor couldn't make it this weekend. I'm staying in a beach house placed at my disposal by Antoine Calvert a few kilometers south of here." She caught a strange look in Keo's eyes. "How about you, sir? Down for the evening or the weekend?"

He didn't immediately reply as his gaze shifted to one side.

"Like you, I'm staying in a beach house placed at my disposal by a friend."

"Would that friend be Antoine Calvert?"

A nod as his eyes met hers again.

"As it happens, yes. Funny that you and I should finally have something in common, isn't it, Dunmoore?"

She gave him a friendly smile that didn't entirely hide a predatory edge.

"It is, sir. Glad we could establish that. Is Admiral Hogue around?"

He shook his head.

"No. This is not her sort of scene, nor has she made close enough friends in Marseilles for invitations to the Topaz Coast."

Words to the effect that Hogue wasn't useful to them sat on the tip of Dunmoore's tongue, but she restrained herself. Still, it was another piece of the puzzle and reinforced her suspicion the all too convenient patrol schema changes originated with the deputy commander of 3rd Fleet, not his boss. Did Calvert have her and Keo meet here tonight so they realized what they had in common was accepting gifts from the most prominent mobster in the star system and a friend of the most ambitious and dangerous politician in the Commonwealth?

Dunmoore and Vincenzo were among the first to slip out shortly after the midnight fireworks, and once the car was on the main road, she let out a soft sigh.

"Did you see Horace Keo?"

"Yes, Admiral."

"He told me Antoine Calvert gave him the use of a beach house as well, something he didn't report. Otherwise, you and I would have known about it."

Vincenzo grimaced.

"That'll raise many questions at Fleet HQ when my report arrives. It's a given Calvert arranged for your meeting tonight, so both of you understood the situation."

"I realize that. And I doubt Keo will have nuked the surveillance network in his villa as you did in mine. He probably doesn't even realize it's there. This makes me wonder what sort of military secrets ended up in Calvert's hands and how much blackmail material Calvert keeps ready in case Keo doesn't do as he's told."

"Either way, sir, I suspect it'll be game over for him once I report back. He placed himself in a potentially compromising situation, and that's a big no-no for a three-star who's the Navy's number two in the Rim Sector."

"Tell them to hold off on the big guns, Chief. I want another patrol change on record with interceptions by the 101st in the affected systems. Once that's established, Admiral Holt can transmit the arrest warrant. I'll take care of Horace myself while you and your cousins hunt down the traitors in our midst and eliminate a few of the more prominent external threats *pour encourager les autres.*"

"Roger that, Admiral. I'll see that the local counterintelligence office gets orders to help. Right now, they don't know I'm one of them on a special mission. But I'll need backup if we're targeting Keo in good order." They drove on in silence for a minute, then he said, "When we get back to the villa, how about you grab a glass of something and look at the stars from the terrace while I do a sweep? Five hours is enough for Calvert's people to plant new surveillance devices."

— Twenty-Six —

When she returned to work the following Monday, after an uneventful Sunday at a villa stripped of surveillance devices for the second time in less than forty-eight hours — Calvert's people had indeed installed a makeshift network — Dunmoore found Keo's attitude toward her subtly different. He no longer seemed as brusque and abrasive, almost as if he now saw her in a different light. Perhaps as a co-conspirator, a fellow victim of Calvert's schemes, or simply someone he thought dangerous at first but who was blithely compromising herself just as he'd done.

Dunmoore debated asking Keo if he'd swept his villa for surveillance devices, then decided it would be best if she didn't because the answer was immaterial. Either he'd done so and had let no military secrets slip or behaved in a manner that could open him to blackmail, or he hadn't, in which case it was much too late. She certainly wouldn't ask if he'd reported the gift to counterintelligence since he clearly hadn't. Otherwise, Vincenzo would have found out.

That Friday, Victor Herault took her to see the most anticipated production of the season at the Opéra de Marseilles. They shared a loge with Sylvie Lassieux and her partner Uta and joined the after party with the cast and a long list of the city's notables — politicians, mob bosses, senior civil servants, wealthy businesspeople, everyone who was anyone in Marseilles.

When Dunmoore checked the cost of a loge ticket afterward, she immediately reported the gift to Holt via Vincenzo's regular messages. A simple forty-cred seat was one thing. The thousand cred price tag for the loge, the champagne delivered by a human attendant, the hors d'oeuvres, not to mention the after party, was another altogether.

Herault had wanted Dunmoore to wear her mess uniform, probably so more people would notice a rear admiral celebrating with Dordogne's wealthiest and most corrupt, but she demurred and donned the evening clothes she'd worn to the casino party. By now, she was convinced meeting Herault on the hiking trail all those months ago had been anything but accidental.

No doubt, the plan had been for Dunmoore to end up in Herault's bed, where he could have compromised her at his leisure. But though she found him pleasant, intelligent, attractive, and an entertaining companion, she'd felt no sexual attraction and had politely fended off every attempt to make their friendship more intimate.

The realization made their time together feel more awkward, but Dunmoore had no choice other than to play the deadly game to its conclusion and not let on she'd figured things out. She wasn't conceited enough to think she could avoid Hanno Berg's unknown fate if Calvert, who had to be the one giving Herault his orders, decided her time was up. Not even with Vincenzo and his cousins from another uncle watching her back. Which meant she had to be ruthless and strike first, making sure she did so decisively.

"Siobhan." Keo entered her office without so much as a hello one weekday morning after the night at the opera and walked over to her desk. "I finished reviewing the patrol schema with Admiral Hogue in light of the latest intelligence digest. You read it?"

"Yes, sir." Dunmoore had seen nothing that would call for shifting ships around, but she didn't protest.

He dropped a data wafer on her desk.

"Here are the changes Admiral Hogue wants. As usual, keep the order dissemination tightly focused and top secret."

"Of course, sir."

Would it be another test, or were the traffickers controlled from Dordogne preparing significant shipments for their suspected hubs on the frontier? Nothing big she knew of had come through since she'd taken up the operations job, so there had to be a massive pent-up demand for the illicit trade further inside the Commonwealth. Not to mention the empty coffers of those financing the ventures.

After Keo left, she ran through the same analysis as before and decided this time they would go solely through the Mission Colony system, where local policing and surveillance were among the weakest in the Rim. Shift the patrol routes of the frigate and corvette assigned there, and a half dozen traffickers could come in and land unobserved. Or, if seen by local traffic control, remain out of reach to local law enforcement for the time it took to offload inbound cargo and take on contraband destined for the Zone. Besides, a half dozen of them, each on a different vector, would overwhelm the pursuit capabilities of the two ships usually on station.

She tapped her communicator.

"Chief, when you have a moment, at your convenience."

The reply came almost at once.

"Right after lunch, Admiral, if that works."

"Sure. See you then. Dunmoore, out."

When he walked in at thirteen hundred hours, Dunmoore signaled he should shut the door and made the hand sign they'd agreed on for classified beyond the heat death of the universe, as Vincenzo had put it.

"What's up, sir?" He asked as he dropped into his accustomed chair and pulled out his jammer, just in case.

"To quote an ancient master of the arcane arts, the game is afoot. This time, it looks like they'll try going through Mission Colony."

Vincenzo grimaced.

"Not a surprise. Every colonial administration controlled by Earth or one of the Home Worlds is corrupt to one degree or another. The people behind the traffickers own enough of Mission Colony's administration to ensure no one notices ships landing in out-of-the-way spots when there are no Navy units around."

"We need to alert the 101st, but so the opposition's people inside 3rd Fleet don't notice, which means I can't communicate with Commodore Pushkin or Commander Yun and let them know since they're probably watching me and everything I do closely."

"I can put in an untraceable call, so that's no problem. But I'm more concerned about the fallout. What will the opposition do to you once they realize we intercepted their latest shipments?"

A shrug.

"Try to kill me, no doubt."

"Then when I call the 101st, I'll see how they might help by extracting you on order should the Pègre put a price on your head. After all, the Marines and dropship pilots aboard Iolanthe are special ops." When she opened her mouth to object, Vincenzo raised his hand. "This is not optional, sir. If I let anything happen to you, Admiral Holt will kill me, and Admiral Kowalski will make sure they never find my remains."

"All right. Understood."

***

Over the following days, Dunmoore felt as if she was being watched night and day, whether by Calvert's people, or other members of the opposition, such as SSB agents or Vincenzo's special operations colleagues, she couldn't say. Nor did she spot anyone paying her more attention than they should. But the die was cast.

Vincenzo had alerted the 101st the same day via means he didn't discuss with her, though neither of them knew what Pushkin would do. Dunmoore hoped he would send several of his Q ships so none of the traffickers could escape and warn their superiors, but she did not know his dispositions. As usual, two-thirds of the 101st's ships were on patrol, while the remaining third, including *Iolanthe*, was in orbit docked to Starbase 30 and undergoing routine maintenance.

Almost two weeks passed before Vincenzo showed up in her office one morning, pulled out his jammer after closing the door, and said, "Four intercepts confirmed. Unfortunately, it turned messy, and the locals saw some of the action in orbit, enough to confirm the traffickers were captured by unknown ships. The commodore's people didn't broadcast a beacon when they went into action or display naval markings, but I doubt we fooled anyone. Or if the people on Mission Colony were, their bosses here won't be. That's if word hasn't already reached them, and they decided it was the 101st's handiwork again. Unfortunately, our friends couldn't pinpoint the trafficker's base on the ground, and it escaped unscathed to report on the action."

A grim smile crossed Dunmoore's face.

"Then the countdown has begun."

"Likely." He nodded. "Which means from now until it's all over, I'm not leaving your side, Admiral. And my cousins, who've prepared a few plans of their own to shake things up, will watch from a distance, ready to eliminate any threats they spot."

"Did Earth send orders relieving Admiral Keo of duty pending investigation?"

"Not yet."

"It would have been too much to hope for anyhow. Firing a three-star needs the Grand Admiral's blessing. But removing Keo might have made Calvert think twice about coming after me." She shrugged. "Oh, well. For now, we go on as before and pretend nothing happened until they make a move, or we hear that they're preparing one."

From that point on, Chief Petty Officer Third Class Vincenzo became her constant shadow from the moment she left Joint Base Dordogne until she was back in the office the following day. He accompanied her everywhere, scanned everything delivered to her house, and lived in one of her guest rooms, though he made himself as unobtrusive as possible.

But neither of them nor the undercover operatives detected so much as a hint of a threat. It was as if the interception in the Mission Colony system never happened, and that, as Dunmoore knew from bitter experience, could merely be because something else was brewing in the shadows.

***

"Good morning, Siobhan." Keo entered Dunmoore's office the way he usually did, without warning or knocking, and dropped into one of the chairs across from her.

She put down the overnight operations log and forced herself to smile.

"Good morning, sir. What can I do for you?"

"It's about that firepower demonstration the 13th Marines and the Dordogne Regiment are putting on at the end of the week."

"What about it, sir?"

"Admiral Hogue would like you to attend in her stead as the 3rd Fleet representative and guest of honor."

Dunmoore's expression didn't change, but she felt a stab of irritation at Hogue sloughing off her duties again. Unfortunately, she'd learned it was a familiar pattern, leaving Keo to run 3rd Fleet as he wished. Keo, in turn, downloaded ceremonial and public affairs duties that didn't interest him to the two chiefs of staff.

"Yes, sir."

"If you take your own vehicle instead of a staff car, you can stay in the area for the weekend. I understand there are excellent hiking trails in the mountains."

"I'll think about it."

Keo jumped to his feet.

"Enjoy the visit. If you've never seen two regiments show the full force of their combined firepower before, it's quite impressive."

"Thank you, sir."

The demonstration wasn't something that would impress an admiral whose battle group had raided the Shrehari home system and destroyed two antimatter refueling constellations. It wouldn't even match the energy unleashed by the might of Task Group Luckner in its first salvo. But attending as the senior naval officer was known as a command performance. She'd make all the right noises, do everything expected of the guest of honor, and chat with the colonels commanding both regiments and their senior officers and command sergeants.

Vincenzo sauntered in a few minutes later for his morning briefing. When the door closed behind him, he asked, "Did the admiral want anything in particular?"

"You and I are heading for Fort Vauban on Friday. I'm the designated guest of honor at the ground forces' annual firepower demonstration."

— Twenty-Seven —

The main gate to Fort Vauban, a vast training area several hundred kilometers north of Marseilles, near the provincial capital of Angers, loomed eerily through the morning mist. Established between the shores of the Western Ocean and an offshoot of the mountain range bisecting Dordogne's main inhabited continent, it encompassed every training environment save arctic and boasted live fire ranges that could accommodate the most powerful ground-based and air support ordnance.

A battalion each from the 13th Marines and the Dordogne Regiment was stationed at Vauban permanently to support individual and collective training for both, including the latter's reserve units. The installation also housed the joint battle school, which offered classes from basic all the way up to command non-commissioned officer and a lengthy list of specialties. It cut down immensely on enlisted ranks traveling to other star systems for career progression courses. Plenty of spacers trained at the battle school on matters that cut across service lines, such as boarding party tactics, explosive ordnance disposal, small arms and battlesuit maintenance, and much more.

Today's events represented the culmination of the annual ground forces maneuvers which brought the 13th Marines and the Dordogne Regiment — reservists included — together for large-scale war games that had swept through the entire military reservation for the last three weeks, supported by starships from the 30th Battle Group.

If the sentries who checked their credentials thought a two-star driving her personal vehicle while a chief petty officer third class sat in the passenger seat was strange, they didn't show it. After a quick sensor scan and a salute, they entered the most extensive training area in the star system and one of the biggest in the entire Rim Sector.

The front end of the base was a small city of its own, with a residential section, a network of classroom buildings and simulators, barracks, offices, armories, vehicle parks, and the headquarters of the Dordogne Division, the administrative formation which oversaw all ground forces elements in the star system. Dunmoore's instructions had been to report to the latter, where she would be met by Marine Corps Brigadier General Dashiel "Dash" Spillman, the general officer commanding.

The gate guards must have passed word that she'd arrived because a nattily uniformed military police sergeant directed her to a VIP parking spot in front of the glass and steel three-story HQ building fronting a huge parade square lined by flagpoles. As she and Vincenzo, clad in Navy battledress uniform with qualification badges, rank insignia, and 3rd Fleet patches, along with blue berets and gun belts, climbed out of her car, Spillman himself came through the front doors. He was similarly dressed except in Marine black with the Dordogne Division's Phrygian cap-wearing rooster patch on his sleeve.

He smiled as they exchanged salutes and then handshakes.

"Welcome to Fort Vauban, Admiral. We're honored to have a war hero like you in our midst today."

In Dunmoore's opinion, Spillman could have posed for a recruiting poster. He was the epitome of the Marine Corps general — stocky, muscular, square-faced, with short, graying hair and deep-set, intelligent dark eyes framing a strong nose. He wore Pathfinder wings on his left breast, and she knew from reading his biography that his war record as a command sergeant and company grade officer had been exemplary.

"It's a pleasure to be here, General. I haven't yet visited your command since taking up my post at 3rd Fleet, and this seems an auspicious occasion." She nodded at Vincenzo. "This is Chief Petty Officer Guido Vincenzo, my branch chief and a shipmate in two of my wartime commands. He was with me during the raid on the Shrehari home system."

They exchanged salutes and shook hands as well.

"Welcome, Chief. My division sergeant major will join us when we begin our inspection tour. He's already waiting at the 13th Marines' tactical command post. My car should come around momentarily."

"What's the program?"

"We'll join the civilian dignitaries at the assembly area and, from there, walk through the lines of the 13th and the Dordogne Regiment as they get ready for the demonstration, which will be in the form of a prepared assault on a dug-in enemy position. Each unit has a little spiel, so it should be informative and entertaining. After the tour, we'll have lunch in the field mess set up at the assembly area for today's event, then move to the nearby observation post and watch as the assault goes in."

"Who are the dignitaries?"

"Top of the list is the Dordogne minister for public safety, representing the president. Then, there's the general commanding the Gendarmerie, the chiefs of police of Marseilles and Angers, as well as the Mayor of Angers. Another dozen senior officials round up the government list. We also invited two dozen prominent businesspeople whose enterprises employ many Dordogne Regiment reservists and veterans of all services."

A boxy, wheeled combat car configured as a mobile command post bearing the call sign 99 in black on its mottled flanks came around the corner, and Spillman said, "There's our ride."

They reached the assembly area, several kilometers from the main base, after a short, smooth trip in the combat car, an older model no longer in use by front-line Marine units. There, they parked beside the bus that had transported the dignitaries from the visitor parking by the main gate. The latter were inside the mess tent, enjoying a cup of coffee, and when Dunmoore, Spillman, and Vincenzo alit, she scanned the faces, recognizing many of them from various social occasions, including Calvert, Lassieux, and Victor Herault.

Dunmoore exchanged a wry glance with Vincenzo as if to say, hurrah, the gangsters are all here. She and Spillman made the rounds, greeting everyone individually, beginning with the dour minister for public safety and ending with Herault, who'd maneuvered himself into the last position.

But if he hoped for a few words with Dunmoore in private, he was quickly disabused of the notion when Spillman asked for everyone's attention, then gave them a brief rundown of the day's events. When that was done, one of his staff officers divided the visitors into groups of ten, each with their guide from Dordogne Division HQ, who led them off to begin the tour.

Mercifully, they'd organized the businesspeople into their own groups since they'd spend more time with the Dordogne Regiment reservists, leaving Dunmoore and Vincenzo with Spillman, the minister, and the top police chiefs.

The various groups returned to the mess tent at different times, so they ate together, which suited Dunmoore. The last thing she wanted in this setting was to socialize with people who might be plotting her demise after she cost them a fortune for the second time. But she noticed them glancing at her often as they enjoyed a hearty if simple, field kitchen meal.

When they emerged from the mess tent and were led up to the observation post, what had been a partly sunny day was quickly becoming dark under menacing clouds blown in from the ocean.

"Did you order that sky to create some extra atmosphere, Dash?" She asked Spillman in a murmured aside as they climbed the hill, which sat on the assault's line of departure, between the two corridors that would be employed by the regiments shortly.

"No. Though I wish we could control the weather some days just to give trainees added misery."

When they reached the field chairs — every visitor got a front-row seat — Dunmoore studied the flat, open terrain in front of them and understood Spillman would not feed the entirety of both units through. There just wasn't enough room.

Nor would it be a realistic assault since the distance between the line of departure and the objective wasn't nearly enough to deploy several battalions in good order. As the civilians took their assigned places, she stayed behind with Spillman.

"I'm not sure a tactical solution that crams two regiments into such a small space would please the directing staff at the War College. How much of each unit will do the battle run?"

He gave her a conspiratorial grin.

"About half. This is to impress the spectators and give the most deserving troops in both regiments a chance to fire off more live ammo in a single go than they do all year long. It also shows the newest recruits, who graduate from their basic infantry course here, today, what a regiment, Marine or Army, can put downrange. The various logistics echelons and combat units not taking part are already back on base, cleaning up and preparing to receive the rest once this is over."

A loud voice welcomed the distinguished guests and announced it would explain the action they were about to witness as the sound of armored vehicles moving through the low scrub on either side reached their ears.

Dunmoore's fine hearing picked up the sound of several ground attack squadrons flying nap of the earth well to their rear. Each regiment had its own organic aviation battalion, which could deliver a mighty thump on any target. Then, the first railgun artillery salvo fell on the notional enemy positions, sending column after column of soil, sand, stone, and vegetation high into the air. Within seconds, the near horizon seemed choked by a wall of flame-lit debris that reminded Dunmoore of nothing so much as the legendary entrance to hell. The civilians variously oohed and aahed as they chattered among themselves when the invisible narrator paused his patter.

Then, four task groups of attack ships popped up less than a hundred meters over them and opened fire with their thirty-millimeter calliopes to the sound of rending cloth. A line of smaller flame-propelled dirt geysers erupted in the target zone, adding to the damage caused by the artillery. One burst and the aircraft peeled off to each side, noses aimed almost straight up as they increased thrust to maximum.

And that was the signal for the ground advance. Heavy armored vehicles crested the low slopes on either side of the observation posts, followed by lighter infantry carriers, and opened fire in controlled salvos at notional targets that might have survived the artillery and aviation pasting.

The air was filled with the crack of heavy direct-fire rail and plasma guns of all calibers. It all seemed fantastic under the glowering sky. The spectators had fallen utterly silent, enthralled by the sheer destructive power of what wasn't even an entire regiment when all was said and done, let alone two.

Even Dunmoore, who'd used nuclear-tipped missiles in massive volleys to destroy starships and orbital stations and dropped kinetic penetrator rods on ground targets, was enthralled by the leapfrogging advance of the continuously firing armored troops while artillery kept raining down. If any civilian spectators had visions of the apocalypse, she wouldn't blame them.

And then the last artillery round exploded, the last volley from the armored vehicles struck the target zone, and even though dust and debris still hung in the air, a sudden and unexpected silence fell over the live fire range as everything came to a halt. The spectators seemed frozen in their chairs, neither moving nor speaking until the narrator broke the spell.

"And that, dear guests, concludes the firepower demonstration. The enemy positions have been thoroughly destroyed by the sheer power of two Commonwealth Armed Forces regiments. Woe to any who would dare attack us. Thank you, and please enjoy the rest of your day."

Dunmoore looked at Spillman with a wry smile.

"That was quite an experience. Warships firing volley after volley of missiles at each other make bigger explosions, but no one can hear the bangs in space. It's just soundless flashes at long distances and not real unless you let yourself think of the sentient lives at the other end. I think your civilian guests will be just a little knocked about by today's experience, though. I know I can feel it."

"Which is why we're headed for the officers' mess and a round of drinks."

At that moment, several lightning bolts tore through the western sky and a rolling rumble of thunder, not unlike an artillery barrage, followed several seconds later.

"In the nick of time too," Spillman added. "This will be a big one."

— Twenty-Eight —

Dunmoore accepted a glass of white wine from the officers' mess bartender and turned to see Calvert, Lassieux, and Herault, all three smiling, as they entered and headed for her.

"That was quite something," the latter said with a tinge of awe. "I did not know our ground forces could wreak so much destruction."

"And that's just a tiny fraction of what a frigate can put out," Dunmoore replied. "But it was still an impressive show."

They ordered their drinks. Then Calvert turned to her. "We're staying at my hunting lodge in the mountains over the weekend, Siobhan. Join us. It's only a short drive from National Highway One south of Angers, at the bottom of a most spectacular valley. You can even bring your security man."

"Yes, please do come," Lassieux added. "The lodge is a perfect place to escape everything, and the alpine vista is spectacular."

Dunmoore glanced at Herault, who gave her a smile.

"Antoine's chef is there, and he's one of the top cordon bleus in the star system."

If Vincenzo had been around, she'd have looked for his reaction. But he was being treated to a drink by the Dordogne

Division's sergeant major in the senior non-commissioned officers' mess next door, so she would have to rely on her instincts. And they screamed, not a chance. That all three were at Fort Vauban for an event where she was replacing Keo at the latter's orders simply seemed too pat.

And a hunting lodge in the mountains, far from civilization? No. It wouldn't do.

"Sorry. As much as I'd enjoy a weekend away, I have commitments tomorrow and must head home once we're done here."

Calvert put on an air of disappointment.

"A shame. We haven't socialized in a congenial spot for ages, it seems. Perhaps another time."

"Certainly." She gave them a rueful smile. "I'm sure there will be plenty of other occasions."

"Without a doubt," Calvert replied, though Dunmoore thought she detected a note of insincerity in his voice.

They engaged in small talk about the firepower demonstration and upcoming social events in Marseilles while sipping their drinks until Dunmoore emptied her glass and placed it on the nearest flat surface. The rest of the guests were in small clusters, Spillman with the minister and the police chiefs.

"If you'll excuse me, I must exchange a few words with my Gendarmerie colleague." She turned to Herault. "A shame about this weekend, but how about we plan a pleasant hike for the one after?"

"Absolutely, my dear."

"Then please have a safe trip to the lodge and a relaxing stay, my friends."

"And you have an equally safe return to Marseilles," Herault said.

Dunmoore turned on her heels and walked away, feeling their eyes burning through her back. She didn't really have anything to discuss with the star system's chief of police but felt an urgent need to get away from what felt like increasingly predatory looks from Calvert and Lassieux. Was it her imagination, or did Herault's last look at her seem a tad wistful?

Not long after, Spillman's staff ushered the guests back aboard the busses, which would take them to the visitors' parking lot by the main gate. Dunmoore spent a few more minutes chatting with Spillman, then said, "It's time Chief Vincenzo and I headed back as well."

"Then let me make sure both of you return to your car without getting soaked. It's coming down like Noah's flood out there."

"Very kind of you."

But when they reached the lobby serving all three messes and the dining hall, Dunmoore could see Vincenzo leaning against her car, both waiting beneath the broad overhang sheltering the main doors and an arc of the circular driveway from the rain. As Spillman said, it was pouring, and although the sunset was still at least two hours away, premature dusk had settled. The main base's streetlights and the interior lights in most buildings around the central mess structure were on, giving Vauban a gloomy appearance.

She shook hands with Spillman, exchanged salutes, and climbed into the driver's seat while Vincenzo took the passenger side.

"Anything interesting come up in the mess?" He asked as they pulled away.

"Oh, yes. Calvert invited both of us to his hunting lodge in the mountains southeast of here."

Vincenzo nodded.

"I know about it from my investigation of his background. Calling it a lodge might be an understatement. Like calling *Iolanthe* a mere bulk freighter. But it is very isolated, at the bottom of a narrow valley, with only one road in and no neighbors for fifty kilometers in any direction."

"In other words, it would make a perfect trap."

"That, and a perfect place to hide a private army with its gear. There's a landing strip capable of taking anything up to something the size of a corvette a kilometer beyond the lodge and hangars or warehouses cut out of the mountainside bordering it. No one I know of has so far infiltrated the place, nor have the Dordogne authorities taken aerial and orbital surveys to see what Calvert is hiding."

"How about the Navy?"

"Neither, but that'll change once orders come from Fleet HQ."

They passed through the main gate and soon found themselves on National Highway One. It ran the entire length of the continent, from the northern steppes to the very tip of the southern point, where both oceans met in a clash of furies that would make even the boldest pre-spaceflight mariner blanch.

"I suppose my instinct called it, then." She said after engaging the autopilot and settling back as the car gained speed, slicing through the dense rain and growing darkness.

"That would be my assessment, Admiral. I'm quite sure Keo sending you in his stead and those three showing up as guests from the Dordogne business community and inviting you to Calvert's lodge was no coincidence. You might well have met an accident hiking a steep mountain trail tomorrow. An unfortunate fall that broke your neck and killed you instantly."

"And you?" She glanced at Vincenzo's somber features.

"It could have gone in many ways. I might have tumbled down the mountain with you and died. Or they might have left me alive to report your accidental death." He shrugged. "We'll likely never know."

Neither spoke for a few moments, then she asked, "If that was the plan, do you figure they've made alternate arrangements to see I don't survive the weekend, or are they going to wait for another occasion?"

"Good question. As always, we should be prepared for anything."

He stared out the polarized window at the wet ribbon of road stretching out in front of them for countless kilometers. Like all cars on the planet, Dunmoore's ran without lights on highways, relying on the artificial intelligence and its night vision capabilities to see even through the worst weather in the dead of night. That same AI system, using commercial grade look ahead sensors, could also see other cars on the road and project their position on the driver console's primary display along with intersections, landmarks, and other roadside features.

"There's the turnoff for the village of Beny and beyond it, the road to Calvert's lodge." Vincenzo pointed at the display.

"Maybe from here on, we should watch our six as well, just in case. The AI wouldn't recognize a tail if it saw one."

"How about you do that while I keep my eyes to the front?" She touched the controls, and a second display lit up, showing the intersection receding in the distance.

A few minutes passed, then Vincenzo swallowed a muffled curse.

"I knew it. Two aircars flying nap of the earth just popped up, one on each side of the road, skimming the treetops. No honest travelers would do that, and certainly not two of them keeping formation. They're at maximum visual range, drifting in and out of sight. The sensor wouldn't have alerted us since they're not close enough to present a threat under normal traffic circumstances."

Vincenzo studied the display intently for over a minute, focusing on one dark shape, then the other.

"I couldn't swear to it, but I figure those things are armed. Nothing big, but something that can bring us to a screeching halt."

"What do you think their plan is?"

He thought for a few seconds.

"Depends. If they want to take you alive so you can die falling off a mountain trail, they'll wait until we hit a narrow stretch of road and box us in. From there, it won't take long to make us stop. If they don't care about leaving a trail of debris on the road along with two dead bodies, they'll have chosen a kill zone somewhere in the most isolated stretch of the highway south of here. The Passage du Clos, that long canyon-like cut we came through on our way up, seems a suitable spot. Either way, they count on our inability to call for help."

Dunmoore pulled out her communicator and checked its status.

"And once again, you called it, Chief. We're being jammed."

"Not everything." Vincenzo produced the surface-to-orbit radio. "This works on naval frequencies they can't block. And I think it's time we called in the cavalry."

***

"Iolanthe, this is Luckner. We are being pursued by two aircars presumed hostile and probably armed. They will either try to immobilize and capture or destroy us. Request immediate extraction. Can you read our beacon, over?"

The CIC officer of the watch roused himself from the study of his upcoming promotion exams and turned to the signals petty officer.

"Who the hell is Luckner? And why are they transmitting over the classified emergency channel?"

"Let me see, sir." He called up the list of action codes, to be opened only when transmitted, and studied his display. "Crap. That's an action immediate, sir. Luckner is code for Admiral Dunmoore. Call the commodore and the captain. Sensors, lock on their signal."

Moments after the officer of the watch had done so, Captain Trevane Devall entered the CIC via the conference room door, which connected with his day cabin.

"Do we have a lock on Luckner's signal?" He asked without preamble.

"Wait one." The OOW consulted the sensor feed and nodded. "We do, sir."

"Signals, let them know we're locked in, and the countdown to extraction has been initiated."

Pushkin stormed through the main door before Devall could alert the standby shuttle crews, with Guthren hard on his heels.

"Get the Luckner rescue flight out the door ASAP, Trevane. I'll take care of traffic control and anyone else who squawks at a starship launching shuttles without permission while docked at the starbase. And we'll just ignore Dordogne Traffic Control entirely."

Devall grinned at the fierce expression on Pushkin's face.

"That's the way we like it in the 101st. Alerting the ready crews now."

"Good. Where is she, and what's the situation?"

"One moment, please, Commodore," the duty sensor tech said. "We're not over the target area at the moment. I'll have to pull the data through the orbitals."

A map of the area south of Fort Vauban eventually appeared on the primary display, showing National Highway One and a blue dot moving steadily southward. Before Pushkin could ask, two red dots appeared almost on top of it.

"I presume those are the tangos?"

"They're the only vehicles within range of Admiral Dunmoore's beacon, sir. Aircars. They're moving at approximately one-hundred-and-ninety kilometers an hour through heavy rain."

Pushkin turned to Devall.

"How long before the flight gets there?"

Devall grimaced. "At emergency descent velocity, just under thirty-five minutes from the moment they clear our space doors. And we'll hear traffic control howl at the breach of every flight regulation covering atmospheric insertion."

"As I said, I'll deal with traffic control."

"Sir." The OOW raised his hand. "Space doors opening."

Pushkin grinned at Devall.

"Nice and fast, Trevane. Well done."

"I've had them at three minutes' notice to move since Vincenzo warned us they were leaving Marseilles this morning."

The OOW pointed to a side display showing an armed transport shuttle flanked by four more heavily armed dropships emerging from Iolanthe's starboard hangar and pointing their noses straight toward Dordogne's surface in a synchronized maneuver.

No sooner had they fired thrusters to begin an almost vertical dive into the atmosphere that the signals PO raised his hand.

"Starbase 30 traffic control are calling and want to know what we're doing in the name of all things unholy."

Pushkin took a vacant workstation and said, "Patch them to me."

Moments later, the agitated face of a lieutenant commander appeared on the workstation's display.

"I'm Commodore Gregor Pushkin, Commander. We are dealing with an operational immediate emergency on the ground. That's what in the name of all things unholy we're doing. I ordered the launch, and no, I cannot discuss the nature of the emergency over an open channel. You may expect the shuttles to return like they left in ninety minutes or less, and they will not respond to your hails."

"With all due respect, sir, your actions are not only in violation of several regulations but are highly irregular. There are no operational immediate emergencies on a world like Dordogne. Otherwise, we would have heard of it."

Pushkin gave the younger man a stiff smile.

"You know what the 101st Battle Group does for a living, right? We do things you'll never hear of on orders you'll never see. And this is a no-duff if there ever was one. Please feel free to inform Admiral Anand of our conversation and tell him I'll be glad to repeat what I just said should he call me. Pushkin, out."

Behind him, Guthren chuckled with undisguised amusement.

"You sounded a lot like Admiral Dunmoore back in the day when she did things against the wishes of senior officers."

A wry smile tugged at Pushkin's lips.

"I learned from the best of the best, Chief."

"Commodore, incoming call from Rear Admiral Anand for you. He's on the link and doesn't sound happy."

Pushkin stood.

"I'll take it in the conference room. There's no need for the duty watch to see this."

Alone, he settled in front of the primary display and said, "Feed it in, PO."

"Coming."

Moments later, the display lit up with Anand's normally saturnine face. Except at the moment, it looked as if he were about to pass a painful kidney stone.

"What can I do for you, Admiral?"

"You can tell me what you think you're doing, Gregor. An operational immediate emergency on Dordogne? Who ever heard of such nonsense? I'm about to have the head of Dordogne Traffic Control yell at me for not being in control of naval traffic and endangering civilians through reckless disregard of regulations. I'd like to know why. Especially since his minister will call Admiral Hogue."

"I'm sorry, sir. But until we conclude this mission, it stays SOCOM top secret. I may not discuss what's happening with anyone, not even Admiral Hogue."

An air of anger briefly crossed Anand's face.

"You special ops people go too far. Dunmoore and you — two peas in a pod, both equally disagreeable, secretive, and arrogant."

"I consider that a compliment, sir. Now, was there something else? I should oversee the operation personally to ensure nothing happens that might hit the newsnets, let alone land on the desks of Dordogne government officials. Once it's over, you may well get an explanation. It'll be top secret, of course, but at least you might understand why I acted as I did."

"Just don't break anything."

"That's my goal, sir. And I'd consider it a personal favor if you didn't report this to the 3rd Fleet operations center until I've recovered my shuttles. I assure you Admiral Dunmoore is fully aware of what's happening."

"Now there's a surprise. I suppose asking you to retrieve your shuttles under traffic control direction so we can placate the Dordognais is a waste of breath."

"It would be best if there are no official records of their mission, sir. Once I've recovered them, the entire incident never happened."

"That's what I thought. I'll let Admiral Dunmoore deal with the Dordogne Traffic Control people. Please tell her that. Anand, out."

— Twenty-Nine —

"The cavalry has launched, sir," Vincenzo announced as Dunmoore took control from the AI so she could weave and dodge around whatever their pursuers were planning until their rescuers arrived, and to hell with the rules of the road. Her car could manage some impressive off-road moves should that become necessary. "ETA thirty-five minutes."

"Composition?"

"One armed transport shuttle and four dropships."

"Okay. We can work with that. Two dropships per aircar. Let's just hope the shuttle pilot has a delicate touch and nerves of steel."

Vincenzo turned his head to look at her. He knew that tone from way back.

"Why, sir?"

Dunmoore gave him a sideways smile.

"Ever done a pickup on the move?"

"I'm not even sure what that is."

"It's when you're trying to land a shuttle aboard a starship booting it out to the hyperlimit at maximum acceleration."

"You have?"

"Part of a carrier pilot's training. Mind you, it's been a long, long time since my last successful attempt. I was but a callow ensign then."

"And this relates to our situation how, sir?" Vincenzo asked, part of him dreading the answer.

"We're going one-ninety on an antigrav cushion down a straight road. The shuttle from *Iolanthe* can fly at the same speed ahead of us. And we're running out of room, especially if your concerns about a potential kill zone in the Passage du Clos south of Colmar are right. Who knows what else is waiting there for us with dampened emissions so they can't be spotted until it's too late? What do you think?"

"We'll reach that stretch of road before help shows up if we keep going like this."

"Right, which is why I'm dropping speed as unobtrusively as I can. And?"

"We can't piss about stopping for an orderly shuttle loading process." Vincenzo stared at her again. "Which means a pickup on the move."

Dunmoore gave him a serene smile.

"I hope I can still remember how to goose the car's drive just enough to make it up the ramp without going too fast and slamming into the bulkhead. A carrier had force field arrestor nets. *Iolanthe*'s cargo shuttles? Not even a tractor-repulsor beam like most hangar decks."

"At a hundred and ninety kays? I'm sorry I asked, Admiral."

"Don't worry, Chief. We'll make it happen, but I need a direct link with the shuttle pilot over your jamming-proof radio."

"Hang on, sir." Vincenzo called *Iolanthe* again and passed on Dunmoore's request.

Shortly after that, a woman's voice came through the speaker.

"This is Sea Eagle One, the big box leading Sea Eagle Flight. You called, over?"

Dunmoore and Vincenzo exchanged a brief grin, remembering a rescue long ago.

"This is Luckner Actual, at the controls of the ground call sign you're tracking. We have two tangos trailing us and more possible tangos waiting near where the road enters a sort of canyon south of Colmar called the Passage du Clos, a stretch I consider a potential ambush zone, over."

"We're tracking your tail, Luckner Actual. I have designated them as targets for my escort. And we're marking the Passage du Clos as an area of concern."

"What I'm contemplating is a hot pickup. The road is clear and straight up to and through the passage, and the weather conditions will make civilian observation from any distance almost impossible. I'm currently settling at one-hundred-and-eighty kilometers per hour. My car is antigrav, and I have experience with carrier hot pickups, though it dates to well before the war. Are you game?"

The pilot chuckled with delight.

"I haven't piloted a hot pickup in years myself, but it's something you don't forget. I'll drop to the deck, match your speed, and keep my ramp's trailing edge zero point three meters above the roadbed. Then it's up to you."

Dunmoore could hear a please don't scratch my bird plea in the pilot's voice, but she sounded ready.

"All right. We have a plan. Contact me over these means when preparing to slide in and match velocities. I'm only operating on night vision sensors, but I'll see you fine. Best if you show no running lights and keep the aft compartment dark."

"Roger that, Luckner. It's what I prefer. We're not supposed to be here carrying out this mission and are flying without beacons. If we can make you vanish with no one noticing, so much the better."

"I will turn off my car's locater once we're within visual."

"Good idea."

"We'll see each other soon, then. Luckner Actual, out." Dunmoore sat back. "And now, all we need to do is hope there will be no oncoming traffic at the wrong moment. Although even the dumbest ground car AI with basic sensors will spot a shuttle in the middle of the road from several kilometers away and take evasive action."

"Or there are tangos ready to block northbound traffic from entering the canyon, and Sea Eagle One reaches us a few klicks before we get there." He glanced at the forward display. "Speaking of oncoming traffic. Looks like a road train, which is fully automated around here. Let's hope we don't meet one of those during the recovery, especially not inside the Passage du Clos. No driver to chicken out and move aside well ahead of time, and not much room to maneuver either. It could get ugly."

The following minutes passed in silence while Dunmoore mentally reviewed the pickup process over and over, playing it out in her mind, adjusting the sequence of her actions to the car's capabilities, imagining how it would go down, and what might happen if an oncoming vehicle appeared, or the tangos did something stupid like attempt to block the shuttle or open fire.

Then, "Luckner Actual, this is Sea Eagle One. We are a thousand meters up and behind your location. Escorts are dialed in on the tangos, and we've spotted two more vehicles of the same type on the south end of Passage du Clos lying doggo with dampened emissions. I've marked them as targets as well. What are your rules of engagement, over?"

"Keep a target lock at all times. If they power weapons or make moves showing they'll try to interfere with the recovery, neutralize. If they open fire, destroy. Otherwise, remain weapons-tight. If there is oncoming traffic, be ready to abort."

"Acknowledged." A pause. "All units have acknowledged. The closest oncoming traffic is fifty kilometers to your south, just beyond the Passage du Clos. Figure seven minutes away. We are on final approach. Keep your eyes peeled."

"Seven minutes?" Vincenzo gave her a skeptical gaze. "Is that enough?"

"Plenty. Make sure your seat restraints are tight."

"Luckner Actual, this is Sea Eagle One. The tangos south of the passage have moved to close off the road. Look for us passing above you at two-zero meters altitude in ten seconds."

"Luckner, acknowledged. Nice of the tangos to clear our runway."

A faint rumble cut across the sound of Dunmoore's car slicing through the wind and rain, and both looked up through the windshield as a black mass passed over them, then glided downward until it was just above the road surface approximately forty meters ahead. They saw the aft ramp come down slowly, exposing an empty compartment whose insides were visible only thanks to their night vision sensors.

"Luckner, this is Sea Eagle One. I'm ready to receive."

"Ack. Stand by."

Dunmoore took complete control away from the AI and gently increased the car's speed by tiny increments until they started closing the distance to the ramp's trailing edge.

"Passage du Clos entrance approaching," Vincenzo announced. "We have little room left before we're hemmed in."

"Noted." Her concentration was entirely on the forward display, where a telemetry grid now gave her relative velocities, altitudes, and the remaining distance.

Suddenly, the night lit up behind them, and two plasma rounds streaked over the car and the shuttle.

"Crap." A startled Vincenzo swore. "What are they doing?"

"Warning shot, most likely," Dunmoore replied absently. "A bit of a miscalculation on their part."

More lights flared behind them but without plasma flying by.

"This is Sea Eagle Three. Two tangos destroyed."

"Sea Eagle call signs, take out the remaining tangos," Dunmoore ordered as the car came within a few meters of the ramp, then added in a lower tone, "No more screwing around."

Then, the front of the car lifted slightly as the forward repulsors reached the ramp, and they crept up at a slight angle, still slowly, bit by bit in relation to the shuttle, even though both it and the car were moving at a hundred and eighty kilometers an hour.

"Sea Eagle One, this is Luckner. I'm on the ramp and now under your control. Entering the compartment."

"Thank the Almighty."

Within seconds, Dunmoore, who was still inching the car forward, and Vincenzo felt the shuttle rise into the air at a low angle. Once she judged her aft end had cleared the ramp, Dunmoore cut the drives and settled the car on the deck. Without her prompting, the ramp rose and locked into place, sealing the shuttle for the return to orbit.

Dunmoore released the controls and slumped back, feeling drained. She glanced at Vincenzo, whose tight features were just beginning to loosen as he processed the fact they were safely aboard.

"That wasn't so hard," she said, grinning. "Not that I want to do it again anytime soon, mind you." She flicked on the radio. "Sea Eagle One, this is Luckner Actual. Slick flying, my friend. We didn't feel a single bump."

"Neither did we," the pilot replied, relief evident in her voice. "Good driving."

"As you said, some things we flyers don't forget."

"Our orders were to take you back to *Iolanthe*. But we can land at Joint Base Dordogne and drop you and your car off."

Dunmoore thought about the options for a moment, then shook her head, even though the pilot couldn't see.

"No. Let's visit *Iolanthe*. Captain Devall can boast about having my car aboard his ship the next time he runs out of war stories in the wardroom."

"Acknowledged. Enjoy the ride. I suggest you stay strapped into your car seats until we land."

"Thanks."

Dunmoore glanced at Vincenzo again. "You won't find many of our old shipmates from the war aboard, but she's still the

Furious Faerie we remember riding into battle. Spending the night in familiar surroundings will give us time to breathe and relax."

***

Devall handed Dunmoore a cup of coffee while Pushkin, Guthren, and Vincenzo served themselves from the eternally full urn in the captain's day cabin, then sat behind his desk while the others settled into the remaining chairs.

"Welcome back, Admiral." Devall raised his own mug. "Sorry I didn't arrange a side party, but there's no protocol for a flag officer arriving aboard an orbiting starship in her personal ground car."

She smiled at the younger officer.

"That's all right, Trevane. Chief Vincenzo and I are not actually here anyway."

The car now sat on *Iolanthe*'s hangar deck beside the shuttle, waiting for Dunmoore's decision on the next steps. An image of the unusual sight was undoubtedly already prepared for the ship's virtual scrapbook, a document that, despite its name, was classified as top secret.

"So, what's the plan?" Pushkin asked. "Considering I've put *Iolanthe*, if not the entire 101st, on Starbase 30 traffic control's shit list and got Quintin Anand furious at me for messing with his perfect record keeping the Dordogne civilian traffic control people happy. Not to mention that sometime in the next day or two, the Gendarmerie and Dordogne Traffic Control will connect four destroyed aircars belonging to one of Antoine

Calvert's gangs with an unauthorized operation involving five armed spacecraft launched from my flagship. Not that I mind, but as you'll recall, SOCOM doesn't like covert operations generating public interest."

Dunmoore shrugged and took a sip of coffee. "I'm the 3rd Fleet chief of operations. Questions will perforce come to me, and I can obfuscate with the best of them. How about I call Quintin and let him know any guff from the local authorities should be redirected to me?"

Pushkin nodded.

"That would be a good idea. It might even stop him from complaining to Keo or Hogue, which I doubt will be helpful right now. Trevane, ask your signals chief to see if he can route the link so it doesn't come directly from *Iolanthe*."

"Will do, sir." Devall stood and passed through the door connecting his day cabin with the bridge.

"Okay. That takes care of the immediate. What comes next?" Pushkin asked Dunmoore.

"Next, Trevane's signals chief will send a subspace message from me to Kathryn Kowalski and Ezekiel Holt detailing what happened as soon as I finish writing and encrypting it. I'm a wee bit at their mercy with wrapping this up. We know Keo's dirty, and today confirmed it. We know who of the suspected Dordogne OCG chiefs are involved and what's been going on. But since there are no doubt serious political ramifications — for example, Calvert mentioned he's a good friend of Sara Lauzier and no doubt one of her financiers — along with SSB involvement, I can't go off and do what I want without a script."

"Too bad. Now would be a perfect time to pounce."

"Sure. But my showing up at work on Monday morning as if nothing happened will spook the lot of them. They don't know what happened, nor will their goons have reported my boarding a shuttle before Sea Eagle Flight wiped them out. As far as everyone on the planet is concerned, I've simply vanished."

Pushkin made a face.

"If you want to uphold that illusion, then you can't speak with Quintin until you resurface. Don't worry. I can weather his or anyone else's opprobrium over the weekend by simply not answering any calls, something a one-time mentor taught me."

She snorted, smiling.

"I wonder who that was."

Trevane reappeared, saying, "We can do it, sir."

"And I've changed my mind on that. I will, however, need your help getting an operational urgent subspace message to Earth as soon as I write and encrypt it. No one on this end can know it comes from me."

"Sure." Devall dropped back into his chair.

"And if you don't mind, Chief Vincenzo and I will stay aboard until Sunday evening, away from prying eyes. Then, after, say, twenty-two hundred hours, your shuttle can fly us, in our car, back to Joint Base Dordogne, this time respecting all the traffic control regulations."

"Can do, sir."

— Thirty —

"Good morning, Admiral."

Gregor Pushkin, alone in *Iolanthe*'s wardroom now that the ship's officers had finished breakfast and were at their stations or in their racks, raised his coffee mug emblazoned with the Furious Faerie. He was sitting at the table beneath the ship's infamous crest, where he, Devall, and Dunmoore used to share meals during her time as flag officer commanding the 101st.

"Morning, Gregor." Dunmoore, after a fitful night in the VIP guest suite, headed straight for the coffee urn, then made herself a breakfast sandwich with what remained on the buffet table. "Anything new?"

Pushkin shook his head.

"No. Trevane's people have been monitoring every known official frequency, and there's no ruckus about last night's events or even the mention of Sea Eagle Flight. If the locals complained, it went no further than Quintin, so we might owe him one."

"I'll speak with Quintin on Monday, and we'll see. Should he have deflected them, I'll make sure he knows I'm grateful."

"It gets better. We scanned the extraction site during our last orbit, and the debris of the four aircars vanished. Someone cleaned up during the night, probably your friend Calvert's people. I suppose leaving wreckage would have roused the Gendarmerie's interest, and stuff like that is harder to suppress, even if you own the nearest station's senior leadership."

Dunmoore bit into her sandwich and chewed slowly, lost in thought. She chased the bite down with a healthy mouthful of coffee.

"Good. The less said, the better when cleaning day comes. There's no profit in making a public spectacle."

"Will it come, though?"

She nodded.

"One way or the other. You might recall how upset our friends on Earth got last time the bad guys tried offing me and put you on life support instead. They didn't get the culprits back then. This time, however? The bastards are ripe for the picking. Besides, Zeke knew something was rotten in 3rd Fleet before my appointment down there, hence me taking over when Hanno Berg unexpectedly resigned from the Navy. It means they're ready to act when I send them sufficient evidence."

"They're ready to act?" Pushkin cocked an amused eyebrow at her. "Or do you mean they're ready to let you act when they have sufficient evidence to convince the CNO?"

She shrugged.

"The latter. Me, Vince, and his undercover colleagues, who are doing the Almighty knows what right now."

"Whatever Vince told them to do last night after we finished plotting."

"Oh, good." Dunmoore took another bite. After swallowing, she said, "I get the feeling things might happen over the weekend that won't make Calvert and company happy. Not after the undercover operatives sent by Zeke with orders to keep me alive heard of the abduction attempt."

"I could always send our embarked Pathfinders to seize the lodge where you and Vince would have died in an accident. They haven't carried out an actual operation in several months and are ready for some action against bona fide bad guys."

A wry smile lit up her face.

"I'll keep the option in mind, Gregor, although I can't see our friends on Earth, let alone SOCOM authorizing it."

"No one's talking about an authorized action."

"We're not talking about any action at all. Let's see what develops." She finished her sandwich and washed it down with the last of the coffee. "I've been thinking about my return to the surface."

"Oh?"

"One of *Iolanthe*'s shuttles, marked or not, landing at the Joint Base Dordogne spaceport after dark under traffic control regulations and disgorging my car where the duty watch can see isn't optimum if I want to keep the mystique around my disappearance alive until Keo sees me in my office Monday morning."

Pushkin nodded. "Agreed."

"A training flight registered with all due consideration for the regs and tracked by Starbase 30 traffic control until it enters the atmosphere, then cooperating with Dordogne Traffic Control throughout its evolution. Find a registered but unused landing pad within a two-hour drive from Marseilles and drop us off there. Vince and I will make our way to my house without being seen by too many people."

"Unless the opposition is watching your house. Got a better place to stay Sunday night, Admiral?"

"Let me check with Vince."

"Or you could land on the base tarmac at oh-seven-thirty Monday morning and go straight to work. You'll be seen, but there won't be time for the opposition to react before you reach your desk."

She tilted her head to one side in thought.

"Intriguing idea. Just one problem, I haven't brought my normal working uniform with me. Showing up in battledress will not only seem strange but potentially give the game away."

Pushkin looked up at the deckhead with a sigh.

"How soon they forget. We'll fabricate uniforms to your and Vince's specifications by the end of the day tomorrow. You'll appear at 3rd Fleet HQ looking like you usually do."

***

"I'd love to be a listening device on the apron control deck as the duty watch sees us emerge from the hind end of an unmarked shuttle in a civilian vehicle."

Vincenzo grinned at Dunmoore as she drove her car down the ramp and turned toward the spaceport's perimeter gate.

"Especially since no one, except perhaps Keo, knew we were missing since Friday."

Both wore everyday Navy garrison tunic and trousers, the 3rd Fleet HQ dress of the day, courtesy of *Iolanthe*'s fabricator, their battledress uniforms in bags on the back seat, and they looked as if they'd just come from Dunmoore's off-base residence.

Neither had been privy to the conversation between the shuttle's pilot and ground control about the who, what, where, and why of Rear Admiral Dunmoore and her branch chief arriving via airlift, but she was sure many puzzled eyes were watching them. Someone was perhaps even making calls to let certain people know the chief of staff for operations had arrived in a most unorthodox manner.

When they entered Dunmoore's outer office, Anna Ramius smiled.

"Good morning, Admiral. Chief. I trust you enjoyed last Friday's firepower demonstration and had a quiet weekend?"

"The demo was quite enthralling. A shame you couldn't come with us. And how was your weekend?"

"Same old, sir. The log is waiting in your queue. No important messages, but you got an encrypted personal from Fleet HQ early this morning."

Dunmoore briefly examined Ramius' face for signs of dissimulation or deceit but saw nothing more than her usual pleasant disposition.

"Coffee, sir?" She asked.

"Please."

Moments after Dunmoore took her seat behind the desk and before Ramius returned with her coffee, a visibly irate Keo marched in.

"Where were you this weekend, Siobhan?"

"Staying with friends out of town, sir. Why are you asking?"

"I tried contacting you. Apparently, there was some kerfuffle with the 101st conducting an unannounced training exercise Friday evening Marseilles time that upset naval and civilian traffic control."

Dunmoore's eyebrows shot up.

"Really? I haven't had time to read the weekend log yet, sir. But if there was a problem, I'll sort it."

"Try to remain in contact at all times."

With that, he turned and left her staring at his receding back. Did Keo sound more than just miffed? Was he aware that Calvert's attempt failed and four of the mob boss' aircars were shot down by 101st Battle Group gunships?

But the overnight logs from Friday to Saturday showed nothing more than a mild complaint from Dordogne Traffic Control about shuttles launched into the atmosphere from a ship docked at Starbase 30 and carrying out an unapproved and uncontrolled flight plan. The senior duty officer noted the incident and referred it back to Starbase 30 traffic control, whose officer of the watch confirmed the shuttles came from the 101st Battle Group and considered the matter closed. Dunmoore doubted the civilian side expected a reply to their complaint. Otherwise, they'd have raised Cain. She signed off on the incident, formally closing it. The remaining logs for the weekend held nothing of note.

Dunmoore closed them and sat back. Minor incidents — which covered *Iolanthe* launching and recovering shuttles without obtaining permission beforehand — didn't warrant the attention of the 3rd Fleet's deputy commander, let alone questions about her location. Especially when the logs showed that the duty officer hadn't even contacted him about the matter.

Of course, Sea Eagle Flight destroying civilian aircars near a major highway during a tropical downpour wasn't minor. But no one had lodged a complaint, and all evidence of the incident was gone by dawn the following day.

She quickly dealt with the remaining correspondence, then called up the encrypted message from Earth, which must bear either Kathryn's or Zeke's signature. No one else used that algorithm.

After reading through it twice, Dunmoore turned her chair to look out the window while she analyzed her orders, signed by the Chief of Naval Operations and countersigned by the Chief of Naval Intelligence. Then, she considered what would likely happen once she carried them out. After almost ten minutes, satisfied she had everything straight in her mind, Dunmoore summoned Chief Vincenzo.

"Close the door and grab a chair."

"Sir."

"It's on. I just received orders from the CNO to relieve Keo of his responsibilities."

"And take him into custody?"

"Not exactly. Here's how it'll go."

When she finished speaking, Vincenzo nodded once.

"I'll fetch a pair of counterintelligence officers."

"And I'll call Commodore Pushkin. We need to make this as slick a move as possible before the opposition wakes up and finds ways of frustrating us. Ten minutes?"

"Should be enough. I'll call the cousins as well. They'll have something prepared just for this moment, especially since they weren't around to help last Friday, which will have annoyed them. And annoyed cousins can get creative." Vincenzo stood. "With your permission."

"Go. The timer starts now."

Ten minutes later, Dunmoore went unannounced into Keo's office and shut the door. He glanced up at her, irritation writ large on his face.

"What do you want, Siobhan?"

"To save your life, Horace."

— Thirty-One —

"I beg your pardon."

She dropped into one of the chairs facing his desk and crossed her legs as she sat back, elbows on the arms, fingertips touching.

"What's going to happen is that you're walking out of this office with me and Chief Vincenzo once I'm done talking. From here, we will head for the spaceport, where you'll be taken aboard one of the 101st's Q ships, which will transport you to Earth and hand you over to Rear Admiral Ezekiel Holt, the chief of the counterintelligence branch."

He glared at her.

"Are you insane, Dunmoore? I'm not going anywhere."

"You will if you want to live, Horace. Otherwise, you'll meet the same fate as Hanno Berg. He was probably murdered shortly after retiring to escape pressure from you and the interstellar mobsters who own your soul."

"That's it, Dunmoore." He pointed at the door, face turning a sickly puce, and spoke in a harsh, staccato tone. "Get out and wait for my order relieving you of duty pending an investigation."

Dunmoore pulled her tablet from her tunic pocket.

"I received orders from the CNO, countersigned by the CNI, to remove you from your position and get you off Dordogne ASAP. Today."

"On what charges?" Keo's face lost its color rather suddenly as he finally grasped the reality of his situation.

"Corruption, treason, accessory to murder and attempted murder, and no doubt an extensive list of lesser items. It's over, Horace. You'll be arrested and charged in due course. But for now, all that matters is getting you aboard a shuttle sent by the 101st and away from Calvert." She placed her tablet on his desk. "The message relieving you of duty and ordering you aboard the ship I name for transport to Earth is on there. Read it."

Keo didn't move or speak, though he kept glowering at Dunmoore as if his overt hostility could chase her away and save his career from an ignominious end.

"Read it," she snapped.

He finally did so, then tossed the tablet back at her with some force. She caught it before it struck her face.

"I suppose they want me alive for interrogation."

"Without a doubt. The Fleet will be interested in knowing how far back this goes, how much you've exposed, and who is involved. There's no doubt in anyone's mind you're guilty. The evidence is incontrovertible."

"And then I spend the rest of my life on Parth. No thanks." He scoffed. "Best if you leave me your blaster and one round and walk out of here for a few minutes."

"As much as I don't mind you committing suicide, that's not an option now. But Admiral Holt is an old-fashioned sort. He might just let you do it after you confess everything. Sending a disgraced vice admiral to Parth is probably not in the cards if only because it would mean a court martial first, and putting all of this on record will not be in the best interests of the Navy. But there's no way back, Horace. We can walk out of here and board a staff car without shackling you, so everybody thinks I'm taking you off to an emergency meeting. Or we can do it the hard way, and everybody's last memory will be of a flag officer led away in disgrace."

He held her eyes for what seemed like an eternity before looking away.

"Fine. Let's go."

"Not just yet. We'll wait here until the shuttle is inbound. I don't know which ship took on the task. That way, I can't reveal anything. It won't be long, though. Commodore Pushkin's pilots are virtuosos, as my rescue from Calvert's goons on National Highway One late Friday afternoon proved. Yes, I spent the weekend aboard *Iolanthe*. Was Calvert sufficiently frantic when he realized both of his gambits failed? Did he take it out on you?"

Keo remained silent and looked away again, jaw muscles working, and Dunmoore recognized the signs of a man turning desperate. She reached under her tunic hem, pulled out her blaster, and placed it on her right thigh, barrel pointing at him.

"Let's not make mistakes, Horace. You wouldn't be the first human I shot and killed. Far from it. Instead, tell me, did you know the beach house Calvert loaned you was filled with surveillance sensors of all kinds?"

Keo's head whipped back. "What? Of course not. I swept the place myself."

"Funny, because I had Chief Vincenzo sweep mine, and he uncovered an entire network embedded in the house's structure, invisible to regular sensors, but not his. Vincenzo's a counterintelligence operative, by the way, sent here to investigate why 3rd Fleet was missing more and more trafficking activity on and across the frontier. When Hanno resigned, Fleet HQ appointed me as his replacement for the same reason. We nuked the surveillance suite in the house with a portable EMP blaster, and wouldn't you know it? While you and I were making nice at Calvert's party, they installed a much less comprehensive backup set. If they bugged one place, they'd have bugged the other.

"Calvert is a man who uses blackmail and non-violent coercion like a virtuoso. I suggest you think back and try to recall anything you said or did at the beach house that might have further compromised your position as deputy commander. They'll ask when you're interviewed; the more you tell them, the better the outcome will be. You may even get that gun with a single round and a closed room."

When his right hand dropped, Dunmoore raised her weapon.

"No, you don't, Horace. Put both hands on the desk."

"If you kill me, they won't learn anything."

"I can wing you just as easily. Of course, you'll be in agony until the starship sickbay patches you up, and as I learned on Friday, it's about a forty-five-minute ride up at maximum thrust."

He complied, never taking his eyes off her.

"You realize you've signed your own death warrant, Dunmoore. Those are seriously dangerous people who aren't afraid of the Fleet."

"Oh, I know. If their plan had worked on Friday, I'd have died before the cocktail hour on Saturday, so whatever I do now won't make things worse. Not for me, at any rate. Tell me, how did an officer with your record fall in with mobsters?"

A shrug, followed by a slump signaling total defeat.

"Slowly at first, then all at once. They woo you with friendship, social status, and gifts and note every weakness, appetite, desire, and ambition. Once they've compiled a thick enough dossier, you either cooperate and keep the good times going, with help to reach four stars if all goes well. Or you just keep going so you stay alive and out of the brig until the Fleet puts you out to pasture and you're no longer useful."

"Generally, people no longer useful don't have time to enjoy life after retirement. Accidents happen, even to those who cooperate and move up the chain of command. I'm sure Sara Lauzier and her ilk would have used you mercilessly if you'd become a four-star at Fleet HQ. And then, one day, her pet SSB would make it all come to an unfortunate end. A shame, really. Which one were you? The enthusiastic traitor or the blackmail victim?"

A bitter smile appeared on Keo's face.

"You'll never find out, Dunmoore. By the time I'm singing opera in a counterintelligence dungeon, Calvert will have made sure you die. See, his people only have to be lucky once. You'll need to be lucky every time, and that's just not statistically possible."

She gave him an amused look.

"Don't worry about me, my friend. The Shrehari, the SSB, and various criminals tried during the war without success. And since then, I've ducked so many assassination attempts, some by better mercenaries than those Calvert employs, it's embarrassing for the whole thug profession."

"Just to change the subject slightly, is Hogue aware of this?"

Dunmoore snorted. "Would you make her aware beforehand?"

"No, of course not. You realize I've been running 3rd Fleet, right?"

"I do, just as I understand she wasn't promoted to four stars and appointed because of her stellar abilities as a senior flag officer."

"Hah." Keo let out a bark of laughter. "The words stellar abilities and Hogue don't belong in the same sentence. She's a political appointment, just like the wastrels running the Fleet before the war, and was sent here to ensure 3rd Fleet didn't stem the flow of trafficking across the frontier. But give her a good deputy, and no one will find out."

"Was your predecessor in Calvert's pay as well?"

Keo narrowed his eyes in thought.

"Not that I could tell for sure, but I think so. The effortless way with which they ensnared me spoke of practice, and I noticed familiar patterns in the patrol dispositions during her time once I realized what they were making me do. They'll try with my replacement as well."

Dunmoore gave him a predatory grin.

"They already did and failed, Horace."

It took him a moment to understand her meaning. Then, with an air of disgust, he shook his head.

"I should have known it would end this way. But good luck surviving long enough to enjoy this office."

At that moment, her communicator buzzed. She retrieved it from her pocket and saw it was Vincenzo.

"What's the word?"

"The shuttle is on final. The car and escort are waiting in front, and I'm in your office."

"Then come and fetch us."

"Ack."

"Dunmoore, out." She stood, weapon still pointed at Keo. "Time to fasten your tunic and slap on your beret, Horace. We're off to a meeting with destiny. You'll go up while going down, and I'll stay down while going up. Once Chief Vincenzo gets here, I'll put my gun away, but he'll always have something on you, so no stupid moves, okay?"

Keo replied with a grunt but climbed to his feet and adjusted his uniform. Dunmoore reached back to snag his beret from the coat tree and tossed it over just as the door opened to admit Vincenzo.

"The admiral's car is waiting, sir."

"Thanks, Chief." Dunmoore smiled at Keo. "After you."

Keo walked through the outer office with a stiff gait to the astonished stare of his now former aide.

"We'll be in a meeting for the rest of the morning, Commander," Dunmoore said in passing.

"Yes, sir," she replied reflexively, though she watched them leave through bemused eyes.

An armored staff car was waiting outside the main doors with one counterintelligence officer wearing a chief warrant officer's bars on his collar, standing by the open passenger compartment door. Another sat at the controls, looking straight ahead.

At Vincenzo's urging, Keo climbed in first, followed by Dunmoore. Then, after a silent nod at the CI officer, he joined them as the man took the front passenger seat. They spent the short ride in silence and arrived at the spaceport tarmac gate just as a boxy shuttle of the same model as the one who'd rescued them was settling. The gate slid open as if by magic while the shuttle's aft ramp dropped, and four uniformed spacers with 101st Battle Group patches on their sleeves, one of them wearing a lieutenant's stripes, emerged. Dunmoore recognized him as *Mikado*'s second officer, a man she recalled being near the top of this year's promotion list to lieutenant commander.

They stopped at the foot of the ramp, and the lieutenant called his small crew to attention. When the passenger door opened, Dunmoore motioned at Keo to get out first. As he appeared, the lieutenant raised his hand in salute, a gesture Keo returned with as much formality. Dunmoore climbed out after him.

"This is it, sir. They'll take good care of you and treat you with the respect due to your rank for the entire voyage. I doubt we'll ever meet again."

Keo gave her a searching look. "So do I. Enjoy the time you have left."

"Thank you, sir." Dunmoore raised her hand in salute. "Goodbye, sir."

He returned the salute, turned, and marched up the ramp, followed by his final honor guard. Once the ramp was up, Dunmoore climbed back into the car.

"Where next?" The CI warrant officer at the controls asked.

"Back to HQ."

— Thirty-Two —

Just before Dunmoore got out of the car, Vincenzo stuck out his hand.

"I'll be busy with these gentlemen clearing out Keo's residence for the next few hours and rounding up his worldly possessions for onward shipment, Admiral. The idea is making him vanish. But I wanted to be the first to congratulate you."

As they shook, she said, "I hope you'll stick around for a while because this is only the end of the beginning."

"No fears, sir. Admiral Holt will recall me when you say so, and yeah, I agree. This isn't over by a long shot."

Dunmoore entered the building, waved at the security guard, and headed for Hogue's office to let her know there was a palace coup, and she now had a new deputy. The inner door was closed when she entered the outer office, and her senior aide looked up, frowning.

"The admiral is busy, sir. I understand you took Admiral Keo to an unscheduled meeting."

"She's busy with who?" Dunmoore asked, ignoring his question.

"Admiral Anand. Something about traffic control issues on the naval side. Shouldn't be long, though."

"Do you have any spare stars in your desk drawers, Liam?"

He seemed surprised. "Yes, sir. And every other rank insignia."

"Keep a star handy, will you?"

Before Dewint could reply, something on his display caught his eye.

"They're done." He tapped a control. "Admiral Dunmoore is in the outer office and wishes to see you, sir."

"Send her in."

The inner door opened, and as Dewint ushered Dunmoore through, she said over her shoulder, "We'll call you in a moment, Liam."

"What is it, Siobhan?" Hogue asked when Dunmoore took a chair.

"I'm afraid you're getting a new deputy commander and an interim chief of staff for operations, Admiral. Horace has been summoned to Fleet HQ urgently and is on his way to a ship in orbit as we speak. He won't be coming back to 3rd Fleet after he's carried out his mission. The CNO appointed me as your new deputy commander." Dunmoore produced her tablet and laid it on Hogue's desk. "The orders summoning Horace to Earth and appointing me as his replacement are on here, signed by Admiral Lowell. Copies should come through formal channels any moment now."

Hogue contemplated her in silence for several moments, eyes expressionless, as she digested Dunmoore's declaration. Then she picked up the tablet and read.

"Countersigned by Admiral Jado Doxiadis, no less. That tells me how grave the situation is. Fine. But why did those orders go to you instead of coming to me?"

"Because they will charge Horace with corruption, treason, accessory to murder and attempted murder, and a lengthy list of other offenses when he reaches Earth. Considering the delicacy of the situation and the need to remove him from Dordogne quietly, the CNO decided I would carry out his orders before informing you. This was just in case Horace had confederates in places where they might overhear before counterintelligence officers could secure him."

"I see. And does that mean the CNO trusts you more than he trusts me?"

Dunmoore gave her a rueful shrug.

"I couldn't say, sir. This truly is a case of I was merely following orders, no explanations provided."

Hogue harrumphed.

"Well, I suppose I will have to raise the matter with Admiral Lowell directly."

"Yes, sir."

"And you're now a three-star?"

"If you would be so kind as to pin the third on my collar, sir, we can formalize my promotion."

"Another matter on which the CNO gave me no say. Who takes over as COS Ops?"

"I would recommend making Freya Horvat an acting commodore and the interim chief of staff. She has the seniority and the ability. One of her commanders can step up to replace her as Alpha Watch director. I'll also keep a close eye on operations for the foreseeable future."

"Very well. Freya Horvat it is." She stabbed her desktop. "Liam, we're promoting Siobhan Dunmoore to vice admiral. She'll be the new Deputy Flag Officer Commanding 3rd Fleet. Please bring me a star and the camera drone. Then prepare orders making Captain Horvat an acting commodore and appointing her as interim chief of staff for operations."

"Yes, sir. Right away."

Hogue glared at Dunmoore again.

"Since you're the one with all the answers, what do we tell people concerning Horace?"

"The CNO ordered him to Fleet HQ, and he won't be coming back, which is nothing less than the truth, albeit not the whole truth."

"Fine. Draft the message and give it to Liam."

At that moment, the aide appeared, trailed by the floating camera drone, and both admirals stood.

"By the stand of flags, please," Dewint said.

Hogue managed a smile as she pinned the third star on Dunmoore's collar and then shook hands with her.

"Congratulations, Siobhan."

"Thank you, sir."

"Liam, Admiral Dunmoore will provide you with a message to all staff and formation commanders announcing Admiral Keo's departure and her appointment in his stead."

"Yes, sir." Dewint turned to Dunmoore. "Congratulations, Admiral."

Word about the change of Deputy Flag Officer Commanding ran through 3rd Fleet HQ like an aviso pushing the highest hyperspace bands. When Dunmoore returned to her old office so she could retrieve her personal things, Lieutenant Ramius stood to offer her congratulations.

"Thanks, Anna. A shame we didn't work together all that long, but I'm grateful for your help."

"Will Chief Vincenzo stay on as operations branch chief?"

"No. I'm bringing him with me as a senior enlisted adviser."

"That's what I thought. I've taken the liberty of moving your personal effects to the deputy commander's office. Lieutenant Commander Takahashi is expecting you."

"Excellent."

As Dunmoore walked out into the corridor, Alvin Maffina appeared.

"I understand congratulations are in order, Admiral." He thrust out his hand. "Well deserved."

"Thanks, Alvin. No hard feelings about my taking over from Horace?"

Maffina chuckled.

"None whatsoever. I've known for a long time that I'm terminal at my current rank. Who's replacing you in operations?"

"Freya Horvat until Earth assigns a permanent replacement."

"Good choice. She's solid and has plenty of years left to climb further up the greasy pole." He lowered his voice. "And one of these days, you'll have to tell me how you made Horace vanish so quickly."

With that, Maffina walked off to the executive dining room for a cup of coffee. When Dunmoore entered the deputy commander's outer office, Lieutenant Commander Takahashi jumped up.

"Welcome, sir, and congratulations. Anna and I moved your dunnage over, and she told me how you like your coffee in the morning."

"Thanks, Margo. Can you have a second desk set up in the outer office? I'm bringing Chief Vincenzo with me as senior enlisted adviser."

"Consider it done."

The rest of the day was a blur as Dunmoore dealt with the finer points of taking on a vice admiral's job and deflecting questions about her predecessor's abrupt departure. Gregor Pushkin and Kurt Guthren called shortly after a hurried lunch to congratulate her, as did Quintin Anand. When she spoke with the latter, Dunmoore used the occasion to thank him for keeping things quiet the previous Friday but offered no explanation, even though Anand clearly thirsted for one.

She spent a good hour huddled with Acting Commodore Horvat once Hogue pinned a star on her collar, doing a quick handover of responsibilities before she had the chance to take an afternoon breather — a cup of coffee on the terrace behind the building.

When Vincenzo finally showed up just after sixteen hundred hours, she was ready to call it quits and head home.

"And?" She asked when the chief closed the office door behind him.

"Keo's apartment is empty. We crated all his stuff and readied it to ship along with his personal ground car. The place was bugged to hell and gone, and I'm sure we'll find Calvert's name somewhere in the mess of ownership changes. Or at least the name of someone who works for him or one of his companies. There's no way a vice admiral can afford something like that overlooking one of the prime stretches of Marseilles harbor. It may not look like much from the outside, but inside?" Vincenzo let out a low whistle. "It's a palace, with every convenience. I'll bet Keo entertained a lot of questionable guests in there."

"Good. And with that, I'd say we've earned a cold beer on the terrace at home."

Vincenzo shook his head.

"No can do, sir. You're a prime target, especially now that you've ousted Calvert's man in 3rd Fleet. Home is no longer safe. I booked you a VIP suite in the base officers' mess before coming in. You'll have to stay there until this is over, and you're no longer at risk. Give me a list of the things you need, and I'll visit your place with the CI guys you met this morning."

Dunmoore knew it was non-negotiable and nodded.

"All right." Then she grabbed her tablet and wrote a list of clothing and items she wanted. "Bring the open bottle of Glen Arcturus and the beer in the fridge as well. No sense in me paying officers' mess bar prices when the VIP suites have all I need to keep myself entertained."

"Will do. You can head for the mess anytime you want. They've keyed Suite 205 to your biometrics, and I scanned it for any pesky intrusions. If that's everything, I'll go fetch your dunnage. Then, I have an appointment with the cousins. After this morning's events, they need to complete their preparations. If there's nothing else?"

"Go ahead."

With Vincenzo gone, she stood, stretched, and called out to her aide.

"Go home, Margo. We can do all of this again tomorrow."

"Yes, sir. Have a good evening."

***

Joint Base Dordogne Officers' Mess, one of three spokes around a common hub — the kitchen and dining hall — with the other spokes being the senior non-commissioned officers' mess and the junior ranks' club, sat on the northeast corner of the base's main intersection. Unlike the other two messes, it also functioned as a hotel for transient officers, with three floors of rooms and suites above the mess itself.

Functional and boxy from the outside, like every other building on the base and every permanent Fleet installation in human space, the mess complex was surprisingly warm and inviting inside and, as Dunmoore found out when she entered suite 205, almost luxurious. She'd brought an overnight bag with her to Fort Vauban, just in case, and left it in the car. It had been convenient aboard *Iolanthe* and would be so again until Vincenzo arrived with her wardrobe and quickly changed into slacks, a short-sleeved shirt, and sandals.

Then she headed down to the mess proper and ordered a glass of white wine from the bar. Most of the fifty or so officers present, either for a quick drink before going home or visiting from other military installations, gave her curious, albeit covert glances before whispering among themselves. By now, the entire planet would know Siobhan Dunmoore had inexplicably become the second highest ranking naval officer in the Rim Sector. Those who saw her in civilian clothes standing at the bar must wonder why she was in the mess, a place she'd rarely frequented.

But no one dared acknowledge her presence, let alone speak with her, which was fine. She took her glass to an isolated table by a window, far from anyone else, and settled in to mentally review her day and plan for tomorrow while waiting for Vincenzo's return. It was still a little early for supper, and she hadn't yet decided whether she would eat in the dining hall or have her meal brought to her suite.

Unexpectedly, her personal communicator vibrated, and she fished it from her pocket. The caller's identity was blocked, but somehow, Dunmoore guessed it would be one of her so-called friends.

"Yes?"

"It's Antoine, my dear. What have you done?"

— Thirty-Three —

"I'm sorry, Antoine. What am I supposed to have done?"

"Don't play the innocent with me, Siobhan. You're as crafty, cunning, and ruthless as I am. First, you vanish on Friday late afternoon, only to reappear on the base this morning. Now Horace has vanished, several people in naval uniform emptied his apartment, and you've taken his place. What have you done?"

"I have done nothing. This is how the Navy sometimes works. Horace received an urgent summons from Armed Forces HQ on Earth and left on the first available starship. A few of my people packed his personal effects and are sending them along on the next transport run while the local judge advocate general figures out how to deal with the disposal of his residence since he won't be coming back. As for me, I was merely the next in line and received my promotion a bit earlier than expected. There's nothing sinister about any of this."

Calvert didn't immediately reply, but she could see him frowning. People of his sort were good at detecting liars, and he probably couldn't quite decide how much of what she'd said was true since she hadn't uttered a single falsehood.

"And where were you this past weekend? Victor tried calling several times, but your communicator was out of contact."

"Why would that be any of your or Victor's concern, Antoine?" She asked with a hint of asperity in her tone. "What I do with my time is of no concern to anyone other than the Navy. But if you must pry into my personal life, I spent the weekend with former shipmates, swapping tall tales and enjoying myself." Again, the truth and nothing but. Her lies were in what she hadn't voiced. "If I somehow insulted you by refusing your invitation to the lodge, then please accept my apologies. You've been a good friend to me, just as you have to Horace."

"No, no, no. You didn't insult me, dear Siobhan. It's just that there was an accident on National Highway One near the Passage du Clos at around the time you would have passed through, and we were extremely worried about you."

"Ah. I see. Well, in that case, all is forgiven. It must have happened later because I saw nothing of the sort. Mind you, in that rain, seeing anything was a miracle. Did anyone get hurt?"

"I couldn't tell you."

Dunmoore could not suppress a faintly amused smile at his answer. Of course, he couldn't say because that meant betraying the fact they were his aircars, piloted by his mercenaries.

"In any case, I'm sure Horace is chagrined that he couldn't make his farewells properly, but when the Chief of Naval Operations summons you, and there's a ship ready to depart, you head out, no matter what. Perhaps he'll transmit a message once he arrives on Earth."

"Perhaps. In the meantime, you and I should meet and discuss a few matters since you now sit in his former chair."

"Oh?"

"There are certain realities I should make sure you understand clearly. But face-to-face, not over a comlink."

"That sounded vaguely threatening."

"Not at all." He tried for a reassuring smile, but it only made him look more predatory.

"When and where shall we meet?"

"How about your lovely beach villa tomorrow after work?"

Dunmoore frowned, then made a face.

"About the house, I decided I wasn't a beach-going admiral, so thanks for the loan, but I won't be returning. And after work during the week really won't do. How about your beach villa on Saturday afternoon?"

He didn't seem pleased but nodded. "Okay. Say at fourteen hundred?"

"No. Let's make it seventeen hundred. I have things I must sort out on Saturday. Oh, and how about you invite all of Horace's friends? That way, we can clear the air with everyone concerned at once. I'm like you, Antoine. I prefer meeting those involved face-to-face. And then you can feed us supper to celebrate."

Calvert stared at Dunmoore with his soulless eyes for a few seconds as if he doubted her sincerity again. But then he nodded once.

"Seventeen hundred on Saturday. I'll make sure the right people attend."

"Great." At that moment, Dunmoore caught sight of Vincenzo in the main doorway, looking for her. "Got to run now, Antoine. I have someone waiting for me. Until Saturday."

"*Au revoir, ma chère.*"

Dunmoore cut the link, shoved her communicator in her pocket, and downed the rest of the wine while waving at Vincenzo.

***

"No, sir. That is not going to happen. Your plan is utterly insane." Vincenzo walked over to her sitting room window and stared at the base.

"I'm overruling you, your boss, and your boss' boss, Chief. Besides, I can pull in assets to ensure the balance of power is entirely on my side. Antoine may be a brutal psychopath under that courtly veneer. Yet, he's hopelessly naïve about certain things, especially since he owns so many cops and government officials who ensure he remains untouchable."

Vincenzo turned back toward her. "Naïve isn't a term I would use to describe the biggest mob boss in the star system."

"I said about certain things, such as what the Armed Forces can and can't do without authorization on a sovereign Commonwealth planet. He didn't give me the impression he has a clue about what happened to us on Friday. We killed his people and shot down his illegally armed aircars, but I suspect he can't quite imagine the Navy did it. After all, planetary laws here and elsewhere forbid us from carrying out armed interventions in civilian police jurisdiction without the government asking for military support."

Vincenzo snorted. "Not that SOCOM ever heard about such laws."

"Oh, it knows all about them, which is why *Iolanthe*'s shuttles were unmarked and the pilots wearing their mercenary suits. Trust me on this, Chief. My gut tells me Calvert is one of those crooks who can't believe the military would so blatantly violate Dordogne's sovereignty and its laws. Will your cousins have time to prepare between now and Saturday afternoon?"

"They're ready to go now if you want."

"Good. Thanks for bringing my stuff. Go home, relax, and have a good night's sleep. I'll make the arrangements for Saturday myself. Just leave me your radio. And I promise I won't leave the base tonight. Heck, I won't even leave my room. I've decided to have my meal sent up."

***

"Blayne."

Rear Admiral Ezekiel Holt, wearing a perfectly tailored gray business suit, the sort considered an almost mandatory uniform by the bureaucrats infesting Geneva as they pretended to govern the Commonwealth, settled on the bench beside Blayne Hersom. Similarly clad, the Director General of the Special Security Bureau glanced at Holt with cold eyes.

"What's this about, Zeke?"

Holt kept his eyes on Lake Geneva's shimmering surface, far below the observation point overlooking the eastern shore.

"Dordogne."

"Thought so. Dunmoore has been making more ripples than usual, even for her. Expensive ripples for many people, meaning she's doing what she does best, collecting enemies by the metric ton. So what?"

"Walk away. Let her clean up Dordogne and the trafficking problem on the Rim frontier."

"Why should I?"

"Because you can only rectify the situation according to your lights by assassinating her. Your last attempt three years ago failed. Sara Lauzier's friends, no doubt aided or encouraged by your goons, tried late last week. They failed spectacularly as well. Four dead, not a scratch on the good guys, and Dunmoore, a vice admiral and deputy commander of 3rd Fleet."

"Good for her. Again, why should I let her clean up?"

"Because we have your number, Blayne. Jado Doxiadis warned you three years ago about trying again. I'm here to remind you of that. Dunmoore cleans up the Rim. The SSB walks away, and no one else gets hurt, least of all your friend Sara."

"And if we don't?"

"Are you and Sara ready to die, Blayne? Because that's the point we've reached. Choose your next steps wisely." Holt climbed to his feet and walked away without another word.

***

"And do you think Blayne will heed the warning?" Kathryn Kowalski asked.

"He might. Sara won't. She hates Siobhan with a burning passion and gets too much of her covert funding from sources that depend on large-scale trafficking, money laundering, and other illegal activities. Not to mention that the products of said trafficking give her the means to control anyone with a taste for the illicit."

"Like Horace Keo?"

"To a certain extent, yes. And more of our fellow flag officers than we'd guess. Not to mention civilian bureaucrats. We'll see how far down the rabbit hole they pulled poor Horace when he arrives on Caledonia and meets one of my crack interrogation teams stationed at Joint Base Sanctum."

Kowalski let out a brief guffaw. "Caledonia? I thought you were bringing him to Earth."

"So did everyone else, Siobhan included. But *Mikado*'s captain will receive orders to head for Caledonia when he drops out of FTL to tack and pings the nearest subspace array. I'm sure Blayne has assassination teams lined up, waiting for Horace's arrival. He'll be sorely disappointed."

"And once he tells your people everything he knows?"

"I don't know yet. That'll be the Grand Admiral's decision, but I'm inclined to revive an old tradition for disgraced officers since Horace wasn't the first to sell his soul and won't be the last. Mind you, if we let him go, the SSB or their hired goons will ensure the rest of his life is short and painful. A reminder for others of his sort that getting caught by us isn't the worst that could happen."

"Let's just hope Siobhan's plan to neutralize one of Sara's largest financial support conduits won't make her life short and painful."

Holt shrugged helplessly. "There's nothing we can do to stop her. Vincenzo made that clear in his latest report. Will it destabilize Dordogne? To a certain extent. Will it mess with trafficking from the Zone? I certainly hope so."

"Will it succeed?"

He smiled. "I know who I'm betting on."

— Thirty-Four —

"Judging by the expensive cars lined up in his driveway, Calvert invited the entire board of directors of La Pègre, Incorporated." Dunmoore looked up from the reconnaissance drone feed on her car's secondary display and grinned at Vincenzo, who sat behind the controls for once. "Excellent. The more, the merrier."

Both wore battledress uniforms with sidearms for the occasion, and the three silver stars of her rank glittered on her tunic collar. Vincenzo still wasn't overly pleased with the plan, but he'd do his duty. Dunmoore picked up the surface-to-orbit radio.

"All Sea Eagle call signs, this is Niner-Niner. Shall we dance, I repeat, shall we dance?"

"Sea Eagle One, standing by."

"Sea Eagle Two, standing by."

"Sea Eagle Three, standing by."

"Sea Eagle Base, standing by."

"Niner-Niner, acknowledged. Heading for the dance floor now. Sea Eagle Two may start approach. Out." She glanced at Vincenzo. "Let's go, Chief."

They pulled up to Calvert's front door, after passing a series of guard posts occupied by hired guns, at seventeen hundred hours precisely. Calvert's butler hurried down the steps to greet her as she and Vincenzo climbed out of the car.

"The guests are assembled, Admiral. They're waiting for you in the main reception room."

If he thought it strange that she wore her uniform and carried a weapon to a Saturday beach house get-together, neither his face nor his eyes betrayed any reaction. Vincenzo reached into the back of the car and retrieved a black case.

"Please follow me."

They took the steps, then walked down the long, marble-floored hallway, heels clicking on the polished hard surface. Dunmoore knew the assembled Pègre chiefs were watching her arrival on the room's large display and wondering why she and her security officer were dressed to kill.

They entered the main reception room to complete silence. The dozen men and women, Dordogne's top mob chieftains and financiers, Lassieux and Herault among them, standing in a loose group, champagne glasses in hand, stared at her as if she were an unwelcome apparition. By appearing armed and in battledress at what was supposed to be a reception, Dunmoore was subverting their expectations and hopefully putting them off balance.

"Good afternoon, mesdames et messieurs," she said in a pleasant but hard-edged tone. "Forgive my appearance, but you'll understand momentarily."

Dunmoore gestured at a settee group large enough for all twelve. "Please sit. This will take a bit to explain."

They turned their eyes on Calvert, looking for guidance, but he was just as nonplussed as the rest.

"What is the meaning of this, Siobhan?" The man finally asked. "I understood we were meeting as friends and allies to discuss how you would take over the working relationship we enjoyed with Horace Keo."

Dunmoore allowed herself an icy smile.

"We are."

"Then why the dramatic getup?" He waved his hand at her. "Surely that weapon is unnecessary."

"Probably. But it helps prevent unfortunate misunderstandings. Now please sit."

"If your intention is showing strength and independence, bravo." Calvert gave her an ironic and silent round of applause. "It succeeded."

At that instant, a highly agitated man wearing a security guard's black slacks and shirt burst into the reception room.

"Monsieur Calvert, the property is under attack. Shuttles are landing on the grounds and disgorging armored troops."

Calvert speared Dunmoore with his gaze.

"Your doing, no doubt?"

"Tell your people to surrender, and they'll live. If any of them are stupid enough to open fire, they will die. Instantly. Do sit before I get impatient." Dunmoore pointed at the settees. "Because when I do, my troopers, who are now in control of this place, will make you comply."

Heavy footsteps sounded behind her, and three of the invaders entered the room. All wore black, unmarked combat armor and tactical harness and carried plasma carbines. Their faces were invisible behind lowered helmet visors, and they exuded a palpable aura of menace.

"We're in control, sir," the one in the middle said. "None of the goons was dumb enough to open fire, so no casualties."

"What is this?" Calvert demanded as he visibly fought to keep his fury under control. "A military invasion of private property on a sovereign world? You've not only lost your mind, Dunmoore. You're about to lose your stars, career, and possibly even your life."

Instead of responding, Dunmoore drew her weapon and pointed it at Calvert.

"For the last time, you will sit as ordered, shut up, and listen. I will have no qualms ending your life, Antoine, just as you tried to end mine last Friday."

He gave her a dismissive look that oozed arrogance in a way only Dordognais of a particular social class could master.

"Oh, please stop with the dramatics, Siobhan. You've clearly lost your mind. As soon as I reach friends on Earth, they'll see that you're removed."

"You still don't understand, do you? I don't work by any rules you might recognize because my rules are those that help me win wars, the big ones and the little dark and dirty ones. Such as my war against corruption and trafficking sponsored by you and your friends here. No one is removing me from my position or taking my stars because once I've done what I came here for, all this never happened. Now SIT."

The last word cracked across the room like the snap of a bullwhip, startling Calvert's fellow mob bosses. The covert Marines at her back raised their carbines and took aim. After a few moments, they obeyed, though Calvert made sure he was the last to take one of the armchairs.

Dunmoore let each of them meet her gaze before speaking, so they understood she held all the cards.

"Listen carefully. I'm about to explain how things will work on Dordogne, its star system, and the Rim Sector from now on. My terms are not negotiable, so save your breath. Your friends in the Gendarmerie, the Marseilles Police, and the Dordogne government won't save you. They won't even help you. And by the time I'm done, they won't acknowledge you at all. I control the strongest, deadliest organization around.

"As I proved just now, I can seize any property you own, detain any of you, your family, friends, and employees at will, and there's nothing you can do about it because you're all criminals of the worst sort — you finance human trafficking. Everyone in the Armed Forces hates your kind with a passion and will applaud any move to punish those responsible. Even extra-legal means because you twist the law to protect yourself from retribution, corrupt those with normal human weaknesses, and condemn those trafficked to an early and cruel death."

Dunmoore let out a cold chuckle as she studied their faces.

"You still don't believe what I say? That I can and will do this? I see it in your eyes. How's your Latin, people? Ever heard of *lex talionis*? If you haven't, look it up when we're done because that's the only law I will follow when dealing with you and your organizations from now on."

"An eye for an eye, Siobhan?" Calvert asked in a mild tone. "Rather primitive, no?"

"Ah, so you have some Latin. Congratulations, Antoine. As for being primitive?" She gave him a distinctly Dordognais shrug. "If it works, it works."

"How can you do all this and escape retribution yourself? The Navy is an institution built on the Commonwealth government's laws and regulations."

"Certainly, it is. But I'm now in your universe, Antoine, and since I'm the strongest boss in this star system, I can impose my will on you. Take the deal I'll be offering in a moment, and you'll continue to live comfortably. Refuse, and I will destroy everything you hold dear because I have the power and the ruthlessness to use it. Those who can stop me are on Earth and will never see proof of my taking over. At least not quickly enough to make a difference."

Calvert made one of his habitual courtly hand gestures.

"In that case, we're listening."

"You and your outfits will end any relations with organized crime outside the Dordogne star system. That includes Protectorate Zone traffickers and front groups set up by the Special Security Bureau. You know who the latter are, so there is no need to look dumb. In other words, I'm letting you continue to operate here but nowhere else. None of your funds will go to non-Dordogne political causes." She gave Calvert a significant look. "Or to finance illegitimate business ventures elsewhere. You may still conduct legitimate interstellar trade. Don't use it as a cover for illegal activities, or I will shut you down for good. Be content I'm letting you stay big fish in a small pond rather than turn you into fish food."

"And what if I tell you to fuck off?" Sylvie Lassieux asked in a querulous tone, speaking for the first time.

"Ah." Dunmoore's predatory smile appeared. "Thank you for volunteering to be an object lesson. I figured you might balk. Chief?"

"Admiral."

Vincenzo opened the case he was carrying and retrieved a holographic projector. He set it up in the middle of the room, then raised his radio to his lips and murmured instructions. Moments later, the image of a rundown warehouse appeared.

"I believe this belongs to you and Uta via a few shell companies, Sylvie? You use it to store many illegal items awaiting distribution or transshipment."

"So?"

"This is yours. My people have traced its ownership, as they have the ownership of everything all of you here possess. It wasn't that difficult. You've all grown fat and lazy, thanks to corrupt cops and bureaucrats. I'd be embarrassed if my security measures were that lax."

Lassieux made a face. "Okay. It's mine. So what?"

"Sea Eagle Three, this is Niner-Niner."

"Sea Eagle Three," a disembodied voice came from the holographic projection.

"Go on Lassieux Alpha."

"Acknowledged."

Nothing happened for a few seconds, then the warehouse simply vanished into a cloud of dust and debris from a controlled implosion. Flames shot up shortly afterward and spread incredibly fast before their eyes.

"What was the value of the goods stored there, Sylvie?"

When she didn't answer, Dunmoore looked at the others.

"Who'll be next while Sylvie mourns all those lost profits? Anyone? We've rigged your major properties for destruction, my friends. I only kill when necessary, but the fruits of trafficking are automatic targets. Take my offer, and you may continue your operations here but nowhere else. Refuse, go back on your word after accepting, and I will destroy you without warning. Is that understood? Or should I choose another example to hammer home my point?"

"You can't get away with this, Dunmoore," one of the other bosses said. "I'll make sure everyone knows you're blowing up our business premises."

"Sea Eagle Three, this is Niner-Niner, fire in the hole on Grenier Alpha."

"Acknowledged."

The hologram of the destroyed warehouse dissolved, and that of an intact building appeared in its stead. It, too, vanished in a cloud of smoke and debris, followed by fire.

"You'll tell whoever wants to listen that a vice admiral is blackmailing you by destroying your operations?" Dunmoore shook her head. "I knew you folks were naïve enough to believe you could get away with crass criminality by greasing palms and coercing people because someone like me can't exist in the stultifying atmosphere of a peacetime Navy. Go ahead, try. But you'll be too busy explaining why the arson investigations are finding traces of illegal substances in the remains of those warehouses. And they'll know all about the ownership since I'll provide them with the evidence my people collected. Now, do I need a third object lesson, or do you understand that, in naval parlance, you're completely and utterly screwed?"

"I don't see how you can enforce this for any length of time, Siobhan," Calvert said. "You will eventually leave. Or have an accident."

"Who says I need to enforce it on Dordogne forever?" She gave him a pleasant smile. "Or that it needs to be me who does so. They sent me here for precisely one task — disrupt your interstellar operations at the source, so the Navy has a freer hand in shutting down interstellar traffickers coming from the Zone. My eventual replacement will be thoroughly vetted and as incorruptible as I am, now that we know how you work things, and he or she will continue as I've started. This is your future, Antoine. I'm now the boss of bosses, and you answer to me. The troopers you see are more deadly, dangerous, and powerful than your goons and mercenaries, even the ones you keep near your lodge. They've killed many pirates, reivers, and slavers in the Zone. More than you could ever imagine, and they won't hesitate for a second. And if you make another attempt on my life, they will wipe out every living thing in your lovely little valley, this beach house, and any other property you own. Now, I will ask each of you whether you accept my terms and acknowledge me as the top boss. Antoine?"

He inclined his head. "Yes."

"Victor?"

Herault gave her a pained look. Dunmoore figured it was because he faced the total failure of his task to seduce her and bring her into the fold. But he nodded as well.

"Yes."

"Sylvie?"

"Damn you to hell, Dunmoore. If my security team were here, I'd have them gun you down like the rabid animal you are."

"Too cowardly to do your own dirty work?" Dunmoore pulled out her blaster and tossed it at the astonished mobster, who let it clatter to the floor. "Go ahead. Pick the gun up and shoot me."

When no one moved, Dunmoore laughed.

"You're nothing but a bunch of worthless, petty thugs who won't even dirty their own hands. How do you folks say it? *Des petits merdeux.*"

She bent over to retrieve the weapon and pressed its barrel against Lassieux's forehead.

"Any last words you'd like to share with us? No? I guess you're not a deep thinker either."

With a slick flourish, Dunmoore holstered the weapon.

"Always remember this moment. Sylvie could have sacrificed herself to kill me and free you from my terms. But she didn't. I could have shot Sylvie with impunity, but I didn't. Chief?"

Vincenzo came to attention.

"Sir."

"We're done here. Break it down, then nuke this place. We can't have recordings of the meeting float around."

"Nuke?" Calvert asked, clearly appalled.

Dunmoore turned to him.

"EMP, Antoine. It'll fry every bit of electronics on your property not protected by military-grade shielding. You'll be welcoming the evening in the best nineteenth-century style. Some of your cars may also be affected, so ask your neighbors if they'll lend you their horses."

"Setting off EMPs on human worlds is illegal."

"Not when they're small scale, focused and directed at legitimate targets. But nice try. You're so cute when you invoke laws you don't obey. There's a future in politics for you. A Commonwealth senator's seat, perhaps? You could always ask your friend Sara. And when you do, please give her my love, and tell her better luck next time."

With that, Dunmoore turned on her heels and left.

— Thirty-Five —

"My Marines said watching you own a dozen top mobsters was a thing of true beauty, Admiral. A shame we couldn't record the operation. I get the feeling we missed the show of the century."

"What operation?" Dunmoore chuckled at Pushkin's mock crestfallen expression. "I will confess I enjoyed myself immensely."

"But what would have happened if this Lassieux creature had picked up your gun and fired?"

"Nothing."

Pushkin gave her a suspicious glare.

"What do you mean, nothing?"

"It wasn't powered. By the time she figured that out, one of the Marines would have winged her, or I would have taken my weapon back."

"I'm sure Vince had a heart attack, though."

She shook her head.

"No. We discussed every potential move I could make beforehand, and that was one of them. This was the most thoroughly choreographed operation I've ever planned. Thank you once again for loaning me your Pathfinders and their dropships. I'll take the blame if someone finds out we used them on a sovereign Commonwealth planet in their mercenary guise."

"Still, I'm happy we didn't need Sea Eagle One again."

"That was just a contingency in case things went spectacularly wrong. I didn't expect to need another extraction under fire."

"What happens now?"

"I fix what I can at the command level and turn 3rd Fleet back into the aggressive war-fighting machine it once was. Vincenzo and his colleagues will go witch-hunting through the headquarters and Starbase 30 and ferret out those who sold their loyalties to the Pègre or the SSB. And we will wait for whatever orders may come from Earth."

"I suggest you ask Kathryn to arrange orders giving you — well, Admiral Hogue, but we know who the real boss will be — tactical control over the 101st. No one on Earth would do it when Hogue asked, probably at Keo's urging so they could make sure they directed us even further away from trafficking activity. But the situation has radically changed, and you're best placed to integrate my activities with those of your battle groups now that we know about the systems they've been using as hubs. I don't have specific orders at the moment beyond the general, go out and find something to kill. Is there a system in particular you want cleansed?"

"How about Mission Colony? It's been a thorn in our flanks since the Shrehari gave it back. Your ships may have intercepted a few traffickers, but there's a major hub hidden somewhere on the surface with the connivance of the colonial administration, perhaps even the governor himself."

"Can do. Get orders out to the local patrol that it comes under my command when I arrive in the system and stays so until I leave."

"I'll give you the orders, and you can present them upon arrival. Since we don't know how deeply they've penetrated 3rd Fleet communications, I won't risk letting anyone find out the 101st is on the way."

Pushkin put on a rueful expression.

"Right. I should remind myself there's still a lot of manure shoveling to do in your HQ. And on that note, it occurs to me you can't live in your house anymore. As in flashing target, if not for the Dordogne mobsters, then the SSB."

"I'm way ahead of you. Or at least Vince is. I'm moving into a vacant senior officer's house in the Joint Base Dordogne residence quarter tomorrow. Vince and his pals are moving my personal possessions over, and I'll be putting my place on the market. Not that I'm afraid of the mobsters."

"You? Never."

"But idiots from the SSB may try sending me up in the middle of the night despite what the Pègre wants, and I'd rather not put my neighbors in the unenviable position of becoming collateral damage."

Pushkin gave her a wink.

"Always thinking of others. That's one of the many things we love about you."

"You give me too much credit. After my performance at Antoine Calvert's beach house, I'd never have felt safe in my home again. After all, he claims friendship with Sara Lauzier, and she already has plenty of reasons to want me dead."

***

"Thanks for meeting me, Zeke."

Holt sat down beside Hersom on the lookout bench and studied the Palace of the Stars complex across Lake Geneva's leaden surface. It was a cold, rainy day, and both men wore overcoats and broad-brimmed hats to keep themselves warm and dry. As always, when he met the head of the Special Security Bureau, Holt wore a business suit rather than his uniform.

"What do you want, Blayne?" He asked in a conversational tone.

"Sara's on the warpath. I tried to convince her she should simply write Dordogne off as a clear loss, but she wants Siobhan's blood."

"Ah. So her friend Antoine Calvert complained about Siobhan taking over the entire Pègre, did he?"

Hersom turned his head toward Holt and smiled.

"If what I heard is even just a fraction of what happened, Siobhan outdid herself and found a truly inventive solution to your trafficking and corruption problem. Cutting off the Pègre's interstellar reach will put a serious dent in the financing of illicit operations worth billions."

"And strangle political financing, Blayne. Let's not forget where a good chunk of the ill-gotten wealth flows after they laundered it in exchange for laws and regulations that keep the illegal trade alive, and the Armed Forces leashed."

Hersom nodded once.

"Indeed. You can see why Sara is furious. She was getting a huge percentage of her donations from people who live off trafficking in the Rim Sector. Dordogne's Pègre was not only one of the major groups fueling untraceable cash into her coffers but also charged with neutering 3rd Fleet's effectiveness on behalf of every OCG involved. Calvert and company were handsomely rewarded to corrupt Horace Keo and others at 3rd Fleet HQ. If Siobhan cleans up and is free to hunt for trafficking hubs in the Rim, everyone will be affected — criminals, money launderers, crooked politicians, corrupt bureaucrats. And that spells crisis for many people here on Earth because it will take years for the various trafficking and money laundering channels to be re-established elsewhere."

"You're free with information today, Blayne. It's not your style to help us, let alone against the redoubtable Madame Lauzier, our next SecGen and your next immediate boss, provided you stick around. What gives?"

"Enlightened self-interest, my friend. Sara is planning a campaign of unrestricted political warfare against Siobhan in particular and the Fleet in general. I've already told her kinetic action against Siobhan is out of the question. So now she wants the SSB to play a key role in bringing Siobhan down and curbing the Armed Forces' operational autonomy."

"Which will rebound on the SSB in an excruciatingly painful way, as I believe my boss might have mentioned in the past."

"I understand that, but Sara either can't or doesn't care. As you might imagine, I'm deeply concerned about my organization's survival and future effectiveness. Thus, my first loyalty will always be to the Bureau, not politicians who come and go."

"The deep state must endure," Holt said in a sententious tone.

"I got news for you. We're both part of the deep state, even if we see things from radically different angles."

"That still doesn't tell me why you're being friendly, and you know how easily I become suspicious of other people's motives."

Hersom let out a snort of amusement.

"Suspicion is your default setting, Zeke. And mine. Sara thinks the SSB is her private plaything and will sacrifice it for political purposes. Oh, she doesn't think of it as sacrificing, of course, because she doesn't understand that while we may thwart you in the opening stages, you will eventually crush us and do so with extreme prejudice. I can resist her only to a certain extent before she ensures the SecGen fires me and appoints someone unsuitable but utterly under Sara's control."

"Meaning for the good of the SSB and your career, you want Sara cut down to size. And the means you've chosen is ensuring her campaign against the Fleet and Siobhan fails by minimizing the Bureau's involvement and maximizing the Fleet's situational awareness."

"Precisely. Siobhan's little coup d'état gave me the perfect opening, so you might say she did me a good turn for once, but don't tell her. She might look for a way of screwing me over again."

Holt allowed himself a smile.

"She just might. And because of that, no promises."

"I'll be suspending SSB operations on Dordogne for a while and withdrawing my agents so that Sara can't force my hand if ever she orders direct action against Siobhan and 3rd Fleet HQ."

"Orders?" Another smile. "You're confirming Sara Lauzier still wields the same power behind the throne as during her father's tenure. Thanks for that. We thought so, but it's nice to know we were right."

"You didn't hear it from me. And that's all I wanted to discuss. Let's stay in touch, shall we?" With that, Hersom stood and walked away, leaving a pensive Holt to stare at the Palace of the Stars where Senator Sara Lauzier was plotting his best friend's downfall.

It was time to speak with the CNO about giving Siobhan the tactical control over the 101st Battle Group she'd requested. That way, she could continue fighting with her own praetorian guard at her back.

— Thirty-Six —

The weeks following that fateful Saturday when Dunmoore forced terms on the Pègre were eerily quiet. The authorities considered both warehouse destructions accidental after their owners paid off the fire service investigators. Nothing was heard about the electronics in Calvert's beach house getting fried by EMP bursts, either.

But Dunmoore no longer received invitations to socialize with Marseilles' crème de la crème, not even from Victor Herault, the man who was supposed to become her honey pot. That suited her. Leaving the base had become a chore since she could no longer travel without an armed escort. And if Admiral Hogue had any inkling of what had happened, she mercifully gave no sign and was content to let Dunmoore take care of 3rd Fleet's day-to-day operations.

Two more of Vincenzo's cousins had appeared on Dordogne, and they, along with Lou, Gus, and Vincenzo, formed her bodyguard. Whenever she traveled beyond the gates, at least two of them would be with her, armed to the teeth. When she didn't need an escort, they worked on ferreting out more of the Pègre's helpers in the ranks, which Dunmoore deemed more critical than her rare visits to a restaurant or enjoying a hike among the vineyards. And so she spent her off-duty hours in the senior officers' residence — a spacious four-bedroom bungalow — she'd drawn from base housing.

It offered all the privacy she could want, thanks to tall walls surrounding the property and a front gate at the curb which remained shut against anyone not on her admittance list. Vincenzo had ensured its security and surveillance network were the best the Fleet could offer and warned the military police that any alarm from Vice Admiral Dunmoore's residence must be checked out immediately.

But loneliness soon overcame her. Without friends on the planet and no way of making new ones, Dunmoore spent most of her waking hours immersed in work, though she only sat at her desk the standard eight to four so as not to give others a bad example by continuously working overtime. Yet everyone knew she was putting in more time after supper at home, based on the number of notes, memos, plans, and proposals circulating the next morning.

The only bright spots were Pushkin and Guthren's visits whenever *Iolanthe* was in port and the occasional party she hosted for the 101st's captains. The unauthorized raid on the suspected trafficker hub hiding in the backcountry behind Ventano, Mission Colony's capital, had been a success with tons of illegal merchandise destroyed, several dozen traffickers seized for transport to Parth, and the buildings and landing strip vaporized by kinetic strikes from orbit. The colonial administration protested at what they called an attack condoned, if not carried out by the Navy, proving at least some of the senior people were in the traffickers' pay. But Dunmoore ignored the copy sent to 3rd Fleet and heard nothing from Earth.

Yet she suspected those weeks were merely the calm before the storm.

***

"Did you hear Sara Lauzier's speech in the Senate concerning the egregious, nay outrageous actions of a Navy gone rogue?" Holt asked as he joined Kowalski at her table in the cafeteria, coffee cup and fruit bowl in hand for his afternoon snack.

"You mean the one that if she'd made it outside the Senate chamber, we'd have sued her for libel?"

"That would be it. She's quite the rabble-rousing orator. Notice who among the honorable senators applauded and who sat on their hands?"

Kowalski nodded.

"The usual split. Sara's playing with fire, and she knows it. But she's counting on the slight Home World majority to support her against the OutWorlders."

"Sara didn't mention Siobhan by name, but anyone who knows what's going on in the Rim Sector now that she's kicked 3rd Fleet into high gear with help from the 101st got the message that Vice Admiral Dunmoore is the biggest, most egregious rogue of all and must be stopped."

"Then little Sara will be deeply chagrined when Siobhan sends her ships and Marines to wipe out the trafficking hubs on several Rim worlds, including our favorites, Andoth and Garonne. It'll be much harder to hide the fact that the Fleet is wielding its broom."

Holt scoffed. A marginal world that subsisted on mining, Andoth's sole habitable zone lay at the bottom of a ten-kilometer-deep chasm slicing through the planet's broken landscape for thousands of kilometers, where the air pressure sufficed to support human life. Much like Mission Colony, Garonne had little by way of population dotting the shores and riverbanks. Most of it was tropical and subtropical forest.

"Why should we give a tinker's damn if the evidence points at us? Andoth has needed a serious cleanup since well before the war, and every senator with over two brain cells knows it."

Kowalski gave him a wry smile. "So mainly those from the OutWorlds, then."

"Cruel, but accurate. Garonne?" He shrugged. "Just as bad as any frontier colony. Let Siobhan unleash the full fury of her 3rd Fleet and see how Sara Lauzier spins that into a diatribe against us."

"Oh, the CNO has signed classified orders to that effect, and since *Iolanthe*'s Pathfinder task group might not be enough, the 101st will take on a squadron from the 1st Special Forces Regiment, both of the latter to be TACON to 3rd Fleet for the operation. Siobhan can decide how many of her own units she'll add to the mission. But the strike force will be under Gregor Pushkin's command unless she climbs aboard one of the 3rd's ships rigged with a flag bridge, brings along a task group to back up the 101st, and directs the operation herself. None of her rear admirals are to be involved since we can't be one hundred percent sure none of them are playing on the wrong side. Horace Keo couldn't have been an isolated case. Siobhan has complete freedom of action to decide on force composition and operational planning."

Holt let out a low whistle.

"Zeb Lowell is getting serious."

"He's always been serious, but your boss got information from the Colonial Office's intelligence service pinpointing trafficker bases on those two worlds. Now he's pushing through the gap created by Siobhan's actions like a good commander and reinforcing success."

"Against Sara Lauzier? Won't she have SecGen Chu pounding on the Grand Admiral's desk?"

Another smile.

"Who do you think green-lighted Lowell exploiting the situation?"

"Best news I've heard all day. And if I were a betting man, I'd say Siobhan will take personal command, and she won't just stop at Andoth and Garonne. Expect the largest scale deployment since the war. She'll make sure the traffickers in several places leave nothing for Sara to present as evidence of the Navy's cruelty."

"You mean the Navy declaring war against the good citizens of the Commonwealth? She'll go there, mark my words. Lauzier knows the only effective opposition against her Centralist cabal is the Fleet, even though we pretend to be non-political."

"Oo-rah." Holt pumped his fist.

***

"An inspection tour?" Hogue stared at her new deputy commander as if Dunmoore had grown a second head.

"And impromptu war games with each battle group, so I can judge their state of readiness."

"Well, I never. Horace didn't do those sorts of things."

Dunmoore gave Hogue an apologetic shrug.

"I'm not Horace, Admiral. But I know this part of the galaxy better than any other flag officer. Do you have any objections if I took a task group from Battle Group 30, say, *Salamanca,* along with a trio of frigates to convey me under Commodore Nieri?"

Hogue made a dismissive gesture.

"Of course not. I'm sure Quintin won't mind, provided they're not just back from patrol and crews need rest. Paola Nieri will be thrilled to get away from the office."

"*Salamanca* and the three frigates spent their allotted turn in spacedock, they've been resupplied, and their crew got time ashore. I'll re-jig the deployment schedule so we can spare all four from training and patrol duty for the next few weeks."

"Then, by all means, Siobhan, head out there, show the flag, and enjoy yourself. I'm hearing you've not been socializing much since you took over from Horace, so you might as well sail for the stars."

Dunmoore inclined her head. "Thank you, sir. With your permission."

"Go and prepare."

"I'll have orders to the fleet for your signature within the hour, sir."

As she walked out of Hogue's office, Dunmoore couldn't help but marvel at how oblivious her boss seemed about the undercurrents of corruption, backscratching, and organized criminality on Dordogne. Vincenzo, who'd remain on the planet during the 'inspection tour' so he could continue sniffing out traitors, had confirmed she wasn't cooperating with the Pègre or the SSB because she did not need to do so. Hogue merely enjoyed the perks of being a four-star and was happy for her deputy to do the actual work.

Her aide, Lieutenant Commander Margo Takahashi, would also stay. Not only did she have a young family who'd rather have her home every evening and weekend, but Dunmoore could see no use for an aide while she struck at trafficker hubs.

In fact, she didn't plan on bringing any staff and would coordinate the operations she had in mind, just like in the old days of Task Force Luckner. If Dunmoore needed help, she could call on Commodore Nieri or *Salamanca*'s new captain, a recently promoted officer named Cord Elias, whom she'd never met. Elias was too young to have passed through her War College classes or experienced RED One's tender mercies.

Dunmoore's top secret orders gave her such wide latitude that she could only assume Kathryn Kowalski had drafted them for the CNO's signature. For her, it meant rampaging across the Rim and taking out every trafficker hub intelligence could pinpoint, without regard for legal niceties that protected the guilty while hampering the pursuit of justice.

A few weeks with the 101st to strike, Task Group 30.1 to provide cover, and C Squadron, 1st Special Forces Regiment, to augment *Iolanthe*'s embarked Marines, coming aboard their own tactical transport, *Ragnarok*, escorted by the corvette *Swiftsure*, would do wonders to clean out the Rim Sector's dark corners.

***

"Welcome back, Admiral." A smiling Gregor Pushkin held out his hand after Dunmoore had been formally piped aboard, and they'd exchanged salutes. "To what do we owe the honor?"

They shook, and she asked with a mischievous smile, "What's the reward for good work again?"

Captain Trevane Devall, with whom she shook hands immediately afterward, replied, grinning, "More work."

"Glad to see standards aren't slipping. Your day cabin, Gregor? And you might as well join us, Trevane."

Once they were behind closed doors, Pushkin poured them coffee and sat behind his desk.

"Do I really want to hear this?"

"Oh, yes." She pulled out her tablet. "First, I'll let you read the orders I received from the CNO. Then we'll discuss your part in the mission. Trevane can look at them as well."

As Pushkin scanned the dry, matter-of-fact orders, his eyebrows crept up. Once he was done, he passed the tablet to Devall.

"Task Force Morrigan, eh? Andoth, Garonne, and such targets as the Deputy Flag Officer Commanding, 3rd Fleet, may find suitable. Did you just get your very own license to declare war?"

"Something like that. Needless to say, no one must find out about this until we're in deep space. As far as everyone in the 101st and elsewhere are concerned, you're off on a routine patrol." She fished a data wafer from her tunic pocket. "Your orders. I wrote them myself. No one else, living or dead, has seen them. And no one other than you and Trevane will until you reach the rendezvous point to join up with *Ragnarok* and *Swiftsure*, who will come under your tactical control for the duration. C Squadron, 1st SFR, will remain under my TACON, even though it'll be in *Ragnarok*."

Pushkin nodded.

"Understood."

"The concept of operations is simple. I'm proceeding on an inspection tour of 3rd Fleet. I will travel in *Salamanca*, the lead ship of Task Group 30.1, which will be under the command of Commodore Paola Nieri, Quintin Anand's second in command. Vince and his merry band of counterintelligence operatives vetted her, and she's no dummy. That purpose and grouping will be announced as soon as I speak with her and Quintin, right after we're done here. As far as anyone, Paola included, knows, you're off doing something and aren't part of anything I'm doing. I'll brief her when we're in deep space as well. The task group and the 101st will marry up at Andoth's heliopause, where we'll coordinate the strike while you send one of your ships inward to reconnoiter Andoth and pinpoint the target. Once we know precisely what we're facing on the ground, I will finalize a plan. But the general concept, for Andoth and any other strike, will be the 101st going in while the task group blockades the planet, intercepting starships and standing by to provide you with extra fire support if needed."

"Wow." Devall gave her an appreciative nod. "I don't think the Navy carried out such a large-scale operation since the war. We certainly haven't."

"The assault on the Garonne trafficking hub will be carried out under the same concept. And if intelligence feeds us one or two more, we'll just keep going."

Pushkin rapped his desktop with his knuckles.

"Admiral Dunmoore rides again."

"Once I've met with Quintin and Paola, I'll let you know when the task group is sailing. You can leave any time you want and head straight for Andoth, but don't leave it too long. I'd rather not cause people to wonder whether your departure and ours are related."

"We can be gone by the day after tomorrow."

"Plan on that, then."

— Thirty-Seven —

"Good to see you, Admiral." Quintin Anand, stocky, bald, dark-complexioned, with thick gray eyebrows and a neatly trimmed mouth beard, briefly came to attention when Dunmoore entered his office, then extended his hand. "Welcome back aboard Starbase 30."

"Glad to be back, Quin. You're looking well."

Anand chuckled.

"Prospering."

Dunmoore turned to the tall, slender, olive-skinned commodore with short black hair and expressive brown eyes.

"How are you, Paola?"

"Just like my boss, sir — prospering. Though I miss riding a command chair aboard a starship."

"Then you'll enjoy what I'm about to discuss."

Anand gestured at the settee group to one side of the office, beneath the reproduction of a painting depicting a long-ago battle between sailing ships.

"Shall we? Coffee, sir?"

"No thanks. I arrived a little early and had a quick visit aboard *Iolanthe* to say hi. Gregor fed me a cup of his best brew."

Nieri nodded.

"He serves a good cup. I was aboard the other day to go over the 101st's latest resupply process, so I could make sure we missed nothing this time."

"And? All was well?" Dunmoore asked as she took a seat.

A quick chat with Alvin Maffina solved that problem. Vincenzo discovered one of the senior officers in the 3rd Fleet logistics branch had developed a grudge against the 101st and was taking it out on her former command through mis-prioritization of parts deliveries. Maffina had assured her it wouldn't happen again.

"Gregor was quite happy. The 101st is ready to sail."

"Good. Now, Admiral Hogue is sending me on an inspection tour of the 3rd Fleet's area of operations, and I plan on engaging the battle groups in a few war games to gain an appreciation of their readiness."

Anand winced theatrically.

"That statement from the former head of RED One is enough to send shivers down anyone's spine."

Dunmoore gave him an amused grin.

"I hadn't thought of it, but if your fellow battle group commanders feel that way, then who am I to disabuse them? You'll be glad I'm exempting the 30th from the tour. There's no need since I'll be sailing aboard a task group made up of your ships currently in port, ready for deployment — *Salamanca*, *Charles Martel*, *Arthur Currie*, and *Jan Sobieski* — to be designated Task Group 30.1 under Paola's command."

Commodore Nieri's face lit up at the news, and Anand couldn't restrain another chuckle at her evident glee.

"I think Paola likes the idea."

"The contrary would have surprised me. I wanted to speak with both of you in person on the subject before the orders come out and give you copies of said orders so you can begin preparing. I'd like to sail as soon as feasible but without rushing. Once all four ships are fully supplied and armed — we will carry the basic war load — Paola and I can discuss the departure date and time. Since I don't want to give any battle group an advantage, I'll be revealing our first stop once we drop out of FTL at the heliopause."

Anand glanced at his second in command.

"What do you figure for departure?"

"They're fully supplied now. Say three days for the last checks and for crew still on leave to return." Nieri turned to Dunmoore. "Tuesday, sir? We can break out of orbit at, say, oh-eight-hundred and be at the refueling station early in the afternoon watch and the heliopause by the end of the evening watch."

"Sounds like a plan. I'll come aboard Monday evening then, at the end of the dog watch."

Nieri smiled again.

"Looking forward to it, sir."

"Oh, and I'm not bringing any staff, not even my aide, so I'll be relying on yours if any staff work needs doing. But as you might have heard from Gregor, I'm pretty low maintenance, and putting up a third star hasn't changed that."

"That would be your reputation, all right," Anand said.

Dunmoore fished a pair of data wafers from her pocket and handed them out.

"The orders going to every battle group and the Task Group 30.1 orders. Enjoy. And since I'm here, Quin, if you want to bend my ear about anything while Paola starts her preparations, you have a golden opportunity. I'm not due aboard the shuttle for another hour."

"Since you're offering, there are one or two matters I wouldn't mind discussing."

***

That evening, Dunmoore went to the opera, her first major outing since bringing the various Pègre bosses to heel. And so far, they'd been either obedient or discreet. Even the Naval Intelligence folks assigned to watch them saw nothing.

She'd decided to appear in Marseilles society after her hiatus because, for one thing, the opera was among her favorites from the pre-diaspora repertoire, Turandot. The soul-stirring and show-stopping aria, Nessun Dorma, always touched her deeply. And for another, she wanted to show her face among the people whose trafficker friends she was about to erase from the galaxy.

Not that they'd ever find out for sure, but knowledge of Dunmoore here one day, gone on a sector-wide inspection tour with a naval task group the next, could only get the rumor mills going once news from Andoth and Garonne spread. A bit of psychological warfare never hurt.

Lou and Gus, disguised as anonymous bodyguards, would watch over her at all times, though she would be alone in the loge. Vincenzo tried to argue her out of the notion when she decided on it shortly after receiving the secret orders but finally relented.

Since the Pègre was quiescent and knew better than trying an assassination in such a public place, only the SSB represented a threat, and Holt had passed along word that its agents were withdrawing from Dordogne for a while.

The Opéra de Marseilles enjoyed an enviable reputation in the sector, and with good reason. It was a production as faithful to the original vision of Giacomo Puccini, the composer, as possible. And, as she knew would happen, Nessun Dorma brought tears to her eyes. Once it was over, all who mattered in Marseilles saw Vice Admiral Siobhan Dunmoore, elegant in her evening clothes, enthusiastically applaud like everyone else.

Though paying for a loge entitled her to a drink with the cast and crew backstage afterward, a perk eagerly sought after by the class-conscious Marseillais, she vanished through the opera house's back corridors under the guidance of her bodyguards. Not only would it add to the story, but avoiding the crowd eased some of Vincenzo's concerns. Besides, she found no interest in being polite to people she'd threatened with annihilation at gunpoint a few weeks earlier.

***

The following Monday, after a quiet weekend during which the 101st broke out of orbit and left for parts unknown, Dunmoore received a message from Captain Elias saying that the ship's pinnace would collect her at the time of her choosing. *Salamanca* was no longer docked with Starbase 30, having completed her final preparations, and since he'd have to send a shuttle to fetch her there if she took the regular run up from Joint Base Dordogne, the shuttle might as well bring her up from the surface.

As a result, Dunmoore decided she would take the evening meal in the cruiser's wardroom and head up directly after finishing her day at the office. A small side party piped her aboard at three bells in the dog watch after the pinnace landed on *Salamanca*'s hangar deck, where Commodore Nieri and Captain Elias greeted her.

"Welcome, Admiral. You'll find everything in good order and as it was when *Salamanca* last served as your flagship," Elias said after they exchanged salutes and handshakes while a bosun's mate took Dunmoore's luggage to the VIP suite.

Dunmoore smiled at him.

"I don't doubt it for a second."

"And you'll be glad to hear Task Group 30.1 is ready to leave. We need not wait until tomorrow morning. The refueling station can take us in the next twelve hours, so if you have no objections, I will get us underway now. Once we've broken out of orbit, we three can sit down for the evening meal in my quarters."

"Done and done, Paola. Let's make it so. And I wouldn't mind watching our departure from the flag CIC. It'll bring back memories."

"I have no doubt."

"Let me get out of your way and settle in while you pass along your orders and get clearance from traffic control."

Nieri nodded as she gestured toward the inner airlock.

"I'll call you a few minutes before we're due."

The VIP suite was precisely as Dunmoore remembered from three and a half years ago when she was a captain facing early separation from the Navy for not regaining her star once too often. And now? Dunmoore glanced at herself in the mirror as she unpacked. A vice admiral, deputy commander 3rd Fleet, about to lead her ships on a raid of questionable legality, but one which was desperately needed. And she understood only too well they had placed her in this position because she was one of the few, if not the only flag officer in the Navy who'd willingly accept such a mission, consequences be damned.

Watching Task Group 30.1 depart with Commodore Nieri in the CIC — she'd offered the command chair, but Dunmoore had demurred — with multiple views, including a video feed from the starbase, was a treat. Supper, once Captain Elias set the ship at cruising stations, was pleasant and enlightening. Both he and Nieri came across as intelligent, well-read, and self-aware officers.

They also gave Dunmoore the impression they suspected the inspection tour was merely an excuse for something more exciting. After all, until recently, she'd led the Navy's foremost raider battle group and had once been the bane of the Shrehari Empire in this sector. And they'd noticed all the 101st's ships previously docked or in orbit had quietly slipped away twenty-four hours earlier. If so, Dunmoore hoped no one else was wondering the same thing.

Dunmoore stayed up to observe the refueling process a few hours later and declared herself satisfied with the speed and precision shown by all four ships before heading to her quarters and a few hours of sleep. After breakfast, she planned on briefing

Nieri and Elias about their true destination, so they could prepare navigation orders for the task group when it came out of FTL at Dordogne's heliopause. Part of her couldn't wait to see their reaction — she'd learned plenty of officers who reached senior ranks in peacetime were averse to risk, and these two had still been lieutenants at the end of the war.

But whether they felt comfortable with the objective or not, the mission would go on.

— Thirty-Eight —

"Let me ask a question," Dunmoore said, pushing her breakfast plate to one side and picking up the coffee mug with *Salamanca*'s crest. "Were either of you figuring we might not be on a genuine inspection tour?"

Dunmoore, Nieri, and Elias were the only ones left in the wardroom. The rest of *Salamanca*'s officers had come and gone and were now either at their duty stations or in their racks.

Nieri and Elias exchanged a telling glance, then the former grimaced.

"Not so much figuring as hoping. Neither of us has witnessed shots fired in anger since the war, but by all accounts — and I know they're classified — the 101st saw plenty of action under your command. And now under Gregor's."

"I don't know if you'll witness any in person on this mission, but you'll be part of a raiding force as the backup to the 101st and, at the moment, as a decoy of sorts until we meet up with Gregor. If the targets wisely surrender, there may not be shots fired in anger, but it isn't a training exercise." When they gave her expectant looks, Dunmoore smiled. "We're taking down known trafficker hubs in the sector, starting with Andoth, our actual destination. It's called Operation Morrigan, and once we join the 101st, the formation will be known as Task Force Morrigan."

As she explained her concept, Dunmoore noticed Nieri and Elias becoming increasingly uneasy.

"Sir, pardon me for asking," Nieri said once Dunmoore fell silent, "but at what level was this mission authorized? Military strikes on Commonwealth or sovereign star system colonies, while not as severely restricted as those on sovereign worlds, are subject to an extensive list of caveats."

"The CNO signed my orders. Presumably, he received his instructions from the Grand Admiral. Beyond that, I couldn't say. But the plan is for surgical strikes that won't harm the civilian population. And by putting these hubs out of business, we'll choke off the flow of harmful substances from the Zone and the trafficking of human beings destined for the worst sort of slavery. The latter alone makes a breach of rules favoring criminals over law enforcement not only ethical but moral."

An air of determination replaced Elias' earlier uncertainty.

"No arguments from me on that subject, sir. If you have the coordinates for our rendezvous with the 101st, I'll see my navigator prepares the plot so we can sync the task group after we cross the heliopause."

Dunmoore fished a data wafer from her pocket.

"It's all on there."

"A question, if I may," Nieri said in a thoughtful tone.

"Sure. Never hesitate to ask me anything. I may not always have the answers or the permission to answer, but I'll try."

"Why the internal secrecy surrounding our deployment? I mean things like leaving port without a destination, orders sealed until we're at the heliopause, a deception plan only you knew about, etcetera."

A sad smile briefly crossed Dunmoore's face.

"We have traitors inside 3rd Fleet HQ, on Starbase 30, and perhaps even inside the 30th Battle Group. People who willingly sell information to the opposition — organized crime groups on Dordogne and elsewhere — or committed indiscretions and are now being blackmailed for information. Counterintelligence is tracking them down, and a number have already been unmasked and quietly removed before anyone knew it was happening."

A light went on in Nieri's eyes.

"Such as Admiral Keo?"

"I can neither confirm nor deny that. The CNO recalled Admiral Keo to Earth. Inferring anything from it would be pure speculation."

Nieri and Elias contemplated Dunmoore for a few seconds, then both nodded their understanding.

"Another question, then. The unannounced launch by *Iolanthe* several weeks ago — one transport and four gunships — that riled both our and the civilian traffic control units, was that part of it?"

This time, Dunmoore's smile held a hint of amusement.

"Yes. And if you're about to ask whether they carried out a military mission on a sovereign world, you'll have to keep wondering because I can't answer."

"Understood, sir. Thank you. I guess reality is a lot stranger and murkier than we think from inside our antiseptic peacetime naval universe."

"You have no idea, Paola."

***

"We're at the correct coordinates," *Salamanca*'s combat systems officer said. "By all rights, the 101st should be here, but we're not picking up anything."

Dunmoore, sitting at the back of the CIC by an unused workstation while Nieri occupied the command chair, smiled at him.

"They're here. Once they've established that the four bogeys without beacons are a Reconquista and three Voivodes, as advertised in their orders, one of them, presumably *Iolanthe*, will light up and say hi. The Q ships have some of the tightest emissions controls in the Fleet."

Moments later, the signals petty officer raised a hand.

"We're being painted by a communications laser."

"By all means, accept the link," Nieri said. "And when you pinpoint its source, return the favor."

The combat systems officer glanced over his shoulder.

"She just lit up, like the Admiral said."

"*Salamanca*, this is *Iolanthe*. We have you on our sensors, and it looks like you also found us. Commodore Pushkin would like to speak with Admiral Dunmoore and Commodore Nieri."

Dunmoore jumped to her feet. "How about we take this in the conference room, Paola?"

"Good idea, sir. Signals, please pipe it through."

"Aye, aye."

Moments after they settled at one end of the table, the primary display lit up with Gregor Pushkin's smiling face.

"Welcome to Task Force Morrigan's first area of operations. You had a good passage?"

"As good as can be expected," Dunmoore replied. "I just hope everyone thinks Task Group 30.1 is off on the inspection tour as advertised and that you did your usual vanishing act, presumably for the Zone. You?"

"All is as one could wish, Admiral. We arrived thirty-six hours ago. *Gondolier* is currently loitering at Andoth's hyperlimit while one of its recon drones is scouting the target area. No news so far. She'll only transmit once she has results."

"And we'll wait here until then. No use crowding the hyperlimit for too long before H-hour."

"Roger that. Give me a sec, and I'll link in Lieutenant Colonel Harry Lothbrok of the 1st SFR aboard *Ragnarok*, sailing just off *Iolanthe*'s starboard beam. He brought three hundred of the Marine Corps' best. We could seize control of Andoth and overthrow its government with that many troopers."

Dunmoore made a face.

"No thanks. Once we extirpate the traffickers, they can wallow in their usual lawlessness without interference."

The image on the display split in two as the square, craggy face of a Marine with short black hair, deep-set blue eyes, and a pugilist's nose appeared.

"Good day, Admiral. Commodore. A pleasure to meet both of you. My Marines and I are looking forward to a little live fire action against actual targets. Since leaving Caledonia, we've spent our time studying the topography of Andoth in the target area and everything else intelligence provided. It should be a straightforward raid, although I don't recommend sending any of your ships into the chasm as close support. It'll have to be dropships and armed shuttles."

Dunmoore nodded.

"That was my assessment as well. What I'd like to discuss with you and Commodore Pushkin once we have results from the recon drone is the altitude at which you and *Iolanthe*'s Marines will be launched. Both ships can fool Andoth traffic control into believing they're freighters, and if you launch inside the chasm, the tangos will have much less time to react. Oh, and by the way, I hope you've come equipped with unmarked everything."

Lothbrok cracked a smile.

"We always do, Admiral. We'll fight in proper Marine uniform someday, but that day isn't coming soon."

"I've placed my embarked squadron under Colonel Lothbrok's command for the duration, Admiral," Pushkin said. "They'll be fully deniable as well once they go in."

"Works for me. Now, let's get the entire formation on the same heading and the same speed while we wait for *Gondolier* to report back."

***

"That looks precisely as described by the intelligence report," Dunmoore said when the images from the recon drone appeared on the conference room display.

A sprawling warehouse complex at the foot of the chasm's north wall surrounded a private landing strip big enough for several small freighters. It was protected by a berm and fence reminiscent of those used by Marines for their forward operating bases. A single road cut through the defenses, joining the Andoth Highway that ran thousands of kilometers from one end of the habitable area to the other.

And it was isolated. The nearest mining operation lay fifty kilometers to the east, the nearest town another ten kilometers beyond that. Clearly, the complex could serve no other function than transshipment. There was no evidence of manufacturing operations, let alone ore or precious minerals extraction.

The chasm was five kilometers wide at that point, its walls almost perfectly smooth and vertical. A large swath of the bottom, mainly along the walls where direct sunlight never reached, existed in a sort of permanent semi-obscurity. To Dunmoore's eyes, it seemed heartbreakingly depressing, with no vegetation other than dull green native scrub breaking up the dun-colored soil and rock.

"A few things to note," Colonel Lothbrok said, breaking the silence. "While the drone picked up plenty of life signs inside the buildings, it spotted no humans for the entire time covered by this recording, which is almost three hours. Nor did it detect ground vehicles. As you can see, there are no ships or shuttles on the tarmac either. One might almost think it was abandoned if it weren't for the life signs indoors. Now, the biggest concentrations, several hundred, are in the buildings marked B4 and B5, which would be consistent with holding pens for trafficked humans. Despite the size of the place, it wouldn't take more than a hundred people to run an efficient transshipment operation. Half of that might even suffice. It's isolated enough for trafficking, especially if the colonial administration looks the other way."

Pushkin scoffed.

"Which it clearly does. How many other sites like this are on the planet? None. This is the only one the recon drone saw."

"Any defenses beyond the perimeter, which I suppose includes sensors?" Dunmoore asked.

Lothbrok shook his head.

"The drone found nothing that would hint at active arrays and, yes, there are sensors. It doesn't mean there aren't any weapon emplacements, just that they can't be major. Otherwise, we'd have detected something. I think they're more worried about ground-based threats such as organized crime than having your friendly neighborhood Marines drop by. The one thing I would say if you'll allow me, Admiral, is that aerial bombardment, especially with kinetic penetrator rods, would be ill-advised. We don't want to trigger a chasm wall collapse that might spread to other inhabited areas."

"Understood. That wasn't my intent, certainly not if there are prisoners, as the life sign readings seem to show. Fire support will come from your organic means only."

A nod.

"It's what I plan on. And now, Admiral, this is your call. As per intelligence reports, the target bears all the characteristics of a trafficker hub and isn't listed in the database of legitimate Andoth businesses."

"As far as the colonial administration's public records show, it doesn't exist at all," Pushkin said. "Remember, every aerial and orbital image of the site in the colonial database shows nothing but unused scrubland."

"All right. We're a go. *Ragnarok* to insert the ground force with the 101st in low orbit, so there's always a ship overhead. Task Group 30.1 to take geostationary orbit above the chasm and blockade any incoming and outgoing vessels. Have you shifted your Marines to *Ragnarok*, Gregor?"

"Not yet. I was waiting for your go order. Give us thirty minutes, then we can jump inward to the hyperlimit."

"Let's make it so, folks."

— Thirty-Nine —

"All ships running silent and on course for their planned orbital insertions," the flag CIC sensor chief reported shortly after Task Force Morrigan dropped out of FTL at the hyperlimit and joined *Gondolier*. "Tracking the orbitals."

A few minutes later, the secondary display lit up with a schematic of the planet and every active satellite around it, each with an abbreviation designating its function.

"No active pings from the traffic control orbitals. They haven't picked up our emergence signature."

Dunmoore and Nieri, who occupied the command chair, exchanged glances.

"So far, so good."

They studied the dun-colored, barren planet with the wispy atmosphere in silence as it grew on the primary display. The chasm, a dark slash near the equator, was its only noticeable feature at this level of magnification.

"And they're trying to make the place a prison colony?" Nieri asked in wonderment. "I get that escape would be well-nigh impossible, but still. A distinct contrast with Parth, where you just drop a seed on the ground, and it sprouts. Here, the food must all be greenhouse grown or imported. Which government of fools would spend that much money feeding prisoners?"

Dunmoore smiled at her.

"Our government. Mind you, the miner's consortium running the place on behalf of the Colonial Office must enjoy the extra income." A thought struck her, and she frowned. "I wonder if any inmates vanish and are declared deceased, their remains cremated."

"Sir?"

"Why wouldn't the traffickers send able-bodied humans into the Zone as slave labor rather than return their ships empty? A little money in the pocket of the prison warden, and a troublesome inmate whose upkeep is expensive, disappears."

Nieri grimaced.

"Now there's a lovely thought. The Commonwealth Correctional Service involved in slavery."

"I wouldn't be surprised at all. There are more nasty doings under the heavens than ninety-nine percent of humanity can fathom." Dunmoore sprang to her feet. "Since the approach is going well, I think I'll grab a sandwich in the wardroom rather than breathe down the sensor chief's neck."

When the chief in question, a grizzled veteran with short gray hair, a seamed face, and a close-cropped beard, glanced over his shoulder at her and smiled, Dunmoore winked at him.

***

"All ships are in position, and *Ragnarok* is lining up for her drop run," Nieri announced when Dunmoore re-entered the flag CIC after a leisurely meal and a quick nap, consciously staying out of sight until the action started.

"Still no movement at the target, no people, no vehicles, though *Gondolier*'s drone is still reporting life signs," the sensor chief added, nodding at the secondary display, which now showed an aerial view of the trafficker hub.

Dunmoore took the unoccupied combat systems officer's chair again. After briefly glancing at the three-dimensional tactical projection where an icon marked *Ragnarok* was preparing to slip into the chasm, she studied the video from the recon drone, hovering above the chasm's lips.

Something was nagging at the edge of her subconscious.

"Chief, please find out how low the drone went during her entire reconnaissance mission."

"Yes, sir. Wait one." Several minutes passed, during which *Ragnarok* entered the chasm on a course toward the target. "The drone never went below eleven kilometers, Admiral, to minimize the risk of it being spotted by the tangos or traffic control, in case they have barrier sensors across the top of the chasm and forgot to tell anyone."

"Thank you, Chief."

"Admiral, traffic control woke up and finally noticed *Ragnarok*. They're demanding she identify herself and her destination." A pause. "Dropships are launching. That ought to make traffic control choke on their demands."

Whoever controlled the drone had been right. There had to be a sensor grid across the chasm's opening, one not listed in the navigation orders for the star system if they picked up the stealthiest tactical transport in the Fleet the moment it dropped below the surface and not before. And that could mean several things, but only one worried Dunmoore.

"Put us on the Morrigan Ground frequency, please."

A few seconds passed.

"You have it."

Dunmoore leaned toward the workstation's audio pickup.

"Ground Niner, this is Morrigan Niner."

A few moments passed, then Lothbrok's voice came through the CIC speakers.

"Ground Niner here."

"Hammer the target with your dropship sensors. Concentrate on the life sign clusters. By now, there's no point in hiding. Report back on any anomalies."

"Wilco."

"Morrigan Niner, out."

"Anything wrong, Admiral?" Nieri asked.

"Something's bugging me, and I can't figure out what. Call it a gut feeling."

Less than two minutes passed before Lothbrok came back on the radio.

"This is Ground Niner. We got ourselves an anomaly. The life sign readings are as diffuse now, at five thousand, as they were from the drone readings at eleven thousand. They haven't resolved into clearer individuals or changed at all."

"Decoys, emitting life sign energy readings," Dunmoore replied as the subconscious nagging became a fully formed idea. "It's a trap. Abort the mission. I repeat, abort the mission. Head for low orbit and wait."

"Roger. Aborting the mission and heading for low orbit to wait."

Gregor Pushkin appeared on the CIC's secondary display moments later.

"What tipped you off, Admiral?"

"In all the time we've had the target under observation, we saw no people, cars, or anything else, yet it's teeming with enough life signs to indicate human trafficking."

"You figure the operation was compromised from the outset?"

Dunmoore nodded.

"Looks that way. They surely knew someone was coming and abandoned ship. Either the complex is booby-trapped to blow up in our faces, or it's covered by a network of sensors that would have shown what could only be an unauthorized assault by Armed Forces personnel on a Commonwealth colony. A political booby-trap if you like."

"Then where was it betrayed?"

"Has to be Earth. My orders were encrypted with a special algorithm no one at 3rd Fleet can decipher. You and Trevane were the only ones to know before leaving Dordogne, and I doubt you've gone rogue on me after all these years. Everyone else found out once we were beyond normal radio range. Any unauthorized subspace transmission would have been logged."

"Where did we — or rather HQ — get the intel from, in that case?"

"I don't know, Gregor. But I'll need Colonel Lothbrok to reconfigure the ground mission into a sneak and peek so we can figure out exactly what's going on down there. Have *Ragnarok* recover the dropships, then remain in her current orbit but go silent. Meanwhile, I'll start drafting a message to Earth informing them someone either read the mail or lied about the trafficking hub."

***

"It's going to be a tad difficult to approach the target unseen, Admiral. There's no cover, and if we're not going to drop right on top of it, there are only two ways in — from the east or the west."

"On second thought, I don't much care about being seen at this point. If they don't know yet we're here, they're at the very least expecting us. And if this is a political instead of a kinetic booby-trap, then we've already given them fodder. I want to know what still is inside those buildings, everything we can about the decoy emitters, and the best way to make the target unusable after we leave."

Lothbrok nodded once.

"Then I suggest a small force — two troops, each aboard its own dropship. They land a kilometer east and west of the target, sweep the area up to the perimeter fence, and then send in their troop Augies."

Dunmoore raised a hand.

"Sorry. Augies?"

"Autonomous ground infiltration and exploitation systems. A lot like the Navy's boarding droids, only with more capabilities and better armored. If the Augies don't detect any threats, then you can decide whether my Marines conduct an in-person search and prepare the place for demolition."

"Agreed, Colonel. Please go ahead with the plan. When will you launch?"

"Two hours, tops. Earlier, if we can. The locals know someone's messing about in orbit even if they can't see us, so the sooner, the better."

"Whenever you're ready, you may execute."

***

Visitors and locals must ignore Andoth traffic control a lot because they stopped squawking about the two dropships entering the chasm without permission after three attempts. Dunmoore suspected the further such intrusions were from the major ports, such as Yavan, the capital, a good five hundred kilometers west of the target, the less they cared. Or perhaps they were paid not to care by people like traffickers.

Once on the ground, the dropships' stealth coating made them quasi-invisible to the naked eye and, with their power dampened, to civilian sensors beyond a kilometer. The Marines themselves, wearing chameleon armor, blended with their surroundings so that the recon drone hovering above the chasm could barely pinpoint them at maximum magnification.

Video feeds from both troop leaders played on the flag CIC's side displays, showing their progress toward the target in real-time. So far, the Marines' battlefield sensors had detected nothing unusual beyond life signs that showed no more resolution at a few hundred meters than at eleven kilometers. By now, they should be able to make out individuals or at least small clusters and detect bodies behind walls in the infrared part of the spectrum, but nothing.

"No question that place is full of decoys," Pushkin, or rather his image on a tertiary display, said with an air of disgust. "Someone definitely betrayed us."

The Marines reached the fence-topped perimeter berm without incident and encountered no other living beings. From the troop leaders' point of view, the environment felt claustrophobic. Hemmed in by ten-kilometer-high cliff walls almost as smooth as glass, one within a hundred meters, the other five kilometers to the south, little sunlight reached the floor, and the sky was just a pale blue ribbon overhead. One getting darker as dusk approached.

"As suspected, there's an active perimeter sensor network, but still no signs of weapons emplacements," one of the troop leaders said. "The main gate is closed but does not appear locked."

"Have your Augie open it," Lothbrok replied.

"Roger. Launching Augie One."

A third video feed appeared moments later, closer to the ground, as the small tank-like machine floating on an antigrav cushion switched from standby to autonomous mode. It glided up to the gate, extruded an arm with prehensile digits and grasped the right-side gate handle. An almost effortless tug moved the mesh panel aside, creating an opening big enough for the Augie.

Dunmoore realized she'd been holding her breath as the low-slung droid scooted in, triggering no alarms or, worse yet, explosions. A fourth video joined the other three as Augie Two entered behind its artificial sibling. But where One turned toward the buildings with the heavy life sign decoy readings, Two went for what looked like a warehouse at the edge of the cliff, near a smaller structure that also emitted fake life signs and evidence of electrical power.

"I wonder..." Dunmoore said in a thoughtful tone.

"Sir?" Nieri glanced at her.

"Was this ever used, or is it all staged for our benefit while the true trafficker base is hundreds of kilometers away, hidden inside a mining complex? Serious question, folks. Am I imagining things, or does the place exude a sense of flimsiness close up?"

"Now that you mention it," Pushkin replied. "It doesn't feel substantial. But prefabricated structures dropped in containers from orbit rarely seem solid at first glance. And they don't really need to be particularly weatherproof either. There's not much wind or rain on this world."

"One thing that strikes me is how uncluttered everything is," Nieri said. "No garbage, no piles of discarded construction or packing material. And it's dusty everywhere, yet I've not seen tracks or footprints yet. Ah, here we go. Augie One is at the first building with the several hundred fake life signs."

The little machine found a door and sat in front of it for over a minute, scanning for threats. Then it extruded an arm again to grasp the handle.

"No booby-traps Augie can detect, and it isn't locked," the troop leader reported.

"Let it enter," Lothbrok replied.

The door swung inward at the Augie's push. It crossed the threshold and into a space empty but for a metallic box on a table at the center. The box was connected to a black cable that snaked across the floor and vanished into a junction box set at floor height.

"Prefabricated panels on a concrete slab," Pushkin said. "Not meant to be permanent. If the other structures are of the same construction, I figure a determined crew could disassemble this entire little base in a day. And that box is our decoy emitter. I suggest Augie bring it with him."

"I'd rather not, sir. Augie will give it as thorough a scan as any, but I think we shouldn't tempt fate. If they rigged anything to go off on us, that thing would be my prime candidate. Besides, if we leave it as is, it might make the opposition wonder."

Before anyone could argue, Dunmoore said, "I'm with the colonel. We'll take only scans and leave everything in place. Every bit of misdirection can help. Besides, I'm almost certain this is a political booby-trap. There are almost certainly many video pickups recording everything happening here, and they're likely so well hidden and at a distance that it would take days to find them. And we have other, more pressing matters."

— Forty —

"A Potemkin trafficking hub?" Admiral Zebulon Lowell's thick eyebrows rose in surprise after Kowalski and Holt relayed Siobhan Dunmoore's report. "Imagine that. Is Dunmoore right about it being a political booby-trap? Are we spying the hand of Sara Lauzier and her tame SSB behind this?"

He, Kowalski, Holt, and Doxiadis sat around the latter's office conference table in the HQ building's top security section.

"I'd say there's a high probability that either or both are the instigators," Holt replied. "That base was abandoned several weeks ago, judging by the dust accumulation, which means by the time we received the intel, it was already out of date. If they're still on Andoth, it'll be far away from the target and probably better concealed behind a mining operation."

"We got the info from the Colonial Office Intelligence Service, right, Zeke?" Doxiadis asked.

"Yes, sir. Since Mikhail Forenza took over as director of field operations, the flow of information between the Colonials and us has been constant and seamless. And yes, sir. I know what you're about to say. They have traitors in their organization. Which isn't a surprise. If we've been penetrated, so have they. I'll meet with Mikhail later today and apprise him of the problem."

A faint air of annoyance creased Lowell's face.

"So we can assume the rest of the sites they fed us will be bogus as well."

"Siobhan is working under that assumption. She's also assuming there's a chance the traffickers might head for the real Andoth hub once Task Force Morrigan leaves, and so she's playing the odds. The 101st stays in the system, running silent, ready to intercept likely ships, while Task Group 30.1 visits the nearest battle group, which would be the 36th, and shows the flag. If nothing else, it might make the opposition wonder."

"You realize, sir," Kowalski said, "that if Siobhan's theory is correct, and I consider it a distinct possibility, we may face another political scandal pushed by the Centralists. We can thank the Almighty that Siobhan listened to her gut instinct and pulled the strike force back at the halfway mark, sending a small recon team instead. Otherwise, I can only imagine the political capital Lauzier would generate by accusations of senior officers going rogue. It's much harder to build a case when all the evidence is of dropships making a brief flight through the chasm, never dropping below five thousand meters, and a handful of unidentified troopers inspecting an abandoned installation, taking nothing, and harming no one."

Lowell rubbed his cheek with one hand.

"Okay. If Andoth comes up, it'll be called a training exercise on public land. After all, there are no official records of the installation. Let them prove differently."

"That was going to be my recommendation, sir. Siobhan might get lucky, and the 101st makes a few good seizures while she's playing pantomime with the 36th, something that'll raise the blood pressure of the financiers."

"And the next target, Garonne?"

"Her approach will be radically different. She might even send the 101st by itself while she visits the 37th Battle Group, whose home port is nearest to Garonne."

***

"An interesting place to meet." Mikhail Forenza dropped on the bench beside Ezekiel Holt. The latter wore a well-cut civilian business suit once again. Forenza, the consummate Colonial Office executive, was even more elegant.

"What? The lookout on top of Montagne du Vuache? Best place to study the city of humanity's original sin without modern interruptions." Holt turned his head and smiled at Forenza. "How are you? And how's the new job?"

"I am fine. The new job is as well. But if you and I are meeting here, I suspect both will be not fine momentarily."

"Cynic."

"How long have we known each other, Zeke? Since the Toboso affair? I'm a realist. Cynicism is but an inevitable side effect of reality unmasked."

"Then I suppose I'm about to reinforce your reality unmasked. You remember finding trafficker hubs for us in the Rim?"

Forenza turned his craggy face, dominated by a sweptback mane of silver hair, toward Holt.

"Why do I think you're about to make life less pleasant than it was a few minutes ago?"

"You have traitors in your organization."

"Don't we all." Forenza's eyes returned to the distant view of humanity's capital and its eponymous lake to the northeast. "Let me guess, our latest intelligence on traffickers didn't pan out."

"They knew we would do Andoth before you even gave us the intel. Siobhan hit a great big goose egg there. We figure someone wanted to record the Fleet carrying out unauthorized military action against targets within the Commonwealth. It didn't work because Siobhan pulled out in time."

"She is blessed with good instincts."

"You have folks working for the opposition in your organization, Mikhail. Far be it from me to offer advice when I'm still hunting down enemies inside the Fleet, but here we are. Siobhan kept the most stringent operational security going into this, and as I said, the Andoth target gave every sign of having been abandoned before we ordered her in."

"Then I suppose I have some wet work in my future."

"Just thought you ought to know." Holt stood. "We're treating every other target designation we received from you as compromised. If they're looking for video of the Fleet breaking the law, they'll find nothing but bitter disappointment."

"They? The SSB, or the Centralists?"

"Is there a difference? Anyone gravitating around Sara Lauzier. We're purging our ranks with extreme prejudice. I suggest you do the same. Until we can be sure again, any intel you pass along will automatically be tagged as suspect." Holt turned his head to glance at Forenza over his shoulder. "And yes, we're aware the opposition would like nothing more for us to be at odds, so stay in touch, my friend, because we can't let them succeed."

"No, we can't," Forenza replied softly as he watched Holt's receding back.

***

"What the hell happened?"

As was her long-time habit, Sara Lauzier strode into Hersom's office without so much as a knock and dropped into a chair.

Hersom, who'd been reading a report, looked up at her with an exasperated sigh. Moving his office out of the Palace of the Stars was becoming more imperative by the day.

"What are you talking about?"

"Andoth. The Navy came, diddled around, and buggered off without giving us any propaganda value. I assume it was Dunmoore since she apparently went off on a so-called inspection tour and has a habit of constantly interfering. How did she figure out the intel on the Andoth hub was bogus?"

"If it was her. I'm sure I said this before, but the senior officers out there, dealing with the realities of a hostile universe, aren't like those from Fleet HQ who gravitate around politicians, seeking favors and advancement. They're smarter, more perceptive, and more alert to danger. The chances of your scheme succeeding were never that good. And now they've uncovered one bogus site, they'll suspect every other one pointed out by Colonial Office intel is fake, and they'll approach them accordingly. The only positive from this is a potential drop in trust between Naval Intelligence and its Colonial Office counterpart. However, the personal relationships between senior officers of both are good enough to mitigate problems." Hersom sat back and studied Lauzier. "I hate to say this, Sara, but your schemes have a maddening habit of failing, probably because they're a little too complex."

"No, Blayne. They've failed because of Siobhan Dunmoore and her friends at Fleet HQ. Take them and Dunmoore out of the equation, and things will go the way they should. But you refuse, so I suppose you're equally blameworthy. You understand your tenure as director general of the Bureau is at the pleasure of the SecGen."

"And you have your hand up Judy Chu's backside, yes, I know that. But I'm sure you also understand that I know enough about your shenanigans to ensure you'll never sit in the SecGen's chair if you try anything against me. We are in a situation they once called mutually assured destruction. So, no. I won't remove Dunmoore or anyone else. Find schemes of discrediting the Fleet that might work, even if smart officers figure out what's happening. For what it's worth, Dunmoore is currently visiting Starbase 36 with her little task group, so she may not have been involved with the Andoth business. Her former command, on the other hand, is a different story."

A furious Sara Lauzier glared at him for several seconds, then climbed to her feet.

"The failure has her fingerprints all over it. We'll continue this discussion later, Blayne. When you've had time to think about what's best for you and the Bureau."

***

Dunmoore's inspection tour of Starbase 36 and the resident battle group's ships currently in port was both educational and tiring. She found no fault with either, and the flag officer commanding, Rear Admiral Katsuro Ishikawa, who'd studied under Dunmoore at the War College, gave her an appropriately dignified reception. She spent many hours listening to his concerns and ideas and found the visit, which lasted all of three days, helpful and not just as a decoy. However, she skipped the war games since the ships in port were in various states of refit, replenishment, and crew leave.

She didn't worry much about security, either. The Andoth raid was done, and the opposition had undoubtedly heard about the results by now. No one other than Pushkin and Lothbrok knew about their next target, and the only one in Task Group 30.1 aware the 101st stayed behind in the Andoth system to ambush unwary traffickers was Nieri.

When Dunmoore finally exhausted her reasons for staying, she ordered the task group on a course for Starbase 37, their next stop, and closer to Task Force Morrigan's second target. However, she expected another collection of empty buildings, abandoned weeks earlier.

Per standard protocols, the flagship queried the nearest interstellar subspace array for messages whenever the task group dropped out of FTL. When they tacked halfway to Starbase 37, Dunmoore received an encrypted message from Gregor Pushkin. Four confirmed traffickers were seized as prizes within Andoth's hyperlimit, and one hundred and forty-two enslaved humans were freed. The lot was on its way to Starbase 36 under prize crews, with *Gondolier* as an escort. The Q ship would rejoin the 101st at the Garonne heliopause, where the rest of the 101st would head shortly.

Dunmoore wanted to share the good news with Commodore Nieri and Captain Elias but knew it would be best if no one in Task Group 30.1 found out. The 101st's missions were still best kept secret. That way, there would be no slips of the tongue which might confirm who was responsible. In these dark and dirty wars, information remained the most valuable weapon of all.

Instead, she merely ordered a change of destination to the rendezvous at the Garonne heliopause. Her inspection tour of Starbase 37 would have to wait.

— Forty-One —

"Blayne Hersom is dead."

"What?" Kathryn Kowalski's head whipped up from her reader when Ezekiel Holt entered her office without warning.

"I just heard via my contacts." Holt dropped into a chair. "When Blayne didn't show up at work this morning and didn't answer his communicator, his chief of staff, Leila Gherson, went to Blayne's residence. Getting no answer to her hails, she entered — the top SSB brass have door codes for each other's homes — and found him slumped in a living room chair. No signs of foul play, no signs of forced entry. Looks like cardiac arrest."

"So Sara finally offed him for not playing her games?"

"Possibly. Or it could well be a natural death. Blayne was in his seventies, and who knows what health problems he might have concealed. As my mother used to say, we get a certain number of heartbeats in this life. Some people get less than others, and when you run out of heartbeats, that's it."

Kowalski grimaced.

"But from your tone, you doubt it."

"Any death convenient for someone like Sara makes me wonder."

"Wouldn't Hersom have dangled insurance over Sara's head to prevent this sort of thing? She's done enough evil deeds in her time, many of them with help from the SSB."

"I'd have thought so. We may still see her skeletons uncovered over the coming days. Unless she found a way of neutralizing the threat." Holt shrugged. "Or it could be a natural death, meaning his insurance policy wouldn't come into force."

"Who takes over?"

"Someone more willing to please Sara, no doubt. It's a SecGen appointment, meaning Sara will see that Chu names whoever she wants."

"And until then?"

"Leila Gherson. Before you ask, we know little about her. She's the proverbial gray woman, a career SSB administrator who remained in the shadows all this time."

Kowalski cocked an eyebrow at her friend.

"Is this Gherson one of Sara Lauzier's minions?"

"Not that we know. But if you're wondering whether she'd be well-placed to nullify Blayne's insurance and arrange for his seemingly natural death, then yes to both questions. We'll likely never find the truth, but the dynamics in this city have shifted rather dramatically with Blayne's death."

"I can't say I mourn his passing, though."

"I do, to a certain extent. He was a level-headed man who understood there were limits to what the SSB could do with impunity. We could talk about things and, if not always agree, then see the other's point of view. Now those on the intelligence side will have to build new relationships with Gherson and whoever gets the job permanently."

A faint smile danced on Kowalski's lips.

"Ten creds it'll be her. A reward for taking care of an SSB director general who wouldn't always bend the knee. As you said, she's well-placed to do Sara's bidding."

"Ten creds it is," he replied. Then his expression sobered. "The biggest question is whether Blayne's successor will abide by the truce we negotiated with him. If the answer is no, then Siobhan becomes a target for assassination once more, and so do we. Sara doesn't forgive those who cause her schemes to fail."

Kowalski scoffed.

"She doesn't forgive or forget anything, period. What do you think might have triggered Blayne's premature end if Sara ordered the deed?"

"The 101st's last series of intercepts in the Andoth system on top of the trap's failure, no doubt. More money vanished than we could imagine, and we collected more intelligence about the traffickers to help us shut down their nests in the Zone. A substantial loss for her side. She could well have run out of patience."

"Will you let Siobhan know?"

"Yes, and I'll make sure Chief Vincenzo prepares for her return, in case she's now back to being the SSB's target number one." Holt gave her a significant look. "I suggest we also take precautions for the foreseeable future, Kathryn."

"You think Sara's new SSB chief would dare?"

"In a nanosecond, if the worst-case scenario unfolds."

***

"Looks suspiciously like the Andoth site." Lieutenant Colonel Lothbrok grimaced. "Same sort of life sign readings, same sort of prefabricated structures around a rammed earth tarmac, all surrounded by a berm and fence. Fifty clicks to the nearest settlement, and only visible from directly overhead."

"Okay." Dunmoore, eyes on the images from the recon drone, tapped her fingertips on the conference table. "Reconnoiter the site as if you were doing a normal infiltration operation. Find out whether there are any actual humans there. If it's vacant, *Iolanthe*, or whichever ship Commodore Pushkin designates, can drop a kinetic rod. If it's occupied by traffickers, carry out a raid under the normal rules of engagement. Once you and any prisoners or rescuees have evacuated, the 101st will drop a kinetic rod."

She let her eyes rest briefly on Commodores Nieri and Pushkin.

"Task Group 30.1 and I will head for Starbase 37, where we will do our job as decoys. Once you've dealt with the ground installation, Gregor, stick around like you did in the Andoth system and wait for traffickers who might think you've cleared out. We will move on to Starbase 38 when we're done on 37."

"And after Garonne?" Pushkin asked.

"Merseaux. We might as well make it three for three."

"And then?"

"We'll discuss it when the time comes, Gregor. But I foresee my cutting the inspection tour short because of pressing business at 3rd Fleet HQ while you head out for the usual."

***

"Thank you for seeing me, and congratulations on your appointment as director general of the Bureau."

Holt sat on the bench beside a middle-aged woman with a pixie haircut. Of middling height and middling weight, with dark hair, dark eyes, and an olive complexion, Leila Gherson was eminently forgettable in a city like Geneva, especially wearing the typical bureaucrat's business suit, gray, like the weather. It was a little chilly here near the Skanderbeg statue lookout on the shore of the lake, in a section of the Palace of the Stars precinct reserved only for those employed by the Commonwealth government.

She kept her gaze on the choppy waters and didn't immediately reply, so Holt did the same and waited.

"Let's get something clear right up front, Admiral Holt. I am not Blayne Hersom. He was a former field agent who sometimes played faster and looser than was good for the Bureau. And unlike him, I rarely meet with underlings, only my equivalents. With the Armed Forces, that would be Admiral Doxiadis. It means this is the first and last time I accept a meeting request from you, and only so you hear a few things from me. After today, if Jado Doxiadis has a message, he can damn well call himself. And while you and Blayne were on a first-name basis for reasons that remain obscure, I will not engage in that sort of false friendliness with members of Naval Intelligence."

Holt kept his gaze on the lake.

"As you wish, Director General. Am I correct in assuming you're aware of the informal truce the late Director General Hersom and I negotiated on behalf of our respective organizations?"

"I am. And it is over."

"Regrettable, Madame. If the SSB plans on resuming its adversarial stance vis-à-vis the Fleet, may I remind you of our respective sizes, strengths, and reach?"

"I'm aware of the disparity, Admiral. However, these days, what matters is political power. Ours is ascendant, and the Fleet's in decline. SecGen Chu has resolved to clip your Grand Admirals' wings and rein in all those admirals who believe they can be laws unto themselves. And she expects the SSB to ensure compliance."

"Judy Chu?" Holt snorted. "Dear me. Has she suddenly turned into a fanatical Centralist? Or is she merely doing as Senator Lauzier wants?"

"Believe what you will, Admiral. The Armed Forces are subservient to the civilian administration in all things, and you will be reminded of it as forcefully as necessary."

"What does that mean, Director General? Will the SSB itself neutralize those rogue admirals?"

"If necessary."

"I see." Holt paused for a few moments. "Are you familiar with a 20th-century admiral by the name of Yamamoto Isoroku?

"No."

"He was one of the finest naval strategists of his time. Certainly of his nation. He led his Navy to stunning early successes against two allied great sea powers, but in the end, he not only lost his life, but his nation lost an existential war."

"Fascinating." Her dismissive tone turned the word into a barely veiled insult.

"Yamamoto left posterity with several trenchant observations, a few of which apply to our situation, Director General. One of my favorites, which predates his country's declaration of war against those powers, said that in the first six to twelve months of the war, his forces would run wild and win victory upon victory. But if the war continued after that, he had no expectation of success."

"What? You're comparing me to this Yamamoto?"

"No, of course not. But he knew what would happen if he followed his government's orders. I'm not sure you do. And therefore, I'll leave you with my second favorite Yamamoto observation, which he made after his first strike against the enemy. It goes like this — I fear all we have done is to awaken a sleeping giant and fill him with a terrible resolve."

Holt paused for a few seconds to let his words sink in.

"We don't want a war with the SSB, let alone the administration. But if you start one, I can guarantee we will end it on our terms." Holt stood. "I'll leave you with one warning. Target our people, and we will take yours out in retaliation. The Fleet has adopted the *lex talionis* philosophy, and we will apply it to our enemies, foreign and domestic. We will not allow political strife between sovereign star systems, especially at the Centralist's behest, to trigger another migration war, and if that means opposing the administration, so be it. Enjoy the rest of your day, Madame Director General."

— Forty-Two —

"I'm calling an end to this exercise in futility." A visibly frustrated Siobhan Dunmoore sat back in her chair after Lieutenant Colonel Lothbrok reported another abandoned or decoy facility, this time on Merseaux. "Three goose eggs in a row clearly prove they played us for fools. Task Force Morrigan is hereby dissolved. Colonel, thank you. A shame you couldn't expend live ammo on the old two-way range. You may return home with *Ragnarok* and *Swiftsure*. Commodore Nieri, Task Group 30.1 will head back to Dordogne forthwith. I'm ending the inspection tour at this point because there are other, more pressing matters I must attend to. And Commodore Pushkin, you may indulge yourself in a tour of the happy hunting grounds. Maybe visiting our favorite free port might be more profitable."

Pushkin nodded once.

"Yes, sir."

"That's it, folks. I wish I could say we will work together again someday, on a mission with actual targets, but I doubt I'll get the chance at a last hurrah leading ships into battle, such as it might have been. In peacetime, a three-star's battlefield is administrative and often political, not one where guns roar and missiles fly."

Lothbrok let out a gentle snort.

"No worries, Admiral. If you knew the number of goose eggs the 1st SFR's squadrons collect in an average year."

She gave him a small smile.

"That bad?"

"Sometimes, it's as if the opposition sees our orders before we do."

"Or they're the ones feeding us fake intel," Pushkin said.

"That was certainly the case this time, Gregor. I hope the folks on Earth will find out how we were suckered into almost giving the opposition a massive propaganda boost."

"At least we snagged a dozen traffickers who thought the coast was clear after we checked out the decoys and supposedly left."

Dunmoore nodded.

"True, and it's not a negligible accomplishment, but I doubt we can make that tactic work again once they figure out what happened. Which they will. The opposition seems to have an inexhaustible supply of insiders who feed it information. In any case, that's all. You may proceed at your discretion. Commodore Nieri, I'd like to head back to Dordogne now."

***

"So how was it?" A smiling Admiral Hogue asked when Dunmoore reported to her office after an uneventful voyage home. "And please sit."

"I only visited three of our battle groups, but they were in fine shape, sir. I found little to criticize. My report should be in your queue as we speak."

"Excellent. Did you hear we have a new chief of staff for operations? Rear Admiral Fernando Juarez. He'll take up his post in four weeks."

"No, I hadn't heard. Does Freya know?"

Hogue nodded. "She does. Have you met Fernando before?"

An amused smile lit up Dunmoore's face.

"I did the readiness assessment on his last command. I believe his last words to me after I gave him his ship's report were, I hope I never see your face again, Dunmoore."

"He didn't pass?"

"Oh, he passed all right. But I always ran a no-win scenario as the last test once I saw enough of the ship and crew. They just never knew which scenario would be the last one. And the cockier a captain behaved as he and his people passed test after test, the harder and nastier that no-win ended up being. Fernando ran a tight ship, and he had a good tactical mind, but he was a little full of himself, so I took him down a few notches. He did not take it well and called me a few choice names within hearing of my team. When I debriefed him, I let him know about those. I wonder how he feels coming to work under me."

Hogue chuckled.

"It'll be interesting to watch his reaction to you when he reports. Other than that, things have been quiet during your absence."

"I was in touch with Alvin and Freya via subspace radio whenever *Salamanca* wasn't sailing FTL and took care of most routine issues that way."

"Commendably diligent. If you have a bit of time, why don't you give me a thumbnail sketch of your written report and tell me your personal opinions of the battle group commanders?"

"Certainly, sir."

***

Lieutenant Commander Takahashi stood when Dunmoore entered the outer office. She'd gone to Admiral Hogue straight from the spaceport, it being early afternoon in Marseilles, and hadn't yet settled in, though her luggage would wait on the front porch of her residence.

"Welcome back, Admiral. You had an enjoyable inspection tour?"

"It achieved its purpose, Margo. And as you might have noted, I stayed on top of the administrivia all along."

Takahashi smiled.

"Everyone noticed, sir. Chief Vincenzo asked to see you when you have time for him."

"Then, by all means, send out a summons, and I shall receive him forthwith." When Takahashi gave her a strange look, Dunmoore chuckled. "Not much for an admiral to do in hyperspace except read, and I brought a few pre-spaceflight classics with me."

"I'll call him right away."

"Thanks."

Dunmoore sat behind her desk and called up her work queue, noting one message from Earth encrypted for her eyes only. But she set it aside and scanned the rest of the list, helpfully arranged in order of priority by Commander Takahashi. Before she could deal with more than the three top items, a knock on the door jamb caught her attention.

"Welcome back, Admiral."

Dunmoore made a come-in gesture, and Vincenzo took one step, saluted, then closed the door behind him.

"I hear it didn't go as well as hoped."

"False intel, though the 101st made a respectable number of intercepts. The bad guys thought we'd clear out after scoring goose eggs. Grab a seat. Margo said you wanted to see me."

"Yes, sir. Did you read the latest message from Admiral Holt?"

"Not yet. It came in while *Salamanca* was FTL, and I didn't bother querying the subspace network after we pinged the last interstellar array."

"Things have changed on Earth. Blayne Hersom died."

Dunmoore's eyebrows shot up.

"Did someone terminate him?"

"Officially, it's death from natural causes, but Admiral Holt suspects they murdered him at Senator Lauzier's orders because of the unofficial truce he'd negotiated between the SSB and the Fleet. The new director general is Leila Gherson, Hersom's former chief of staff. Admiral Holt figures she's in Lauzier's pocket and will do whatever the senator wants. And the first thing to go was the truce. You're to consider yourself a prime target."

She sat back.

"The SSB will gun for me again?"

"Not Bureau agents, sir. La Pègre on behalf of the Bureau, as before. When I got the message, I told our cousins to see what the word on the street was. Rumors in certain circles speak of ending the accord you forced on them, which probably means ending your life. Admiral Holt is certainly taking it seriously. Three more cousins showed up yesterday, sent from Earth aboard an aviso that rode the very highest hyperspace bands. One of them is a woman who physically resembles you, and with a bit of facial disguise, she's your twin. Goes by the name Jill. The other cousins are Tanya and Domingo. I felt the latter two are Marines, but Jill is Navy, probably a chief petty officer or a warrant officer. She has the lingo down pat — I tested her. She seemed amused by it. If you pardon me for saying so, Admiral, you and Jill should get along just fine."

Dunmoore made a face.

"Body double, huh? That's a first for me. What will the arrangements be?"

"That's one thing we need to discuss. Jill's orders are to be your shadow, act as a decoy when needed, and take a bullet if necessary."

"Take a bullet? Isn't that dramatic and unnecessary?"

Vincenzo shrugged.

"I didn't write up her orders. The brass on Earth wants to ensure you stay alive now that the SSB is under new management, and that's what the cousins and I will do."

"For the next two years or however long I stay at 3rd Fleet?"

"If necessary."

"I can't see myself being a prisoner of Joint Base Dordogne for the foreseeable future, Chief."

He nodded.

"We — the cousins and I — understand that, but you will always have an escort, and there are places you can no longer risk visiting."

"Who decides where I can't go anymore?"

"The cousins, based on their threat assessments, but mainly Jill. And, sir, she'll be living with you."

Dunmoore let out a soft sigh.

"No privacy either for the foreseeable future."

"At least until we're sure we've neutralized any threats against you."

"When do I get to meet this Jill?"

Before Vincenzo could reply, Dunmoore's communicator chimed — Commander Takahashi.

"Yes, Margo?"

"There's a Chief Warrant Officer Jill Bradigan here with orders assigning her as your personal assistant."

Dunmoore and Vincenzo exchanged a glance, then the latter nodded once.

"Please send her in, Margo."

Vincenzo turned in his seat as the door opened to admit a tall, slender woman wearing a Navy-blue garrison uniform with the three silver bars of a chief warrant officer second class on her collar. Her silver-shot copper locks beneath a beret worn at the same rakish angle as Dunmoore affected were an almost exact match to the latter's hair, both in color and style.

Bradigan's height, body shape, and even her movements as she entered the office, came to attention, and saluted, were eerily familiar to Dunmoore. But her facial features, though similar, were different enough to ensure no one would think them twins. At least not at first or even second glance.

"Chief Warrant Officer Bradigan reporting to Admiral Dunmoore as ordered."

"Welcome, Warrant. At ease, and please take a seat." Dunmoore and Vincenzo locked eyes again just long enough to confirm it was indeed Cousin Jill, an agent from Naval Intelligence's Special Operations Section.

"Thank you, sir." She glanced at Vincenzo. "Nice to see you again so soon, Chief."

"Likewise, Warrant. I just finished briefing the Admiral on your addition to her personal staff."

"Good. That'll save time."

Bradigan met Dunmoore's eyes without hesitation as the latter studied her, searching for more similarities between them. Dunmoore quickly realized that they differed in one major, if not immediately obvious way, at least not to casual observers. The agent's gaze was entirely empty of human feeling, as if a great void lay behind her black pupils — the eyes of a remorseless killer.

"Admiral Holt sends his best, sir. He asked me to tell you the faulty intel came from the Colonial Office and that he had a chat with the man you rescued from the late SSB director general during the war."

"Mikhail Forenza?"

Bradigan nodded.

"He's the Colonial Office Intelligence Service's director of field operations nowadays. Admiral Kowalski also sends her best and suggests you duck whenever Chief Vincenzo tells you to do so."

"Or you, for that matter, since I understand we'll be inseparable."

"I won't just tell you, sir. I'll do whatever is necessary. Admiral Holt said if something happens to you on my watch, I may as well never come back."

— Forty-Three —

Anyone who asked why Dunmoore suddenly got a chief warrant officer as a personal assistant was told Fleet HQ sent Jill Bradigan instead of a second aide-de-camp. That usually ended the questioning. No one dared ask why Bradigan lived in a guest suite in Dunmoore's official residence, and anyone who looked into the agent's empty eyes for more than a few seconds no longer felt the urge to wonder about anything. But she was so utterly unobtrusive that Dunmoore often forgot that her security guard and body double lived with her.

Even Admiral Hogue swallowed the cover story. Not that she cared much, provided her deputy took care of 3rd Fleet's day-to-day business and kept the boring administrivia from reaching her desk. In fact, Dunmoore quickly confirmed her earlier impression the admiral was simply marking time until her appointment ended so she could retire gracefully and with full honors. That Dunmoore ran 3rd Fleet so efficiently without bothering her with details was the icing on the cake.

Bradigan and Vincenzo still disappeared during working hours, the former making sure Dunmoore would recall her before leaving the building. Meanwhile, 3rd Fleet military members, along with civilian staffers, abruptly retired, quit, or were reassigned and shipped out on the first available naval vessel. Yet more remained, but counterintelligence expanded its reach with each arrest as it dug deeper into the Pègre's dark corners. Still, Dunmoore hadn't been allowed to leave the base during the evenings and on her days off. Vincenzo took care of the shopping, and Bradigan headed into town on her behalf if she needed clothing.

On a Saturday afternoon, three weeks after Bradigan's arrival, the agent suddenly appeared in Dunmoore's living room wearing Dunmoore's face, startling her. She'd been reading indoors because of the persistent rain rather than enjoying her private, walled-in garden and hadn't heard a peep from the agent.

"What's up, Warrant?" Dunmoore carefully closed the book and put it on the side table. "And yes, that's me, but I'm used to seeing myself in reverse in the mirror, so you're a little spookier than I expected."

"We decided to lay a trap, sir," Bradigan replied in Dunmoore's voice. "Gus and Lou got wind of Calvert's gang being on standby to make you die in an accident the next time you left the base. They received orders from off-world paymasters that leave them no choice but to obey and ensure they're successful. And they've been keeping tabs on all gates for the last few days."

"Those paymasters being the SSB?"

Bradigan nodded, just as Dunmoore did, which added to the eeriness of the situation.

"Most likely. The Pègre wouldn't make a move against you without being compelled. At least not yet. Your taking them down is still too fresh in their memories."

"Be careful."

"It's not us who need to take care, Admiral." Bradigan's predatory smile, so like her own, sent a shiver up Dunmoore's spine. "Please don't leave the residence until one of the team or I return. You cannot be seen by anyone while I'm impersonating you. Don't even answer calls unless it's an emergency. I'd get Vince to sit at your door with a plasma gun, but we need him to make this work. Oh, and we're taking your personal car. It may not come back in the best shape, if at all, so my apologies in advance."

Anyone watching the front of Dunmoore's house would have seen her leave in her car, dressed in the casual slacks and blouse she usually wore when not in uniform.

Shortly before midnight, a car Dunmoore recognized as Vincenzo's pulled into her driveway. She'd spent the rest of the day and all evening fretting about what was happening beyond her control and had the displays in every room keyed to show the front of the residence.

Vincenzo, wearing dark civilian clothes, climbed out on the passenger side, looked around, then walked to the front door. At Dunmoore's orders, it opened, and he stepped in just as she reached the foyer.

"Mission accomplished, sir. Chief Warrant Officer Bradigan would like you to come with us. You'll be safe with Lou and me. At least for tonight, or until the opposition figures out what happened. Can you put on dark clothes, please?"

A distinctly curious Dunmoore complied and climbed into the car's aft passenger compartment. The agent known as Lou sat at the controls, but his facial features, at least what she could see in the shadows, were subtly different. If the neighbors were still awake and looking out, they would have seen Dunmoore leave twice that day without coming back in between, but she doubted anyone would have noticed the anomaly.

"Where are we going?" She asked as Lou put the car in motion.

"We tricked Calvert's assassination team into targeting Chief Warrant Officer Bradigan and led them on a merry chase, at the end of which they fell victim to our ambush. Three of them died. We disposed of the bodies, and they'll never be found. We captured another five and interrogated them. One died during the interrogation, but they confessed to being Antoine Calvert's top so-called removal specialists."

"There's no doubt who they work for?"

Lou shook his head.

"None whatsoever. We're also specialists in our own way, and interrogating people who aren't conditioned is one thing we do better than anyone else."

"With that and other information, we raided Antoine Calvert's private residence, leaving another seven of his goons to meet the Almighty. Thankfully his wife was away. Calvert joined his four surviving goons in our custody, and that's where we're headed. Jill thinks you ought to witness her carrying out the orders given by Admiral Doxiadis."

"Oh."

Dunmoore immediately understood what would happen and sat back, wondering how she felt about it. But after a few moments, she reminded herself the dark and dirty wars she'd fought with the 101st hadn't ended for her just because she sat behind a desk rather than in a CIC command chair. And Calvert fought on the enemy's side, as evidenced by the assassination attempts. If the Fleet's senior leadership had decreed a policy of retribution, then she would make it so.

They left Marseille's lights far behind them as the car raced north and toward the interior until they reached a farm darkened save for light coming through the front door windowpane.

"Who owns this place?" Dunmoore asked as they pulled up to a dilapidated house next to an equally sad-looking barn.

"A shell company we set up shortly after Gus and I landed," Lou replied. "Every operation needs a safe house. This is ours, codename Marguerite. The interior is in better shape than the outside, and we gave it a few upgrades."

They climbed out into a warm night air redolent of pine and lavender.

"Your car is in the barn, but I'm afraid it didn't escape unscathed. We will buy you a replacement and dispose of this one in the morning."

Dunmoore gave Lou a curious glance but remained silent.

"Please follow me."

The agent led them into the house, where a plain-looking woman of average height and average build with a forgettable face greeted her.

"Admiral. We haven't met yet. I'm Tanya, one of what Vince calls the cousins. My partner Domingo, Gus, and Jill are waiting for us in the interrogation suite downstairs. The other two team members are out, cleaning up any traces of our operation."

Tanya turned and headed for an open door at the far end of the corridor, where stone stairs led into a lit basement. There, behind a metal door, Dunmoore found her double along with the other agents quietly watching four banged-up Pègre soldiers and Antoine Calvert strapped to metal chairs with plastic restraints. All five were wide-eyed, muzzled, and stark naked.

When Calvert realized he saw two Dunmoores — the one who'd interrogated him and the new arrival — he jerked against his restraints while making muffled sounds. The mob soldiers, who bore the hangdog look of defeat, merely eyed her curiously.

Bradigan straightened and nodded.

"Admiral. Welcome. We had an interesting evening with these gentlemen, especially Monsieur Calvert." She reached out and ripped off the latter's muzzle. "He'll answer any question you might have since he's still under the influence of the interrogation drugs. I wanted you to hear the truth from his mouth."

Dunmoore studied the man for a few moments, reading fear and loathing in his eyes.

"Did you try to have me killed for the second time today, Antoine?"

"Yes." His voice cracked. "And it would have worked if it weren't for your psychopaths, especially your double."

"I thought we had an agreement."

An unattractive sneer twisted his lips.

"We only went along with you until we found a way out."

"What changed?"

"Friends asked me to have you killed in return for certain assurances and guarantees."

Bradigan took a step toward Calvert.

"Don't make the Admiral drag it out of you, Antoine."

Calvert reared back in fear, at least to the extent his restraints allowed.

The agent smiled at Dunmoore.

"Monsieur has a low threshold for pain. Go on, Antoine."

"We received word from Earth that you were once again a target for assassination and that with your death, our former interstellar trafficking and money laundering activities could resume under the same or better protection as before."

"Protection from who? The SSB?"

Calvert nodded.

"Yes. And friends in the Senate."

"Such as Sara Lauzier."

"Yes. We were forced to comply with you when the SSB withdrew from Dordogne. But they're back under a new director general who dislikes you as much as we do. You were to die in a motor vehicle accident — it's how we dispose of people. The police would have investigated and concluded there was no foul play because we own so much of them."

"I see." Dunmoore tilted her head to one side. "You keep saying we, and I know you don't have royal pretensions, Antoine. Who is this we?"

"My professional colleagues, like Sylvie and Uta Lassieux and the others you threatened at my beach house. By the way, replacing the electronics your goons fried cost a fortune."

"Are you saying they'll come after me as well?"

"If I fail? *Certainement.*"

Dunmoore glanced at Bradigan, who shrugged.

"Not a problem, but you'll stay under tight security for a while longer. Maybe the idea that obeying the SSB means death will convince the other mob chiefs that respecting your terms is a better choice. Did you have any more questions for Calvert? We conducted a more fulsome interrogation on matters of interest to our superiors."

Dunmoore turned to Calvert again, then shook her head.

"No."

"In that case," a small-bore blaster appeared in Bradigan's hand, "time to carry out our orders."

The weapon coughed five times in rapid succession. Tiny black holes appeared on the foreheads of Calvert and his men, and they slumped forward, dead.

"Let's get you home, Admiral. We'll take care of the bodies. They will find Calvert clutching a death card in one of his homes." Bradigan produced a playing card, an ace of spades with a laughing skull in the center. "The goons will simply vanish along with the rest. That'll give us a head start on making the rest reconsider their life choices."

Dunmoore let out a soft grunt.

"Remind me to never piss you off, Warrant."

A wintry smile lit up the agent's face.

"I may be a psychopath, Admiral, but I only act on orders from my superiors. And since they deployed us to keep you alive, I doubt they'll order your termination."

"What a comforting thought."

— Forty-Four —

Jado Doxiadis, wearing a dark gray coat over his equally gray civilian suit to cut the wind coming off Lake Geneva on a chilly day, sat beside Leila Gherson on the bench by the Skanderbeg statue overlooking the leaden waters.

"Glad you didn't send that obnoxious errand boy of yours, Admiral."

"Holt?" Doxiadis asked in a conversational tone. "He's too busy rolling up your networks for a little chin wag on the palace grounds."

"So, you're responsible for my stations and contractors going dark? We suspected as much, but thanks for confirming."

"No thanks needed, my dear director general. This is a war of your own choosing. I have no problems acknowledging my victories after the fact, hoping you might see reason like Blayne eventually did. Antoine Calvert's death is entirely on you, as are the deaths of everyone involved in the attempt. Try again with another mob boss, and the same will happen."

Gherson scoffed.

"You should keep in mind that my people only have to succeed once. Yours must succeed every time, my dear admiral."

Eric Thomson

"And yet you will still lose a war of attrition, just as surely as Admiral Yamamoto did."

Disgust briefly flashed across her face.

"Not you as well."

"Did you ever hear of a twentieth-century philosopher named George Santayana?"

"Must you Naval Intelligence people make everything a history lesson?"

Doxiadis turned his head toward her and smiled.

"How funny you should use those very words. George Santayana's most famous aphorism states those who cannot remember the past are condemned to repeat it. That's why we study history with such great intensity, so we do not commit the same mistakes repeatedly. You should think about that before sending your janissaries into battle against us again. We anticipated your attempt on Admiral Dunmoore and countered it easily. Then, we applied *lex talionis*, and Antoine Calvert is no longer among the living, along with his best soldiers. We will do the same against any other mob boss you commission to assassinate a Commonwealth Navy vice admiral. And should you try anything against senior officers here on Earth, such as the man systematically destroying your operative networks, I guarantee we will apply *lex talionis* against you personally."

She turned her head as well to lock eyes with him.

"You threaten the administration's top security adviser with assassination? Take care, Admiral. Take good care."

"Oh, I will. If your actions are sufficiently egregious, we might even focus on the one giving you your orders."

"You wouldn't dare."

"Look down at your chest."

"Why." Despite the question, she did so and saw the small red dot of a targeting laser above her heart. Gherson's head came up abruptly, and she scanned the far shore, where the putative sniper would be hiding.

"Don't bother, Leila. Our people can take out any target within line of sight, no matter the distance. And we don't care about trying to disguise our terminations as deniable accidents or natural deaths. Such as poor Blayne's murder at your hands."

"What do you want?"

"I want the truce back in force. You don't try killing our folks using proxies or your own agents, and we won't make you feel the pain personally."

"But you'll still attack my people out there?"

"Only if we find them spying on us or interfering with our business. Or aiding criminals inside the Commonwealth and beyond its sphere. That was the deal we had with Blayne. If the SSB steps outside the law, you take your chances with us. But assassination is off the table. Period." Doxiadis produced a playing card, an ace of spades with a laughing skull in the center, and dropped it in Gherson's lap. "Otherwise, my people will deal out more of these."

He stood.

"I'll let you mull it over. Give my regards to Sara and remind her that when Clausewitz wrote war is a mere continuation of politics by other means, he didn't mean waging war against your own Armed Forces."

***

"And now on to force protection matters." Vice Admiral Siobhan Dunmoore looked up from her tablet. "You all heard about Antoine Calvert's murder three weeks ago."

Admiral Hogue, the two chiefs of staff, Maffina and Juarez, and Command Chief Petty Officer Grechkov nodded. The newsnets had been overflowing with stories about the assassination by parties unknown. Dunmoore was impressed that the Gendarmerie kept the death card found in Calvert's hands from becoming public knowledge.

"Overnight, two more reputed organized crime bosses, Sylvie and Uta Lassieux, were killed in their home by parties unknown, along with several security guards. The Marseilles Police and the Gendarmerie, as well as our military police and counterintelligence units, fear an all-out gang war is brewing. At the latter's advice, I'm raising our force protection level to orange. All Armed Forces elements on Dordogne will issue heightened personal and unit security orders. We don't want our people caught in the crossfire should this incipient gang war spill into the streets. Questions?"

When they shook their heads, Dunmoore moved to the next item on the agenda. She hadn't known what happened until the reports came in that morning. Only that Bradigan had vanished during the evening after warning her to stay put until her return, after oh-three hundred.

By common accord, Dunmoore no longer asked where the agent went or what she, the rest of the cousins, and Vincenzo did under the principle of plausible deniability. But she knew Lassieux had sent assassination teams to catch her when she left the base. Or rather, the moment Bradigan, wearing Dunmoore's face, left the base to troll for mob killers. Either they hadn't yet received word from the SSB to stop, or the new director general had ignored all warnings.

When the executive committee meeting wrapped up, Dunmoore headed back to her office, where both Vincenzo and Bradigan were waiting for her, sipping coffee and chatting with Commander Takahashi.

"Got a moment, Admiral?" Bradigan asked.

"Sure. Come on in."

When they were behind closed doors, Dunmoore waved at her conference table.

"Sit. Busy night?"

"A tad," Bradigan replied. "I hope the two death cards we dealt will get through to the rest of the Pègre bosses. Mind you, with the two biggest OCGs on the planet facing a leadership vacuum, they'll be busy fighting each other for larger slices of the business while looking over their shoulders night and day. Incidentally, Gus heard from his police contacts this morning that the cops are spooked by the death cards and understand this isn't actually gang warfare among the various Pègre factions but outsiders cleaning up the trash. The gang war theory is merely for public consumption."

Dunmoore's eyes narrowed in thought as her fingertips tapped the tabletop.

"Could we send the remaining bosses a death card as a warning? They'll surely know the police found their dead colleagues clutching one."

Bradigan shrugged.

"I don't see why not. They're meant as a bit of psychological warfare, after all. Perhaps they'll understand capitulation is the only way to survive. Consider it done."

Almost a week passed without further incidents or any suspicious tails on Dunmoore's new car when Bradigan took it for a drive around town. Then, unexpectedly that Sunday morning, Dunmoore received a call from Victor Herault on her personal communicator.

"Thank you for answering, Siobhan," he said when she saw his face on her display.

Dunmoore caught movement out of the corner of her eye and saw Bradigan listening from the living room doorway, out of the video pickup's range.

"To what do I owe the honor, Victor? I'd have thought that after the events of the last few months, we weren't on speaking terms anymore."

He chuckled in his semi-seductive way and smiled.

"I'm merely an envoy. My friends deputized me to tell you they surrender and will, from now on, religiously observe the terms they accepted that afternoon in poor Antoine's beach house. No more attempts on your life. You will henceforth be safe from them, although they cannot speak for agents of an unnamed organization headquartered on Earth."

"Then I suggest your friends speak to their unnamed contacts and ensure the latter comply with this surrender. Otherwise, someone might need to break open a fresh deck of cards. Perhaps those contacts could send a message to their superiors advising them of my warning."

He inclined his head.

"I shall do so. And now that I've delivered my message, can I tempt you with a ramble through wine country, punctuated by lunch at the charming vineyard restaurant where we first met?"

His expression and tone were so disingenuous that Dunmoore couldn't help but laugh.

"I wish I could, Victor. But even if I were to trust you, my people never would, and that might spoil the mood. Your friends aren't the only ones with humorless security staff."

"Then we might share a glass of champagne at the opera or at a charitable event someday when all this has quieted down, and we can once more interact like civilized people. Thank you again for taking my call, Siobhan. *À bientôt.*"

The display went dark, and Dunmoore turned around to face Bradigan.

"Comments?"

"Only that we'll always have a healthy supply of the ace of spades, Admiral."

— Forty-Five —

Siobhan Dunmoore re-read the message signed by Grand Admiral Zebulon Lowell, promoting her to admiral and appointing her flag officer commanding 3rd Fleet, replacing Admiral Eva Hogue. The latter was retiring after a long and distinguished career.

And after less than two years as a vice admiral. She'd certainly made up for her decade in the wilderness as an increasingly overage and bitter post captain on the verge of early retirement. If anyone had told her twenty years ago that she'd follow in Admiral Hoko Nagira's footsteps again, she wouldn't have believed it.

And she'd finally caught up with the prodigy who was once her signals officer in *Stingray* a lifetime ago. Kathryn Kowalski had also received her fourth star and was taking command of the 1st Fleet, meaning she wouldn't even leave Earth and could keep working her intrigues at Armed Forces HQ and in Geneva.

Dunmoore went through the rest of the messages. Oliver Harmel — one of the good guys — was getting his third star and returning to Dordogne as deputy commander. Dunmoore couldn't have asked for better. Gregor Pushkin, who'd received his second star earlier, would stay in command of the 101st for another year. Fortunately, Rear Admiral Fernando Juarez also turned out to be one of the good guys, proof her friends on Earth were intent on ensuring 3rd Fleet's senior leadership was of the highest caliber. Juarez had long since forgiven her for the brutal no-win scenario, and they still joked about it.

Dunmoore had pushed through many changes after counterintelligence extirpated most of the traitors — some always escaped detection. But more work remained before the formation would be proofed against indifferent or venal flag officers after she left. Her efforts had stemmed the flow of wealth in and out of the Rim Sector. However, enough still circulated from the Protectorate Zone to keep corruption among public and military officials endemic despite the 101st's best efforts.

Before Dunmoore could climb to her feet and see Hogue, the latter walked into her office smiling.

"Congratulations, Siobhan. I couldn't have asked for a better successor to care for my legacy, a much improved and more effective 3rd Fleet."

A wry smile crossed Dunmoore's lips as she stood and accepted Hogue's handshake. If she wanted to claim Dunmoore's work over the last two years as her legacy, that was fine. Everyone who mattered knew the truth.

"Thank you, sir."

"I'll alert Chief Grechkov to draw up the change of command ceremony plans. He'll have us organized in no time."

"Yes, sir. If I may ask, where are you retiring to?"

"My home planet, Arcadia. I'll probably dabble in the family firm. Maybe run for public office, but star system only, not federal. Traipsing across the Commonwealth is no longer as attractive as it once was. Besides, there are other Hogues vying for federal office, and we mustn't all congregate in the same place."

Not that Hogue did a lot of traveling, Dunmoore thought. A few trips per year within the Rim Sector for ceremonies and high-level meetings, nothing more. Certainly nothing compared to the number of light years she'd traveled over the past twenty-four months on real and fake inspection tours of the sector and her battle groups.

"Then let me wish you a pleasant and relaxing retirement, Admiral."

"And you a successful and pleasant tour of command — fair winds instead of stormy seas."

About the Author

Eric Thomson is the pen name of a retired Canadian soldier who served more time in uniform than he expected, both in the Regular Army and the Army Reserve. He spent his Regular Army career in the Infantry and his Reserve service in the Armoured Corps. He worked as an information technology executive for several years before retiring to become a full-time author.

Eric has been a voracious reader of science fiction, military fiction, and history all his life. Several years ago, he put fingers to keyboard and started writing his own military sci-fi, with a definite space opera slant, using many of his own experiences as a soldier for inspiration.

When he is not writing fiction, Eric indulges in his other passions: photography, hiking, and scuba diving, all of which he shares with his wife.

Join Eric Thomson at www.thomsonfiction.ca

Where you will find news about upcoming books and more information about the universe in which his heroes fight for humanity's survival.

Read his blog at www.blog.thomsonfiction.ca

If you enjoyed this book, please consider leaving a review with your favorite online retailer to help others discover it.

Also by Eric Thomson

Siobhan Dunmoore

No Honor in Death (Siobhan Dunmoore Book 1)

The Path of Duty (Siobhan Dunmoore Book 2)

Like Stars in Heaven (Siobhan Dunmoore Book 3)

Victory's Bright Dawn (Siobhan Dunmoore Book 4)

Without Mercy (Siobhan Dunmoore Book 5)

When the Guns Roar (Siobhan Dunmoore Book 6)

A Dark and Dirty War (Siobhan Dunmoore Book 7)

On Stormy Seas (Siobhan Dunmoore Book 8)

Decker's War

Death Comes But Once (Decker's War Book 1)

Cold Comfort (Decker's War Book 2)

Fatal Blade (Decker's War Book 3)

Howling Stars (Decker's War Book 4)

Black Sword (Decker's War Book 5)

No Remorse (Decker's War Book 6)

Hard Strike (Decker's War Book 7)

Constabulary Casefiles

The Warrior's Knife (Constabulary Casefiles #1)

A Colonial Murder (Constabulary Casefiles #2)

The Dirty and the Dead (Constabulary Casefiles #3)

Ashes of Empire

Imperial Sunset (Ashes of Empire #1)

Imperial Twilight (Ashes of Empire #2)

Imperial Night (Ashes of Empire #3)

Imperial Echoes (Ashes of Empire #4)

Imperial Ghosts (Ashes of Empire #5)

Ghost Squadron

Printed in Great Britain
by Amazon

46535189R00225